'As much a ride as a read, th[...] something absolutely show[...] expectation and defies it – to [...]
JANE [...]

'I did nothing else until I finish[...]
SOPHIE HANNAH

'Wow. Swanson gives us what few writers can – a thriller with heart'
CHRISTINA DALCHER

'An unforgettable tour-de-force. Imaginative, terrifying, beautiful. Do not miss this one'
CHRIS WHITAKER

'Vast, playful, ingenious ... It's a book as much about writing as about loss and hope ... but Louise Swanson takes that idea to audacious extremes, finding real soul amongst the dream logic and textural trickery'
SFX

'Unsettling, twisty, emotional, and so expertly written that you live every dark, discomforting moment with its protagonist. Expect this book to be a highlight of the year'
CULTUREFLY

'This beautifully written book blew my mind. Takes "what if?" to a new level'
JANE CORRY

'Absolutely enthralling, incredibly clever, brutal and heartbreaking. This deserves to be the book everyone is talking about'
C.J. TUDOR

'A bewitching story about the power of fiction and redemption. Unlike anything else I've read – utterly breathtaking'
CATHERINE COOPER

'A book about the importance of storytelling. A little bit magic, a little bit dark, and a lot emotional. I adored it'
AMANDA PROWSE

'Inventive, original, moving, with a unique premise and a heart-wrenching drop-the-book twist'
TAMMY COHEN

'A shocking portrayal of a world undone. Swanson's writing is powerful and thought-provoking'
LAUREN NORTH

'A chilling and moving tale that will strike fear into the heart of every book lover. The ending blew me away'
MARK EDWARDS

'An intriguing premise and a genuine didn't-see-it-coming twist. It made me think about how we tell stories, how we occupy them and how stories can ultimately change us'
ARAMINTA HALL

'Simply devastatingly good – I may need some time to recover'
CLAIRE ALLAN

'Shocking, powerful, topical, and utterly compelling'
JOHN MARRS

'Every twist was perfectly executed. A fantastic thriller'
HEATHER DARWENT

'A masterpiece of storytelling, with a plot that relentlessly draws you in, and then twists and evolves into something utterly unexpected ... Breathtaking'
PHILIPPA EAST

'Oh wow ... I could not put it down! Intriguing, captivating and utterly heartbreaking – such a brilliant book'
SUSI HOLLIDAY

'A beautifully written tale which had me enthralled from the start. Hugely imaginative, original, and ultimately incredibly moving, *End of Story* is wonderful'
AMANDA JENNINGS

END OF STORY

OF

STORY

LOUISE SWANSON

HODDER

First published in Great Britain in 2023 by Hodder & Stoughton
An Hachette UK company

This paperback edition published in 2024

I

A CIP catalogue record for this title is available from the British Library

Paperback ISBN 978 1 529 39613 3
eBook ISBN 978 1 529 39611 9

Typeset in Bembo by Manipal Technologies Limited

Printed and bound in Great Britain by Clays Ltd, Elcograf S.p.A.

Hodder & Stoughton policy is to use papers that are natural, renewable
and recyclable products and made from wood grown in sustainable forests.
The logging and manufacturing processes are expected to conform
to the environmental regulations of the country of origin.

Hodder & Stoughton Ltd
Carmelite House
50 Victoria Embankment
London EC4Y 0DZ

www.hodder.co.uk

This book is dedicated to the storytellers; the authors,
the musicians, the playwrights, the poets, the artists,
the photographers, the actors, the dancers, and the painters;
and most of all, the parents and caregivers who tirelessly
send their small ones into dreamland with a bedtime story.

If you tell a story well enough, it's true.
Fern Dostoy

Writing is the only way to be heard without screaming.
Shelly Dean

When we're gone, all that's left is the stories we told.
Lynda Harrison

What is there without art? Who are we when we cannot express?
Cass May

Part One
Denial

If you tell a story well enough, it's true.

This sentence came to me every time I started a novel. I typed it beneath whatever the working title was in that moment. An italicised reminder when I opened the document late at night to resume, coffee steaming on the desk nearby, and a single cigarette waiting as reward for hitting my word goal: very Paul Sheldon. These nine words chided me while I ruthlessly edited every first draft – pruning flowery words, tightening passive verbs, moulding metaphors, letting my voice rise. These nine words forced me to address plot holes, character motivation, the denouement. Only when I finally submitted the manuscript to my publisher did I delete them.

If you tell a story well enough, it's true.

But I haven't written a story for a long time.

No one has – or at least if they have, they haven't shared it with the world. The celebrated career I enjoyed for a brief but bright three years is over. The three books – two bestselling – that garnered pages of reviews, won the British Fiction Prize, took me to all the big festivals, are over. My role as the first ever British Fiction Laureate is over. The novel is over. If I wrote one now and shared the fact on social media, I'd be trolled, reported and banned. If I wrote one now and tried to publish it, I fear for the consequences. My books, along with many others, have been burned in mass bonfires across the land, the flames licking and swallowing our precious words.

I dreamt about those flames last night.

And I woke this morning *compelled* to write, sentences bursting out of me, despite my fears, despite the fires, despite it all. I've realised that I cannot live in denial of the written word any more.

So, I'm writing. I am a writer. My laptop isn't safe though. They could be watching me. A physical pen it is. Yellowing pages in a physical notepad I've had for years, four daffodils on the front. Neat handwriting on the lines provided. At my desk. Coffee but no cigarette. Lamp on low next to me. Door locked. Curtains shut. Just me. Darkness devouring the outside world with both hands.

I will write.

If my words are discovered by the wrong people, I could incriminate anyone I speak of. I could lose everything I have; not that it's much. But they can't accuse me of writing fantasy. Because this is not a novel. No denial: I'm going to tell you how we got here, to this world without fiction. No denial: I'll tell you about my life, dull as it now is, lonely as it now is, painful as it now is.

No denial: I will speak.

I need to or I think I'll go insane.

Friday 2 November 2035 – 7.23 a.m.

It's the middle of another November heatwave. The pavement is melting. At midnight, it was as soft as playground rubber beneath my feet when I carried an empty milk carton to the end of the garden, held my nose, and dropped it in the recycle bin. I hate the smell of milk that isn't cold. Buttery and rich, like pungent glue, it puts me in mind of when poorer children got a free bottle at school breaktime. My mother once told me the crates stood in the corner of the classroom for hours, until the cream curdled.

When I finished writing here at my desk last night and was finally falling asleep, the fridge made a sound like an industrial nail gun. I almost fell out of bed. Thinking someone had broken in, and terrified *they* knew I'd been writing, I grabbed the lamp and crept into the kitchen.

No one there. The fridge was silent. It must have been failing for a while because my lettuce has been browning faster than usual, and my Coke hasn't been chilled for weeks now. Laura next door keeps telling me to get a SuperFridge, but I wouldn't trust it. I like my old one. I don't have any sort of voice assistant either. I can't undo – or whatever the proper word is – my Internet because since 2030 every building has it. But I haven't opened my laptop for months. I only turn my smartphone on once a week to order groceries. I wonder if I'm the only person who stays offline.

The last time they came I got questioned, and they asked why I avoid it.

I didn't answer. I don't have to.

Now it's dawn. I'm drinking strong tea at my desk, electric fan blasting cool air onto my face, recording the death of the fridge in this notepad. This feels like where I should write. Of course, facing a bare wall and no view and no books, it's a far cry from my old desk, that large oak thing that saw the creation of so many words. There, I was surrounded by physical books. It was a house of stories.

They crowded onto every available shelf, line upon line upon line, crushing those beneath, merging endings with beginnings, fighting for a place in my heart.

I had a place in hearts too then.

I'll have to get a new fridge. Go to a store. See if my Finance Score will let me spread the cost. A cleaning job doesn't cover much. I work five mornings a week at the Royal Hospital, scrubbing conference rooms and corridors. They don't know who I am. Since minimum wage hit an all-time high last year, many small companies went bust. Now some pay you a lesser salary if you're prepared to take half in cash. It suits me. I was able to give a false name. I do a good job, keep quiet. But it means my Finance Score is low because it only considers the small part of my salary that goes into the bank, and my dwindling savings, which is what's left of my Starting Out Sum. That was the grant given to me to help until I got a job; it was given to all fiction authors, editors, anyone who lost their jobs as a result of the ban.

I'm supposed to be at the hospital for my shift in an hour. I bike. I can't afford a car. Not even an old diesel thing. Those AV autonomous ones can't be trusted, and since 2030 they are all you can buy new. Self-driving cars form about eighty per cent of those on the road now. At least there are bike lanes on every street, though not all AVs recognise this and injure hundreds of cyclists a year. Are humans better behind the wheel, with their tics and emotions? I don't know. Does a driverless vehicle remove all human responsibility if an accident killed a child?

When I wrote fiction – long, *long* ago it feels – I had a routine. I'd wake late, as my life permitted then, start the coffee machine going, respond to emails, drink more coffee, and then write. I'd take a break for lunch and return to the page afterwards, an unfinished sentence awaiting me, so I had no choice but to complete it. That was one of my tricks. Never finish that last sentence. Let its mystery be the thing t—

Oh, there's someone at the door.

My heart. Shit. I'm still on edge from the fridge scaring me last night.

Wait, I'll—

Friday 2 November 2035 – 9.18 a.m.

I'm back.

I thought it might be *them*, the tall one and the short one. They don't come often now, but I dread an appearance. Instead, it was a young man waiting on my doorstep. A mock-vintage van was parked in the street behind him, the kind that's popular with the return of 'old-fashioned' specialist services. *Fine-Fayre* was engraved on the side in gold lettering, above a picture of a 1990s family drinking tea and eating biscuits. Laura next door orders from them. She said having friendly folks delivering treats, instead of soulless couriers who don't look you in the eye, is her week's highlight. I recognised the young man. I've seen him wheel up to her door a few times.

'Good morning,' he said from beneath me. 'Have you ever considered buying teabags from somewhere other than a supermarket?'

'It's barely eight-thirty,' I said.

'Would you enjoy having tea delivered directly to your door?'

He was in a wheelchair. The scar on his right cheek must have been semi-corrected by some sort of too-late surgery. As I stared at his face, I noticed that the joined expanse between his eyebrow and jaw resembled shoelaces when you first try to tie them as a child, where one part of the shoe's leather is pulled tighter than the rest. Politeness sent my gaze to his thick brown jacket with a gold trim and the words *Fine-Fayre* stitched into the pocket. My eyes travelled down to neat brass buttons, the same gold trim above the cuffs, and finally to his shiny products laid out in a wicker basket in his lap, where the criss-crosses of weave mirrored his facial injury.

'Our tea is competitively priced,' he continued.

'Did Laura send you?' I looked towards her house. She's been checking up on me more recently. It unnerves me. It's so hard to trust anyone.

He didn't reply, simply studying me.

'She feels sorry for me. I hope that's not why you're here.'

More studying, no words.

I wanted to ask if he was deaf as well as unable to walk but I'm not cruel. Yet there was something about him that triggered me. Maybe it was the heat. Maybe it was the off milk. The dead fridge. The idea that he pitied me, that I wasn't sure why he was here.

'We offer a full-money-back-guarantee if our products aren't perfectly to your liking,' he said. I couldn't place his accent. He spoke carefully as though no one had ever listened to him before. 'Our biscuits were described by *Love Baking* magazine as an utter delight.'

'Do I look like I give a fuck about biscuits?' I surprised myself; I don't often say fuck these days, and here it is within a few pages. I do realise that I'm not coming across well. But this isn't a novel. I'm not perfect. I'm not in denial about this. I had to admire the tea man for not flinching at *fuck*.

I realised I was irritated at me, not him.

Irritated that I was afraid, always afraid, when people came to my door.

Why was he so insistent? Why *me*?

Could I trust him? It would be nice to have someone to trust.

'Might I ask how you drink your tea?' he said.

'Hot and strong – hate weak crap.' I gave him that.

'Tea that lasts then.' He paused. 'And how many bags would you say you consume in the average week?'

'Who adds up teabags?'

He glossed over my remark. 'I think we have the perfect teabag for you. Strong tea lovers rave about these. This blend reheats in the microwave and still tastes as fresh as when it was first made. It's not like no-label tea that reheats and quenches your thirst in a lazy way.'

'You should be a writer.' This came out before I could think. 'Look, I can't buy your tea. I've no money.'

He studied me again. I thought for a moment that he recognised me. I prepared for it to show on his face; to stretch that
scar taut. But his features remained even. Hot air simmered above
the road. November. Not even nine a.m. And already it was twenty-five degrees.

The tea man took a small gold packet from his basket. 'How
about I leave a sample and give you time to think?' he said.

'I don't need time to think,' I said.

I closed the door and leaned against it, breath held, and waited
until I heard van doors slamming and the buzz of his wheelchair
ascending to the driver's position. After a minute or two I went
onto the step to check he had gone. Electric vans are so quiet that
I can never tell. They creep up on you like tragedy. The street was
deserted. I wondered if I'd imagined him; made him up like I used
to make things up.

As I turned to go back inside, I saw it. A flash of gold on the wall
separating me from Laura. A piece of sunshine. He had left me a
sample. He was real. The gift touched me, but I buried the emotion.
I couldn't risk it.

Why had he knocked? Does he feel sorry for me, living alone?
The nerve; *him* pitying me.

I carried the gold packet to the kitchen – ignoring my useless
fridge – and put it next to the kettle. I must go to work now. I
can't decide if it's safer to take my notepad with me or to slot it
back in the incision I made in my mattress. I don't like the idea
of it not being in proximity at any time. I'll take it with me. I'll
finish later.

Putting pen to paper and recording my life, I feel human again.
When I write, I'm the purest form of me. How different can this be
to creating fiction? It still has to make sense. I'll hide leitmotifs in
the prose. I'll play with the words.

Now, to work.

I'm back. No time has passed. Not enough to count.

I was about to leave the house. That's when I saw it. On the hallway windowsill. A single boy's blue and white trainer. One for a left foot. Not branded. Not expensive. Scuffed enough to have been worn lots. Around the size that would fit an eight-year-old – at least I imagine so. I reached for it, imagining my hand going right through it, like a hologram. But it was real. How did it get there? Who put it there? The tea man? Laura? Is it a cruel joke?

But they don't know my pain.

How could they?

Is the tiny fleck of blood on the sole real or di—

I'm at my desk again.

My hand aches from writing. It's a new experience for my fingers. Something I've not done for years. Midnight means nothing. The heat does not lessen with the late hour. Aside from this poor, overworked fan that stops me melting like the Wicked Witch of the East, the house is silent, the fridge especially. I binned the rest of its tepid contents earlier, gagging at the rubbery cheese. I didn't get chance to buy a new one today. I got distracted.

I'll tell you about it.

And then I'll tell you more about the books; the fiction ban.

I biked to work, my shirt dampening beneath my rucksack, the air on my face a blast from an open oven. Above, the winter sky was as blue as the stripe on the small trainer in my hallway. I almost hit the kerb. I had forgotten. Briefly. I cradled the shoe in my palm before I left the house, and then put it in the kitchen near the dead fridge. Why just one? Where's the other one? Who *put* it on my windowsill? My heavy heart and barren womb had me realising I maybe knew *why* – I just didn't know who. It's a cruel mockery of my childlessness; of the son I've longed for and never had; of the tests that found no physical flaw.

But who knows about that?

There is no pain like wanting a child. The clock ticks. Then the clock dies. I'm fifty-two. Out of time. Even with the extension of NHS-funded IVF, the National Institute for Health and Clinical Excellence (NICE) recommend that it can only be offered free up to the age of fifty. I could pay for it. They don't care if you're single. But I don't have that kind of money. And I'm resigned to it now. It is my lot.

At the traffic lights, a beautifully made-up woman studied my tear-stained face with pity from her air-conditioned car. She stopped speaking animatedly on a phone, something that's no longer a crime because of AVs, and frowned as if to ask, 'Are you OK?'

I wasn't. I was thinking about the leg that might wear the blue and white trainer, the boy owner of that leg who might run in those shoes, chase a ball, chase a girl, a boy, chase the wind. The woman's car was blue too.

I got to work, brow damp, heart still heavy. The other cleaners are pleasant, but I keep myself to myself. I began my duties, taking my cleaning trolley in the lift to the top floor. It's not lost on me that my third book – the one that changed my life – was set in a hospital. Did I set out to end up here? No. I just saw the ad and applied.

The NHS is the best it's been in years. At least that's what the politicians and their news channels tell us. Advances in technology – and lessons learned after Covid-19 – have apparently improved its efficiency. For five years health has been monitored digitally by the NHS App. Skin implants are currently being trialled, but many hate the idea of something so invasive. I do. I don't have the app either. I never will.

While cleaning Conference Room 3a, I faced my nemesis again.

On the long white table – next to a twisted Coke can pierced for some reason with a pair of eyebrow tweezers – was a glass of milk. Half full of room temperature evil; buttery liquid glistening with putrid moisture. According to my shift report, the last meeting in here finished yesterday at three, so it wasn't likely to be fresh. I put the crumpled Coke can into the bin bag tied to my cleaning trolley. Then I polished the table, ignoring the milk. When I could make out my flushed reflection in the veneer, I finally held my nose and reached for the glass.

The door opened at that point with a life-disturbing squeak. Two men and a woman filed into the room. I recognised Mr Patrukal (a squat surgeon with thinning red hair) and Mr Shrivel (a flirtatious orthopaedic surgeon who often makes appraising reference to my appearance), but I didn't know the willowy blonde woman. My index finger stopped inches from the milk. I snapped it back to my apron pocket and the glass went over, spilling milk across the surface. Rancid drips plopped to the floor. The trio stared at me.

'Sorry,' I said, flustered.

I mopped it up with two cloths, and then wrung them out over my bucket, retching at the stench.

'We need you to vacate the room, Mrs...?' The willowy blonde – who when she leaned close had breath like off dairy produce – tilted her head slightly, encouraging me to complete the sentence.

'Mrs D-Dalrymple, but call me Fern,' I responded. 'There's no meeting scheduled in here as far as I know.' I looked again at my report and shook my head, annoyed because I couldn't leave the hospital until I'd done every room on my list. 'I still have to clean the fridge, wash the windows, and empty the—'

'She can continue,' said Mr Shrivel, warmly. 'Fern has worked here for five years; she won't trouble us, not with that lovely disposition.'

His behaviour could be classed as sexual harassment, which if proven is punishable by a short prison sentence. But in my sterile, lonely world I find this appraisal of my personality rather ... *kind*.

Mr Patrukal waved his hand dismissively. 'Really, I think not for this.'

'I don't have any meetings on my report,' I repeated, like they would simply shrug and leave me to quietly finish my work.

'It was arranged last minute,' said Mr Shrivel.

Mr Patrukal glared at him, like these five words revealed some great secret. 'She'll have to leave,' he said.

'Do you mind?' Mr Shrivel asked me, with a conspiratorial smile, as though we were both humouring the other surgeon. 'Just this time.'

I shrugged. 'Do you know how long you'll be?'

'An hour at most, Fern,' he said.

I wheeled my cleaning trolley out of the room, feeling their eyes heavy on my back. I could tell they were waiting until I closed the door after me before they spoke. Probably some top-secret medical development that wasn't for the ears of a humble cleaner. Not that I was interested. I went back an hour later and the room was empty, only a stained coffee cup, three crumbs, and one awry chair evidence they had ever been there.

I don't have a stammer by the way – *D-Dalrymple* – but I sometimes forget that's my name when I'm here. I chose one beginning with D so that when I almost say *Fern Dostoy*, I can at least repeat the D and say the name I'm known by now.

Once upon a time Fern Dostoy wasn't just my name; she was a writer of novels. Of books that are now digitally erased, physically destroyed. But not all of them. I avoid social media and online news, but I know that reports regularly emerge of pre-2030 novels being found in basements and lofts and garden sheds. One day, the government will have their way though. With fiction no longer being printed – and with every physical paperback being hunted, surrendered, destroyed – our words are dying.

I still have a copy of my final novel, however.

Technological Amazingness: that's what it was called. It was one of the Big Four that changed everything. I can't let it go. I'm not recording here where it is right now, but I keep it like you keep the silver shoe charm your dying mother put in your hand with her last breath. I promised to tell you about how the books got banned. And I will. I'm not in denial, I just need to take my time and ma—

Saturday 3 November 2035 – 2.46 a.m.

I'm back. Not at my desk, but in bed. I can't sleep. The heat. The words. They won't let me. I didn't finish the story of what happened yesterday.

I will now.

I cycled home from work, painstakingly slowly, sweat drips clouding my vision. The temperature had soared to a breath-stifling thirty-nine degrees. I had to stop twice to wipe my face with my sleeve. The second time, I leaned my bike against a tree and rested in the shade. Voices drifted my way, carried, it felt, on the blast of heat. I looked about for the source but saw nothing except a quiet, mid-afternoon street. I chained my bike to the tree's narrow trunk and walked towards the nearby square, where cafes and shops surround a marble fountain. A long queue spilled out of the ALLBooks doors.

This is the UK's only bookstore now; a glitzy corporate chain. Indie bookshops were another casualty of the death of the novel. They couldn't compete with the low price of non-fiction in ALL-Books or with their vast budget and monopoly on advertising. It never fails to cross my mind that ALLBooks could not be a more misleading name for a place that doesn't sell fiction. SOMEBooks would cover it better.

Why the queue though?

No sooner had I wondered this than I realised what the people in line – quiet, heads bowed as though awaiting admittance to a funeral – were holding. Novels. Colourful, different-sized, tattered, brand new, hardback, paperback, beautiful *beautiful* novels. Some I recognised as ones released just weeks before the ban, never having the chance to find their place in the literary world, now clutched in hot hands for the last time.

I knew then why they queued.

Book Amnesty Day.

The first Friday of every month is the one day when you can hand in your pre-2030 books without fear of recrimination. Though they are no longer sold or published, it's hard to monitor whether people still have old ones. Plans are to end the amnesty by 2037, that all fiction will cease to exist by then. For now, you can turn up at any bookstore – which, of course, just means ALLBooks – and surrender your illegally owned words.

I joined the queue, curious to see what books they had, longing to see novels, *any* novel, in the flesh. I've never taken part in Book Amnesty Day. Laura next door has. She went last month with Edie Lane's erotic bestseller *Take Me Any Way*. I was removed suddenly from my previous house by two government officials, the tall one and the short one as I call them, both of whom now interview me when they feel like it, to make sure I've not indulged in any further writing. I don't know what happened to my vast collection of novels, the copies signed by the author and the unique, special editions that would have been worth a fortune before the ban. Were my beloved books burned? I still can't bear to think of it. When I walked around the house I was taken to, the one I live in now, I sobbed against the bare walls. Even now, at times, I touch the white expanse and pretend I can feel the raised, glossy spine of a book, of many books. I imagine I can pluck one from the shelf and get lost in a world that isn't this one.

A voice interrupted me from my reverie. 'You don't have a book,' said a woman holding three ancient, clearly much-loved Stephen King novels.

I looked at my hands as though expecting one to appear. 'Oh. Wrong queue. I just want to buy a … um … a medical dictionary.'

'You don't need to wait in line then,' she snapped.

I nodded. And stepped inside. I haven't been inside an ALL-Books since 2033 when a desperate need to be near physical books of *any* kind consumed me. Then I touched the shiny surfaces of the mostly hardback tomes and grieved for the lost freedom of creating my own world. Now the shop's air conditioning felt heavenly. I let it cool me for a second before I took a breath and approached the bookstands.

They're still displayed A to Z by the author's surname, still categorised by genre, and still have little review cards tacked below where staff have chosen a favourite. Underneath a biography about boxer Mac West – title *Pulling No Punches* – Sienna had written 'This is a brutally honest and eye-opening account of his career to date'. I smiled. An honest book. I often think that biographies are the closest thing to fiction that is published. They at least tell a story.

A voice broke into my thoughts. 'He's my hero.'

At my side, a small boy wearing a red T-shirt with a silhouette of Mac West on the front grinned at me, two teeth missing. He only looked about six.

'Your hero?' I repeated with a smile.

He nodded vigorously. 'Mum said she'll buy me it,' he said.

'Will you read it yourself?' I asked, impressed.

He shook his head. 'Some of the words are too big.'

'Will your mum it read to you then?'

He shook his head again. 'She won't,' he whispered conspiratorially.

'Why?' But I realised why as soon as the word was out. She was probably afraid to. Could even reading non-fiction to a child be classed as storytelling, something the current school curriculum actively discourages?

'She's not supposed to, is she?' he said, and it broke my heart.

He was too young to remember a time of bedtime stories. Too young to have had a parent sit on the bed and smooth down his hair and kiss his forehead and begin with *Once upon a time*.

'Not made-up stories, no,' I said. 'But she can read you this book.'

'Sometimes,' he said softly, and I moved closer, 'my big sister and me hide under her duvet and she tells me stories about talking elephants and flying cars. I usually fall asleep before the end, so she has to tell me the rest in the morning.'

I longed to kiss his cheek, to hug him, but much like with sexual harassment, touching a child that isn't yours – even just to help them up after a fall – is punishable by a short prison sentence.

The children of our land are sleepless. I watched a documentary late one night that followed two doctors who are having to prescribe sleeping pills for eight-year-olds, which means zombie kids in class the next day. They blamed climate change, overly stimulating computer games, hidden additives in the vitamins all children under ten must now take, the materials used to build our furniture. Despite it being the most obvious cause, not one of the doctors or politicians or parents interviewed for the programme suggested it could be down to the simple act of not telling them a bedtime story. Would I have dared say it, if interviewed? Probably not. But that's what I think. Reading aloud to children stimulates their imagination. It soothes them. Helps them understand the world. This is an undisputable fact. If it's fiction, all the better. The warmth, safety and joy created by snuggling up with your child and giving them an imaginary world can never be underestimated.

But no one says it.

Children always pay for what we do; for our mistakes. When there's a recession, they starve. When there's a water shortage – like the drought of 2032, when lush lawns fried, and dry trees caught fire – they dehydrate. When the government make decisions, they're the last to be considered.

'Tell your sister,' I said to the little boy, 'that she shouldn't stop the stories.'

I might not have a child, but I worry about the nation's children. When I grew up in the 1980s and 1990s, I fell asleep to the sound of my mother's voice whispering the words from *Peter Rabbit* and *The Witches* and *Now We Are Six*. If I had a son, now, in this only-the-truth, no denial world, I'd secretly make stories up for him. The forever end of fairy tales wouldn't stop me.

I suddenly pictured the strange blue and white trainer on my hallway windowsill and looked down at this boy's feet. Smart black lace-ups. I smiled.

'*Mac*,' came a shrill voice. 'Stop bothering the nice lady.' A large woman with long plaits marched up to us.

'It's fine,' I said. 'Honestly. He wasn't bothering me.'

'You definitely want it?' she said to him, nodding at the biography.

'Please,' he said.

She reached for it — the last copy — and they headed to the counter. He turned to look at me one last time, a *shhhhh* finger over his lips.

I returned my attention to the people queueing with novels. An assistant was letting them in a few at a time. They then went to a separate counter where a large plastic container awaited their paperbacks. A wiry woman with hair as thin as her frame looked down at the 2029 Shelly Dean novel, cradled in her arms as though it was her own infant. *Army of Lovers* depicted a utopian future where it's discovered that love, when allowed to be shared freely between all consenting, of-age humans, has hidden codes and healing powers. Like my third novel, it was another one of the four banned books that changed everything; one of the Big Four.

'What happens to these books?' the wiry woman asked, unable to surrender hers.

'No idea,' said the assistant. 'We seal the container, and someone picks it up.'

'I can't do it.'

'You *must*.' The assistant looked nervous.

'I... can I come back next month instead?'

'I really don't think that's permitted.' The assistant would have known the penalty, the possible prison sentence for owning this book. The expression on her face suggested that she felt immense pressure to make sure she did her duty.

The wiry woman slowly handed her black, cream and red book over and moved away, palms still up as though hoping for another book to drop into them.

'Next,' called the assistant.

I turned to go back to the shelves and crashed into someone. The first thing I saw was my own book. *Technological Amazingness*. It was a first edition; one with a picture of a doctor holding his own dripping, bloody heart up, the gap in his chest permitting the view of an empty, sterile hospital ward behind. My hand went to my chest, as though to stop my heart escaping too. I *ached* for my book. For the whole thing. For the writing of it; for the late nights, the early mornings, the passion, the typing until my fingers throbbed; for the first sight of it when early copies arrived; for the praise, the glorious praise. It was all I could do to not reach out and take it from the man who was now studying me intently, eyebrows untamed and beard bushy.

'Oh my God,' he hissed.

I saw it. He recognised me. I shook my head, panicked, but his blue eyes were sky warm, not ice cold. He touched my arm and I savoured the human contact. He suddenly pulled away as though he realised the action could be condemned.

'We adore you,' he whispered.

'You...?' I blushed.

'Your hair is short ... a different colour ... but I still knew.'

Involuntarily, I touched my neck.

'We hold secret book groups.' He leaned close.

'You do?' How this filled me with hope. *Secret book groups.* God, I missed them. Meeting readers in their own homes, drinking their coffee, eating their home-made cakes, talking literature until the sun set. I'd gone to so many, back in the old world.

'We loved the Big Four.' He paused. 'They'll never destroy them all,' he said, near my ear, breath warm. 'And even if they did ...' He tapped his head. 'We'll not forget them. If we keep talking about them, they don't die. You book is my all-time favourite. I feel ... it's such an *honour* to see you, to meet you. Fern Dostoy. British Fiction Laureate. *You.*'

I looked around, afraid every head would have turned at my name, but the low hum of conversation was white noise that drowned out our illicit encounter.

'*You have no humanity. You have no heart. You have no right. No, but we have the ability, we have the hands, and we will make it right,*' he whispered.

He had memorised my words.

But here, in this bookshop, I had none.

'This one is just to keep them happy,' he whispered.

'Sorry?'

'One of our book group members thinks we're being monitored.' He spoke so quietly I could barely hear. 'This is to throw them off, if we are. I have two more copies of your book. I'll bring another next month. But they won't get my final copy. Ever.'

I wanted to cry.

'Do you have a message?' he asked.

'A message?'

'For the group.'

'Oh. I... um...'

'Anything?'

'Thank you.' It was all I could think of; how I felt.

'Would you visit us?' He struggled to keep his voice down.

'I ... I couldn't. It's too ... *risky*.' But I wanted to. God, I wanted to.

'I understand,' he conceded. 'I didn't know you were still in the area. There was a rumour on social media that you had moved to Greece.'

'Was there? I don't go online much.'

'Do you want to hand that book in?'

We both jumped apart. An assistant pointed at *Technological Amazingness*. 'You're the last one,' she said. The queue had dispersed. The plastic container was full of books. He nodded and without a word he followed her. I watched him hand my book over. Watched it go in with all the others. Watched him leave the shop, turning to look at me one last time, a *shhhhh* finger over his lips like the six-year-old boy earlier.

Then I picked a book off one of the shelves – any book, I didn't even look at it – and paid for it and returned to my bike and pedalled home. I put my package on the kitchen work surface near the dead fridge. As I left the room, something made me stop. An absence;

sensed before confirmed. The blue and white trainer. I spun around. It wasn't there. I looked in the musty fridge, on the floor, on the windowsill. Gone as though it had never existed at all.

Had it?

Was I losing my mind?

Am I losing my mind?

I need to rest my hand now and sleep for a few hours. Then I'll tell you more about how the books ended up be—

Saturday 3 November 2035 – 6.28 a.m.

I'm drinking my Fine-Fayre tea black because, well, no milk. The circular bag fits into my mug like it was designed for it. The leaves have freed an undeniably fresh flavour. It's early, not even light. I'm sitting in bed, no sheet and three pillows.

The books.

OK. This is how it started. I hate to give it truth on this paper. But I must if I'm to tell the full story. I'll summarise in a few pages hopefully, like a teen's essay for a school exam. But there's much more. I *will* share that.

I just need to ease myself into it.

Physical books made a comeback after the rise of eBooks in the 2010s. We returned to our love of the glossy cover, of the smell of the page, of the chance to meet the author and have them sign it. Reading grew in popularity during the 2020 and 2021 lock-downs. Though the arts were financially neglected during Covid-19, with theatres closing and film production coming to a standstill, novels survived, victorious. Their popularity grew from the debris of limited entertainment. They were all we had.

But towards the end of the twenties, the government grew afraid of their power. They were turbulent times with a major world pandemic, climate change, crippling recession, the growth of extremism in politics, the oppression of minority groups, and hard-won disability and BAME rights being cancelled. An avalanche of novels addressed these themes through fiction.

Four – the Big Four as they became known – stood out.

Together, they sold a hundred million copies in the UK alone.

Author Lynda Harrison – in her 2028 best-selling novel *The Final Adjustment* – had a fictional prime minister enforce herd immunity during a deadly worldwide pandemic, not just to eliminate the old and weak but to finish the creative industry, silencing it for good.

Then, in 2029, we had Shelly Dean's epic *Army of Lovers* and Cass May's *The Rebel Girls*. The latter was a love story between

24

two women from opposing extreme left and far right parties, who brought a lawless nation together, until one of them – not the one you might expect – changed her mind and betrayed her lover by selling their story, causing the final abolition of many LGBTQ rights.

My novel – *Technological Amazingness* – was set in a hospital. It was the first thing I wrote, during a time of intense grief, but it took five years and two books for it to finally be published. I was angry at how the Covid-19 pandemic had been handled; angry that the virus had taken the one I loved; tired of vulnerable people losing out on life-saving treatment because of impossible targets the government set the NHS in order to get funding.

I wrote the story of a fictional medical team who came up with two extreme ideas to ensure they got funding – The Pre-Surgery Care Mortality Policy and the One Death Policy. The former was the requirement that patients were already dead pre-op so recorded deaths by surgery were zero. Perfect. No one died on the table. Funding increased. The latter was the requirement that every UK family volunteered one member for euthanasia each year, thereby eliminating thousands of people from using the NHS. I wanted to present the idea that a seemingly ridiculous and outrageous policy could be implemented. Show how insane the world had gone.

My book was compared to *Animal Farm* and described as 'angry, shocking, utterly compelling, and necessary' by *The Times*, but the Big Four were bestsellers because people loved and hated them; they divided the nation, causing discussion online and on topical news shows, discussion that led to violent protests across the country. In 2029 Lynda, Cass, Shelly and I were guests on a panel called The Future Now at the Edinburgh Book Festival. As it concluded, eight members of the new Anti-Fiction Movement set fire to the tent, injuring sixteen attendees and destroying all the books. This growing movement was headed by Ade Woods, a controversial journalist outspoken in his belief that fiction caused more harm than good. He often used my book, *Technological Amazingness*, as example of the damage, especially when three hospitals were burnt down by vigilantes who believed that the fictional team in my novel were inspired by real surgeons.

That was the start.

The government used this moment to justify a new campaign to first censor fiction that questioned their policies, and eventually remove it. And by the middle of 2030, all fiction was banned. You might ask, how do you enforce such a thing? Well, it begins with falsified reports showing the damage fiction does to our young. With 'highly-esteemed' professionals announcing that school children need a more regimented education, not an endless story time. With reports by Ade Woods, and then others, attributing violent protests and a rise in crime to fiction books, particularly books like ours.

The government likely knew it would be impossible to control all fiction. The only answer? Ban it.

At the start of 2030, tens of thousands of novels were removed from circulation. Small publishers and indie bookstores folded. The government's argument became that words written by 'mutinous' authors muddied the 'truth'. That this was not freedom of speech but freedom to lie and deceive and mislead.

My life as a writer was over.

Now, the only books to be published are factual: science, biography, nature, medical, psychology, history. These are wonderful books. But we need novels too.

Even TV 'stories' were affected. Fictional programmes were eventually outlawed, from soap operas to drama serials. Only reality TV, documentaries, game shows, and news programmes were produced, and even those were heavily monitored.

There you have it, in summary.

There were, of course, times I thought it might not happen, times when groups protested, when someone of esteem spoke out defending fiction, when opposing political parties came close to changing legislation but were stopped at the last minute, when a documentary explored the benefits experienced by terminally ill patients who were read stories, though opposition then quickly disappeared. I still often ask myself aloud, 'How the hell did it actually happen?' Yet, looking back over history, so many unthinkable things – inhumane events you would never imagine occurring – have happened. You have to live through it to believe it.

Now, here we are. Here I am. In bed. Notepad slowly filling, hand aching.

No denial.

This is the truth and I ca—

Saturday 3 November 2035 – 10.28 a.m.

I got up eventually and went to the kitchen. For a moment the brown package on the work surface made me stop in my tracks, heart tight. What the hell was it? Who put it there? Then I remembered the book I'd bought in ALLBooks the day before and hadn't even looked at yet. I put the kettle on, popped the second of the three teabags in my sample pack into my mug, and picked the package up.

Inside was the newest edition of Stephen Hawking's *A Brief History of Time*. I smiled and held the silver and black hardback to my heart. One of the few books I love that survived the madness. Maybe I'll read it again.

I opened the glossy cover. Something white fell to the floor with a whisper. A small card. I picked it up. In the top corner was a graphite sketch of a sleeping baby on a cloud, an upside-down book his pillow. Central was a bold headline: BEDTIME STORIES FOR THE RESTLESS (09887 555777). My curiosity fired, I thought about switching on my smartphone and dialling the number

No. *No.*

I read the small print beneath the headline, moving my mouth around the words and stirring the stagnant kitchen air:

> *Happy-ever-afters are here. Call this number between*
> *6 and 9 p.m. if you still believe in the fairy tale and one of*
> *our many calming storytellers will send your restless child*
> *into a blissful, contented sleep with the tale of their choice.*
> *(This number is untraceable and will not show on your bill.)*

I smiled. The thought of reclining on a bed and hearing someone read aloud made my eyelids deliciously heavy. I turned the card over. In the top corner was a graphite sketch of an adult reading from a large book. There was more text beneath.

28

If you still believe in fairy tales, we need you.
Do you want to be a calming storyteller?
For more details, meet us near the last statue
at 5 p.m. on the second Monday of the month.

Who put the card inside the book?

Surely they couldn't be in every single one; ALLBooks would be shut down.

Reading fiction to a child can result in a full investigation by the social services, and possible removal of said child for an indefinite amount of time. Laura next door told me the horror story of the eight-year-old son of a friend of a friend who was put in care for six months after his father found a Roald Dahl in the loft and read it to him in the garden, where he was overheard and reported.

A powerful chain like ALLBooks wouldn't risk association with something that advocated story time. It must have been the assistant. I sat at the kitchen table, steam curling from my black tea, and tried to recall who served me yesterday. The transaction had been so fast, so perfunctory, with me eager to leave. A woman. Young. Nails painted mint. That's all I can recall. What did she see in me that had her thinking I'd be interested?

And what is the last statue?

For more details, meet us near the last statue
at 5pm on the second Monday of the month.

Maybe it's the last one they built before they stopped?

Statues were in the news for a while. Back in the twenties there was outrage when the sculpture of slave trader Edward Colston was pulled down and replaced with one of Marcus Rashford, a young black footballer who campaigned for free school meals for children in poverty. Other statues accused of being racist were defaced. It divided people. Some argued that they glorified racism; others argued that it was part of our history. Slowly, over the last few years, many have been destroyed or put in museums. Not all of them, I don't think. There's the Pages statue, by the river. I'm sure it's still there. I can't bear to think of it. It's such a simple, small thing, but special. It certainly wasn't the last one built. They erected yet another dedicated to Shakespeare at the end of 2029. Was that the last?

Perhaps this clue is designed to wheedle out the serious story-tellers from those who might make trouble. But the risk, giving out such a card to arbitrary people. Was I randomly selected? Maybe the assistant recognised me. I made my opinions public before the ban; I said it was a blatant attempt to suppress freedom of expression, that the government wanted to control their version of the truth. I was outspoken then. I swore. I rebelled. I fought. Look at me now. *Look at me now.*

Is the Bedtime Stories card a test?

I daren't turn my smartphone on and search online. It's not worth the risk.

I shivered despite the thermometer already touching thirty degrees and looked around my kitchen – at the plain cupboards, the loveless walls and the quiet, dead fridge – as though someone might be watching me read the card; as though a hidden filming device might be deciphering my face for a positive or negative reaction to the words. That was unlikely – *wasn't it*?

What if Bedtime Stories is a way of ensnaring those who flout the fiction rules? I put the card on the table. Sweat trickled from my forehead, down my nose. What if I figured out what the last statue is, went along to this place, and the tall one and the short one were waiting there for me?

After all, Shelly Dean – author of *Army of Lovers* – has apparently been missing for more than a year. It wasn't on the news. It isn't likely to be. Laura next door told me. She saw it on some social media site that's since been pulled. An anonymous blogger shared that he had 'personally been informed' that Dean's family reported her absence after three months without contact.

Is it true? My gut tells me it is. And I'm not sure I want to know where she is.

I put the card in the drawer, intending to also put it out of my mind.

Without thinking, I went to the fridge, fancying cereal for breakfast.

I'll have to get another one, especially during this heatwave. I can't live on packet foods and microwave meals for the rest of my life. Or maybe I can. It would mean never again spilling milk, never again trying to erase the stink before spoilt dairy infused the air. I can smell it now, even here at my desk. People wince at farmyard scents, at overflowing sewers, at overturned wheelie bins. Not me. I can tolerate any putrid odour. But not warm, days-old, off milk.

Oh.

There's someone at the door. Shit. *Them*?

I'll be ba—

It was the Fine-Fayre tea man. Sitting in his chair on my path, wicker basket in his lap, like the witch in Snow White hoping to get me to eat a poisonous apple.

'Did you enjoy the tea?' he asked.

He hadn't closed my gate properly and it swung back and forth with a rude squeak. Next to it tiny buds sprouted from a plant, promising colour any day. My tulips, however, were alive with brazenness. Flowers never know when to bloom any more. They should be dying now we're going into winter, but random heatwaves followed by sudden cold snaps confuse them.

'How do you know I drank it?' I studied his facial scar and then his useless legs. His earth-brown hair was neatly cut around the ears and brushed to the side. One strand escaped the others, rebellious. He returned my gaze. Said nothing. 'It wasn't too bad,' I eventually admitted, filling the silence.

He smiled as though I'd said I would buy two thousand and handed me a larger gold pack from amongst the condiments. 'These particular teabags are two pounds and nine pence for forty and—'

'I didn't say I wanted any,' I said.

' – and this week's special offer,' he continued regardless, 'is a free bag of Nutty Speckles when you spend ten pounds.'

'They're not free then, are they?'

'Free when you spend ten pounds.'

'As I said, not free then, and I'm already broke.' I paused. '*Nutty Speckles*? What the heck are those?'

'A thin, oaty biscuit peppered generously with tiny nut-free nuts, and with a dash of citrus.'

'Who thinks of these names? They're … *creative*.'

He continued as though I hadn't asked the question. 'Forty teabags at two pounds and nine pence works out as just five pence each. You'll find most supermarket brands cost twice that and they lack the quality of our bags. If you like them I ca—'

'Are you done?' I asked.

He stopped abruptly.

'This is harassment you know,' I said. He had fired the old me. The me who fought, who questioned, who mostly hid now, within the sad skin of this pathetic docile creature.

He reversed his chair with a whirr and turned to leave.

'What kind of salesman *are* you?' I called after him. I wanted him to stay, even though he irritated me, even though I wasn't sure I could trust him. Company is company. It's the weekend and I probably won't speak to a soul until work on Monday.

He paused at the gate.

'How have you ever sold a single thing if you just crawl off like a sad puppy when I tell you to?' Questioning him like this made me feel alive. 'They can come up with those fancy product names, but they can't train you to persevere?'

He returned to my step. His brow was damp. The hot air was so still, so close, that I felt if I reached out, I'd be able to hold it in my palm.

'You must be roasting in that thick jacket,' I said.

'I'm OK.'

'There must be a thinner option?'

'We just have two of these.'

I surrendered then. 'I'll take one pack of teabags. Wait there.'

I got my credit card, put it to his phone and waited for the tick. He passed me the large gold pack, then seemed to think. He went back into his basket and handed me some Nutty Speckles.

'I didn't spend a tenner,' I said.

'It's fine.'

'I don't want *pity* Nutty Speckles.'

'All new customers get a welcome gift.'

'You never mentioned that.'

'I have now,' he said.

'I might not be a new customer though. I might not want any more teabags.'

'Keep the gift anyway,' he said.

'If I *did* want more … what would happen?'

'I'd call by whenever you'd like me to.'

'I suppose you can come back in a week.' I sighed like he was testing my patience; like I was doing him a huge favour. 'I might want some more by then.'

He swiped his smartphone's screen. 'Next Saturday? Same time?'

'Maybe not at the crack of dawn.' Sarcasm.

He typed the info into his phone. 'Noon?' he asked.

'I suppose.'

'Can I take your name?'

'Do you have to?'

'But what will I call you?'

'Call me whatever you like,' I said, 'but if these biscuits upset my stomach, I'll sue you.' And I shut the door.

I took the gold package into the kitchen. I gasped and it fell from my hand, landing at my feet, the foil cool against my ankle. The small blue and white trainer was back. On its side, on the windowsill, one lace slightly muddier than the other, a red speck still visible, like it had been sitting there all along. Had it? No. *No.* It was on the hallway windowsill last time. I approached slowly, afraid it might move.

Who had put it there?

I stopped in my tracks. The tea man? He came before I saw the shoe yesterday. (Was it only yesterday?) But he didn't leave my sight – and he didn't today. And why would he? He doesn't know me. Did Laura next door come in the back while I was distracted? Did she suggest the tea man come to give her the opportunity? But *why*? It makes no sense.

I couldn't bring myself to touch the shoe this time.

It brought to the surface emotions I didn't want to look at.

I went to lie on the bed, feet bare, electric fan on full, pointing at my face. Due to the unpredictable climate, new houses are automatically fitted with air conditioning these days, but mine is an eighties build and I don't have the money to update it. It was barely lunchtime on a Saturday and the hours loomed ahead of me, empty, lifeless.

My days are mundane, my routine the same every week. Work Monday to Friday. Switch my smartphone on once a week to order groceries and check my bank account and see if anyone has called or messaged, which never happens. Even the two government officials hardly ever call by to interview me anymore.

They never warn me of a visit. They just turn up – one tall, one short – uneven on my doorstep, waiting until I admit them. The last time was six months ago. We sat at the kitchen table. The tall one asked about my current reading material – Demi Moore's 2019 memoir, borrowed from Laura next door and proven by a hardback on the bedside table – while the short one searched the house, not caring to put back tossed underwear or overturned bins.

Eventually, the fan's whir lulled me to sleep. As I drifted off, I wondered, if I had a son, what would we do for the day? Go to the park. Ride bikes. Climb trees. Pick apples. Watch one of the many factual children's shows on the two speciality under-eight channels. Bake apple tarts with our haul. Eat them in the sun on the back step.

Would I secretly tell him stories?

Would I dare?

I dreamt hard. It was the kind that disorients you. That holds onto your sleeve as you begin to wake and begs you not to forget.

There was a boy. Maybe eight, chunky the way they are before their baby fat becomes lean pre-teen flesh, with cheeks ripe for squishing and reddish-blond hair damp from some game or exertion. He wore one shoe: a blue and white trainer on his right foot. Did I have the other one? I couldn't see my real-world windowsill because I wasn't in my house. I was in his. He sat cross-legged in a bedroom, a smartphone in one hand and a small white card in the other. I recognised it – the Bedtime Stories card. He looked at it, then tapped the number into the phone, brow furrowed in concentration.

35

After a moment he said, 'Hello, I'm Hunter.'

Hunter. I smiled.

He paused. Waited. 'Hello? Is that a somebody?' His lower lip dangled with such innocence that I teared up. 'Hello?' His lip wobbled and I couldn't bear it.

Someone talk to him, for God's sake.

He pressed END CALL and dialled again. 'Hello? Is the story lady there? Hello? Why can't you hear me?'

'I can hear you,' I said softly, not expecting a reaction.

But he turned. Looked at me. Saw me. Smiled. I melted.

I woke, not wanting to, hating with sudden venom this sterile world of cold words, wishing if not to be dead then to be stuck in my dreams, to be in a place where a small boy's smile made me feel there was hope.

I imagined putting my blue and white trainer on his other foot like the prince when he finally located Cinderella and they belonged together fore—

Saturday 3 November 2035 – 2.55 p.m.

Apparently, there was no medical reason for my infertility, the implication being that there was something wrong with my mind, my heart; that I wasn't trying hard enough. I was married for eight years, to Cal, and we *tried*; ninety-six months of enjoyable and then eventually desperate effort. I thought I was pregnant once but never told Cal. I wanted to cherish the moment before sharing it. The test's faint line said I was a real woman. That I had *tried*. For eight days I was a mother. My breasts ached; my tummy swelled. Then nothing. The doctor said false positives often happen.

Keep trying, he said. *Keep trying*.

But my ovaries slumbered like Sleeping Beauty, except no kiss stirred them.

Cal died of Covid-19 in June 2020. He was admitted to the hospital on a Tuesday with a mild cough and a temperature, laughing it off, saying he'd be home for dinner and to keep it warm, open the wine. By Thursday, he had gone. Just fifty years old. I couldn't be with him. I never got to say goodbye. There were ten people at the funeral, socially distanced, grieving quietly. I haven't seen his parents since. We weren't close. Our lack of children means there is nothing to bond us.

I keep Cal's photograph in a small silver frame by my bed. I hardly look at it, so long has it been there, as everyday now as a tap or a door handle or a light switch. He never lived to see my success as a writer. He never lived to see my part in ending all fiction. He never lived. I haven't loved a man since. I miss him, deeply, but I can't dwell on it or I will never again get up in a morning.

I planned the child I would have with my school friend Ella during Biology; she wanted two, didn't care what, and I wanted a boy who'd have reddish hair. I still see him exactly that way when I can't sleep. I could draw my imaginary boy here in this notepad. A few careful strokes and he'd come to life without the need for IVF. I often described him to Cal, who said, 'one day,' and kissed my cheek. That one day never came but we had many others that were special too. We didn't have much, but we had hope. We painted over the cracks in our cheap first house and we made a large chicken go a long way. We had nicknames for one another, and we fed on sarcasm when we were crabby and wanted to lift one another. I miss laughing. I miss the old life. I miss Cal.

I miss me.

It's afternoon now. The heat is unbearable. The fan has followed me from desk to kitchen to desk, though it makes little difference. Laura next door knocked at two with the remains of an apple pie and some cream.

'I won't eat it all,' she said. She would. She's a large lady. She's tried every NHS diet with no success and has had to pay the Obesity Fine at least three times, poor woman. Bringing a pie to my door was an excuse. To check on me. To be nosy.

'It's no good giving me cream,' I said, without thinking.

'Why?'

'My fridge broke.'

'Oh no.' She peered round me as though I might invite her in to see it. 'They'll replace it, won't they?'

'I doubt that. It's about twenty years old.'

'You should get a SuperFridge. I couldn't live without mine. It tells me how many calories there are in—'

'I don't want one.' I took the pie but ignored the cream.

'I've got one of those mini fridges in the shed. You can borrow that. Nothing special, old as anything, but it'll keep your milk and margarine cold.'

I agreed and she dropped it off an hour later, clearly hoping once again to be invited in. I plugged it in and waited for it to cool. Once it did, I opened the door and stood in front of it for ten minutes. I looked at the blue and white trainer still on its side on the kitchen windowsill but didn't touch it. My grocery delivery arrived at its four o'clock slot and I put salad and Coke and margarine on the two shelves. I checked the milk's use-by date. Five weeks away. God knows what they put in it to make it last so long. I have a rule that I won't drink it if the use-by date is within four days. I can't risk the slightest chance that it's off, not that it ever gets close to that date anymore when it lasts a month.

I can't stop thinking about Hunter.

I'm at my desk, Fine-Fayre tea next to me, with a splash of cold milk. I tested the tea man's theory that this blend tastes just as fresh after being reheated in a microwave as it does when first made. I hate to say that he's right. I even tried a Nutty Speckle. It wasn't the worst biscuit; crumbly and sweet, but unusual.

Writing with a pen reminds me how much I miss the physical letter. Folding the paper, putting it in an envelope, sending it and awaiting a reply. In the nineties I had a French pen pal and kept our exchanges in a shoebox. Now, the soft scrape of pen on paper soothes me.

I've just been to check on the blue and white trainer. Still there.

I can't stop thinking about Hunter.

Did I really dream him? Was it the heat? I can *see* him as clear as I saw Laura on my doorstep earlier, as real as my dead fridge dumped now near the shed, as vivid as my fiction used to be when I wrote it.

I've stuck the Bedtime Stories card in my notepad. It'll make it easier to hide it if the tall one and the short one turn up to interview me. I picture all the children out there, desperate for a story. Just before the fiction ban, a report suggested that parents should read to them until they were eleven. Many had stopped when they hit six. Those kids expressed how much they missed 'precious and cosy' reading time. There was strong evidence of a link between the nightly bedtime story and success in education.

What do parents do now at bedtime? Switch on the TV? Watch a dull documentary or biased news show? Leaf through non-fiction? Today, those younger than five will never even have seen a physical storybook. What world is this that they haven't? I can't bear it. I must do something. The old me, she'd do something. I must find this Bedtime Stories place. But the risk. They watch us, even outside. I'm only safe in here.

But what is safe? It's work. Eat. Sleep. Denial. Work. Eat. Sleep. Denial. This isn't a life. I can't bear it. I must *do* something.

I need to figure out what the last statue is, and maybe I wi—

Monday 5 November 2035 – 3.29 p.m.

I'm just home from work.

I didn't feel like writing yesterday. Some days I don't even want to think, let alone string words together. Some days I long with physical pain for the time before 2030. I'm on my second cup of Fine-Fayre tea in an hour. I wonder if they put extra caffeine in their bags to get new customers hooked. I finished the Nutty Speckles yesterday. I miss them. Maybe they're peppered with caffeine too.

Today was odd. I was scrubbing a yellow stain off the window in Conference Room 3a when the same trio from Friday disturbed me again; the willowy blonde, Mr Patrukal, and Mr Shrivel with his customary appraising smile. 'Fern,' he said, warmly.

'You want me to leave again?' I was annoyed, knowing my sheet said the room was empty all morning.

'I don't,' said Shrivel at the same time as Patrukal started with, 'Yes, I thi—'

Mr Shrivel whispered in his ear, glanced at me, and awaited a reaction from Patrukal. 'OK, *fine*,' he said, as though it was anything but. 'If you make some drinks, you can finish what you need to do here.'

'Three coffees,' said the willowy blonde, taking a seat.

I pushed my trolley into the corner of the room where a large fridge and limescale-encrusted kettle forms an insignificant kitchen and began preparing coffee. I heard chairs scraping, a zip opening, the ping of a laptop firing up, but I didn't turn. Discretion; I love that word. I formed it silently in my corner. I can be as discreet as soft net curtains hiding an illicit encounter. I can be invisible. That's how you harvest stories from the conversations around you.

'Sorry to have been obscure on Friday.' Without turning, I knew Shrivel's voice. 'I know we didn't get to finish our meeting beyond introductions and sharing our backgrounds with Dr Brane, but I think that serves us well.' He was clearly speaking to Patrukal, and

41

now must have turned his attention to the willowy blonde. 'Good to have you with us again Dr Brane.' So that must be her name.

'My pleasure,' she said, voice musical.

'You'll understand shortly why I wanted to get to know you better, Dr Brane, and you us. I'm both excited and nervous by what I'm working towards. I want us all feeling familiar and on the same page before I share my … well, my *vision*.'

'Quite,' she said.

I carried three coffees to the table and placed them centrally, with a bowl of sugar to sweeten the sour. Dr Brane had long, pearly fingernails and I wondered how impractical they might be in exploring human crevices. Perhaps I was jealous; my fingernails never grow and are ruined by bleach and disinfectant. My hair used to be blond and flowing, but now it's short and mousy with streaks of grey. I'm no longer Fern Dostoy, writer of books. I'm Fern Dalrymple, cleaner of filth.

'Milk?

I looked up from the lustrous nails. Patrukal was staring at me, the whites of his eyes yellowing at the corner. 'Are we to have milk?' he asked.

'Oh. Yes. Sorry.'

I got the milk from the fridge. It was in a jug. I winced. How could I know how long it had been there? I couldn't bear to sniff it and check. I took it to the table. Let them take the risk with it.

'NICE think this is an idea with great potential,' continued Mr Shrivel, pouring milk into his and Patrukal's cups. I felt sick watching the creamy liquid merge with black. Dr Brane put a hand over hers. I returned to my corner. 'They said that if I can get a team together, do the retrospective quantitative research and build some statistics, they'll take it even more seriously.'

I know – from my research for *Technological Amazingness,* and now having been a ghostly presence at countless meetings here – that NICE is the National Institute for Clinical Excellence. I've heard all this medical jargon a hundred times. I've cleaned gooey stains off windows and dog shit off the floor while doctors discuss NHS protocol and malpractice suits. I've ignored surgeons who quickly straighten their clothes and remove hands from the inner thigh of a smiling colleague when I enter a room. I've cleaned up used condoms, abandoned sandwich wrappers, broken lipsticks. I witness NHS madness as a cleaner. I had to imagine it as a writer. It's a shame I didn't work here before I wrote *Technological Amazingness*. The ridiculous Pre-Surgery Care Mortality Policy and One Death Policy I created for the book might have been extreme, but the behaviour of the characters and the lengths they went to for funding, that wasn't far wrong.

'I won't agree to be part of anything until I know what it is,' said Dr Brane.

'This milk.' It was Mr Patrukal, indignant. 'I think it's off.'

Mr Shrivel continued as though he'd had no interruption. 'NICE agree that I should be the project manager. I have the interest of numerous government officials too; I'll share their details with you if and when they agree to back it.' He paused and I sensed he'd glanced over at me, wiping the fridge, maybe remembering I was still there. 'What I'm proposing will significantly aid the Department of Health's 2040 *A Healthier Nation; A Stronger Nation* policy. As you're aware, one of the four targets is to reduce heart disease, cancer and strokes by half in those under sixty-five.'

I paused, my cloth dripping onto the floor. Shrivel's delivery, some of the words, they could have been straight out of my book.

'What I'm proposing will challenge everything you previously thought,' he said.

'Why us?' It was Mr Patrukal. 'I'm sorry, but while I consider myself the best in my field, you must surely know that though I'm still on duty, I'm under investigation – and Dr Brane is only working part-time until her court case.'

I dared to glance at them; she looked put out at his sharing this. She looked over at me and said to Patrukal, 'I think *she* needs to leave.'

43

'It all sounds exciting,' Patrukal continued as though he hadn't heard her. 'Ambitious. But if you're being mysterious to engage us, you can quit. Be upfront. I've to be in surgery in an hour.'

'I will,' said Shrivel, patient. 'I have to lay the groundwork first. You see, this could be considered … well, *unethical*. This is my greatest problem. The NSF is going be the real challenge.'

This is the National Service Frameworks. They establish measurable goals within set time frames for the NHS in England, aiming to raise quality standards and to identify key interventions for a service or care group, such as people with long-term conditions. See how I can quote these things after five years here?

'Is this to do with the Tarquin Smith-Jones case?' asked Mr Patrukal. 'The pregnant thirteen-year-old boy?'

'No, no,' said Mr Shrivel, indignant. 'I've no time for flamboyant experiments. My proposal … at first, you may greet it with shock. You will question both yourselves and me, but then, when you find the right answers therein, I'm sure you'll be as excited as I am.' The words came out of Shrivel's mouth as though it had taken effort to make sure they were in the right order. A chair scraped. He was on his feet. I wrung my cloth out. 'Listen, please, with an open mind. Hear the many pros for my idea, let them sink in, and then open your thoughts to the future possibilities. I believe that if you join me in piloting this, we will be at the forefront of the greatest moment in medical history.'

The room fell silent. I glanced over my shoulder. Shrivel stood, legs apart, before his rapt audience, like a priest delivering a sermon. A phone rang, shrill, rude. Dr Brane fumbled in her jacket pocket and found it.

'I have to get this,' she said, and left the room.

'I should go too,' said Patrukal.

'We must resume,' said Shrivel, insistent. 'Soon. I'll email you both.'

And then I was alone with him.

'I need to finish the rest of the room.' I wheeled my trolley into the centre.

'Of course, Fern.' He smiled warmly. 'It must seem we are strange creatures?'

'Sorry?'

'Doctors. Surgeons. All of us. You see us at our worst. Behind closed doors. Behind the mask.'

'I don't really think about it,' I said. 'I'm just here to do my job.'

He seemed to consider something. 'You're very discreet. I may have a special role for you in the near future.'

'I'm happy with this role.' I collected the empty coffee cups. What on earth did he mean?

'No ambition for more?' he asked. 'No big dreams, Fern?'

Those are over, I thought.

'You're very like the last statue,' he said, on his way towards the door.

My heart stopped. Was it a test? Did he know about the card in my book? 'The what?' I asked, trying sound casual, barely interested, but hoping he would answer.

'Nothing.' Had he meant to say it? Did he now regret doing so? I tried so hard to read his face. 'You're just … well, an enigma. Like a remnant from time gone by.' He opened the door. Did he know who I was? Or was he giving me clues for the last statue? I felt sick with fear, but tense with excitement too. When he had gone, I polished the table and mopped the floor, and tried to keep my hands from shaking.

Now, my Fine-Fayre tea is cold next to me, the air is still as hot as a packed gym changing room, and my hand aches from writing all of this. But I feel more alive than I have in months. Years. Since they took away the books and ended my ca—

Wednesday 7 November 2035 – 12.01 a.m.

It's late but I can't sleep. I wonder if I'm drinking too much Fine-Fayre tea. Maybe I'll stop drinking it in the evening. Even one sheet on top of me is unbearable. The pillow is damp with sweat. If I write for half an hour, it might settle me.

It used to.

My last two days at work were uneventful. I didn't clean Conference Room 3a. I didn't see Shrivel or his companions. When I got home earlier, I made a salad, stepping from one foot to another because my feet hurt; this must have triggered the realisation that the spot on the kitchen windowsill was empty. The blue and white trainer had gone. I stared at it. Had I moved it without knowing? I knew the answer. No.

I searched the house, found nothing.

The shoe is gone. I don't know what the last statue is. I can't stop thinking about Bedtime Stories and Hunter.

Am I losing my mind?

I'll tell you about a better time.

It isn't just reading fiction that I miss. It's writing it. I don't see any of the writers I knew back then – I'm not allowed to communicate with anyone from that world now – so I've no idea if they feel the same. But they *must* do. I miss the festival panels, passionately discussing ideas and themes and upcoming projects, signing books for readers, drinking with other authors in the bar afterwards. We never saw it coming. We never believed it could happen. Who would have done?

I miss Lynda Harrison, writer of *The Final Adjustment*.

Before we both became famous, we had a similar journey. Our debut books barely made a ripple. Mine – *A Sort Of Homecoming* – was released in 2026, a month after hers. We did a launch together at an indie store because both books addressed themes of childlessness, and clicked immediately. At the end, as the last of the few attendees were leaving, she said to me, 'It's not about how

46

many came, but how much they enjoyed it.' I laughed, knowing we'd both been disappointed in the small turnout, but still given them a hundred percent. 'Let's set a limit of five next time,' she said.

She always made me laugh. She always kept me going.

My second book, like the first, was written in the cramped box room in the flat Cal and I had shared before he died, a place where we once again made do with the worn soft furnishings already there and laughed at the old-fashioned toilet with an overhead flusher on a chain. The words on the first page were my reminder: *If you tell a story well enough, it's true.* I deleted them before submitting *The Dark Room* to an agent who had expressed an interest. It was bought by a big publisher and released in March 2028. It hit number one in fifteen countries three weeks later. The *Guardian* said it was 'the perfect escape from today's brutal landscape, lifting readers with a hopeful story about a photographer who recreates lost images for grieving humans'.

Though she was yet to find success with her next book, her big one, Lynda was overjoyed for me. She came to all my launches and events. Toasted my sales and rave reviews. I began to be recognised, to have people approach me in the supermarket, pointing to my novel on the shelf and saying I'd made them cry.

It made *me* cry.

I finally left the tiny flat and bought a Grade II listed townhouse with views over the river. I wished Cal had lived to see it; to enjoy walls that were smooth and toilets that were of this century. It was there, in my new study, that I opened an old file on my laptop and started reading it. Shivers ran along my neck like cold fingers on a keyboard. It was something – barely even a book – that I'd written after Cal died. *Technological Amazingness* was the title. I'd been angry. Immersed in grief. When I had the idea of a medical team who come up with the Pre-surgery Care Mortality Policy and the One Death Policy, I'd been so tired I was hallucinating.

High on the success of book two, I edited this one.

I had a feeling.

I need to see it. Now.

I've just been to get it. My one copy. It isn't the beautiful first edition with a picture of a doctor holding his own dripping, bloody heart up. They removed those copies from my house, and the hardbacks with the heart monitor that flashes when you move the book from side to side. This is a cheap edition, mass produced to meet demand; I grabbed it and hid it on my person while the tall one and the short one permitted me to get some toiletries before they led me from my home on the river. The pages are yellowing. The cover is so faded that the doctor, in his crown and God-like robe, looks exhausted. Like always, I let it fall open a random page and read the first line there:

> *There is no direct punishment for breaking the Hippocratic Oath,*
> *but someone always pays. The fee is rarely met by the*
> *one who has no ethics, rather by the one who has no clue.*

The first page is the same as the first in all the other versions.

It says: *For Cal.*

For a moment, I miss him so acutely I think I'll be sick. I turn the small picture of him face down, unable to look into his eternally laughing eyes. I turn the fan up. I need to put the book back in its secret place. I won't say where in case this notepad lands in the wrong hands, which is ridiculous with all the other incriminating things I'm sharing. But if they find this, I want my last copy of *Technological Amazingness* to remain. To exist, unfound. I'm going to try and sleep n—

Friday 9 November 2035 – 6.51 p.m.

Today I almost asked Laura next door about the last statue. The question almost came out of my mouth. She called by to get her apple pie dish back, which I had to quickly wash because I hadn't finished eating it. I wanted to ask about the blue and white trainer too. Did she know anything about it?

'Did you send that tea man to me?' I asked instead as she walked away.

'Oh, you mean—'

'Don't say his name,' I cried. 'I don't want to know.' I wasn't sure why. 'Did you send him to me because you felt sorry for me?'

She stopped at the gate, frowning. 'Why would I feel sorry for you?'

What could I say?

'No, I didn't send him.' She closed the gate. 'He does have some delicious biscuits though, doesn't he? Those Toffee Tickles. *Lovely.*'

I came inside and stood in my tiny hallway listening to the sounds of the house; the mini fridge humming, the fan whirring, my heart beating inside my chest. The heart is the sound of a house; if we are home, it's there, always. I never wanted this place though. It was where they brought me when they led me from my beautiful townhouse; when I was forced to surrender everything that I'd made from the books. It's where I've lived since. I've never had the inclination to paint the walls or hang pictures. I'm here physically but not emotionally.

What is the last statue?

What is it?

I feel like when I know, I'll have already known wh—

Saturday 10 November 2035 – 2.44 p.m.

When he came today, the tea man was late. He left my gate open again. It was immobile in the windless air. The budding flower by the gate had blossomed, brightening the wall with red.

'Were you born in a field?' I asked, a phrase my mum always used to say.

He turned and looked at it, then back at me. I glared at him. He wheeled down the path, closed it, and returned to me, not a glimmer of complaint crumpling his face. Is this what irritates me about him? How level-headed he is? Yet Cal was that way. So why would it annoy me? It should comfort.

'You're late. You said you'd be here at noon.'

Someone had cut his hair badly. One ear hid behind an overlooked inch and the other was exposed fully. Had it been an attempt to lessen the irregularity of his scar? The hope that adding patchiness elsewhere would detract from it.

'I'm sorry,' he said. 'One of my customers was having a bad day, so I stayed with her for a bit longer.'

'I might go back to supermarket teabags if you're not careful.'

'That would be a shame,' he said. 'It's a poppy, you know.'

'What is?'

He motioned to the red flower by my gate. 'They normally bloom in June.'

'It's the weather,' I said.

'I like daisies.'

'Daisies?' I repeated.

'The flowers.'

'I know they're bloody flowers.'

'Such a simple thing. Resilient and pretty. They're edible too, you know.'

'Oh, God. Now you're going to tell me you sell a biscuit with some sort of soft daisy centre.'

He smiled. It lit up my dull path. Creased his eyes. Melted my heart. 'No,' he said. 'Not yet anyway.' Then he rummaged purposefully in the wicker basket before pulling out a bright yellow packet of biscuits. He held them out. 'You look like you might enjoy a Lemon Crackle though.'

I ignored the yellow packet. 'How does someone *look* when they might enjoy a Lemon Crackle?'

When I still didn't take it, he put it back in his basket and studied me again. 'You look – and excuse me for being presumptuous if I'm wrong – a little sad today.'

'I'm fine. You don't even know my name.'

'Do I need your name to know if you look sad or not?'

'I'm tired if you must know.' I was. I hadn't slept until late again. 'I reckon it's all the caffeine in these teabags. Do they put it in the Nutty Speckles too?'

'We only use natural ingredients in our baked produce.' He paused. 'Maybe you're ill. There's something going around. A lot of my customers have it. I have lemon teabags that soothe the throat.'

I laughed. 'Tea's no remedy for tonsillitis.'

'I agree. The best cure for an aching throat is to release what's stuck there.'

'My throat's fine!'

'Something must be lodged there.'

'*What*?'

'You've to release what's there.'

'So you're a doctor *and* a tea salesman?'

'Just a tea salesman.'

If this story were fiction, he'd be a non sequitur. Simply put, this means *it does not follow*. An illogical or unexpected turn in plot or dialogue with no explanation, sometimes used to make readers laugh, or to mislead them. A character who appears randomly, no foreshadowing, no obvious reason for being there. But the tea man is real. He was here today. He is not a blue and white shoe.

'What the hell are Lemon Crackles anyway?' I asked.

He smiled as though he'd won an argument I wasn't aware was going on. A second smile. I can't deny how it touched me. But I need to remember that I can't be sure I can trust him. 'They're a crunchy, soft-centred biscuit with tart lemon pieces sprinkled throughout. Popular with those who like a bit of bite. They go well with a stronger teabag like the ones you have. Something about the—'

'I'll just take my teabags.'

He handed me the gold pack and I put my card to his smartphone until it pinged. As I leaned closer, I wondered why he had to use a wheelchair.

'Thank you, Mrs—?'

'Nice try,' I said.

'Next Saturday at noon?'

'You'll be punctual this time?'

'Yes.'

He turned to leave and reached the gate.

'Fine-Fayre!' I cried.

I suddenly didn't want him to go. I felt the world might not end up how it should be if he left. That he might never return. He irritates me and yet his *smile*. His visits feel like they were on the cards all along. He's not just a non sequitur. He's a motif; a recurring element of symbolic significance. I just haven't figured it out yet.

'You can bring me some Nutty Speckles next time,' I told him.

'You liked them?'

I ignored the question. 'And you'd better give me some sort of discount price for bulk buying.'

'Wouldn't it be more sensible if you knew my name? Then you'd not have to shout *Fine-Fayre* at me when you need something else.' He paused by the gate, his reflection in the silver van a polished twin.

'I don't want your name.' He'd want mine and that might be dangerous.

'Have a nice day,' he said.

'Come back.' I waited while he did and then spoke more softly to him. 'If I said the last statue to you, what would you say?'

'I'd say it should never have gone.' He spoke sadly. There was no clue in his face that he knew why I was asking; that he had dark reasons for being here.

'It's gone?'

'You didn't know?'

'Would I be asking if I did,' I snapped. 'Where was it … *before* …?'

'By the river,' he said. 'The last one they took down.'

Not the last one built, but the last one taken down. I knew then. Because he said the river. I just hadn't known it was gone. How had I not known? I watch the news occasionally. It was probably on social media, but I never go there. Gone. My knees felt weak. My heart too.

'When did they take it down?' I asked.

'I think … a couple of years ago.' He looked thoughtful. 'It's a miracle it stayed until then. The council fought to keep it. Even if those books are banned, I think we should always remember them.' He paused. 'I do.' He held my gaze and then glanced around and changed his tone to a more cheerful one. 'Have a nice day. See you next Saturday at noon.'

'Not a minute later.'

I went inside and shut the door.

I took my teabags into the kitchen. I pressed them to my chest when I saw it: the blue and white trainer, back, on my windowsill, as though it had been there all along and I had wrongly thought it gone. I ran back outside but the Fine-Fayre van was pulling away. What's the point in asking him? He didn't disappear from my sight. He can't have put it in my house.

This time I grabbed the shoe and hurled it at Laura next door's small fridge. 'You are not here!' I cried.

It's still on the floor where it landed. I won't touch it. I won't look at it.

The last statue; I'll think about that.

Now I know where to go if I want to find out more about Bedtime Stories. But I must decide if I'll dare go on Monday. If I'm caught doing such a thing, the consequences … I can't imagine.

I see Hunter in my dream asking, 'Why can't you hear me?' And I see myself saying, 'I can hear you'. And I see him turning, looking at me, seeing me. Smiling.

I have to go a—

Monday 12 November 2035 – 4.02 p.m.

I've been home from work for an hour.

It was uneventful. Conference Room 3a was empty except for two sugar sachets in the centre of the table. I cycled a different way back, along the river, grateful of the cool breeze it gave my face. The statue is indeed gone, barely a dent in the parched ground marking its once-upon-a-time existence. Apparently, it was the last one. I didn't stop cycling. I couldn't face that empty spot.

I'm at my desk, fan on, Fine-Fayre tea my regular companion. I wish I'd bought some Nutty Speckles now. I'm still ignoring the blue and white trainer by the fridge. Maybe it'll be gone by Wednesday like last time.

Let me tell you about the last statue.

It was erected in 2029 to celebrate the soar of the Big Four. The delicate sculpture was a spiral of stainless-steel falling pages, tiny punctuation marks and letters flying away from them like butterflies. The square marble base had quotes from Lynda Harrison, Cass May, Shelly Dean, and me on each of the four sides. Mine was the words, *If you tell a story well enough, it's true.* My editor revealed to the world that I wrote this at the top of every manuscript and deleted it once finished, and they thought it the perfect phrase to represent me.

There was an unveiling in April 2029. Lynda, Cass, Shelly and I were there, with our editors, agents, a few close friends, members of the press, and some other literary stars. We toasted the future of great books with champagne and speeches, the soft springtime sunshine on our faces and the new leaves greening on branches overhead.

It was one of the most joyful days of my life. Probably my last perfect moment. I leaned close to Cass for a moment, clinked my champagne glass to hers, and said, 'I can't believe they dedicated something like this to us. I didn't invent anything or save anyone; I just wrote a book.'

'Believe it.' She smiled. 'Enjoy it.'

Afterwards, Lynda and I shared more sparkling wine at mine.

'They're our children,' she said softly, cheeks flushed, ashy hair awry now.

'What are?' I asked.

'The books. The children you and I never had.' She put her glass to mine. 'I can live with that.'

At that moment, I could too.

And now it's all gone. The statue, the books, the joy.

How could I not have clocked that the Pages monument, as they called it afterwards, was *the last statue*? The mysterious clue did briefly trigger the sculpture in my head, but I didn't know it had gone. I haven't thought about the unveiling in ages. If there's no reason to think about something, we don't. I rarely go along the river. Perhaps I avoid that spot without realising I am. In this fiction-free world I try not to think about what once was.

Until now; here on this page I must because I want to share what happened, to make sense of it, own it, and record what's still happening.

It's 4.30 now. If I want to be at the last statue by 5 p.m. I need to leave. Is that what will happen?

Should I go?

Should I ch—?

Monday 12 November 2035 – 9.30 p.m.

I went. And I'm back. I won't sleep for hours, I know that. So much to think about. So much in just a few hours. Let me settle. Make some Fine-Fayre tea.

Then I'll write.

I cycled down to the river. Though it was almost dark, being mid-November, the heat was still suffocating. Dripping with sweat, I chained my bike to a railing. Each clink echoed my heart. Fear I could understand. But why did I feel guilt? Maybe because when something is banned – even if you know the ban is wrong – it tarnishes that thing forever.

At 4.59 p.m. I stood as near to the parched ground residue of our statue as I dared. I had a plan. If someone official approached, I'd say I had lost my way. If someone ... *creative?* ... arrived, I'd take the chance. Would they approach me? And what if someone else turned up, someone like me, wanting to volunteer?

They didn't.

Then, at 5.02 p.m., a figure emerged from the shadows, dry grass crunching under feet. The area was badly lit so I couldn't see what kind of person it was; safe, not safe? How could I be sure? She came closer. *She.* And I knew I was safe; I knew *her.* I saw her recognise me too.

'*Lynda,*' I said, my heart about to crack.

I hadn't seen her in years. She shook her head, put a finger over my mouth, and pulled me firmly but with care towards the trees. I let myself be taken. We reached the road where a vehicle waited, and she bundled me into the passenger seat and got in behind the wheel. It was an ancient car, a 2017 Citroën Picasso, not an AV, so I felt safe to speak.

Once we shut the doors, she pulled me into an embrace. I hadn't been hugged in such a way for a long time. I was overwhelmed. It was like when we were allowed to hug again after Covid-19;

nervous at first, then gulping down the affection like thirsty, fevered children with a large glass of juice.

'Fern Dostoy,' she said, eyes wet. 'Oh, my heart when I realised it was finally you. I've been waiting so long.' Her hair was scattered-ash grey, paler now, and the skin around her eyes was lined, like an inviting piece of notepaper.

I squeezed her back. How good it was to hear my real name on the lips of someone I loved. I could almost imagine for one euphoric moment that it was the old days; that she might come back to my house, and we might drink wine, discuss the books we were writing, plan book club events together, and laugh, laugh, *laugh*. 'It's really you, my dear friend,' I said. 'How *are* you? What have you been doing?'

'Waiting for you,' She paused. 'I knew you had the card and prayed you'd come.'

'Waiting for me? You *wanted* me to come?'

'For fuck's sake, woman, of course. But you never went to ALL-Books. Until that day. Tinsley's had a card to give you since we started Bedtime Stories a year ago. That's why she got the job there. She was looking for *you*.'

'Those little cards aren't given out generally then?'

'Yes, but they're not quite the same. We should go. Give me another hug, woman.' She squeezed me; it was years of love. Then she started driving. 'We created that card especially for you with the extra bit on the other side, so you'd hopefully come. The rest of them just have the *Happy-ever-afters are here* side, so children can ring for a story. We leave them in schools and libraries and whatnot. Most are probably destroyed ... the rest find their way home ... and of those, some parents let their kids call us . . .'

'This fucking world,' I said. 'I hate it. That this is what you have to do, in secret.' I felt like the old me. Lynda made me feel that way. 'If anyone was going to kick back, it'd be you.'

'And now you can too,' she said.

'But what if someone official calls the number?' I asked. 'It says on the card that it's anonymous, but can't you be traced by someone who knows how?'

'No. We have an encrypted telephone network of our own. I think it goes through the dark web. I don't fully understand how it works but we have an expert team who do all that stuff.'

'How do you fund it all?'

'The phone calls – there's a fee when people ring. But *we* all do it for nothing – the readers, the tech people, the good folks who give us their basements.'

'Basements?'

'That's where we answer the phones.'

'Wow. It's so …' I didn't know how to finish. I was overwhelmed.

'I know. It's been quite the journey.'

'How did you even start it?' I asked.

'I caught my neighbour Ellie upset one day in the garden.' Lynda's voice broke. 'She couldn't soothe little Mabel. Nothing worked. She cried for hours. Ellie said that the night before she'd whispered aloud what she remembered of a story her own mother told her, about a sad prince, and Mabel fell asleep. I knew I had to do something. Many volunteers have kids themselves and hate not being able to read to them at night.'

'But why did you want me so badly?' I asked.

'Who else tells stories like you do?' She smiled. 'And why wouldn't I use this excuse to find you?'

What could I say? 'Where are we going then?' I asked, excited now.

'Tinsley's house. We take calls in her basement. There are similar hidden rooms all over the city, and in other cities too.'

This thrilled me. It thrills me now to write it here. The idea of spoken stories defying the ban; phones ringing; words bouncing; tales shared. 'Do you get many calls?' I asked.

Lynda nodded, sad. I saw us suddenly, launching the debut novels that failed to make any mark on the world, crying together over our childlessness, and how it was too late for us. I understood the pain in her face. I knew it too. 'Thousands,' she said. 'We're overwhelmed.'

'And you set the whole thing up?'

'Cass and I,' said Lynda.

'Cass *May*?' I grinned at the mention of my old friend.

'Yes. She runs those in the south. I've spoken to her, but we haven't met in person for years. It's just too risky.'

'Is she OK?'

'Yes. Well, as OK as we can all be in this world.'

'And what about Shelly? Where is she? Do you know?'

Lynda shook her head. 'I haven't been able to ask her family what's going on. I'm afraid to. I don't want to put them at risk. I only know from someone at Bedtime Stories that she was interviewed by *them* one day and then gone the next.'

I shivered despite the car's warmth. '*Them*,' I whispered. 'The tall one and the short one.'

Lynda nodded. I had always known it wasn't just me they visited. They check up on all authors, editors, agents.

'Maybe Shelly…' I tried to come up with something plausible. 'Maybe she'd had enough and went away somewhere?'

'Maybe.' Lynda sounded about as convinced as I felt. 'They come and interview me a lot. I dread it now. How about you?'

'Six months ago was the last time,' I said.

'They must be happy with you.'

I shrugged. 'I can't believe it's really you,' I said softly.

'It is,' she said. 'And it's *you*.'

'Do you write still?' I leaned close as though someone might be listening, which was silly after what we'd just discussed, and impossible in a car this old.

'No,' she admitted. 'I'm afraid to. But Bedtime Stories fulfils me.'

We chatted about our lives in recent years – I had little to say in this regard, while Lynda was retired and still with husband Tom – until the car pulled up at a nondescript house, one of the many, many super economy new builds designed to get twenty-somethings on the property ladder now that the average house in England costs £480,000.

'These houses don't have basements,' I said.

'This one does.' Lynda opened the door. 'What better place to hide an underground room than in a house that *doesn't have one*, eh?'

I followed her inside. It was clearly a family home. Toys were abandoned on orange kitchen tiles and unfinished plates of food were left on a table and shoes were by the door. I paused in the hallway. One blue and white trainer. Alone amongst the other pairs. I picked it up. Chest tight. Tinsley came down the stairs, saw me, and smiled.

'Oh, that's Miller's,' she said. 'Hi, I'm Tinsley.'

I recognised her now. Young. Nails painted mint. She opened a door to what looked like a cupboard, picked up the coats covering the floor, and then a rug, revealing a flap that pulled up. Steps there led into the dark. Lynda took the blue and white trainer from me, gave it to Tinsley, and led the way down. Tinsley didn't come. As I descended, I saw her feet, mint nail polish on her toenails too.

'She doesn't tell stories,' said Lynda. 'She provides us with the room, as do so many other important helpers. She used to be a children's bookseller so imagine how much she dislikes working in ALLBooks now? But she does it to reach potential storytellers, hopefully enlist them.'

'Why doesn't *she* read on the phone lines?' I asked.

'She said she feels guilty when she can't even read to her own children,' said Lynda. 'But she wants to support us in this way.'

The basement was large. Three doors led to what looked like a toilet, a tiny kitchen and a bare room with four large beanbags scattered around. In the centre of the main space were a couple of old sofas and in the corner was a large, cluttered desk. The rest of it was divided into four cubicles where a phone sat on each desk and a rack of books hung on the partition wall. I went straight to the books, picked up *When We Were Very Young* by A.A. Milne, and sniffed the pages with a greedy gulp.

'They love the classics,' said Lynda, behind me. 'Meet Jasmine and Alfie.'

I realised there were two other people in the room also.

'Jasmine is our team leader, and Alfie is a storyteller, like me, and like you'll be.'

I said hello to a young woman in a striped vest and matching scarf taming wild hair, and to an older man whose blue eyes sparkled.

'And this is Fern Dos—' started Lynda.

'—toy,' finished Alfie with a huge grin. My name – or the remainder of it – on the lips of someone else felt good. 'Oh my God. It's really you.'

I laughed. It was so odd to be her again. It was so long since I'd experienced the attention her books garnered. I suddenly saw myself at a prize ceremony, milling about, meeting people, in awe of the grand venue, my achievement, high on champagne. The writer who'd won the previous year said to me, 'Congratulations. Enjoy it. It's probably not forever.' Had they known what was coming?

'I loved your book,' said Alfie.

'Thank you,' I said.

'We'll be turning the phones on soon,' Jasmine interrupted. It was just past quarter to six. She sat on one of the sofas and the rest of us followed. 'I'll give you a quick account of what we do, and then you can listen in, maybe take a call before we finish at nine?'

'How do you stay safe?' I asked her, looking up, thinking of Tinsley, the risk she was taking with her family home.

'We only have a maximum of four people per basement,' Jasmine explained. 'We all arrive and leave at slightly different times. We're hidden down here but if we were caught coming into the house, we're just coming for dinner with Tinsley. We each have a story to explain how we know her. You met her at ALLBooks and bonded over a love of the Bible.'

I laughed. I couldn't help it. Jasmine didn't.

'You should familiarise yourself with it if you don't know it well already,' she said.

I stopped laughing.

'When we answer the phones,' she continued, 'we say, Bedtime Stories, what's your favourite? This immediately breaks the ice with the child. If they don't know – and many don't because they're too young – we give them a summary of a few books and let them choose. Really, it's up to the reader to use their intuition and assess what genre or theme the youngster might enjoy based on age or gender. Local calls automatically come through to here, so you'll get regulars. If you build a rapport with a particular child, or don't finish a story and want to resume, they can call you back and ask for you. But do try not to get too attached.'

'Why?' I asked.

'Some of our readers have done. It never works out well.'

'How so?'

'We had a young woman who built a great relationship with a little girl. She rang for a story every night for weeks. Then she stopped. No warning. We never knew why. It often happens. But the reader was devastated. She took it personally and never came back.'

'That's sad,' I said quietly.

'Always remember, this is for *them*, not for you.' Jasmine studied me as though to impress this into me. 'As a reader, take it slowly. Pause if the child laughs, answer questions, and be prepared for them to hang up mid-story if they're tired, or to ask for a different one if bored.'

'Do you have kids?' asked Alfie.

I glanced at Lynda on the opposite sofa, caught her eye. 'No,' I said. 'Does that matter?'

'Oh no,' he said. 'I just wondered. I don't either, but I get a lot out of doing this.' He seemed to recall Jasmine's words earlier about it being for them not us, and added, 'Because of the joy I bring to them.'

'Is there a time limit?' I asked. 'I mean, can we tell them a story all evening?'

'Most either fall asleep or end the call within an hour,' said Jasmine. 'But we do stop at nine, so if you have a child lost in your story, and time approaches that hour, gently wrap it up somehow, even if you have to change the words.'

I nodded.

'Not all our callers are wakeful children. One is a grown man, Jamie, who rings from his sickbed and likes to hear the story of Mr Pink-Whistle. We've numerous regular adult callers.' She paused. 'It's almost six. Any more questions?'

I shook my head.

'I'll turn them on,' she said.

One by one, they started ringing, each ringtone different, causing a disharmonious song. Alfie, Lynda and Jasmine went to them. Words overlapped: *Bedtime Stories, what's your favourite?* I tried to listen to each of them. Alfie spoke gently, clearly to a child he knew. Lynda sounded like she had a new caller, one who was unsure. Jasmine had a more no-nonsense approach, leading the way by suggesting *Alice's Adventures in Wonderland* or *The Secret Garden*.

When they each began to read, tears filled my eyes. The voice is different when it reads. The words are different when lifted from the page. The air holds its breath when a story is told. Needing a moment alone, I went into the empty room next to the kitchen and closed the door after me.

How had we done this to the children? Made this world.

I sat on one of the beanbags in the empty Bedtime Stories room. There was a phone on the floor nearby. On a worktop in the corner was a carton of milk. I could smell it. Rank. Fetid. I knew it was off. I had to get out of there.

Then the phone next to me rang.

I stared at it.

I picked it up.

'Bedtime Stories, what's your favourite?' I spoke the line, nervous, like I was typing a phrase I shouldn't be into an Internet search engine. I realised there weren't any book racks in here. What was I supposed to read?

'I've heard them all. I'm tired of them.' It was a boy. 'Got any new ones?'

'What stories do you like?' I scanned the floor where grey cord offered no inspiration, looked at the closed door like it might open onto a prologue.

'Ones I haven't heard,' he said, exasperated.

I lifted the beanbag and looked underneath for a book. Voices continued to rise and fall in the other room, like a long ago tireless analogue Internet connection signal, trying and retrying, trying and retrying. The readers read and the restless listened.

'What *have* you heard?' I asked him.

'All of them,' he sighed.

'OK. Let's see what new stories we have.' I paused so he might think I was selecting one. What was I going to do? I filled the time by asking, 'What's your name?'

'Hunter,' he said.

'I know,' I said before I could stop myself. Because I did. Then. 'I'm eight.'

'I know.' Because I did.

'How?' he demanded. 'You're new.'

I need to pause here. I need a drink. I need to cry. I need to make tea. I need to cry.

I'll come back and write more wh—

Monday 12 November 2035 – 10.29 p.m.

I can still smell that off milk in the room. It's ruining the moment. Hunter. Did I really have the dream about him? It feels impossible now. Like I just made it up, as foreshadowing. But if I look back through these pages, it's there. He's there. Before he called me tonight. If this were fiction, you'd complain that it's too much of a coincidence, to have the boy I dreamt of call me at my first Bedtime Stories session. Readers often told me they had trouble with my 'twists of fate'. But this isn't fiction. And I can't explain it. I can only live it. And when he said his name was Hunter, I melted, and I—

I covered my nose because the smell of tepid milk was suddenly overwhelming. 'I just … had a feeling,' I said to him. 'You sound eight. You sound like a Hunter.'

'Do I? Oh, good. You sound like … I dunno. A crazy lady.'

I laughed.

'I shouldn't say crazy,' he said. 'My mum said the word is offensive.'

'Not to me.' I smiled.

'You're a new one.'

'I am.'

'At least it's not Jasmine,' he whispered, as though she might somehow hear.

'What's wrong with Jasmine?'

'She always sounds dead bored.'

I smiled.

'Are you gonna tell me a story then?'

'OK. Yes. Let's see.' I recalled Jasmine's suggestion about using our intuition, but how could I do anything without a physical book? I've never read to a child. What do eight-year-old boys like? I wanted to entertain him. Make him happy.

'What's the title of my story then?' he asked, impatient.

'What would you like it to be?'

'I don't have the book, you do.'

'Yes. True. But … I'm still deciding. What type of stories do you prefer?'

'Ones where there's danger and adventure.'

'Of course.' I took my hand away from my nose, winced at the milky smell, and opened my palms as though a book rested in them. Maybe it would help. 'This story is called . . . it's . . . *What Happened to All the Bloody Books?*' I intuitively felt he'd love my curse but still nervously waited for him to reprimand me.

He giggled. 'I have to sit on the naughty step if I say that word.'

'I'm on a naughty beanbag,' I said.

'Will the story answer the question?'

'I don't know.'

'Haven't you read it before?'

'No.' I looked at the lines criss-crossing my palm. The dairy stench was too much, and I had to cover my nose again. 'Are you sitting comfortably then?'

'I'm in the crap chair at my mum's desk. She goes out to badminton on Mondays and Thursdays and that's when I ring there.'

'Doesn't she want you to have stories?' I asked.

'Nah. She's not bothered. I asked her if she ever read to me, you know, when we still had storybooks, but I don't think she did...' His accent was similar to mine, and I wondered how close by he lived. I remembered Jasmine saying earlier that local calls automatically came through here.

'Didn't she? That's ... sad. Why not?' I felt I had to defend her. That there might be a valid reason. 'Maybe she felt shy or she wasn't very good at it?'

'She was probably too busy. She is now. I see Josie my nanny more than her. What's your name anyway?'

Was I allowed to give it? I hadn't asked that. 'Fern,' I said anyway.

'Go on then,' he said.

'What?'

'The story.'

'Oh, yes.' I suddenly felt the weight of expectation. What was I going to tell him? Maybe I should have admitted there were no books in the room, but I was afraid of losing him. So, with nothing to guide me, I tried to make something up, hoping he couldn't tell. 'Once upon a time, long ago, books were physical,' I said. 'And ... they were legal too. And back then the words inside the pages ... they knew where to go and who to pair up with.' What was I saying? He wasn't four. 'Basically, the stories were vivid and sensible and turned out well. The best ones didn't even include pictures because the stories were so good, they weren't needed. Anyway, these physical books lived very happily on shelves and in cupboards and beside children's beds and—'

'This is one weird story,' interrupted Hunter.

'Is it OK?' I asked.

'It definitely doesn't sound like one I've heard before.'

'You didn't want one you'd heard before,' I said.

'True.'

'Shall I carry on?'

'Suppose.'

Was he bored? What was I going to come up with next to keep him? At that moment the door opened, and Jasmine came in the room. 'What are you doing?' she asked, clearly confused.

'The phone rang,' I said. 'I thought I should answer it.'

'That's impossible – it's not one of the Bedtime lines. This is the room where we relax. That's a secure line directly to drivers who pick us up if we need it.'

'I have to go,' I said to Hunter. 'I'm on the wrong phone.'

'When will you be back?' he asked.

'When can I come back?' I asked Jasmine.

'Who are you talking to?' she demanded, coming to take the phone off me.

'I'll come back on Thursday,' I said quickly to Hunter.

'I'll ring then,' he said. 'Crazy Lady.'

I smiled. He had gone. Jasmine took the phone off me. I stopped smiling. She listened to it.

'Well, he's gone now,' I said.

'That's impossible,' she repeated. 'No one can ring in on this line, only out.'

'Well, they did,' I said. 'A boy called Hunter.'

She studied me like I was a specimen under a microscope. 'Do you want to come back into the other room and take some proper calls now?'

69

I suddenly felt exhausted. Spent. Ready for my bed like I hadn't been in years. I hadn't even told a full story. Would Hunter sleep after a mere paragraph?

'I think I'll go home now,' I said. 'Is that OK? Can I come back on Thursday?' I had to see if Hunter called back.

Jasmine left the room without a word. I followed her. In the main area, Lynda and Alfie were on the phones. Jasmine went to the cluttered desk, found something in the drawer and gave it to me. A small card with Tinsley's address on it.

'Memorise it,' she said. 'Then dispose of it. You must make your own way here from now on. Come on Thursday by five-thirty. We'll go from there.' She spoke like I was a naughty child. 'I'll call you a driver now. Tinsley will let you out. She's your friend now. You both love the Bible.' She went to the phone in the other room. I was dismissed. I wanted to say goodbye to Lynda, but she was describing a giant's castle in the sky.

When I got home, they were waiting for me.

The two of them.

The tall one and the short one.

On my step. Stance erect, two black shadows in the dark, mismatched but identical twins. It was eight-thirty by then. They had never come at night before. I thanked God the driver had dropped me at the Pages statue and I'd biked home. I was no longer tired. I'm not now. I'm angry. I'm going to call the next part 'Anger' before I tell you about them. No denial; only anger now and th—

Part Two

Anger

'Fern Dalrymple,' said the tall one.

It was statement not a question. The tall one always says it when they arrive, as though I might have forgotten it. It was the third time tonight someone had said my name, but this one brought no joy. The wrong name, on his lips, made me feel sick. But I nodded, as I always do, and opened the door to let them in.

'Where were you tonight, Fern?' he asked. He always asks the questions. His face is smooth, as if he's had some sort of laser surgery. I couldn't give him an age. They both wore black suits again. It might have been comical – like something out of that old *Men in Black* film – if it wasn't so unnerving.

I carried my bike into the hallway. 'I just fancied some exercise.' I hoped my voice sounded casual. I was desperately anxious about the card in my rucksack pocket with Tinsley's address on it. Had they ever searched my bag? They've never caught me returning from anywhere. I'm always home when they come.

'Is this something you do now at night?' asked the tall one.

He might ask the questions, but the short one is far more menacing in his silence. He has never spoken during the visits. Not once. He rarely takes his eyes from mine. Tonight, the same. I couldn't look at him. I didn't need to to know that his auburn hair was brushed flat and neat, and his matching eyebrows were equally as orderly.

'Sometimes,' I lied. I needed to lay the foundations of an excuse for imminent trips to Tinsley's house. 'It helps me sleep.'

'Trouble with insomnia?' he asked, like he cared. 'Why might that be?'

'My age,' I said. 'The start of menopause and all that.' That would shut him up. Even now in these liberated talk-about-everything times, many men still hate talk of anything intimately feminine. 'Would you care to go into the kitchen?' So civil, like they were out-of-town friends passing through.

73

When they went ahead, I sneaked the card from my rucksack into my jeans pocket. They have never searched me, so it felt less risky. I put my rucksack on the table where they sat, as is custom, and I switched the kettle on. The short one searched my rucksack, rough, probing, pushing tissues and mints aside. I hoped he couldn't hear my heart pounding.

Then I realised the blue and white trainer was still on the floor near the mini fridge. Had they noticed? How would I explain it? I remembered that Hunter had worn a similar one in my dream, his other foot bare. Had I dreamed that because I had this one and my mind was speculating the location of the other?

'How have things been, Fern?' asked the tall one, tone level.

'Same as usual,' I said.

I remember the first time they came to see me in this house, without warning, almost five years ago; my acute anxiety at the surprise visit. They were back. They had been before – when they brought me to live here – but I'd hoped that was it, even though the tall one had explained that they would be visiting anyone who'd ever written or published fiction. It was all part of ensuring that we followed the new rules. It would go on until they were sure we'd fully complied. At first, they came every other month. Recently it has been more like twice a year. I guessed they were satisfied with me now … who knows?

'Still working at the hospital?' asked the tall one.

I nodded. 'Tea?'

'Yes, we both will, thank you.'

I didn't need to ask how they had it. Both with milk and sugar. I got the carton from the fridge and poured it into their cups but not mine. I couldn't stomach it. I glanced at the shoe again. Could I remove it without them noticing?

'What's that?' asked the tall one.

'Ah … I'm not sure,' I stammered.

'Not sure?'

'I mean, I found it on my step the other day. I wasn't sure what to do with it. I just brought it inside, thinking maybe a local child had lost it and might come knocking.'

'Bring it here please,' he said.

I did, with his cup of tea. He turned it over in his hand, peered closely at the strange speck of red. Then he gave it back to me without comment. I put it on the windowsill and joined them at the table.

'This is Fine-Fayre tea, isn't it?' said the tall one.

Was it a loaded question? Had *they* sent the tea man? Was it a test?

'Yes,' I admitted. 'My neighbour gets it and said it's very refreshing.'

'I agree,' he said. 'I enjoy it too.' I always felt more on edge when he was civil. Like he was trying to lull me into security and get me to accidentally confess some crime. 'Have you been reading?'

He always asks this. 'Yes,' I said. 'Stephen Hawking.'

'Good choice. Anything else?'

I shook my head.

'Where did you purchase it?' It was a ridiculous question when ALLBooks was now the only bookstore.

'ALLBooks,' I said. 'Last week.' I wondered then if I should set up an alibi for going to Bedtime Stories and say I'd got chatting to Tinsley there. I didn't have chance. He came at me with another question.

'And have you been writing?'

'No.' I felt sure my no sounded more like a yes.

'Do you *want* to write again?'

'No.' I could barely say it.

'You know what's going to happen now, don't you?' he said.

My throat was dry. The question sat in my stomach like a too-heavy, carb-laden dinner. Did he want me to answer? I couldn't.

'My colleague will search the house.'

'Of course.' I tried to breathe evenly.

75

A bead of sweat trickled down my forehead. I thought about the notepad hidden inside my mattress. Has he ever searched the bed? I tried desperately to recall if I'd ever retrieved my bedding from the floor. I didn't know. The short one got up and disappeared. I should have taken the notepad out with me like I often do when I go to work. But then, no, he would have found it in my rucksack.

'Are you OK, Fern?' asked the tall one.

'Yes,' I said too fast. 'It's just been so hot.'

'It has. It's set to stay this way for weeks.'

I could hear drawers being pulled out, wardrobe doors opening, my bathroom cabinet being rifled through. Then footsteps on my bare floors and the coffee table in my living room going over. I tried not to let my face react.

'I see that you still appear to prefer not going online,' said the tall one.

The short one returned to the kitchen, shook his head at the tall one, and sat back at the table. He hadn't drunk any of his tea.

'I don't like all the negativity on social media,' I said. 'And I never know which news is true.'

'The government news website is the only place you'll find the truth,' said the tall one, not a hint of irony. 'Now, Fern, before we leave you in peace, we need to inform you of a new law that will come into effect at the end of the month. I'm concerned that you won't know about it if you don't avail yourself of the important information on our site.' He finished his tea. 'As you already know, the penalty for attempting to purchase a novel is fifteen thousand pounds, a prison sentence for a second offence. It was hoped that such a deterrent would be enough to prevent occurrences of this crime.' He sighed, as though disappointed in the actions of an unruly child. 'It would appear not. This last six months, eighty-three people were fined and a further forty imprisoned.'

To me, this sounded like a relatively small number of people. Brave people, I thought. Brave, creative, marvellous people. I saw a report on the BBC, perhaps a month ago, about three women and one man who attempted to sell their novels online. Would I dare do it? Not only write one, but attempt to sell it? No. I didn't even have the courage to admit to my *non*-fiction, my sort of diary. And then I was angry. Furious that this was the world now. That I'd just accepted it. That they had taken my words. Stopped me writing more. But I just avoided eye contact and tried to suppress this sudden rage.

'We realised that we need harsher penalties.' The tall one touched my arm, so I was forced to look at him. 'If, Fern, for example, you were to write a novel – even just start one – I would have no option but to take you to one of our new re-education centres.'

Re-education centres. Two innocent enough words. But spoken in the soft, cool way the tall one said them, they were as ominous as *concentration camp* or *aversion therapy*. I thought of Shelly Dean. Had she already been taken somewhere like that? Was that where she was?

'I haven't …' I stammered, my rage melting into fear. 'I wouldn't …'

'I know that *now*, Fern. You've proven yourself to be very obedient. But let us say the muse overtakes you, as the creatives often described it …' This was said with abject mockery. '… then you would need a reminder that such activity is criminal. That reminder would be an indefinite time spent in one of our new re-education centres.'

I felt sick.

'This would not be a choice. You would leave this house, your belongings would be donated to local schools, and any family – though we know you don't have any – would be told they can never communicate with you again.'

Just for writing a story, I wanted to scream.

'Well, this was lovely, as always.' The tall one stood; the short one did too.

'Thank you.' Ridiculous words that I hated myself for saying.

'I trust you'll follow the *real* news on the government page a little more often?'

I nodded. They went into the hallway, and I followed. At my door, the tall one turned and said, 'We look forward to seeing you again soon. Tell me this, Fern?' He paused. 'What was it about writing that you loved so much?'

He had never asked me such a question before. I noticed the use of past tense – what *had* I loved it, not what *did* I love. I was afraid to answer. Would I incriminate myself? For a moment, I imagined they could see my thoughts. That technology capable of doing so had been created – apparently, we are close to it.

'You can be honest,' he said. 'I'm genuinely curious.'

'The escape,' I said softly.

When I closed the door after them, I slumped to the ground, stemmed angry sobs with my fist. They had only stayed half an hour. It felt like days.

This is what my answer to his last question should have been: I like to go somewhere else when I write. When I create another world, I'm transported from a dull desk, a difficult situation, a tragedy, the tedium of daily life, to another place, another time. When I look up off the page – take a breath like I've been underwater for a long time – the alien room often surprises me. Because I've forgotten it exists. I remember; I'm me. This is where I really live. But by going somewhere else, I've made my existence more bearable. When I write fiction, I believe every single word.

And it is over.

It is over and I ca—

Wednesday 14 November 2035 – 4.30 p.m.

I didn't feel like writing yesterday. Work was uneventful – unlike today, which I'll get to – yet I couldn't settle when I got home. Perhaps if this was fiction, if it was the escape I used to enjoy and I could make anything happen, I'd rush to my desk no matter what. Even a half-finished last sentence on the page doesn't always compel me.

This is real.

Surely it can't be coincidence that the tall one and the short one turned up the very night I left the house for the first time. I was often called the mistress of fluke in fiction, but this doesn't feel like a positive sign from the universe. Biking home from my first Bed-time Stories, I'd been hopeful, buoyed, determined to go again and wait for Hunter. Their visit destroyed that. I'd wanted to lie on my bed and relive Hunter's call, imagine another, dissect and enjoy the after-effects of my unusual evening.

Instead, I thought about turning my phone on and research-ing re-education centres. But I was afraid. The idea had me waking repeatedly during the night, unable to breathe.

What good would it do me to know the true horror?

I'm angry again today. It surges at random times, like I've heard hormones do in the days after giving birth. I just tore the paper writing that sentence. Hunter's phone call was a flash of light and they have dimmed it. I'm afraid to go back to Tinsley's on Thurs-day in case they return, and I'm angry that I'm a coward. Maybe I should make something to eat and then come back and tell you about work today, because that is a whole other oddity.

I'll do that.

And brea—

Wednesday 14 November 2035 – 6.28 p.m.

The blue and white trainer has vanished.

I just made beans on toast and noticed the absence. I've been to check again. It's not on the kitchen windowsill. It's not anywhere. Did the tall one and the short one take it? No. Stupid question. It was there yesterday. I saw it when I washed the dishes. And it's definitely real because the tall one held it.

I've become comforted by its presence rather than unnerved by the lack of explanation for its arrival, disappearance, return, disappearance, return, and disappearance again. Now I can only hope it will return once more.

I'll drink Fine-Fayre tea and tell you about work. It might help me make sense of it because right now my world isn't something I could make up without readers questioning my sanity. I'm beginning to think that the endless heat is affecting it. It's certainly affecting how I function; I'm clumsy, slow, tired. It takes an age just to write a paragraph now, but I won't let it stop me.

When I entered Conference Room 3a with my trolley, they were already there – Shrivel, Patrukal and Brane, forming a triangle at the table, laptops open. The room fell silent when I opened the door. Despite having to clean the room, I just wanted to run. It's nine days since they let me stay to make them drinks, since Shrivel strangely said he might have a 'special role' for me.

'Come in, Fern,' he cried. 'We'd love coffee, if you will?'

I dreaded the large fridge, a jug of undated, curdling milk. But in I went, trolley wheels squeaking. All the windows were open, but the air was still stagnant with long-time heat. Was the air conditioning broken? I switched the kettle on and while I waited for it to boil, I scrubbed a grease stain off the worktop. My three roommates simultaneously studied their laptop screens.

Then the fire alarm sounded, shrill, urgent, disrespectful.

'It's just a practice drill,' cried Shrivel over the din, stilling Patrukal in his seat with a hand on his left shoulder. 'I was warned that it would happen today; we've no need to leave. Finish reading the plan.'

The siren sounded for a full five minutes. There was a similar interruption by one in *Technological Amazingness*. It foreshadowed the big reveal in Chapter Eighteen. During this real-life blast I delivered three coffees to the table and went back for the jug. The milk in it was yellow. I gulped down the nausea that I'm sure has intensified recently. Maybe it's the heat that I'm blaming for everything else. Maybe menopause. No one looked up from their laptop.

'No milk for me,' said Dr Brane.

I removed a wasp-yellow mark from the window and began on the sink. I suddenly remembered the special home-made remedy my mum created and affectionately called Sour-to-Sweet, that included lemon, salt, and ginger, and eliminated most stains. The only spillage that evaded its magic cure was milk; nothing eradicated that smell. She died before my book success. Though I wish she had witnessed it, I'm glad she and my dad are no longer here in this horrible world.

When the alarm stopped, Mr Patrukal shook his head and said, 'Seeing it written up here in full doesn't make it any less wrong,' at the same time as Dr Brane said, 'You're still serious?'

'Many thought Alexander Fleming had lost his mind when he suggested that a substance he'd discovered on mould would change the medical world,' said Mr Shrivel.

'Fleming's discovery hardly compares with this.' Patrukal again. 'You expect us to take it seriously? I thought maybe you'd invited us here today to admit it was some sort of ... well, test, I guess. To see if we would easily abandon our ethics.'

Shrivel laughed. It was cruel, shrill. 'Your *ethics*?' he said. 'This from the man who on the twenty-eighth of April, during a kidney transplant, left two paperclips and an empty Sprite can inside a thirty-six-year-old mother of four?'

'Is that why you asked me here?' said Patrukal. 'Because you couldn't possibly ask anyone without a bit of a ... history.'

'*History*?' Shrivel laughed. 'Is that how we're phrasing it now? Show me a surgeon without a history and I'll show you a hospital cleaner.' He looked at me. 'No offence, Fern.'

What could I say? I finished the sink and started the floor. A cup crashed down, a chair scraped back, and I looked up from my position on my knees to see Shrivel, out of his seat, stance erect, striding the length of the table. Dr Brane watched him with narrowed eyes.

'Didn't you read all the positives?' he said. 'Let me remind you that my policy guarantees that no patient dies on the table – statistically any operative procedure could be declared one hundred per cent safe. My policy reduces the need for expensive equipment and costly aftercare, saving the NHS millions and thereby making this an entirely attractive proposal. Transplants would not depend on a donor. No blood is required. It takes pressure off staff – any procedure would take hours rather than days, with regular breaks not only allowed but encouraged. Imagine it. Think of the funding we'll get. The awards the hospital could be given. *We* could be given.'

I carried my bucket to the sink, poured grey water into the drain, hands trembling, chest tight.

'I won't listen to any more.' Dr Brane closed her laptop, though her bottom still appeared glued to the seat. 'It's pure lunacy. What about the Hippocratic Oath? What about the good of the patient?'

'The good of the patient?' Shrivel shook his head. 'From the woman who had sexual relations with the fifteen-year-old son of a patient in intensive care – *during* a shift.' Then he appeared to change tactic and spoke more calmly. 'Look, you're both being impulsive. You're not opening yourselves to the possibilities. You've just read all the pros. What more do you need?'

'I'll never take part in this,' said Patrukal. 'And I doubt you'll find anyone who will.'

Do you realise that what you're proposing means just about anyone could perform surgery? What need would there be for an anaesthetist? Dr Brane and many of her colleagues would be redundant.'

'If her court case doesn't go well,' said Shrivel, 'she could be anyway.'

'I'm going to wake up in a minute and find that I've fallen asleep in front of the TV at home,' said Dr Brane. I pictured her there, gently snoring, hair falling over her shoulder like waves.

'Yesterday,' said Shrivel, 'I spoke to Daniel Mills who, as you'll know, is the current health minister. He expressed interest a while ago. He says he'll help me get the NSF on board.'

'You're serious?' Dr Brane's face was a picture of disbelief.

'*Daniel Mills*? He'd back this?' Patrukal now.

'Yes. And I *will* get this off the ground. My name will go down in medical history. You're telling me you don't want to be a part of that?'

'I just … I can't …' said Patrukal.

In *Technological Amazingness* the government supported two policies and within a year they came into effect. As I gave the windows a last polish, I began to realise that my book had not been that far from the truth.

'I did forget one vital thing,' said Shrivel when Dr Brane and Mr Patrukal stood and pushed their chairs under the table, picking up coats and grunting their indignance. I tidied my trolley, so they didn't think I was trying to listen. 'I have a good friend at CineTime, and he wants to make a ten-episode documentary, following us when we get this off the ground.' CineTime is the biggest streaming service in the world, more popular than dwindling cinemas and every other online service.

Suddenly, the fire alarm sounded again, but this time no one moved. Patrukal looked to Dr Brane and she looked to Shrivel.

'CineTime?' Patrukal spoke when it was silent again and put his laptop back on the polished table, its reflection doubling his workload.

'Yes,' said Shrivel.

'Our names… they'll be next to yours?' Mr Patrukal was barely audible.

'You'll be my team,' said Shrivel.

They both looked at Dr Brane, who had covered her mouth and was shaking her head. 'I'll not be any part of it,' she whispered. 'You've no humanity. You've no right.'

I stopped tidying the trolley.

Dr Brane collected her things and left the room. I stared after her lithe body, carefully styled hair and crisp clothes, touching my apron and rounded tummy as though to shape them into something else. Though I bike everywhere, I'm not young anymore. I admired Dr Brane for standing her ground. Her stance reignited my fire. I need to be brave. Stick by my plan to return to Bedtime Stories.

'It matters not,' said Mr Shrivel to his remaining colleague. 'She's an anaesthetist and there are many others. Dr Wilkins could be an option. I'm happy that you've finally seen the light, so to speak.' He patted Patrukal on the shoulder. 'Now, I must leave, so walk with me and we'll discuss further meetings. I'm away next week.'

As they headed for the door Shrivel turned and glanced at me.

'I'll catch you up,' Shrivel told Patrukal. Then he came over to me. 'I imagine you're curious about our plans?' he said.

I shook my head, not wanting any involvement.

'As I said last time, I may need someone like you.'

'I'm very busy,' I lied.

'We'll see.' He smiled. 'No one with any sense would shy away from something like this. It could change your life, Fern. After all, you …' He appeared to think again.

I was itching to ask, me? Me what? But I refused.

'Take care,' he said. 'I'll see you after next week.'

I'm off work next week too and I'm glad. I didn't like how he studied me when he said my name. I didn't like how he lingered by the door as he left and looked back like he wanted to say something else. I didn't like the things he never quite said.

I biked home, tempted for a moment to go by where the Pages statue once was, but too tired and hot to pedal all the way around.

And now it's almost 8.45 p.m. and dark. The Fine-Fayre tea is cold, and the room is hot despite the fan. My hand aches. I'm done writing. I've shared my day, my thoughts, my all; I'm purged. I'm afraid of a knock on the door, of any sound that could be that. I'm angry that I'm afraid and have lived this pathetic existence so long.

But I'm excited about tomorrow.

Bedtime Stories. Will I go? Yes. Let my anger steer me there. Let it be the wind on my back, let it pedal my wheels. Will Hunter call? I don't know. But I must find out. If the tall one and the short one come and take me away afterwards, then so be it. What life is this anyway if I remain the same? If I keep quiet. If I obey. If I never tell another sto—

Thursday 15 November 2035 – 8.04 a.m.

I woke when it was still dark this morning and drank my Fine-Fayre tea black, standing on the back doorstep, enjoying the brief chill in the air before the heat soars. Despite having a mini fridge that works perfectly well, my aversion to milk is now a repulsion. I don't simply dislike it – it fills me with dread. I just reread that word three times. *Dread*. Such an intense choice. But it does. I feel now like if I drink it … I don't know. Something. Something … not good.

I thought about the British Fiction Prize as I stared into the dawn gloom.

When *Technological Amazingness* was longlisted in July 2029, six months after its release, and rose to the top of the bestseller lists, I stood at daybreak on the creamy stone doorstep of my too-big house, alone, wishing Cal could share my joy.

There was a way he looked at me when we first met. It was like he feared that if his eyes left my face for a second, I'd change, leave.

Passion like that doesn't last forever. It's impossible. Knowing someone intimately for a long period kills mystery. It's like fire when it first catches. It sparks. It's excited to have life. Then, eventually, it flickers to a gentler rhythm. This is good. This is deeper, more fulfilling. We flickered like that until his death.

I wished that morning, as now, that I'd been able to give Cal a child. I wished I had that piece of him. Would it have been a boy like Hunter? Am I hanging all my buried grief on a boy at a phone line?

But I was ecstatic to have been longlisted for the British Fiction Prize. Lynda, Shelly, and Cass were also on the list. We congratulated one another, in disbelief at our 'luck'. To celebrate, we decided to host a free book club event at Piccadilly Waterstones, inviting readers from all over the country. Barely anyone turned up. They had been targeted by members of the Anti-Fiction Movement, receiving death threats, and being told that fiction was 'an insidious danger to our country'.

The government had recently started their campaign to censor fiction. They used the heated discussion and outrage that our books had caused against us. The Big Four were blamed for random looting, the rise in arson attacks on buildings, online trolling, an increase in crime, unruly children. I remember someone on a social media platform saying the four of us were being controversial in our books because we were 'ugly as fuck'. Such a petty thing, but it got shared millions of times, and it stung. Ade Woods appeared on every political show, adding his voice to the cause. I was furious. I was never asked to speak in defence of our fiction, to insist that our books were not trying to incite violence or hatred. On my own platforms I tried to be heard, I *tried*. But every time I spoke up, my message was always drowned out by the abuse, by the trolls, until eventually I got reported for 'being hateful', when all I'd been doing was highlighting *their* hate.

When Lynda, Cass, Shelly and I found out we had all been shortlisted for the British Fiction Prize in September 2029, it was petrol on the fire.

But we had supporters too. I got messages from readers all over the world who had loved my novel. People came up to me in the street and told me personal stories about how the government's lack of NHS funding meant they had lost loved ones or lived with chronic pain. They said they loved that *Technological Amazingness* was now highlighting such things.

I'm proud to this day that thirteen children's hospital wards were saved because of the book, and the donations I made from its royalties.

I won the British Fiction Prize in November 2029. Even writing these words now, long after, I can't believe it. The ceremony at the Guildhall in London was a blur of faces I'd only seen on black and white photos inside hardbacks, and the occasional spark of colour in a face I knew, like the Big Four writers, and my agent and editor. The night wasn't without drama. Police had to guard the doors and stop Anti-Fiction protestors getting inside. The speeches were subdued; it seemed those in the publishing industry were nervous. But when the master of ceremonies said my name as the winner, my joy obliterated the tension. I turned to someone and said, 'They must have made a mistake.'

I woke the next morning to the glass award sitting on my hotel room dressing table. I stood with it before the mirror, to forever impress the visual image in my head. It wasn't only the physical award; it was what this prize *meant*. In winning, I was appointed British Fiction Laureate, a first, a new honour that meant I would write literature to mark and celebrate a variety of situations. Publishers wanted to push back against the Anti-Fiction movement, to show how important and relevant novels were, how much we still needed them.

My first project would be a children's book inspired by stories working class kids had written. The current Children's Laureate had recently resigned – a situation shrouded in mystery, with her stating only that she 'needed time away' – so, until she returned or another was chosen, I would be a voice for the young. A voice for everyday people.

Winning changed my life.

But not how it should have done.

The government didn't want me to be heard.

And that was the nail in fiction's coffin.

My handwriting is barely legible today, my hand is shaking so much. Last night I woke over and over, replaying the curious scene at work yesterday. I'm glad I won't see Shrivel for a week. I hope when I do, I won't witness more of what sounds like a dangerous idea.

I'm exhausted and I still have to go to work. Then to Bedtime Stories to try to bring fiction back to li—

I've been home an hour. I had to sit a while and think before I could set down on the page my day. This is how it can be with words. My mum used to shake a jigsaw box before resuming her incomplete puzzle on the kitchen table. She said the pieces emerged more randomly that way; the challenge was greater. I sat quietly on the back doorstep earlier, the darkness bleak and hot, in the hope that the pieces might settle. There's already enough challenge in finding their order.

I left for Tinsley's house at 5 p.m. It's a fair bike ride. She lives on the city's outskirts, and I knew I might need to stop and drink water. I wondered about riding the opposite way for a while to confuse anyone following me, but that would have doubled my journey. At the house, I wondered where to put my bike; in the end I chained it to a tree on the opposite path. I felt conspicuous knocking on the door, thinking at any moment the tall one or the short one would appear from nowhere.

Tinsley answered and ushered me wordlessly inside. I glanced at the pile of children's shoes by the door. No blue and white trainer today, like in my house. She lifted the flap in her hallway cupboard and down I went to the basement, noticing on my way that the mint nail polish on her disappearing feet was chipped.

Soft voices rose to greet me. I was glad to see Lynda, on a sofa with a can of Coke, a fat white bandage around two of the fingers holding it, Jasmine at her side, nodding at whatever Lynda was saying.

'Fern.' Lynda smiled as soon as she saw me, but it seemed forced.

'I didn't know if you'd be here,' I admitted. 'Hi, Jasmine.'

'I come whenever I can,' Lynda said. 'Do you want tea?'

I nodded. 'No milk though.' My water bottle was empty. It was five-forty. While she made it, Jasmine asked how I was. The question felt loaded with something I couldn't figure out. Then, before I could respond, she said, 'There doesn't appear to be a fault with the phone in the time-out room. It hasn't rung since you said it did.'

I noticed the words were *since you said it did* not *since Monday night*.

Lynda handed me a black tea, her bandaged fingers scraping mine. 'It was certainly odd,' she said. 'I've never heard it ring before either.'

I faltered in believing my own truth. Maybe I *had* imagined it. 'Jasmine heard me talking to him,' I said.

'I heard *you*,' said Jasmine. 'But there was no one on the line when you gave me the phone.'

'He'd gone,' I defended. I imagined if I told them I dreamt about Hunter before the call, they'd think me insane, so I didn't mention it.

'Obviously, he somehow got through to there instead, bless him.' Lynda caught my eye and patted my shoulder, clearly to show she believed me. 'What was his name?'

'Hunter. He's going to call tonight.'

'Don't think I've had a Hunter before,' she said. 'Maybe it was his first time and he mis-dialled or something …'

'Impossible,' snapped Jasmine, and Lynda glared at her.

'It wasn't his first time,' I insisted. 'He said he'd spoken to you before.' I looked at Jasmine. She simply shrugged.

'Anyway,' said Lynda, 'are you excited to be back?'

I nodded, even though Jasmine's interrogation annoyed me. 'What happened to your fingers?' I asked Lynda.

Her demeanour changed. The cheerful facade dropped but so briefly that only a good friend would notice. Then she was jolly, dear Lynda again in a flash. 'Oh, nothing,' she said. 'I cut them on one of those new cheese grating things.' I didn't believe her, but I wasn't sure why she would lie.

'Glad I stick with old-fashioned utensils,' I said.

'Any questions before we start?' interrupted Jasmine crisply.

'I did wonder,' I admitted, 'whether it's OK to just chat to the child. By that, I mean, well, if they ask us things, can we answer?'

'I wouldn't recommend more than your name,' said Jasmine. 'Remember what I said about not getting attached. You're the story. You're not *you*. Right, we should get on. It's just us three tonight. Alfie's sick.'

At six o'clock the phones began to ring. Lynda and Jasmine went into booths, leaving me to respond to a third. I pressed green. For a moment I forgot how to respond. 'Bedtime Stories, what's your favourite?' I asked eventually.

It was a girl, voice squeaky, insistent about what she wanted; the story of *Snow-White and Rose-Red*. I found a copy in the rack. A lump rose in my throat. It was a late eighties edition, yellowing with age, font dated; the exact one my mother read to me, once upon a time. Now I had to read it to this girl. I wanted to do it as well as my mum did.

I read the prose slowly, impersonating the voices of each character as best I could. I'd never thought myself a very good orator when I read at book festivals. I did a workshop once with an actress who told us to look at the line on the page, take it in, and then look up and say it to your audience. 'Connect,' she said. 'Don't be afraid of that pause. They'll wait.'

The little girl waited for me. She fell asleep before the end, but I took this as a great sign. I smiled at the sound of her even breaths and hung up. As soon as I did, the phone rang again. None of us left the booths for an hour. Some children needed half an hour of *Charlie and the Chocolate Factory*; most needed just a couple of minutes of a fairy tale. I found it exhausting, especially switching stories, having to bring a different character to life when I'd just found the rhythm of the previous. But the fulfilment. It was … profound. Not unlike the moments when I had completed a particularly tricky paragraph, satisfied I'd put magic on the page.

In a quiet moment, I wandered into the time-out room. Lynda and Jasmine were still on calls, Lynda's fat white fingers like a bookmark between pages. No milk on the worktop this time, thank

God. I looked in the cupboards. Packets of biscuits, teabags, random sachets of exotic coffees.

Then the phone near the beanbag rang.

I went to the door to ask if Lynda and Jasmine could hear it too, but they were still telling stories. I needed them to bear witness. It continued to ring. I sat on the beanbag and answered it.

'Bedtime Stories,' I said softly. 'What's your favourite?''

'The rest of the one you started the other night, Crazy Lady,' he said.

Hunter. I had known it would be.

'Hello, Hunter,' I said.

'I want the rest of *What Happened to All the Bloody Books.*'

I laughed so hard I was sure Lynda or Jasmine would come in. 'Maybe we shouldn't say bloody. I was naughty to call it that.'

'I like it. Better than all the stupid titles most books have.'

My agent and editor said at first that *Technological Amazingness* was an odd title for a book. That no one would buy anything called that. I stood my ground, arguing that it fitted the ludicrous element of the story, that a doctor had used the phrase to describe his 'life-changing idea'.

'Would you read a book called *Technological Amazingness*?' I whispered to Hunter.

'Bloody yes,' he said. 'Can you tell me that one?'

'I don't have it here – and it's too adult for you.'

'Anyway, they're all gone,' he said.

'What are?'

'The made-up books.'

'Yes.' I paused. 'Hunter, can I ask … when you called here, did you just ring the number on the card?'

'Yeah. What other number would I use, Crazy Lady?'

I needed Lynda to come in, but I could hear her telling the tale of some horse who didn't like his new farm. 'It's just … you came through on a different phone. It doesn't matter. What have you been up to then?' I knew I was supposed to get on with the story, but I loved listening to him.

'School,' he said in a bored voice. 'Marley Robinson spilled chocolate milk all over me at break and said it wasn't his fault 'cos Rosie Smith pushed him and anyway I nicked his last week. It stinks now.'

Suddenly I could smell it too; I gagged and covered my mouth.

'You OK?' he asked.

'Y-Yes,' I managed. 'It's quiet there. Are you alone?'

'Yes.'

'But you're only eight.'

'I don't mind.'

'I do.' I was angry. 'Where's your mum?'

'Badminton.'

'And your dad?' I asked.

'He left a long time ago,' said Hunter.

'Any brothers? Sisters?'

'Nah.'

'I thought you said you have a nanny?'

'I do, Josie, but not all the time.'

'What if something happens to you?' I asked, and then realised it was insensitive and I might worry the poor boy.

'It never has,' he said.

'You're often alone?'

'Sometimes.'

I wondered what Jasmine's protocol was on something like this; child neglect. Surely, I'd have to report it. But how? Who to? I'd ask.

'The story then?' he asked. 'That's what I rang for.'

'I wasn't sure you'd enjoyed it last time,' I said.

'I keep thinking about it.'

I realised that this could be the children's story I never got the chance to write. The one I was supposed to use real kids' stories to inspire. Here, Hunter would be my muse, and the story I never created then would be born in this room.

'That's wonderful,' I said. I couldn't recall exactly what I had told him. Maybe I should make notes each time, but I had no paper. 'Where did we get up to?' I asked him.

'You'd done about when books used to be physical things and when they were legal.' He said the word legal like he was proud to have remembered it. 'They didn't have pictures in 'cos they were so good they didn't need 'em. And these books were on my shelves and in my bedroom.'

'OK.' Where should I go with it? I tried to recall sitting in front of a blank screen when I wrote novels. How I found the story by actually writing it. I'd have to do that now. 'So, one day,' I began, 'maybe three or four days into the story, the main boy, whose name was Hunter, and he—'

'Bit weird,' he interrupted.

I smiled. 'That's why I thought you'd like this one.'

'OK.'

'Hunter lived with a very kind mother and father who knew the great importance of physical books and who introduced new ones every week. They bought them from a variety of bookstores – because there were loads back then – and from charity shops and at library sales. They knew exactly wha—'

'What does Hunter look like?' he asked. 'This matters.'

'Oh. I think a description might come later but … well, he's chunky, but you know, in a good way, like he'll be a strapping lad when he grows up. His hair's reddish blond, though he tells everyone it's more blond. Blue eyes. Not tall yet, but who knows?'

'Too weird,' he said.

'What do you mean?'

'You just described me.' He paused. 'But my hair really *is* more blond.'

Goosebumps crawled up my back.

'Can you see me from there?'

'No.'

'Weird.'

'Weird,' I repeated.

'Crazy Lady. Go on then.'

'What?' I shook my head, tried to concentrate again.

'The story.'

'Yes. OK. Well, one day, very late in the morning, Hunter woke up … everything felt different. Even before he'd opened his eyes. Like he could smell the change. Then he opened his eyes. And something in the room was very wrong.'

'What was it?' Hunter sounded full of wonder. My heart melted. I wanted to reach into the phone and ruffle his mostly blond hair.

'Well, for a start, the window was wide open, and his blue and white curtains were fluttering in the breeze. Then there was Hunter's favourite chair, one that rocked, where his mum used to read him stories when he was a baby and couldn't sleep. Now, he often curled up there with – ' I tried to think. ' – with Geoffrey the cat and his favourite physical book, which was … about …'

'A superhero who can make time go backwards.'

I smiled. 'Yes. That one. Anyway, everything else in the room seemed the same. The posters were on the wall and the laptop was on the desk and Geoffrey slept on the end of the bed. Then he realised—'

'*What?*'

'Where were all the books?' I added extra drama to my voice. Left the question hanging in the air.

And then Lynda came into the room.

'Just a minute,' I said to Hunter. 'Lynda, it rang again. It's him.' I beckoned her over. 'Say hello.' She took the phone from me and said, 'Hello there,' into it. Then again. Then she handed it to me and said, 'There's no one there, Fern.'

I snatched it back. 'Hunter? *Hunter?*' He had gone. 'He was there,' I told Lynda. 'He *was*.'

'I believe you,' she said gently. 'Maybe he got nervous? He'll call back.'

I felt sick. The putrid odour of milk rose from the beanbag. I stood, afraid I'd retch. Jasmine appeared at the door. The phones

95

rang angrily behind her. 'I need you,' she said. We followed and I went into a booth. I read *Goldilocks* to a little boy; then *The Witches* to another; then I started *The Railway Children* for an older girl. Then it was nine o'clock and we were done.

'What was going on in there?' Jasmine motioned to the time-out room.

Before I could speak, Lynda said, 'We were just catching up. It's been years since we've been able to see each other.' I realised she wasn't going to mention Hunter.

Jasmine didn't look impressed. 'Right, well, I'll leave first.'

When she had gone, Lynda hugged me, hard. I felt everything in that affection – the past, the now, our losses, our friendship on hold for so long.

'They visited me Monday night, after I got home from here.' I didn't need to tell her who.

Lynda paled. 'What did they want?'

'Just the usual check-up, it seemed. Do you think they know I came here?'

Lynda shook her head but didn't catch my eye. 'They probably want us to *think* they follow us all the time, but if they had time for that, why wouldn't they have already stopped me coming here after all this time?' Why did I feel like she was reading from a script? 'They *have* to still interview us occasionally, don't they, but I imagine they have more important things to do than follow a couple of has-been writers.'

'Speak for yourself.' I smiled. 'Do you think—?'

'What?'

'That they're waiting for us to do something worse than this? That they're thinking, let them read their stories. Let them feel they've won. But we *know*. We're waiting for what you do next.'

'You've read too many books,' said Lynda.

I laughed. 'God, I wish.' I paused. 'Do you know anything about these new re-education centres?'

She shrugged. 'Only what I've seen online.'

'And what's that?'

'No one ever comes back. Don't you go online?'

'No.'

'Why not?'

'They'll see.'

Lynda nodded. I motioned to her fingers again. 'They must hurt?'

She shook her head, a little too briskly, and changed the subject. 'You should leave next, and I'll go in five minutes.'

I headed to the door. 'Shall I come back on Monday?' Hunter's mum plays badminton Monday and Thursday.

'Are you sure you want to?' Her eyes shone with affection.

'Of course. Why?' Pause. '*What?*'

'I … oh, no, nothing. I just … want you to be sure.'

'I am.' I hadn't asked Jasmine about the protocol because Hunter had admitted he was alone. But then, she didn't even believe he had called. 'See you Monday.'

Biking home, I dreaded two shadows on my doorstep, one short, one tall. I rode up to the house, slowly, from a different direction to throw them off. I planned my story. I loved a night-time bike ride. I loved the inky sky. I loved the quiet streets. I would find the rest as I went. It's what I do.

But I had no visitors.

Now it's after midnight and I wish Hu—

Friday 16 November 2035 – 2.03 a.m.

My mum had a framed picture of Van Gogh's sunflowers on the hallway wall when I was a child. I couldn't understand how it was just a print and not the original. 'But how can you be absolutely sure it's not the real thing,' I asked her once.

She said, 'If you saw the real thing, the colours would jump off the canvas at you.'

Her words haunted me. I thought then, 'That's what I want to do. One day I'll write, and I'll make the colours jump off the page.'

And I did.

I *did*.

But they're all washed away now.

Except when I told Hunter the story.

Then, I saw flashes of sunflower; I saw those three shades of yellow in the painting and nothing else; I saw them leap an—

Saturday 17 November 2035 – 2.26 p.m.

When there was a knock on the door earlier, I panicked and thought it must be *them*. Thought, they've come to take me to a re-education centre. I wasn't writing at the time, but I grabbed my notepad from the mattress, slipped it down the back of my skirt, and hid the rest beneath my top. It should be safe there. The tall one and the short have never searched me though I'm sure that one day, inevitably, they'll check the mattress.

I opened the door – my heart buzzing like I'd swallowed an old-fashioned alarm clock – and blinked in confusion.

The Fine-Fayre tea man sat in the usual spot, two strands of his hair damp, wicker basket of condiments on his knee, scar cutting his cheek in two. Gate properly shut. The return of my non sequitur on wheels. Then I remembered. Of course. Saturday. How had I forgotten? In between visits, I hardly thought of him. It's like he took our shared moment away in the basket with him. I looked at the time. Three minutes past twelve.

'You're late again,' I said.

'It was twelve when I knocked,' he said.

'You terrified me, hammering like that.'

'Like what?'

I realised it had actually been a gentle rap; exactly how the tall one and the short one knock. That was why I'd overreacted. 'I should report you to your superiors for giving me a bloody heart attack.'

'I apologise.' He seemed to think. 'How would you like me to knock in future?'

'It doesn't matter.'

Next door, Laura was trimming the hedge with a softly vibrating device; she kept peering over every so often, then disappearing like a wind-up toy with a failing battery.

'You seem angry,' Fine-Fayre said.

'I'm fine,' I snapped. 'Don't tell me … you've got teabags that will calm down a hot, tired menopausal woman?'

He smiled. It was as bright as sunflowers. It was impossible not to smile back. I still can't figure out what it is about him. I still can't be sure I trust him. But he incites something in me. A need to keep him on his toes, a desire to get a reaction.

'I do have camomile tea, which is reputed to calm anxieties.'

'I'll just take my usual caffeine-filled bags, thank you.'

'We have a special offer on this week.' He went into his basket of wares and took out a delicate teacup and saucer decorated with festive trees and rows of holly garlands. 'You can have this exclusive bone china set *free* when you buy three packs of our new Rich and Regal percolated coffee.'

'I don't want coffee.'

'I can speak to my manager, see if she'll let me give you one next time for buying three packs of teabags instead.'

'It's fine. I don't like teacups. I prefer a mug.'

'OK.' I could see him deciding what to say next. I'm beginning to anticipate his moves. Read his expressions. 'How about some Fruity Frazzles today?'

'Dear God,' I said. 'What the hell are Fruity Frazzles?'

'A soft, cake-like biscuit with surprising layers of sensual strawberry, pleasing peach and bitter blackcurrant, topped with a light sprinkling of brown sugar, that lingers long after the final bite.'

'Do you learn these lines by heart?' I asked. When he didn't respond, I said, 'Go on then, I'll have three packs.' I could take some to Bedtime Stories on Monday.

'You asked me to bring you more Nutty Speckles too.'

'Did I?'

'Yes.'

'OK, those as well.'

He took out my now usual gold pack, some Nutty Speckles, and three glossy bags flecked with orange sparkles. He patiently scanned each item and said, 'That'll be ten pounds and seventy-nine pence, please.' I've observed during our few interactions that his facial scar hardly moves when he speaks, as though he's learned to fit talking around its inconvenience. I couldn't take my eyes off the long, thin, imperfect stripe.

'I know you're looking at my scar,' Fine-Fayre said.

'I'm not,' I lied, moving my eyes elsewhere.

'I don't mind – it bothers other people a lot more than it both-ers me.' I insisted that it didn't bother me at all, and he said gently, 'I think it does.'

'You think I don't have bigger stuff to worry about?' I regretted the outburst immediately. I like our banter but that had been too open. Laura stopped trimming the bush. Had she heard me? After a few seconds, she resumed. At that moment, his device pinged, twice.

'Your card's been declined,' he said.

I was mortified. I had no idea why. What had I bought recently? Nothing. Had they stripped me of my overdraft as they often did when they randomly felt like it? Thank God Laura's trimmer had been buzzing when it occurred. 'Is it OK if I pay you next time?' I knew I had no right asking for any favours after my nastiness.

'We're not supposed to.'

'Well … then … I can't buy anything this time…' I handed my items back.

He didn't take them. 'I could say you weren't in. That I left the teabags in your greenhouse.'

'I don't have one.'

'You can pay me next time.'

'Why are you kind to me?' I asked softly, suddenly afraid I might cry.

He didn't answer. Instead, he wheeled his chair backwards before turning on the path; he let go of the basket and it tipped slightly. The teacup – sitting atop the mass of curiously named produce – fell. I saw it in slow motion, the way you see things when you're remembering them rather than as they happen. The smash when it hit the concrete was louder than expected. Laura paused her toil again and called, 'Everything OK?'

'Fine,' I snapped.

'Oh, oh, gosh, *gosh*.' Fine-Fayre tried with difficulty to bend down.

'Leave it, I'll sort it out,' I said.

I went to the kitchen and found the dustpan and brush.

'Let me help you,' he insisted.

'Don't be silly, I'll do it.' I looked up at him as I collected the tiny pieces of china. I realised that few people probably saw him from this angle. That mostly he had to look up. Be lower. Be beneath. I wanted to stay there for longer. See him that way. Let him be the bigger one. The scar ran under his chin, like a stream continuing down a hill's curve. Eventually I got up and emptied the fragments in the wheelie bin. He watched as though I was disposing of a beloved family pet.

'It's only a cup,' I said. 'Don't look so bereft.'

'They know exactly how many I've got. They'll see that the number I don't have doesn't match the coffee I've sold.'

I smiled. 'Does that even make sense? Tell them the miserable creature whose name you don't know at number seventeen stole one.'

'I couldn't do that.'

'I don't care.'

'I'll just tell them I accidentally smashed it.'

'They'll believe that, you clumsy bugger.' I paused. 'Will they really be that bothered about a broken cup?'

'We have to pay for all losses or breakages.'

'How much for a cup?' I asked.

'I don't know until I tell them.'

'Put it on my bill then.'

'I can't do that. Just pay me for your purchases next time.' He continued down the path. He stopped at the flowers bordering the fence. My front garden looked like a summer day despite it being just five weeks until Christmas. 'Yellow tulips are an expression of cheerful thoughts and hope.'

'Those are red,' I said.

He nodded. 'All flowers have meanings, you know.'

'If you believe that kind of stuff.'

'Daisies symbolise purity. They're my favourite. When given as a gift they represent loyal love and whisper, *I will never tell.*'

'Flowers don't talk.'

'Symbolically. Can I take one?' he asked.

'What?'

'A tulip.'

'Sure.' I wanted to ask who it was for. 'What do the red ones mean?'

'Perfect love.'

No such thing, I almost said. But then I thought of all the mothers who described what they felt for their child as absolute love; how they said it was unconditional, that they would die for them. It did exist. I'd just never known it. I wondered if Fine-Fayre had kids. Like he was inside my head, he said, 'My daughter likes red tulips.'

He had a daughter. Did he have a wife? A husband? An anyone?

I watched the van pull away and went back inside.

The shoe will be back, I thought. *If today is like the other times, it'll be back again …*

I hurried to the kitchen. Looked on the windowsill. Came back into the hallway, looked around. Searched the living room, even though it had never been there. Eventually went outside, hoping, hoping, hoping. No blue and white trainer. No blue and white trainer. No blue and white trainer.

I cried until I fell asleep, hot an—

Sunday 18 November 2035 – 6.09 a.m.

Do I exist if I don't write?

I often feel that things didn't really happen unless I put them down in this notebook. Life overwhelms me if I don't explore it here in syllables, vowels and consonants, if I don't give it some sort of meaning through rhythm and rhyme. We're influenced, both consciously and subconsciously, by everything that happens to us. I make sense of my world on this page. I can be honest and show no one. It's painful at times, but it gets the pain out. It's safe to do so.

Except it isn't anymore.

They have taken this simple act from us.

I'm angry – angry, angry, *angry*. Writing used to fill my days. Reading used to fill my nights. And that filled my heart. What now? Now, hot days, even hotter nights, and just my thoughts and this page.

I keep thinking about these re-education centres. Where are they? Are there more than one? The idea of such a thing turns my stomach like bad milk. I watched the late news on the BBC last night, but no mention of them. Would such a thing be reported publicly? Probably not. Six years ago, words like *re-education centre* wouldn't have affected me so. Back then I dared to resist change.

Three months after I won the British Fiction Prize, I had a visit.

It was the first time I met the tall one and the short one.

In the weeks before that, still high on my win, I had shut myself away, trying to start my first book as British Fiction Laureate, reading some of the children's stories that were to inspire me, crying at their tales of being hungry without free school meals, uplifted by their descriptions of how bedtime stories soothed them.

The world outside was changing but I ignored it. I shut the curtains. Muted my social media. Put Lynda, Shelly and Cass off when they repeatedly suggested we get together and celebrate my win. On an essential visit to the supermarket for groceries I noticed the shelves that usually housed the fiction paperbacks were looking depleted. I asked a member of staff why, but she had no idea.

The next time I visited, they had been filled again, but with tens of copies of the same book. It was yellow and black, angry-looking, like a wasp. Had the words WARNING: NO WARNING across the top. And the title, *Technological Truth*, beneath. Then the author's name below: *Ade Woods*. Ade Woods, journalist and leader of the Anti-Fiction Movement. I was incensed. What the hell? The title was clearly mimicking mine.

And mine had been removed.

I grabbed a copy, full of fight, and stormed home. I skim-read *Technological Truth*. Each chapter broke down exactly how each big book in the last ten years had used fiction to trick, deceive, and anger readers, including mine.

I binned it in outrage.

Then I called my agent, demanding to know whether she knew about this book and why Ade Woods had been allowed to so clearly mock (that was how I felt) *my* book. She said there was nothing she could do. She didn't sound like herself. So, I called my editor, asked her. She didn't sound as outraged as I felt. She sounded afraid. Muted. Quiet. 'Things are changing, Fern,' she said. 'We can't take on any new authors until this Anti-Fiction Bill is finalised. They're monitoring everything we do. We have no idea what it's going to mean … but we're … *scared*.'

I hung up, nervous now myself.

How the hell was this happening?

The next day I called Lynda, Cass and Shelly, leaving messages when they didn't answer, inviting them over for supper that night, saying I wanted to talk to them about all these changes, ask what they knew.

I went to the door at seven, expecting them.

I thought perhaps the two men in dark suits were police officers and feared someone had died. Instead, they showed me some sort of government identification – which I didn't really take in, being more concerned about my quiche burning in the oven – and asked if they could speak to me. I didn't fear them then. I had no reason to. I can hardly recall what I thought of them.

They followed me into the kitchen. They may have made small talk, agreed to a cup of tea, it's hard to be sure now. Then the tall one picked up the glass British Fiction Prize trophy on my mantelpiece. 'We'll be taking this, Mrs Dostoy,' he said.

'I'm sorry?' I dropped the quiche I'd just removed from the oven. I remember that. It splattered all over my tiles, still bubbling away inside.

'Your book violates new laws that will come into effect next month.' The tall one spoke like we were discussing the best price for new home insurance. Hadn't my editor mentioned some sort of new bill? Yes. 'The British Fiction Prize has been cancelled. This award is now invalid.'

'Sorry, *what*?' I dared to be outraged back then.

'We're here to ask you to stop writing.'

'I have visitors coming.' I don't even know why I said this. 'You'll have to leave.'

'You don't. They won't be coming.' It was the tall one still, my award in his hand. The short one hadn't said a word. He just watched me, the way a tiger might watch a gazelle as it prances unaware.

'What? *Why*? I'm going to call Lynda right no—'

'That won't be happening.' The tall one grabbed my arm as I went for my phone, his grip surprisingly strong. That was when I first tasted fear; just an appetiser. When I suddenly wished Cal was still alive, that he might march them off the premises. 'You will not see your author friends again. They have also been informed.'

'Is this a joke?' I relaxed a little. It had to be. 'Did Shelly send you? To wind me up?'

'I assure you, this is no joke. Don't you watch the news, Fern?'

'I've been trying to write,' I cried. 'I'm supposed to be writing a book for childr—'

'That won't be happening now.'

'But I'm the British Fiction Laureate. I have t—'

'Not anymore,' he said.

'What? Who the hell *are* you?' I demanded. 'I want to speak to your superiors.'

'That isn't possible. You are to stop writing. Today, this is just a polite request. Once the new codes are law, it will be a formal instruction. If you have started a new work, delete it. We will check that you have on our next visit. Your three previous novels will be removed from circulation in the next few months. You are not permitted to promote them now in any way.'

'Who do you think you are, coming into my home, trying to take my award, telling me wh—'

'If you create a scene, this won't end well for you.' The tall one approached me. He opened his jacket enough for me to see the gun. Now the main course of my fear arrived; a carb-heavy, dense meal. I looked at it and then him. 'I have the authority to arrest you if you resist, and we can detain you as long as we see fit if you don't comply. It will be seen as an act of rebellion.' He smiled, warmly. 'It's not really so bad. There are other careers.'

'But … I don't understand. How is this *possible*? I'm on *Woman's Hour* next week talking about the new children's book, and I'm going on a book tour next month.'

'It's cancelled.'

'*What*? No one told me.'

'I'm telling you. You and those other three. I always disliked the Big Four as a collective name'

'But you can't just … *stop* us writing. It's what we do.' I paused. 'It's because we're women, isn't it?'

'Your gender is irrelevant.'

'But I don't understand why? What harm are we doing?'

'Plenty,' said the tall one. 'We've never seen so many hate crimes and violent protests like we have this last year.'

'But that isn't down to us. People are annoyed about the NHS being underfunded, about the government trying t—'

'You're wasting your time,' he said. 'You will stop writing. We will return to make sure. You won't hear from your publishing house. They are no longer allowed to operate. Don't contact them. Don't contact any other writers. Don't contact the other so-called Big Four. Don't write. We'll be back next week.'

They left, with my award.

I stood in my kitchen for ten minutes, the quiche still bubbling at my feet, not moving. I tried calling Lynda, then Shelly, then Cass, and no one answered. I said aloud, 'What the hell?' I went into the street to see if the world looked different. It didn't.

But it was.

I would later learn that supermarkets no longer stocked *any* fiction, that bookstores had closed until further notice, that popular TV and radio shows that reviewed the latest novels had been cancelled, that libraries were being emptied of everything in the fiction section, and that large vans were pulling up outside schools to take away their fairy tales. I would learn that teachers who resisted were arrested and served six months in prison, that librarians who united to protest were beaten to the ground by police officers, that anyone who tried to order novels online received a hefty fine within days.

The first thing children learn to write is their own name. Over and over. This is who I am, they're saying. Don't forget me, don't ignore me, love me, they're pleading.

My name is Fern Dostoy. And I'm a writer. And I will write.

Whatever the price and wh—

Monday 19 November 2035 – 3.51 p.m.

I'm used to drinking my Fine-Fayre tea black now. It has a kick that milk dilutes. Keeps me sharp when my eyes grow tired of writing. Laura next door's mini fridge has started buzzing. It's hard to know whether I've only just noticed or the mechanism is failing in some way. It'll be no great loss if it dies. I'm weaning myself off dairy. I opened the fridge door earlier and just seeing the milk – not even smelling it – I retched in the sink. I'd think I was pregnant if it wasn't for my age and lack of sexual activity.

I'm off work this week. I didn't know what to do with myself today. Long ago, I'd have caught up on reading, listened to the latest audiobook, browsed the Internet, or visited writer friends. I often wonder if they think of me too.

Instead, I wandered up and down my overgrown garden. I saw Laura in an upstairs window; she was hoping I'd cut the grass. I like its wildness. It's my one freedom, letting the weeds devour the space. The sun is not letting up on its late heat. When I couldn't stand it anymore, I came inside.

I hoped the blue and white trainer would be back, but it wasn't. Despite the oddness of its appearance, I hate the thought of never seeing it again. I can't explain it. I don't even care that I don't know who's leaving it in my house, or why. For the rest of the afternoon, I sat at the kitchen table with the fan on full. I tried a Fruity Frazzle – it was far too sugary to finish – and counted the minutes until I might speak to Hunter.

Would he call?

This worry nagged at me.

And now I must leave for Bedtime Stories and—

Monday 19 November 2035 – 11.51 p.m.

I left early for Bedtime Stories and went via the river in case I was being tracked. Then I took a less obvious route for the rest of the journey, lights off, down passageways behind shadowy houses, pushing my bike through wilting allotments. Like last time, Tinsley ushered me wordlessly into the house, and opened the basement flap. This time I could hear children in a back room somewhere. I tried to see them as I descended the steps but had to make do with shrill laughter; ghosts in a distant attic.

The basement was empty. I was the first to arrive. It was only five-fifteen. I had no sooner glanced at the clock than the phone in the time-out room rang. I ran to the beanbag, closing the door after me, and answered it.

'Bedtime Stories,' I said, 'what's your favourite?'

'*What Happened to All the Bloody Books*, Crazy Lady?'

I smiled. It was Hunter. Hadn't I known it would be?

'That's a long story,' I said, sadly.

'Is it? How many pages?'

I frowned, confused. Then I remembered. That was the title of *our* story, and where I'd finished it last time. Once again, I'd have to try to recall what I'd told him, then build on it enough to keep him happy.

'Did I come through on the weird phone again?' he asked. I could hear an odd squeak, squeak, squeak.

'You did. But I'm here, so I suppose it doesn't matter. Is your mum there?'

'She's at badminton.'

'Of course. And your nanny … what was her name?'

'Josie. She's … somewhere.' Squeak, squeak, squeak again.

'What's that sound?' I asked.

'My mum's chair. It spins. I'm at her desk. This is where I come for stories.'

'Wouldn't you rather be in bed in case you fall asleep?' I almost said that was where I had stories read to me as a child, then realised it was insensitive to describe something he'd never experience.

'Nah,' he said. 'This room smells most like my mum.'

Such simple words. So telling. My heart. I uncurled my legs and shifted. The beanbag suddenly lost its support. I could picture Hunter there, see a large oak desk, a chair that was on its way out and slowly sank the longer you sat in it, a plant that his mum forgot to water, that fried in the direct sunlight from the sash window, a blue and white trainer on the floor, and photos of Hunter aged two, four, seven, in a row, like a picture story of his growth. I saw it as clearly as I saw my novels when I wrote them.

'What does she do as a job?' I asked him.

'Something computery.'

'Does she know you ring here?'

'Nah.'

'Would she mind?'

'Nah.'

I smiled. 'But Josie's there, yes?'

He didn't answer. 'So, where did all the bloody books go then?'

'I'll tell you,' I said. 'But tell me first ... how well do you sleep?'

'Why?' Squeak, squeak, squeak. Did he fidget when he was bored or interested?

'I keep seeing on the news that children can't sleep at night.'

'I stay up late,' he said. 'I go on CrashLand.' I don't even know what that is. 'I'm on level eighteen and I have five hundred tanks, though Marley nicked ten last week.'

'Aren't you tired at school?' I asked.

'Sometimes. I fell asleep on the PE mats today and Mr Woodward made me stay behind.' He paused. 'But I slept good after you did the story last time.'

'Oh, I'm glad. Can you remember where we got up to?' I asked it playfully, hoping he'd think I was involving him rather than that I'd forgotten.

'Everything in Story Hunter's room was the same,' he said, 'except the books had gone.'

'Oh yes.' Damn. This was hard. I looked around the room for inspiration. Nothing. I'd easily pictured where Hunter was sitting, surely this should come to me too. 'OK … Hunter crept downstairs because it was still very early, and he didn't want to wake his mum or dad. In his house there's a bookshelf between the kitchen and the hallway, and that was empty too. But nothing else in the house had gone. Or moved. It was all very strange. Then he noticed that—'

'I can't hear the pages turning,' said Hunter.

'Sorry?'

'The *pages*. Jasmine always turned them dead rough. You're more … careful.'

I wondered whether to grab a book next time so I could create an accompanying sound effect. 'OK … so … Hunter decided to become a detective and hunt down the book stealer. He—'

'What did he notice?' asked Hunter.

'Sorry?'

'You said earlier, *Then he noticed that* … But you didn't finish it. You can't cheat. I wanna know.'

'Oh. Yes. Then he noticed that … when he went past the hallway mirror, he no longer had a reflection.' I shivered. I don't know where this idea came from, but it landed in my mind, like a memory.

'*What*? That's crazy! How?'

'Let's see,' I said. 'Hunter went up close to the mirror and touched the place where he wasn't. His hand met empty space.' As I said it, I could see it. The story now unrolled like a new carpet in front of me. 'How was it possible? Where had he gone? He ran, scared now, to the bathroom mirror. Emptiness there too. It was the same when he sneaked into his mum and dad's dimly lit bedroom and leaned close to their mirror.'

'Spooky,' said Hunter.

'I know. He was a boy with no reflection. And he wondered, did that mean he wasn't real anymore?'

'There's one way to find out.'

'What's that?'

'See if his mum and dad can see him.'

'You're very clever.' I smiled. 'That's what he did. Hunter sat on the edge of the bed and waited for one of his parents to wake up. After a while, his dad snorted, shuffled about, and reached for his phone. Hunter waited because he was afraid. Then his mum moved too, and she sat up first. She looked at Hunter. He smiled. She didn't smile back. He realised that she wasn't looking at him – she was looking right *through* him.'

'Sometimes I feel like that.'

'Like what?'

'Invisible.'

'Oh, that's awful.' I wanted to kiss his forehead. 'When?'

'It doesn't matter.' His voice was small. No squeak, squeak, squeak now.

'It does to me,' I said.

'Carry on with the story,' he said.

'Maybe this one's a bit too dark. Shall we do something jollier?'

'No,' he cried. 'I want to know about where the books went. Where bloody Hunter's reflection went!'

'Who makes you feel invisible?' I tried again. Was this dangerous ground? Jasmine warned about getting attached. But I was just looking out for a lonely kid like any decent adult should.

'My mum.' He spoke so quietly that I held my breath.

'How?' I asked.

'She's never here. I mean, she is, sometimes. But it's like … like she's not really. She's always on the phone or saying *just a minute* or waving her hand at me to go and play CrashLand.'

'Maybe she doesn't realise.' I wanted to make him feel better. 'If she has lots of work, and it's just her, it must hard. Tell her. I bet she'll feel terrible and try harder.'

Hunter didn't speak.

'Should I continue the story?' I asked him.

'Yes,' he cried.

Then the door opened, and Lynda came into the room. It was five-forty-five. 'Wait a moment,' I said to Hunter. Nothing. He had gone. Damn. 'It was him again,' I told her. 'He always hangs up if someone disturbs me.'

'It rang again in here?' She came to the phone and studied it. Her two fingers were still bandaged; the material was stained with old blood. 'Strange.' She shrugged and turned her attention to me. 'How are you, my friend?'

I stood, hugged her lightly. 'OK. Did you tell Jasmine about Hunter's call in here last week?'

'No. I saw no reason to. She's off tonight. It'll just be you, me and Alfie.'

'I'm worried about him,' I said.

'Alfie?'

'No, Hunter. He sounds lonely. No one has time for him.'

'You can't go down this avenue,' said Lynda kindly. 'You can't get involved. It'll compromise the whole thing. This place only works if we're totally anonymous. Remember, if anyone found out he rang here, he could be taken away from his mother. We give them the stories they need, and that's all.'

I nodded. She was right. I wondered if he'd try again and get through to the regular helpline phones when we turned them on.

We went into the main area as Alfie came down the stairs, face pale. 'We need to be quiet,' he hissed. 'The police were knocking on the door as I came down. Tinsley shut the cupboard after me before answering it. We can't turn the phones on. We'll have to wait until she gives us the all clear.'

'Shit,' said Lynda softly.

'Has this happened before?' I whispered, feeling sick.

Lynda nodded. 'Only once. It wasn't the police though, just someone from a political party. They left after half an hour.'

'What if they look in the cupboard?' I said, panicked.

'Tinsley always puts the coats and stuff back on top of the hatch,' whispered Lynda. 'This house isn't supposed to have a basement, remember, so they won't even think of it. It'll be fine. We just need to sit tight.' She didn't sound convinced though. Fresh blood stained her bandage now. She realised too and tried to hide it.

'Are you OK?' I asked. 'Should a cut still be bleeding like that?'

'It's fine.' She seemed irritated to be asked about it.

Alfie sat on one of the sofas in the centre of the room, and we joined him. In silence, we strained to hear what might be going on upstairs. It was eerily quiet.

'What do you think they want?' I whispered.

Alfie shrugged. 'You don't think—?'

'What?' asked Lynda.

'They followed me here?'

She shook her head.

'How can you be so sure?' he asked.

She didn't answer. Something was off about her response. It was like she *knew* they couldn't have followed him, but she didn't want *us* to know that. I think now, after hours of consideration, that I'm wrong. I trust Lynda with my life. She is one of us; the good people. But does she know something that she wants to protect us from?

'What time did you get here?' Alfie asked me quietly.

'Oh, early. I biked here and kept to the back streets.'

'It'll be fine,' said Lynda. 'Tinsley will come soon; it'll be something and nothing.'

Fifteen minutes later and no Tinsley. I thought about the re-education centres. About Shelly Dean having been missing for so long. About the notepad hidden in my mattress, and that maybe

I should have brought it with me. Lynda's finger kept bleeding into the bandage, like a growing sketch of a rose.

'I have Fruity Frazzles.' I remembered them in my bag.

'You have what?' Despite the tension, Lynda smiled.

'They're a sort of fruit-flavoured cake. My tea man delivered them.'

'Oh, I've tried those,' whispered Alfie, wrinkling his nose. 'My husband got me some. Awful things.'

I laughed and immediately covered my mouth. We all looked up. Waited. Still quiet above us.

'I'll try one,' whispered Lynda.

We didn't dare put the kettle on and risk clinking cups. She ate it, slowly, her face a picture of unsureness.

'What if she doesn't come for us?' said Alfie.

'Who?' I asked, dumb.

'Tinsley. What if it gets to nine, and she hasn't come down? How long do we wait?'

I looked to Lynda. 'Look, I don't know,' she admitted in a low voice. 'This has never happened before.'

'Isn't there some sort of protocol?' I asked.

Alfie and Lynda looked at one another. 'Not really,' he admitted. 'I mean, there's food in the cupboards, a bathroom, water—'

'We can't stay *forever*?' I hissed.

He didn't answer.

'It's the risk we've been taking I guess,' whispered Alfie. 'We've taken it for granted that we come and tell stories and it's all lovely and satisfying. But discovery would be dangerous for every one of us.' He paused, looking suddenly aghast at his own naivety. 'I suppose, I never considered it in full. I felt … infallible. Like it would never happen – being caught.'

Do I feel that way? Is it foolish?

When it got to eight-fifteen, we had been silent for a while. There was nothing to say. I thought about all the children not hearing a story. It made me angry. How dare anyone deny them that?

I thought about the book I'd been supposed to write for them as British Fiction Laureate, and my anger melted into ache; sad, nostalgic, tearful ache.

A crash above. Our eyes raised in wide unison. The muffled sound of crying. A child. Then it went quiet. Louder again, more needy. What the hell was happening?

Then the hatch opened, and light flooded the stairway. We didn't move. I glanced at Lynda and saw the same fear in her eyes. Would we be united in a moment that changed our lives? I saw minty nail polish and my heart stilled. Tinsley. Not a police officer. Alfie stood, approached the stairway. Her cheeks were flushed; she wrapped her arms around her chest as though to self-comfort.

'I'm sorry,' she said, flustered. 'I had to gather myself. Then the kids were playing up because I'd neglected them.' She shook her head. 'A woman up the street, she was robbed. I know her. They wanted info. It took forever.'

'Poor you.' Lynda stroked Tinsley's arm. 'It must have been horrible. Is there anything we can do?'

She shook her head. 'Do you mind leaving? I need to settle the kids.'

'Of course,' said Lynda. 'I'll let Jasmine know what happened tonight.'

Tinsley went back upstairs. Alfie called a driver on the other phone; Hunter's phone, as I thought of it. Lynda said she was parked on another street. My bike was chained to a tree. It was time to go.

'I'll leave first,' said Alfie.

Lynda and I were left alone. We faced one another, shrugging at the same time, like we were one another's reflection. 'Has it made you think again?' she asked me.

'Think again?'

'About coming here.'

'No.' The answer came out before I could stop it.

Lynda had been so joyful to see me that first night, hugging me with passion. The second time, something changed. There was reluctance behind the joy. What happened in between? Now she seemed keen to put me off coming to Bedtime Stories. Why? Did she know something?

'I feel like you don't want me here anymore,' I admitted.

'Oh, no, I *love* seeing you.' She seemed torn. She shook her head and said, 'I'll see you on Thursday then?'

'Yes. Or …'

'What?'

'We could meet up.'

'No.' Lynda's negative response came as brusquely as mine had earlier.

'I know we're not supposed to … but we could meet somewhere isolated. The woods near—'

'No,' repeated Lynda. 'It's too risky. I care for you too much to put you in that situation. We could jeopardise this.'

I nodded. 'You're right. I'll see you Thursday.'

I took the same backstreet route home, and approached my house from the opposite direction, fearing a tall and short shadow on my doorstep. But all was quiet. I didn't switch the lights on, intending to go straight to bed, but an unusual shape on the kitchen windowsill stopped me heading upstairs. The mini fridge buzzed, sputtered, and resumed buzzing. I went to the window. It wasn't an unusual shape. It was the one that I'd missed. The single blue and white trainer. I held it to my chest. I knew I wouldn't sleep.

I'm here, at my desk, black tea cold, shoe in front of me.

I need my anger.

But right now, I'm sad and I wish th—

Wednesday 21 November 2035 – 4.45 p.m.

The anger is back. I woke with it hot in my throat like the start of tonsillitis. I'd tossed and turned all night. Did I, like the children, need the stories in order to sleep? At some point in the night the fridge must have died. This morning, I was greeted with a pungent smell, an absence of buzzing, and the knowledge that I'd have to open its door at some point and face sour milk.

Mid-afternoon, a hearty rap on the door interrupted me binning its putrid contents. I almost dropped the milk carton. Rapping, again. I frowned. It didn't sound like how the tall one and the short one knock. I marched into the hallway. Laura next door? I'd have to tell her the fridge had broken.

It was Fine-Fayre, brow speckled with damp.

His scar looked redder than usual, or was his skin simply paler today? His jacket had creases along the arm, like he hadn't had time to iron it. Did a partner usually do it? I looked at his left hand – no wedding ring, not that it means much these days. Was his appearance unusual because it was a different day to when I usually see him? Was this his Wednesday persona?

'Why were you so loud?' I asked.

'I tried not to knock how I did last time.'

Of course. Then I remembered. I didn't pay him last time. I checked my account at the weekend, and I'd forgotten to allow for my annual ARF – that's the Author Rectification Fee that all writers now must pay, supposedly to put back what we took away. I moved some money from my dwindling savings. Anger flared again at the nerve of him, returning to make sure he got his money.

'I'm not going to do a runner,' I said. 'I'll still be here to pay on Saturday.'

'I'm not here for that – I brought you this.' He took one of those festive teacups from his basket.

'I told you, I prefer a mug.'

'Give it to someone for Christmas,' he said.

'I don't have anyone.'

'Oh.'

'What happened with the one you broke?' I now felt sorry for him. Anger was better. Pity didn't sit well with me.

'I paid for it,' he said.

'How much?'

'Fifteen pounds.'

'For *that*?' I flung an arm at the cup, still in his hand.

'Ten for the cup. Five for the breakage.'

'You had to *pay* because you broke it?'

Fine-Fayre ignored the question and pulled out a leaflet from between some Coconut Crunches and extra-dark Brazilian coffee. It was some sort of application form emblazoned with the words *The Perfect Gift or Treat!* 'You've bought enough teabags now to qualify for entry in our big annual prize draw,' he said.

'How many did I buy?'

'Enough.' He smiled and it was almost as bright as his Saturday smile.

'What do I win then?' I sighed.

He read the leaflet. I watched his eyes skim the text, his frown line fine, not yet a permanent fixture like mine. 'The first prize is a hamper full of Fine-Fayre goodies ... the second prize is a slightly smaller hamper full of Fine-Fayre goodies ... third prize is a Fine-Fayre voucher for twenty pounds.'

I laughed. 'I think I'd rather lose.'

He took a gold pen from his pocket. 'It's free to enter and it's regional, so you have a high chance of winning.'

'It doesn't include Fruity Frazzles, does it?'

'You didn't like them?'

'No one did.' I studied him, pen poised hopefully. 'Your scar looks sore today.'

He clicked the pen as though I'd said I would be *delighted* to enter. 'I just need some details from you.'

'Have you been scratching it?' I felt sad when I visualised him doing so, possibly hurting himself.

'Can I have your phone number please?'

'*Why*?' No, I couldn't risk feeling sad for him. I still didn't truly know if I could trust him.

'I need it so they can contact you if you win the prize draw.'

'I just told you, I don't want to enter.'

'You could give it to someone as a gift,' he suggested again.

'And I told you, I don't *have* anyone.'

'I just need to take your name please.'

'Nice try,' I said.

'You could give a false one.' He held my gaze. Did he know my surname *was* a false one? 'As long as we have your correct number so we can call if you win.'

'What happened to you?' I asked, more kindly. 'Is the scar anything to do with you being in this wheelchair?'

'You could just give me one of your initials,' he tried.

'I only bought your teabags because I pitied you,' I cried.

I didn't expect the words. They weren't even true. He had annoyed and fascinated me the first time he knocked. Now I even felt sad for his sore scar. But there was no pity. I regretted my harshness immediately. What did I want? A reaction. An argument. *Something*. I don't know.

Fine-Fayre wordlessly put the application form back in his basket. 'Do you want to pay me what you owe now?' Did this mean he wouldn't come back? Did this free him from the obligation of my visit? I put my card to his device, waited for the ping.

I didn't want him to go. I wanted to say something to cancel my cruelty.

'Take another tulip,' I cried. 'For your daughter.'

'They're dying,' he said, sadly.

They were; their green stems arched down, like tired old men. I hadn't watered them, and it hadn't rained since a brief, hot storm five nights ago. 'I'll water them,' I said. 'They'll revive. You can have one next time.'

'I'll see you on Saturday,' he said.

'Yes. Saturday.' The relief that he would return washed over me.

He backed his chair up and turned it to leave.

'I'll take the teacup,' I said.

He handed it over. Our fingers touched momentarily.

'I'm sure I can find someone to give it to,' I said.

On his way to the van, Fine-Fayre put his basket on my wall so he could close my gate carefully, securing the latch and then tugging on it to check it had caught. I watched the van leave and went inside. I'd left the milk on the worktop. I vomited at the stench and the—

Thursday 22 November 2035 – 7.03 a.m.

It's early. I'm drinking black tea in my festive teacup. I like the soft tinkle it makes each time I put it back on the saucer. I've been thinking about tonight. Bedtime Stories. I don't *have* to go. I could resume my dull, routine, safe life. Rip up this notepad. Tell Fine-Fayre not to come any more. But I don't *want* to resume dullness, routine, safety. The re-appearance of the blue and white shoe has only cemented this, and I don't know why.

I *will* go tonight.

I must tell the stories. They are a song we all know. I read once that the ability to understand sheet music is not essential in creating an opus. Many composers produce a masterpiece without the capacity themselves to read musical notes. It's about needing to; being compelled to; about ear, instinct, rhythm. I *must* tell Hunter the rest of his story. If I don't he—

Thursday 22 November 2035 – 10.32 p.m.

On my way to Bedtime Stories, I cycled past ALLBooks.

Little silhouettes, dark against the dying November light, queued out of the door: children. I slowed down to try and see why but it was impossible. I stopped in the square, near the marble fountain, and approached the shop on foot. In the window, a yellow poster screamed words in bold black. The two colours were wasp-like, very *alarm*, very *warning*, very *stay away*, very *I've seen these before*. They said that Ade Woods would be in the store at 4.30 p.m. – in fifteen minutes – to sign his new book, *Technological Truth For Tots and Teens*.

I reread the six words.

Then again.

I felt sick. Woods' first book, *Technological Truth*, has now sold more than my British Fiction Prize winner, and is upheld by the government as a beacon of light in this new world. He still appears on many a political panel, advocating endlessly the 'joy in truth', though I avoid watching him. The Anti-Fiction Movement has died out. It fulfilled its aim. We are free of fiction.

And now his insidious ideas were clearly being repackaged and delivered to the young, to children who had already missed out on story time for over five years.

I approached a girl in the queue; she was maybe ten. 'Is this a new book?' I asked her, motioning to the poster.

'No, but it's the first time he's been here,' she cried.

'Is he worth reading?'

'I haven't read it yet,' she admitted, 'but everyone says it's dead good.'

'What's it about?'

'How like stories are lies and they used to damage us ... and how big our brains are now we only read stuff about real things. It's got Four-D pictures in it too and there are all these hidden clues in them. And no one has like *ever* solved it ...'

I wanted to tell her *no*, stories are how we *get* to the truth. *No,* stories are how we light up the neurons in our brain, make our hearts dance, access our emotions, connect, learn, live. I wanted to scream, *no*, I was going to write you *all* a story, once upon a time. *No*, I was going to use the very words you children wrote down as inspiration, your joy and your fears and your hopes and your lives.

But the queue moved, and she lost interest in me.

I had to leave or I'd be late for Bedtime Stories. As I cycled, hard, I thought about the other authors out there, somewhere in the dark. How were they coping? Did they ever see the people they'd created in their books wandering around the real world? Did they shiver at the similarity of scenarios? Did they wonder which came first – their story or reality? Ade Woods using one word from my book title was not plagiarism, just as Mr Shrivel's big plan causing such an extreme reaction in his colleagues could not possibly be lifted right off the pages of my bestseller.

Still, I don't like these strange occurrences.

I got to Tinsley's, sweat dripping down my back. I was the last to arrive. Lynda, Alfie and Jasmine already sat on the sofas in the main basement area.

'Bloody Ade Woods,' I said, without even saying hello.

'What now?' they said in unison.

'He's written a children's book.' I was still in shock.

Alfie nodded. 'I know. He's bloody everywhere at the moment.'

'Right now, he's in ALLBooks,' I said.

'Yeah, he's on tour,' said Jasmine. 'I reckon the government asked him to create a kids' version of his book because they know that Bedtime Stories exists, and they need a strong anti-fiction message to reach kids directly. He's young, good-looking, has a strong voice, and he cleverly paints a world where fact is the most exciting story you can tell.'

'It still pains me,' said Lynda softly, 'that they believe fiction is some sort of evil trickery.'

'That isn't it,' said Alfie. 'They didn't like the freedom it gave. They didn't like you writers having a voice.'

Lynda didn't respond; she looked sad, tired. I noticed then that the bandage on her fingers had been replaced by a snug black glove that appeared to be made of some sort of half rubber, half cotton material.

'What happened?' I motioned to it.

'Oh. They think it hasn't healed well. I need this to support the bone.'

'After cutting it on a *cheese grater*?'

'It's six,' said Jasmine, and Lynda looked glad of the interruption. 'We just discussed what happened here last time – I'll update you if we get a moment, Fern. But now, what we came to do …'

And so, we began. Once upon a time. In a distant land, long ago. Far away, in a wood. There was once a prince. There was once a princess. A wish was made. A wish was granted. A wish ruined it all. And then they all lived happily ever after. Our words merged in the air. Stories intertwined. An end harmonising with a beginning. But I was distracted; my attention was drawn to the time-out room, to how soon I could say I needed a coffee and escape there. A lull gave me chance just after eight. I was the only one without a call. Before another could delay me, I grabbed the nearest book, hurried into the other room, and shut the door.

Did I know the phone would ring immediately?

I think I did.

'Bedtime Stories, what's your favourite?' I sank into the beanbag.

'You already know, Crazy Lady,' he said.

'What made you ring at this exact moment, Hunter?'

'What do you mean?'

'Why right this minute?'

'Um …' That familiar squeak, squeak, squeak. I knew where he was. I could see it. 'I was eating a cheese and tomato sandwich. Then I went to the toilet. Then I did some homework. Then, just a minute ago, I realised I didn't want to play CrashLand, I wanted a story …'

'Is your mum at badminton?'

'Yup.'

'And Josie?'

'Doing washing.'

She was there. Good. 'What was your homework?' I asked.

'Crap. English. Hate it. We have to write a report on our favourite book.'

'And which one is yours?'

He paused. 'It's the book you've been reading to me, but I can't write about that, can I? It'll have to be about that one by the *Technological* mister. He so copied that book you mentioned the other time, the one you can't read me 'cos it's adult.'

'He so did,' I agreed, with a smile.

'Wonder what they'd do if I wrote my homework about *What Happened to All the Bloody Books*?'

'You mustn't.' The idea chilled me to my core.

'I won't.' He sighed like I was stupid, and then tutted for an exclamation mark. 'I know what happens. Marley at school told me they take you away.'

'This is just between us.' I thought of something. 'Do you tell your friends you've rung here?'

'Duh, yeah,' he cried. 'Loads of my mates ring. We don't tell the teachers. We're not dumb.'

I nodded. 'No, you're not.'

'Can we get on with the story then?'

'Of course.'

I knew where we'd got up to. I remembered the last line, exactly, word for word. *He realised that she wasn't looking at him — she was looking right* through *him*. I said it again, slowly, with heavy menace, while opening the book I'd grabbed so he could hear the pages.

'That's so spooky,' cried Hunter.

'I know. I got shivers too. Well, let's see what he's going to do.'

'Be loud. Move the duvet. Knock things over!'

I laughed. 'OK.' I readied myself. 'Hunter stared back at his mum, hoping the weight of his glare might be enough to have her see him. But she yawned and stretched and got out of bed and walked right past him, like he was …' I had to think so I turned the page to buy time.

'You're clumsier today,' observed Hunter.

I smiled. ' – like he was a sheet of clear glass. His mum went downstairs, and after a moment his dad followed, also seemingly unaware of Hunter, sitting on the bed. He was so stunned that he pinched himself, to check if it was a dream. No. He was real. He followed them downstairs. He went to pull the books off the hall-way shelf onto the floor, to grab their attention, and remembered. No books. They were gone. He suddenly wondered if whoever had taken them had taken him too? It was as though he had somehow been flattened in the night and stuck inside the pages and stolen away with the words.'

'I love that,' said Hunter, sounding sleepy.

'You might not if it happened to you!'

He giggled. It was enchanting.

'Are you happy?' I asked him suddenly.

'Yes,' he said. 'This story is good. Don't st—'

'No, are you *happy*?'

'What do you mean?'

'I know today's world is strange, but are you OK, Hunter?'

'I guess so. Our house is nice.' He yawned. 'Mum always gets me the best trainers and lets me eat what I want for tea and we have nice holidays even though I'm always bored 'cos it's just me.' He paused.

'*But?*' I prompted.

I looked up to see Jasmine in the doorway. Damn it. I'd barely had time to speak to him and I knew he'd be gone now. We'd hardly got any further with the story. It could take forever, and who knew if we had that long. Next time, I need to take his phone number. No. That might put him in danger.

'Who were you talking to?' she asked, eyes narrowed.

I had to trust that Lynda hadn't told her about the last time Hunter called. 'Oh, it was one of those sales robots.'

She didn't look like she believed me. 'I don't understand how. That line only goes out.' The main phones rang behind her, demanding we begin another fairy tale. I followed her into the main room, resumed a seat at a phone, and continued the tailored drama.

At nine, I was exhausted. It's surprising how dry your throat is after talking non-stop for three hours. Alfie had to leave straight away so went first.

'I have to go next,' said Jasmine, 'but just time to let you know, Fern … earlier I was telling the others … Tinsley's quite shaken up by the other night. Even though it had nothing to do with this, it made her realise the risk she's taking with her family home. She said we can use it for another two weeks but after that, we need to find somewhere else.'

All I could think was that Hunter wouldn't be able to call me. 'Do we have anywhere else?'

'There are ten other call centres in the city, but no room for us to join them. We need to work on finding somewhere. I'd offer my house, but there's no basement or suitable loft space. Lynda, as an ex-author, can't risk it. Nor you.'

'How can we find somewhere then?' I asked.

'We're asking around,' said Lynda.

'I have to go.' Jasmine pulled on a faux fur coat. 'See you next time.'

'God, I hope we find somewhere else,' I said to Lynda.

'Maybe …' She trailed off, sounding sad.

'What?'

'Maybe it's a sign. Maybe we should let this one go. Plenty of other centres. And maybe … it's time I stepped down.'

'*What*?' I couldn't believe what I was hearing. 'You started this. You and Cass. You were so happy when I arrived. You spent all that time hoping I would join you. But since …' I thought about it.

'Since you cut your fingers, you've been … odd. Different. What happened, Lynda? What changed you?'

'Nothing,' she snapped. 'Maybe last time, with Tinsley, made *me* nervous too.'

'No, you were different before that.'

'I'm just … tired. Let the young ones do the stories.'

I went to hug her. She let me but it was a submission, not joyfully received. I'd only been here four times, but already I couldn't imagine not coming. She pulled free and picked her bag up off the sofa. 'See you on Monday,' she said.

'So you'll be here?'

She nodded, resigned. 'For now.'

'Lynda?'

'Yes.' She paused at the door, black-gloved hand awkwardly about the handle.

'I've been writing.' I don't know why I said it. I wanted to tell someone. I wanted to say it. Share it. Hear it spoken.

She turned to look at me. I've seen many expressions on her familiar, beloved face in the past, but this one threw me. Fear. It greyed the normally warm skin tone. It slackened the usually full lips.

'Not fiction,' I said quickly, wanting to quash her obvious distress and wishing I'd never admitted it. 'A diary, I suppose you could call it. Just … my everyday life.'

'Which parts of your life?' she asked, almost inaudible.

'All parts. The dullness. The heat. Work. This tea man who visits me.' I paused. 'Coming here.'

'Delete it.' Lynda strode towards me.

'No.'

'You must.' She grabbed my arm with her gloved hand and winced. 'They'll see it on your laptop. They probably already have. That's probably why they came the other night.'

'It's not on a laptop. I'm not stupid. It's in a notepad, which I hide.'

'They'll find it. Probably already have.'

'They searched last time and found nothing.'

'I mean when you're not there,' Lynda said.

I felt like I'd just been dropped by one of those fast-falling fairground rides. 'You mean …' I couldn't finish.

'The visits when you're there are just to keep you on your toes. The ones when you're *not* are when they find what they're looking for.'

They come into our homes. No. They can't. That's illegal. (I'm laughing now as I write at the fact that I was even shocked when Lynda told me, after all that has happened, after all they've done.)

'But if they *had* found it,' I said, 'surely they'd have followed me here. They'd shut us down, take us all away.'

'Not necessarily.'

'What do you mean?' I was even more confused.

'They want us to continue.'

'What? *Why*?'

'You have to carry on as though you haven't realised they know. Understand? Do a few more of these Bedtime Stories and then stop. Make your excuses. As long as you're not here when the other stuff happens, you should be OK.'

'The other stuff?'

'I don't agree with it,' said Lynda.

'With what?'

'The government *want* us to carry on telling our stories here, to let us think we've got away with it. So then, when we take things further, it'll make sure the fiction ban is never *ever* lifted.'

'What do you mean?' I was angry now.

'We're going to burn down every single ALLBooks store in the UK.'

'*We?* You mean … the Bedtime Stories team? *No* … That isn't what we're about.'

'It isn't what you and I are about,' said Lynda, sadly. 'It isn't what most of the team are about. But some … they're angry.'

'How do you know all this?'

'Jasmine told me.'

'No, how do you know the government know about Bedtime Stories and want us to continue?'

Lynda didn't answer. She shook her head. Kissed my cheek tenderly. And headed for the door. 'Earlier, with your diary, I wasn't mad about you jeopardising this place,' she said. 'It's already done. I was mad because I don't want you to jeopardise *you*. Come back a few times, and then leave, before the anarchy starts. I am.'

'I was so happy when I arrived,' I cried. 'You were too.'

'I didn't know about these plans then.'

'But how do you know so much about what the government know?'

'See you Monday.' She disappeared up the basement stairs.

I don't remember the bike ride home. My head buzzed with all the new information. I could hardly get my breath. What would I do if they were waiting for me, the tall one and the short one? I needed time to prepare. To compose myself. To be able to act as though I knew nothing of what I now do. No one there. Just dry leaves dancing in the idle breeze, not a care in the world.

I'm at my desk. I started writing at 10.32 p.m.; now it's almost midnight. I'll never sleep. I can hardly hold the pen. Most of these words are a scrawl. I can't believe they come in the house when I'm not here. It's a violation. If they found this notepad last time and read it, they put it back exactly how it was. And if they find it again, it'll be a miracle if they can make sense of tonight's pages.

Should I stop then?

Is there any point if they've already seen my life so far? They'll know I still have a copy of *Technological Amazingness*, even if I didn't record where I keep it. Do I now edit what I say? Why? They'll read this paragraph and know what I know. I've written it. I can't unwrite it. I could cross it out but that only draws attention to it, and maybe they have a way of reading what's beneath.

I'm going in circles.

I'll take it with me. Yes. Every time I leave the house.

Then I can still be as honest as I want to be.

Why haven't they come for me?

Hunter. Shit, *Hunter*. Have I jeopardised him? I just flicked back through previous entries. They can't know from this which Hunter. There's no surname. I don't know where he lives. Shit – I can't leave Bedtime Stories without being able to speak to him somewhere else. If I go to another base, how will he be able to get me when he calls? I need to finish his story. I have to think of a way. Something that doesn't put him at risk.

The blue and white trainer is still on the desk.

Shit. Did *they* put it in the house?

The tall one asked me about it last time they visited. Was it a test? Did he know where it had come from? If Lynda is right, they've been in here while I'm out. But the shoe, I was home the first time it appeared. Maybe the next time too, I can't recall without looking back at old pages. But why a single, slightly worn child's shoe? It doesn't make sense.

But what does?

This. Only this now. Writing. I'll continue to record my story here but now I'll—

Saturday 24 November 2035 – 2.03 p.m.

I didn't write yesterday. I couldn't. I didn't even get out of bed. I didn't wash. I didn't eat. I slept on and off, dreaming of fires and explosions and burning books and charred victims, likely exacerbated by the temperature. I grabbed my picture of Cal and dozed with it under the pillow, whispering questions I wished I could ask him in that vulnerable moment: Is everything going to be OK? Can you see me where you are?

On the weather report this morning the blonde avatar – whose name I can't recall – said the heatwave is likely to continue into December. At least the washing dries in half an hour on the line. I saw Laura while I was hanging it out, told her the fridge has died but I'll replace it.

'Don't worry,' she said. 'It was only a spare one. There's currently a big sale on SmartFridges.com.'

'It's OK, thanks. I'm going dairy free.'

'Everyone eventually does it.' She sighed, seeming almost nostalgic. 'I miss the days when you weren't judged for enjoying something that an animal has birthed or shat.'

And she went inside.

Just before noon, there was a knock on the door. I ran and got my notepad and shoved it down the back of my jeans. If it was them, I had to act how I always do. But how is that? Meek. Compliant. I opened the door with what I hoped was an I'm-exactly-who-I-was-last-time expression.

Fine-Fayre sat in his wheelchair, hair neatly bowl-like about his head, basket full, scar less angry. I was determined not to look at it this time. In his absence, I'd briefly forgotten the cruel words I'd said to him. He was like a book that I put aside while I went about my daily life. Now the guilt flooded back.

'You're early,' I said, but not unkindly.

'I had one visit less than usual,' he said.

'I ended up using the teacup,' I admitted. 'I quite like it after all.'

'My scar has nothing to do with me being in this chair.' He had obviously been thinking about my blunt question last time.

'Oh.' I had to compose myself. 'I … you don't have to exp—'

'You didn't win the competition I'm afraid.'

'What competition?' I was thrown off again; I'd thought he was going to explain his injury.

'For the hamper,' he said.

'Oh. That. How the heck could I *not* win something I *didn't* enter?'

'I entered you with a fake name and my phone number.'

'What did you call me?'

He paused, like he wanted *me* to say my name. 'Mrs Tulip.' He looked at my wilting flowers.

I laughed. I couldn't help it. It felt good. There's not much to smile about right now. In that moment, with him there, smiling too, I felt hopeful. 'What if I'd won the hamper? I'd have been disqualified with a fake name and your phone number.'

'You didn't win. It doesn't matter.' He went into his basket. 'Do you want your usual teabags? Would you like a sample of our new Ravishing Raisin loaf?'

I laughed again. 'How do you keep a straight face with these names?'

'It's good with marmalade on.'

I studied him. 'Don't you ever get bored of just selling tea?'

'I won't be doing it forever.'

'No. I suppose. If you have other dreams.' I paused, wondering if he'd share them. 'Well, I hope your replacement has a better haircut than you. You look like Blackadder,' I teased.

'Who's Blackadder?'

I realised he was too young. I was only small when the series was on TV so didn't get a lot of the humour until reruns in my teens. I liked how much my mum laughed. 'I'll take the teabags,' I said, 'but I don't want biscuits today.'

'That's a shame. The Nutty Speckles are half price.'

'No wonder.' I smiled again. He handed me the gold pack. I took it. Put my card to his phone. Heard the satisfying ping of payment accepted. 'Your pity was ill-placed,' I said gently.

'Sorry?' He fumbled with his phone.

'You'd no reason to feel sorry for me. I know you did. That's why you first came here, isn't it? You knew I lived alone.'

'No. It isn't.' His gaze was unflinching. 'It's you who pity *me*. But I don't mind. It happens a lot.'

'I don't,' I snapped. 'I know I said that awful thing last time, and I feel terrible now, but it was just a reaction to the thought of you feeling that way about me.'

'I was in the care system a lot as a kid,' he said.

What was he talking about now?

'My mother had learning difficulties, so my sister and I lived in all manner of places. A boy in one of the care homes cut my face. He told me it was a pen, so I let him draw on me. But it was a pen knife. I was ten. It wasn't tended to right away. The doctor who then stitched it up did a pretty bad job.' He shrugged. 'It was hard as a teenager. I got picked on.'

'That's awful,' I said, zero pity, only compassion.

'But now … well, it's just me. My face. My life.'

'And the wheelchair?' I asked, still curious.

He didn't respond.

'Do you ever think about having those SmartLeg things that walk for you instead of the chair?'

'I didn't come to your door because I pitied you.' He ignored the question as he so often did. It's almost like he doesn't hear them. 'I came because I … admire you.'

'*Admire* me?'

'Because I recognised you.'

I went cold. 'You …?'

'I was delivering to Mrs North (that's Laura next door) and I saw you, pulling the wheelie bin out. I couldn't believe it. On a street as bland as this one. *You*.' He caressed a pack of Lemon Crackles. 'So you see, I could have given your real name in the competition, but I thought it might show up on the system as an alert or something, and I'd not be allowed to return to you.'

I can't get in trouble for being recognised but I'm encouraged (this word suggests choice) to keep a low profile. Change my surname. Alter my appearance. It's to protect me as much as the world from my 'awful, hate-inciting, controversial' book. I need to be forgotten. I belong to the past. I must shush.

'What's my name then?' I asked, quietly.

'Fern Dostoy,' he said.

And I knew then I could trust him.

For a moment I imagined what it might be like to kiss him. To lean down and put my mouth to his. To touch his face, run my fingers over his scar's pleats and ridges, then feel his flat, smooth skin in contrast. A fly buzzed in the hallway behind me, urgent, distracting. I opened the door a little wider for it to escape.

'Yes,' I said.

'*There are no limits to what we can do,*' he said softly. '*Our abilities and technology are infinite. But "we can" is not ethical, not emotional, not a follower of instinct. Someone has to say no to us. When no one does, we scratch yes into the flesh of every human who can't afford better.*'

He was quoting my book. It was eerie, hearing him whisper words I'd not heard in so long. 'All these visits,' I said. 'Why didn't you say something?'

'I used to read you instead of studying.' His eyes dimmed with nostalgia. That made him, what, late twenties? So young. I could be his mother. 'I had a place booked on your last book tour before they cancelled it. And I was so excited about the news that you were going to write a children's book.' He paused. 'You inspired me to write a novel.'

I felt sick. He could be in danger. 'Where is it? You should be so careful.'

'No, back in 2029. I was supposed to be writing essays about Chaucer. Then ... well, there was no one to send it to. No one to read it. Fiction was over. I deleted it. I was scared they'd see it.' He was going to leave. I saw it in the way he studied the controls on his chair.

'What was your book about?'

He shook his head and reversed.

'I love your tea,' I said when he reached the gate. I wanted him to know I trusted him. To know I had never meant to be so cruel.

I didn't close my door until the mock-vintage vehicle had disappeared around the corner. Then I leaned on it and thought about checking that the blue and white trainer was still on my desk, but I didn't because I knew it was. I *knew*. It's mine now. I don't need to leave this sentence half complete to bring me back to the page today: I don't need to let its mystery be the thing that calls me because I am hooked.

Sunday 25 November 2035 – 3.30 p.m.

After the tall one and the short one took my British Fiction Prize during that first shocking, quiche-dropping visit, everything happened quickly. Now, sitting here writing in this world, I'm accustomed to passivity, but back then I resisted. At least for a few weeks. Until they returned.

By then it was April 2030.

I had tried to get hold of my editor and failed. I'd last seen her at the British Fiction Prize ceremony. Thinking back on it, she had been quiet that night, and she hadn't been in touch since I'd spoken to her briefly when I'd seen Ade Woods' book in the supermarket, and called her to demand what was going on. Calls now went to the answering service; then I got nothing as though it no longer existed.

I panicked.

In March, I went on the train to my publishing house. The shiny building was locked. All the electronic posters that once ostentatiously advertised upcoming novels had gone. I peered inside a window – the reception was bare, stripped of all furniture and artwork. Not even a coffee machine. Other publishing houses were shut too. I wandered the streets, desperate to find one open, so I could go inside and ask someone how the hell this had happened so fast.

Had I been blind, shut away those weeks trying to start the children's book?

Had I ignored the signs, never believing something like this could happen?

The new laws the tall one had said were coming into effect must have actually happened.

I continued ringing Cass, Lynda and Shelly to see if they'd had the same strange visit, how they were, what they thought. Nothing. Nervous, I travelled to their homes, and each was empty. Curtains, sofas, photographs, books, *gone*. Fear came full force. Not an appetiser, not the main course, but a banquet.

Where the hell were my friends?

139

On my way home from Lynda's empty flat, I passed boarded-up bookstores on the high street. I parked up and approached the window of one. Police stickers criss-crossed the wood as though it had been the scene of a crime. At home, frantic, I went online for answers, frenziedly typing a variety of questions. I found articles on an assortment of news sites, some fiercely questioning this new anti-fiction law and what it would ultimately mean for freedom of speech, others praising the speed with which the government was 'ridding the country of insidious extremism in the form of today's so-called literature'. The comments beneath were mixed, but I noticed those that heatedly criticised the new ruling were swiftly taken down. Sometimes words disappeared as I was reading them and had me questioning my sanity.

And then the tall one and the short one returned.

I was ready for battle. I still believed it was a fight I could win. They had papers that meant the government now owned my home, along with my car, furniture, and all the books. I asked to see them but was refused. I demanded they let me speak to their superiors but was told that failing to comply would result in a prison sentence.

I ran before they could stop me, into the living room, to my bookshelf. The short one was upon me as I grabbed for it; my dear, celebrated, beloved *Technological Amazingness*. I struggled. He struggled. Prised it from my hands, my beautiful first edition with the picture of a doctor holding his own dripping, bloody heart up.

'No,' I shrieked.

But it was pointless. I was given ten minutes to pack some essentials. Choking back sobs, I couldn't think straight and tried to grab what I thought I might need for somewhere I didn't know I was going. I found one of the cheaper, mass-produced copies of my book in the bedside cabinet and slipped it down the front of my trousers. It was a good job I did because they searched what I'd packed, removing my smartphone and laptop.

'You won't need those,' said the tall one. 'You'll get new ones.'

'This can't be happening,' I said.

'It is,' he said.

'But only three or four months ago … it was … *normal*.'

'You really should open your eyes, Fern. This has been coming for *many* months.'

And then they led me to a black car waiting outside, some dog shit stuck to one of the chrome wheels. I tried again to run. The tall one locked me in a painful grip and reminded me he had a gun that he was prepared to use. I gave in. I didn't look back as the car pulled away. I couldn't. I was numb. Anger died. Resistance faltered. I watched the streets fly past, watched a woman carry books out to her wheelie bin, watched a large van plastered with the waspish yellow and black *Technological Truth* poster delivering boxes to a supermarket, watched my old world die.

I don't want to write any more today. I still can't believe that only six years ago I had a shelf full of books and the freedom to read every one.

Monday 26 November 2035 – 3.43 p.m.

I woke this morning with dread heavy like undigested bread in my stomach. I knew I had to go back to work. My simple job has never bothered me before. There's satisfaction in making clean the dirty. But as I biked there, I thought again about the odd meetings I'd witnessed in Conference Room 3a, the déjà vu of their words, the curious way that Mr Shrivel seemed to not want to say something in full to me. I was also worried about Bedtime Stories later, and the changes that loomed. As long as I could get into the time-out room and speak to Hunter, that was all that mattered.

I wheeled my trolley towards Conference Room 3a, having left it until last. *Please let it be empty, please let it be empty, please let it be* . . . They were there, seated around the large table: Mr Shrivel, Mr Patrukal, and a red-haired woman I'd not seen before. I went in. Cool air greeted me like a welcome winter ghost. They must have fixed the air conditioning.

'Shall I come back?' I hoped Shrivel would nod.

'No, do come in, Fern, please,' he said warmly.

I pushed my trolley across the streaked floor, knowing it would need more than one scrub. They already had drinks, so I hoped to do my work without interruption. I started on the fridge.

Shrivel coughed twice. I still wince at anyone doing so without a face covering. 'Mrs Sargeson,' he said to the new guest, who I assumed was a surgeon too from the title he used. 'I'm leading the way with two new policies. Mr Patrukal is part of my team, and we have full backing now from the NSF as well as NICE and Daniel Mills. I'd like a woman with us. I'm sure you'll be just as excited about it as we are and say yes.'

'I'll have to hear the policies first,' said Mrs Sargeson.

'Of course.' He glanced at Patrukal. 'Have you an open mind?'

'Always,' she said, no emotion evident in her voice.

'And are you ambitious?'

I looked up from washing the fridge door handle.

She frowned. 'Odd question.'

'Well?'

'Yes, I am.'

'Good. I think we *all* are.'

Mr Shrivel looked at me as he said it. Smiled. Kept his eyes on me for so long that I felt uncomfortable. Then he stood. I waited a moment and then I did too. I got the polish and began on the wooden surfaces. Shrivel strode the length of the table so that Patrukal and Sargeson had to look left and right as he passed, like spectators watching a tennis ball. Then he addressed them.

'I have come up with the Pre-Surgery Care Mortality Policy and the One Death Policy – or ODP as I like to call it.'

I dropped my polish with a crash. All eyes shot my way. What the actual fuck? Was this some sort of joke? Set up at my expense. But why? I was nobody.

'And what do they involve?' asked Sargeson.

I expected Shrivel to ask me to explain it to her I expected him to say, 'Oh, we're having a bit of fun at Fern's expense – she can tell you what they are, she invented them in her novel.' He didn't.

'The former,' he said, 'is the requirement that all patients are dead pre-operation, and the latter is the requirement that one person in every UK family volunteers a single member for euthanasia each year.'

Silence except for the whir of air conditioning. I took a step closer to the group. Mrs Sargeson opened her mouth, but nothing came out. Eventually she managed to expel some sputtering-in-disbelief words. 'You expect me to take seriously a proposal for *dead* people undergoing surgery? Why would any of us perform life-saving surgery on someone who is *deceased*? Why would you even suggest it?'

'The Pre-Surgery Care Mortality Policy has many positives,' Shrivel said. I whispered the words along with him; the scriptwriter just ahead of her actor. 'It guarantees that no one dies on the table;

statistically any operative procedure could be declared one hundred per cent safe. It reduces the need for expensive equipment, overpaid surgeons and costly aftercare, saving the NHS millions. Transplants wouldn't depend on a live donor. No blood is required. It takes all pressure off staff – any procedure could take days rather than hours, with regular breaks not only allowed but encouraged.'

'Can I just confirm that you're actually suggesting all patients should be *dead* before surgery?' Sargeson tugged on her russet hair like a toddler in distress. 'I heard it right? This isn't a joke?'

'Am I smiling?' asked Mr Shrivel.

I looked. He wasn't. I felt light-headed. Weightless; like I might float to the ceiling. Now he'd say, 'Nah, I'm joking. You all read our Fern's book years ago? You know the story,' and they would laugh heartily with relief at his tomfoolery, and I'd start scrubbing the floor.

'Even if I presume this isn't a bad joke,' said Sargeson, 'you're suggesting dead patients on a surgical table and the non-require-ment of surgeons … to a group of *surgeons*. Where would that leave us … *me*?'

'On my team.'

'I don't think so.'

'Do you not see the beauty in it?' Mr Shrivel held his palms open like the Jesus statue my mum used to have in her living room. I imagined blood there, dripping.

'*Beauty*? It's insanity,' hissed Sargeson. 'Even if anyone agrees to such madness, how will it work?'

'They *have* agreed to it,' Shrivel reminded her.

'It's not as outrageous as it sounds.' Patrukal spoke for the first time. 'Once you know what it could achieve.'

'But how will patients *be* dead? Are we to wait until they are? How would we know who's worth waiting for?' She shook her head. 'I can't believe I just asked that.'

'We don't have time to wait.'

'Are you suggesting …?' She couldn't finish.

'We have to ... *ensure* that they are deceased pre-op,' said Shrivel. 'This is the part the NSF had the greatest trouble with ... at first.'

'The *greatest trouble*?' cried Sargeson, sarcastic. 'I'll say.'

'They came around.'

'You really think you can enforce this? It's not only unethical but illegal, and I still don't see what you can think it achieves. Yes, yes, you listed those *positives* (dripping with sarcasm here) for saving money and time on surgical procedures, but that's not enough to justify ... murder.'

I went back to my corner and sat on a chair before my legs gave way.

'It's not murder.' Shrivel sighed as though she was a child. 'These people would have died at some point. We're just ... bringing that date forward.'

'We're *all* going to die at some point,' said Sargeson. 'How far will this end up going?'

'Another positive is that – as we all know – one of the four main 2040 targets is to reduce heart disease, cancer and stroke by half in people under sixty-five,' said Shrivel. 'Both policies will mean we hit this target.'

'Both policies?' Sargeson looked confused. Then she clearly remembered the other one.

'The One Death Policy is likely to have families choosing a member who's already ill, thereby ensuring said member who undergoes voluntary euthanasia doesn't die of the heart disease, cancer or stroke that might have killed them. Thereby, greatly reducing deaths by said diseases.'

'Families will never agree to it,' cried Sargeson.

They will, I thought. *They will if this is anything like my original fiction* . . .

'Once upon a time, families were against immunisation.' Mr Sargeson smiled as though recalling a happier, long-ago land, a fairy tale. 'They came around to the idea. It once seemed impossible that injecting a person with small amounts of influenza would save them from it. This is much the same; a revolutionary idea that might scare people at first. The One Death Policy will save many from agonising convalescence and suffering.'

'But your policy means killing people who don't even *have* these diseases,' cried Mrs Sargeson. 'Families might select members they had an argument with last week – or whoever didn't wash the pots last night.'

That line wasn't in my novel. I liked it though. For a moment, I imagined editing it. Then I shook my head. This was madness. This was real life, not the pages of a book.

'More than one in two people get cancer,' said Mr Shrivel. 'They're great odds.'

'Sorry?'

'One in two people selected for voluntary euthanasia might have died of cancer.'

'I'm not listening to you anymore.' Sargeson stood. 'They should arrest you.'

'They should give him an OBE,' said Patrukal.

She didn't dignify that with a response. She grabbed her leather coat and bag and headed for the door. When it slammed after her, Shrivel turned to Patrukal and shrugged. Then he turned to me, still on my chair, not sure what was happening, hoping I'd passed out finally from the relentless heat, except it was chill in here, chill like my heart, and this was no hallucination.

'Can you give us a minute?' Shrivel said to Patrukal.

'Sure.'

When we were alone, he approached me. 'We should dance, Fern Dostoy,' he said. 'Dance with me.'

'You're insane.' I remained in my seat.

'You wrote it,' said Shrivel with a chuckle.

'As an observation,' I cried. 'As satire. To rip apart and address what was happening to the NHS. Do they know you stole your ridiculous ideas from a banned novel?'

'Of course.' He danced alone, a mini tap dance, his shoes clacking on my not yet clean floor. 'I told them from the off.'

'You knew who I was when I started here.'

'I did.' Tap, tap, tap. 'I read *Technological Amazingness* in 2029. I thought it was genius. I never agreed with the banning of all fiction, but hey, who am I to argue?' Tap, tap, tap. He moved his hands, grotesque claws, one higher than the other, as though controlled by a puppeteer; up, down, up, down. 'I didn't think it fair to address you as Fern Dostoy when you have to keep a low profile. I didn't want to embarrass you. But your ideas niggled at me ...'

'You can't blame me for this,' I cried. After a moment: 'Why didn't you tell me your full plan the first time I was in here with you all?'

'I enjoyed watching you realise. It was ... satisfying.'

I felt sick. Glared at him. 'It doesn't make sense. They banned a novel that suggested this in mockery but they're going to let you actually *do* it.'

'Perhaps that's what they intended all along.' He paused his bad Fred Astaire routine. 'Did you consider that? They hoped that a virtuoso like me would be brave enough to do it. Listen, Fern, there's a place for you on our team. Our mascot, if you like. After all, you came up with it.'

Now I stood, outraged. 'I did not. I wrote a *novel*.'

'Very George Orwell,' he said.

'Fuck you.'

'Oh, Fern. They might let you write again. You could chronicle our progress. Be our voice. Think of the headlines. Writer of *Technological Amazingness* backs plans to bring her banned novel to life.'

'I don't back them,' I said. 'You've read the book. You know how it turns out. If you do this, everything will get a lot worse.'

'It won't be that way for us, I'll make sure.'

'I want no part in it,' I said.

'Your loss.' Shrivel ended his dance. 'I'm so disappointed in you. But I won't trouble you again. I'll let you do your work here, a nobody, invisible, as before. I just hope—'

'What?'

'I just hope you have a lot of family members to choose from when the One Death Policy comes into effect. How on earth will you choose who dies, Fern, when there's only you?'

I pushed past him. Ran. Reached the toilets in time to hurl into a sink. I never went back for my trolley. I left the hospital half an hour early, biked home, sobbing, hardly able to get breath. I paced the house, unable to settle, tearing at my hair. I wanted to write. Vomit out my day but I needed to give better care to the words. So, I sat at my desk and tried breathing deeply; in, out, in, out, in, out. When my heart slowed, I picked up the pen and wrote what you have just read.

I am living my book.

I am living my book.

I am living my book.

And now I have to go to Bedtime Stories and create another tale for a little boy who feels invisible. Time for bargaining: I'll make a deal with you, my page, my god. Remain hidden so that I can be visible to Hunter; remain hidden so I can save him.

Part Three

Bargaining

Monday 26 November 2035 – 11.57 p.m.

I don't know where to start. I don't know how to set it down. How to tell you it all. But I'll try.

I'll begin.

Are you sitting comfortably? I'm not. I don't know if I'll ever be comfortable again. We drink tea for comfort during the darkest times. But my milk-free Fine-Fayre brew, sitting on the desk in my delicate festive teacup, steaming like autumn fog, isn't doing the job. I've made a deal with the night; I whispered, darkness, stay as long as you want if you let me just . . . I don't even know what my side of the bargain is.

I didn't take my secret route to Bedtime Stories earlier. What's the point? They know. They've known all along. They let me think I was free, like a caged lioness released onto the wider landscape of a fenced safari, thinking she is liberated. I cycled the main city streets, brazen, notepad in rucksack, blouse sticky, hair damp, trying to sweat out the nightmares from last night where Shrivel deftly danced along a hospital ward, Patrukal shadowing as his Ginger Rogers, flames flaring off their tap shoes. Then I caught my breath when flashes of a brief, more pleasurable dream about Fine-Fayre came to me; I kissed him, and he touched my cheek so tenderly that I never wanted it to end.

But it did. I woke. To a sick, heavy dread.

I was the last to arrive at Tinsley's tonight. Wordlessly, no nail polish on her toes, the pile of children's shoes by the door orderly, she let me into the basement. Lynda sat on one sofa with Alfie, her hand still gloved in black, and Jasmine sat opposite, all holding steaming mugs of coffee. It was five-fifty-four.

'We're just having a quick meeting,' said Jasmine. 'Join us.'

I sat next to her. All I could smell was the fetid milk in her coffee. I put a hand over my nose.

'Problem?' she asked.

'I've developed an acute aversion to dairy. Even the smell of it. Sorry. What were you discussing?'

She glanced at Lynda, who looked at me, eyes sad, gloved hand cradled in her lap like it was a black kitten she must let sleep. Did Jasmine know I knew about the upcoming plans to burn down the ALLBooks stores? Had Lynda told her? I guessed Alfie knew if they both did.

'We're finishing here on Friday,' said Jasmine.

'*Friday*?' I didn't understand. 'But you said two weeks.'

'Tinsley wants us to leave sooner. Look, there's some stuff going on. There's no time to explain now but Lynda said she'll tell you afterwards. I'm not sure if you'd like me to, but I can look at trying to get you a slot with another team?'

'I don't know if I'll continue,' I admitted. Hunter was my only concern. I had to hope he called so I could ... I wasn't sure what.

'A storyteller on another city centre team is leaving,' continued Jasmine, 'so I'm joining in her place. And you're moving away in a month with your husband's new job, aren't you, Alfie?'

'Yeah.' He nodded. 'I'll find a new team there. Though I guess, with all that's going on, it might not be for long ...'

Jasmine looked at the clock. 'I didn't realise the time. Damn. We should get the phones on. I guess that's what we're here to do.' She paused. Exhaustion clouded her eyes. 'At least, most of us.'

And we told our tales. We moved from phone to sofa to phone to sofa, a cycle of seasons, swapping seats, sharing story-time springs, summers and winters. We began with Enid Blyton and ended with C.S. Lewis. We gave the happy-ever-afters and were rewarded with soft snoring, giggles, and questions. Alfie's impression of the Big Bad Wolf made me smile. I realised, not for the first time, that fiction is magic. That we *do* forget our lives when we read it, share it, hear it. I was briefly swept away from a world of restriction and control to a land of imagination and freedom.

Then I noticed Lynda was having trouble at times, having to now answer the phone with her left hand, which I knew wasn't her writing hand. I caught her eye when she dropped it for the second time, and mouthed, 'You OK?' She nodded and continued describing a secret attic where the mice ate stolen cheese and made toys for poor children out of scraps discarded by the Queen.

Just after seven-thirty I had a breather between calls and went to the time-out room, telling Jasmine I 'just needed five'. I sank into the beanbag. My hand was waiting at the phone when it rang. I didn't even say, 'Bedtime Stories, what's your favourite?' I knew the answer. It was my story; ours. It was *What Happened to All the Bloody Books?*

'It's me,' said Hunter. 'Is it you, Crazy Lady?'

'Of course,' I said. 'How are you?'

'Yeah.' He sounded unsure.

'Yeah?' I smiled. 'That's no response.'

He giggled.

'Who's home with you?' I asked.

He didn't answer. Instead, he said, 'You know last time, you asked why I rang at that exact minute?'

I nodded, then quickly added, 'Yes.'

'Well, this time it was dead weird.' Squeak, squeak, squeak. His mum's chair. As always. 'I forgot it was Monday because we didn't go to school today because of the strike. And I was on CrashLand and I finally got to Shark Island and I was dead happy and then someone whispered in my ear *Crazy Lady*. I thought Marley was messing about 'cos he'd been playing too. So, I turned it off and rang and it was you. Was this the right minute?'

'It was exactly the right minute,' I said.

'Can we do the story then?'

'Of course. I need to talk to you first.'

'What about?' he asked.

I hadn't planned what I would say. I didn't even know what I was going to do. I only knew I couldn't let him go. I couldn't leave without some sort of link. 'This Bedtime Stories call room is closing on Friday.'

'Aren't there other ones?'

'Yes, but there's no room for me there.' It wasn't true, really. 'And … look, Hunter, I don't know how long Bedtime Stories will go on for.'

If the ALLBooks arson goes ahead, it's safe to assume the government will close us all down, and I can't imagine anyone trying to run something like this again. This chokes me as I write it. How will the children sleep? What hope is there for them? Will parents have the courage to fight back, to read to them in secret?

'How will I find out where all the bloody books went?' Hunter's voice was small, and it broke me. 'How will I know if Hunter gets his visibility back?'

'We'll find that out, I promise.' I looked at the door, praying no one came in. 'Don't hang up. Even if you hear another voice.'

'I never hang up,' he said. 'You do.'

'*I* do?'

'Yes. You're talking and then you disappear.'

'I thought it was you,' I said.

'No, it's you, Crazy Lady.'

Odd. I'm sure it was him. I'll read back through these pages when I have a moment. Sometimes I wonder if I recorded things exactly as they happened. If I was influenced by my mood, by the heat. Can I trust my own words?

'What will I do?' he said quietly.

'What do you mean?' My heart broke at his sad tone.

He didn't answer.

'Hunter?'

'I'll miss you if you're gone.'

I couldn't speak. Knew my voice would break. 'Look,' I said eventually. 'We'll find a way to talk after Thursday, I promise. I'll be here then so call me. I guess … well, you'll know when to.' I paused. 'Would you like to stay in touch after that?'

'Yes,' he said, eagerly.

I realised that I was overstepping boundaries if I did. He's a child. I'm an adult who isn't his parent. Touching a child who isn't yours – if witnessed and reported – can result in a prison sentence. I'm on dangerous ground. But I can't ignore the feeling I've had since I dreamt of him wearing the other blue and white trainer (which, as I write, is still on the desk in front of me), since I sensed him waiting for me on the phones, since I started our story; a feeling that I must keep him safe. I don't even know what the danger is. But, also, I didn't want Hunter doing something he wasn't OK with.

'Do *you* want to stay in touch?' I repeated.

'Yes.' He was firm.

'OK. Do you have a smartphone that's just yours?'

'Yes, but I don't really use it.'

'Are you happy to give me your number?' I asked.

'I don't even know it,' he said. 'I'd have to find my phone and turn it on and look.'

'OK. Do you want to get it?'

I waited, watching the door, bargaining with the universe; please let no one disturb us and I'll surrender any moment after this one.

'Got it,' he said eventually.

'Are you definitely happy to give me your number?'

'I have to find it first.' He sounded like he was concentrating. I heard the device come to life, got mine from my bag and fired up the rarely used thing. After a while he reeled off some digits and I scrambled to put them into my phone. He repeated them, more slowly, and I created a new contact – HUNTER – and added his number.

'What you gonna do?' he asked me.

'What do you mean?'

'You gonna call me then?'

'I guess so.' I wasn't even sure. 'Do you definitely want me to? I don't have to. It's only if you want. That's the most important part.'

'Yeah. I don't really use this smartphone, but I can keep it with me now.'

I smiled. Whatever happens, I have a way of talking to him.

'Why?' he asked.

'Why what?'

'Why you wanna talk?'

'Maybe I can tell you more stories,' I said.

'That'd be cool. Can we do that now?'

'Of course. That's what I'm here for. Where were we last time? Do you remember?'

'Hunter was going to pull the books off the shelf to make his parents see him … and then he remembered, there are no books!' His excitement was infectious.

'Of course. You remember well.' I realised I'd forgotten to grab a book so I could create the sound of the pages turning. 'OK … Hunter's mum and dad began making breakfast in the kitchen – eggs and bacon and beans, which smelled delicious and made him realise he *did* exist because his senses were still acute.'

'It's making my tummy rumble,' said Hunter. 'We never have bacon or eggs now and I miss it.'

I smiled. 'Did they think he was still sleeping?' I continued. 'Would they soon call for him? Yes. And then what would he do? They wouldn't *see* him. Hunter ran back upstairs and grabbed the duvet from his bed, planning to wrap it around himself so he'd appear, ghostlike, to them. Geoffrey the cat leapt away in surprise.'

'Can the cat see him?'

'Well, of course. This had Hunter wondering if he was only invisible to his parents. What if others could see him? At that exact moment – as often happens in the best books – there came a knock on the door. He abandoned the duvet and ran downstairs. His mum had opened it. The postman stood with a parcel. "Is that for me?" asked Hunter, remembering the new book he'd ordered. "Yes," said the postman, handing it over. "Who are you talking to?" asked his mum.'

'Me,' whispered my real Hunter, sad.

156

'Yes,' I said. 'But the postman said, "The boy." Hunter's mum looked at the parcel, confused. "There is no boy," she said. "Just the parcel ... sort of ... floating in the air. I don't understand." Then she shouted Hunter's name up the stairs. "I'm here," he said, in front of her. She ran past him in a panic, up the stairs, and when she returned, she screamed, "Hunter, where are you?" His dad ran into the hallway. When he saw the parcel, he seemed mystified by its existence. "I'm here," Hunter said again. No one heard him. The postman had gone. His mum reached out for the parcel and—'

'Fern.' I looked up. It was Lynda. Hunter had gone. Whoever had ended the call, it didn't matter. I only had one more shift. But I had his number. It was OK. 'Him again?' she asked.

I nodded, full of emotion.

'You should come back to the phones really,' she said, kindly.

I did but all I wanted was to talk to Hunter. I think the children sensed this because they kept asking me to stop reading after a few pages and then they hung up.

Tuesday 27 November 2035 – 1.46 a.m.

I needed a breather from writing. I know what's coming.

At nine, we were done. My penultimate session. Jasmine seemed in a hurry to get away, and Alfie followed soon after, saying that he'd see me on Thursday, perhaps with goodbye cakes.

'Will I see you?' I asked Lynda.

'Yes. I'll come. For you.'

'Good.'

'One more time,' I said.

'One final time.' Her voice broke on the last word.

'What did Jasmine want you to tell me?' I asked.

'About the arson plan for ALLBooks. She doesn't know I already did.'

'OK.'

'Are you still writing your diary?' she asked.

'Yes. I have it with me.' I motioned to my rucksack on the sofa. 'What's the point in stopping now if they've already been in my house and seen it?'

'You need to know what they're capable of.' She wrapped her arms about her chest as though cold.

'What do you mean?' I felt sick, like someone had milk nearby.

'I wasn't fully honest.'

'What do you mean? When?'

She looked at her black-gloved hand, then at me. She motioned with it for me to sit down and then she sat on the opposite sofa. The silence wanted to be filled. The room waited for a story. And she told me one. The darkest I've ever heard. This is it; this is Lynda's story. How she told it to me. Or at least, how I recall that she told it to me. If it was in a TV show, there would now be a trigger warning. I remember a proposal before the full fiction ban to have trigger warnings in novels, which I found ridiculous. Real life doesn't have a trigger warning. I did not have one when Lynda spoke. She didn't when what happened to her happened.

But I guess this is yours.

'They didn't warn me,' she said. 'They just did it. It was two weeks ago, the day after you started here. They visited. We were at the table in my kitchen, an oak one I love that I got cheap at a charity shop. One minute they were asking me if I'd been writing, like they always do, and before I could open my mouth, the short one pinned my arm to the table. Tom wasn't there. They knew that. I think I screamed, more in shock than to get help. The tall one took something silver from his pocket. Circular. Sharp. With a black handle. I had no idea what it was. Then he switched it on, and the silver part became a tiny spinning blade. The short one was still holding my arm down. The tall one said that they knew about Bedtime Stories. He knew I was reading to children. He said I should carry on as normal, tell no one they had visited. He said they knew about our arson plans (at that point I didn't even know what they were) and he said if I told anyone they knew, he'd come back for the rest of my fingers. *The rest*, I thought, still dumb. Then he brought the rotating silver blade down to my hand. It was quick. I screamed even though the pain didn't hit for about three seconds. Blood soaked into the wood. Later, I couldn't get it out. I had to get rid of my lovely oak table. The tall one wrapped lots of thick gauze round my hand and taped it down. Then he placed my two fingers in a plastic bag and put them in his pocket. All I could think while he told me to visit a medic as soon as they had gone and have the wound checked out was: *my fingers are in his pocket*. And then they left. That was it. They took my fucking fingers, Fern.'

When Lynda finished her story, she exhaled. I had no words. I looked at the black glove and then her contrasting ashen face. 'Your fingers,' was all I could say. I leaned forward and cupped my hands around them but didn't touch in case I hurt her. 'Your poor, beautiful, book-writing fingers. Does it hurt now? Oh my God.' Then the rage came. 'They are fucking animals.'

She nodded.

'Fucking animals,' I repeated. 'I want to kill them.'

Lynda didn't speak.

'I'll make them pay,' I said.

'How?' she asked softly. '*How?*'

I realised my anger wasn't helping her. 'Are you OK?' I asked. 'Is there something they can do to build new – ' I struggled to say it. ' – fingers? I've seen what miracles they can do at work.' I remembered Shrivel's plans and felt sick. Maybe she was better off staying away from any sort of surgery.

'They throb, like they're still there.' I noticed she didn't look at them as she spoke. 'I have a splint, so it looks like I have fingers inside this glove. They're healing over, the, you know, stumps, and soon I won't have to wear this glove anymore. But I … don't know… if I'll dare…'

'Why didn't you *tell* me what they did to you?' It was hard to keep the emotion out of my voice.

'I couldn't,' she said. 'I didn't want to put *you* in danger. I only am now because our time here is coming to an end. I'm so relieved you're leaving, that you'll be safer – but sad it was brief.'

'I still can't believe it. How *dare* they do that to you?'

'I've sort of come to terms with it,' she admitted. 'It could have been worse …'

'How? It's …' I couldn't find words.

'I'm OK,' insisted Lynda. She looked around the basement, at the bookshelves and the phones and mugs waiting to be washed. 'I was so joyful when Cass and I started this. I can't understand why some want to ruin it by burning down bookstores.' She obviously wanted to change the subject now. 'Isn't the world terrible enough already?'

'When the tall one said they knew about our plans … is that what he meant?'

'Yes.' Lynda sank back into the sofa as though she wanted to be swallowed by it. I just wanted to hold her like a child. 'I pretended to Jasmine that I'd heard about it through gossiping team members, and she admitted she'd been informed by . . .' Lynda's voice trailed off; then she resumed with jollier and forced effort. 'Jasmine said she'd been nervous about telling me, knowing it has never been what I wanted for this venture. She doesn't agree with it either and suggested we call a mass meeting to urge them not to go ahead. But they didn't want to listen.'

I shook my head. 'No wonder Tinsley doesn't want to host us anymore.'

'She was already scared. Finding out about the arson plans was the icing on the cake. Oh, Fern. What a world.'

'Do you think there's anything we could have done so we didn't end up here?'

Lynda looked at me; I knew exactly what she was thinking, because the same thought came to me. 'Not write our books,' she said.

'And would you do that?' I asked.

She smiled, like the old Lynda. 'Hell, no.'

I didn't feel so sure. I wanted to tell her that *Technological Amazingness* might be coming true, very soon, but it still felt like I had dreamt Shrivel dancing across the floor of Conference Room 3a. I did last night, after all. If I said it aloud, Lynda would think me insane. But this moment wasn't about me.

'Do you know *when* they're going to burn down the ALLBooks stores?' I asked.

'On the next Book Amnesty Day.'

'But that's ...' I worked it out. 'The seventh of December. A week on Friday. Seriously? They can't kill all those poor decent folks. We have to *do* something ...'

'They're going to do it before the shop opens. They don't want to hurt anyone; they just want to make a point. Destroy the shops so that none of the remaining fiction can be returned to them.'

'But the government know. They'll be caught. Imprisoned for life.' I realised something. 'Tell Jasmine they know. Then surely, they won't do it and risk capture. We could stop it.'

'I've already told her. Yesterday. She knew too. She said they think it's happening at Christmas ...'

'How do the government know *any* of it? Do they listen in?'

Lynda took a breath. 'They know because ...' She paused. 'Cass told them.' I gasped. 'She *had* to. They took four of her fingers, one by one.'

'*No,*' I cried.

Lynda nodded. 'She was clever though. She told them it was planned for Christmas time when the stores are the busiest. She knew they would believe that – it makes the most sense.'

I was aghast. I thought I might be sick.

'When she found out about this awful plan, she knew it was futile trying to change their minds. But she managed to persuade them to at least do it when the store's empty.'

That was fair enough. But still, I can't get on board with destroying them, open or not. I can't accept the burning of *any* books, fiction or not. Books are books, and these are all we have now. And what if someone is passing and caught in the blast? Are they going to make sure no members of staff are there, early? Tinsley works there. I'm sure she'll make sure no one is. But still.

'I have to go,' said Lynda suddenly, standing.

I stood too. What was left to say? What was left at all?

'Next time,' was all I could manage.

'Our last time,' she said quietly.

We hugged so tightly that I struggled to breathe, Lynda holding out her black-gloved hand to avoid it being crushed, me feeling I should mirror this action in solidarity. Now, as I put these words down, tell you this terrible crime, I can barely see the lines for my tears. The ink is going to run. They'll read this notepad one day again and it will be a soggy mess. My hands are shaking. My hands are shaking. But at least I have my fingers.

Tuesday 27 November 2035 – 7.18 p.m.

I was in trouble at work today for leaving half an hour early without explanation. I had to pretend I was ill. I suppose I was. I had a breakdown. I didn't say that though. I'll look for another job. I can't afford to hand my notice in without having another one lined up. I asked new girl, Felicia, if she might clean Conference Room 3a for me and I did the toilets no one wants to do on Floor Nine.

While on my knees, scrubbing a particularly gruesome toilet, I heard a tap-tap-tapping in the corridor and froze. Shrivel? Dancing? Teasing me? I left the faecal stain and tiptoed to the door. The corridor, left and right, was clear except for a nurse pushing a trolley. A plastic belt dangled from the patient, hitting one of the spinning wheels, tap tap *tap*. I returned to the job. Looked at my hand as I scrubbed. How lost I'd be without it. Without fingers. I would bargain hard to keep them. Offer a foot perhaps.

An eye? An ear?

Poor Lynda. I can only imagine her terror. How do I know the tall one and the short one won't want two – or *four* – of my fingers next time they call by? How should I behave to stop it happening? Like usual. But what is usual? Meek. Quiet. Do they know I know they've been in the house when I'm not here? Do they know I know they know about the diary and Bedtime Stories?

Be calm, Fern. Be calm.

I recited this mantra while I finished cleaning, but my precious fingers trembled like I had Parkinson's disease.

At the shift's end, on my way out of the hospital, I passed an empty cubicle in the A&E department. It was yet to be cleaned. Emergency staff had clearly been trying to save a life in there. Had they succeeded? Blood covered the bed, some of it thick, like congealed gravy with bits of meat still in it. Stained clothes were scattered across the floor, some cut up as though for a Halloween costume. They looked small. A child's? About Hunter's age? One shoe sat in the corner, denim, perhaps removed, perhaps fallen.

I averted my eyes. Hurried away. Specialist cleaners deal with those rooms. I can deal with shit and insane surgeons and soiled fridges, but I could never mop up a child's blood. Yet I chose to work in a hospital. On the fringes of the drama. It *was* a choice. I could have cleaned offices or cafes or schools. I took this job.

Now, I'm close to done.

I biked towards the square and ALLBooks. The Ade Woods poster had gone. There were no queues. It was just a Tuesday in the middle of a hot November afternoon. I locked my bike to a fence railing and went inside. Tinsley was at the counter and glanced my way but suppressed any reaction to seeing me. I found what I wanted: *Technological Truth For Tots and Teens.* When I paid, Tinsley lowered her eyes. She still had fingers.

I will now pay attention to these things.

As I left the store, something on the ground caught my eye. A tiny white card. I knew before I picked it up that there would be a graphite sketch of a blissful baby on a cloud and the words BED-TIME STORIES FOR THE RESTLESS on it with the phone number nearby. I knew that unlike the unique one created just for me, it would be blank on the back. I put it in my pocket. I cried as I biked the rest of the way home, the tears warming on my cheeks in the blistering sun.

I put my new book on the kitchen table, still wrapped in the brown ALLBooks bag, unable to look at it yet. Then I watched the main news. I shouldn't have. A mother of three has been imprisoned for secretly selling old Harry Potter books in the playground. A seven-year-old child with autism has been removed from the home of an esteemed lawyer who is reported to have been reading fiction to her because 'it was all that calmed her down after a busy day'.

And then the avatar newsreader said, 'Proposals for a new NHS scheme have been outlined at a meeting between leading surgeons and the health minister, Daniel Mills. The One Death Policy, if it goes ahead, will ensure that deaths from cancer, heart disease and

other chronic ailments will be more than halved, and possibly eliminated, by the year 2045. More on this is an exclusive interview with
Mills at ten p.m.'

It was real.

I thought suddenly of the phrase I used to type at the start of
every manuscript.

If you tell a story well enough, it's true.

I told it well, and now it's coming true.

I turned the news off and came to my desk. I'm here now.
Writing. Staring at the wall. Sipping black tea. Trainer in front of
me. Still. It has remained. I keep thinking of that other solitary
shoe amidst the bloodshed of that A&E cubicle. I took the
Bedtime Stories card out of my pocket earlier and placed it next
to the trainer. I think of Hunter and my heart rate slows. I think
of Fine-Fayre and it misses a beat. I think of Hunter and it settles
again.

Wednesday 28 November 2035 – 10.45 a.m.

I rang in sick at work today. I simply couldn't face it. I had very little sleep last night. Too much to think about. No room for it all. Felt drugged this morning. I lay in bed until nine – late for me – and remembered when I first came to this house.

The tall one and the short one came to my previous home – that beautiful place with river views and high ceilings – and they led me away, bearing nothing but the essentials and a copy of *Technological Amazingness* hidden down the front of my trousers. When they took me up the overgrown path to this compact and sparsely furnished terraced house, they told me it was home now, that there was enough food in the cupboards to last a week and a fully charged smartphone in the bedside cabinet drawer.

'I know your husband and parents are gone,' the tall one said, 'and that you have no children. It will therefore be relatively easy for you to assume this new life. Do not contact anyone from your previous life. Look for work. Menial would be best. Fewer requirements and less chance of you being promoted and becoming notable in any way. You are no longer of note.'

I was given details of a new bank account, into which they had deposited the Starting Out Sum to help me for a while.

'All authors, editors, agents, publishers receive this,' said the tall one.

I wondered then where they all lived now. In similar nondescript homes?

Helping us meant controlling us. Curiously, the account was in my original name. I never understood this when they encouraged me to change my surname and my appearance. It was as though they wanted to end my old life, have me keep a low profile, but not fully protect me. When I got the job at the hospital, I told them I was Fern Dalrymple, even though my bank account is in my old surname.

I often think that if people do realise who I am – if they're not fans or haters – perhaps they don't acknowledge me through fear of association. Perhaps the tall one and the short one knew this. Perhaps they left me with my own name because they wanted me to have to make extra effort to become invisible. Or maybe they wanted me to suffer; to remember every day who I once was.

Before they left me here in this house that first time, the tall one said, 'We'll return in a week and check how you're doing, Fern.' It sounded friendly, like he cared, but I knew it was my behaviour – not my emotional or mental well-being – they were interested in. 'Keep your head down. If you cross paths with another writer or editor, do not speak to them. Do not write. Read only factual books.'

'What about the friends I had where I used t—'

'To them, you do not exist,' he said. 'After our next visit, we'll call by whenever we see fit.'

And they did. They asked how I was finding my new life. What could I say? That it felt like since coming to this house I'd lost more than my books, my livelihood, my furniture, my friends. I'd lost me. That I barely had a reaction now to this new world, to the news that a writer I'd met a few times in 2029 had been imprisoned for self-publishing a book online, to the disappearance of my favourite writing magazines and book review columns, to the sight of novels being burned in parks, an act encouraged by the government. I was embarrassed by how quickly I submitted. Accepted. My writing had been my strength, my crutch, my all, and without it my light dimmed.

The tall one and the short one eventually visited less frequently. Perhaps they saw my docility. Perhaps they had bigger problems than me. Am I a problem now?

I think I could be.

Earlier, I got up just after nine, made a brew in my Christmassy teacup, grabbed my notepad and took them into the garden.

I sat on the stone doorstep, which is a shady spot until noon, and sipped tea until my head cleared. Then I wrote this morning's entry. I feel better. I always do when I write, even this difficult stuff.

Shit. There's someone at the front door. *Shit.*

Wednesday 28 November 2035 – 12.09 p.m.

It was them. The tall one and the short one. They left an hour ago.
I'm still shaking. I can hardly use my hand. It will be slow going.
Bear with me. I'll do it.

I *must.*

I answered the door. They stood on the step, the two of them, legs slightly apart, the sun bouncing off matching gold-lensed glasses. I couldn't be sure, but I felt they were surprised to see me. That Laura pottering about in her front garden had stopped them simply walking in.

'Good morning, Fern,' said the tall one, removing his eyewear.

He didn't ask for an invite – they never do – and was the first to enter the premises, with the short one close behind, two black-suited soldiers marching to my funeral. I followed them into the kitchen, my lower back damp where the notepad was tucked into my jeans. They assumed their usual positions at the table, and I switched the kettle on. I bustled about, getting cups, spoons, sugar, anything to distract myself from wanting to run and never stop.

'Not at work today, Fern?' asked the tall one.

Had they come thinking I'd be out? To search the place in my absence? Yes. I knew it now. They had presumed I'd be at the hospital.

'I … I'm not feeling too well.' It was hard to keep my voice even.

'I'm sorry to hear that. What appears to be the trouble?'

'I … um … women's issues.' I hoped this answer would shut him up. Mentioning menopause last time seemed to.

'How have things been otherwise, Fern?' he asked, tone level.

'Same as usual,' I said.

'Still biking at night?'

'Sorry?' I was confused.

'Last time we were here, we caught you returning from a late bike ride.' The words *caught you* seemed heavy with judgement, or maybe it was how I heard them. 'You said it helps with your insomnia.'

'Yes. I still go a couple of times a week.'

'And you sleep better?'

'Oh, yes,' I lied.

It was a game. An act. A play. I made up a story for Hunter, and I could do it for them too. They both knew where I had been that night on my bike. But I danced along, followed their lead, Ginger Rogers to the tall one's Fred Astaire. Shrivel came into my head. Did they know my fictional policies were being brought to life? They must do. It was on the news. It's happening. The kettle boiled and I realised I didn't have any milk to offer them for their tea.

'I'm sorry, I've no milk. This fridge broke.'

'You don't have much luck with fridges, do you?' said the tall one. 'We'll take them black.'

I carried their drinks to the table, trying to keep my hands steady as I placed two mugs in front of them. I didn't want to draw attention to that area of my body in any way. I wanted to hide them in my pockets but felt that would be too obvious. I moved back to the worktop area, leaned there, mindful that my notepad was hidden above my rear and not wishing to offer too much chance for them to see that area.

'Have you been writing, Fern?' asked the tall one.

'No.' I was sure the word was a gulp that gave me away. It wasn't that I was afraid they knew I had been – that was likely – but that I was afraid they knew that I knew; that this was just a charade and any moment they were going to pounce on me, pin me down, and take my fingers.

He studied me. Was there the briefest flicker of a smile or did I imagine it? 'And how about reading?' he asked.

'I bought *Technological Truth For Tots and Teens*.' I knew this was OK to admit. If there was a post-fiction-ban curriculum, I felt sure this book would be on it. 'But I haven't looked at it yet.' I took it out of the bag last night and put it on the coffee table in the front room. I think perhaps I wanted to avoid it; put it where I rarely go. I'm not even sure why I bought it. Perhaps I want to know what's being fed to our children.

'Great choice,' said the tall one. 'Make sure you read it and we can discuss it some time. It's wonderful that he has rewritten his classic so that younger readers can enjoy it too. I must say that the original is one of my all-time favourite books. My favourite chapter is the one about how the greatest danger with fiction is that when it exists there's every chance it can be mistaken for truth. Because it's put in the mind of the reader. And they believe it. Whereas facts are safe. Science is safe.'

I wanted to argue that facts were dangerous when dictated and decided for us. But of course, I kept quiet. The tall one sipped his black tea. The short one had barely had any of his.

'Can you imagine,' said the tall one, 'if the dangerous ideas explored in novels actually came true, Fern?'

I couldn't speak. It came to me in that brief silent moment.

I realised.

They *needed* someone like Shrivel. Someone who would actually do it. Someone who would bring to life the ridiculous NHS schemes from my book. Then, they can argue that fiction truly *is* dangerous, *and* cull many of the vulnerable in society in the process. I'm not going mad. But I didn't say a word, I just shrugged, my heart beating.

'Have you been watching the real news?' he asked.

Last time he encouraged me to. I was about to say yes but I realised they would have checked my online activity and know I haven't visited the government page. 'I tend to watch the BBC news,' I said quietly.

'You'll get a more accurate report on our page. There's a lot going on, isn't there?'

'I guess, yes.'

'There are a lot of law-breakers out there, Fern. A lot of people who think we're not taking note. Four more people have been imprisoned since we were here two weeks ago.'

Because they don't agree with what you're doing, I wanted to scream. *Because this is madness. All of it.*

'But we're opening a new re-education centre next month.' He said it like he was speaking about an all-inclusive holiday island in the Indian Ocean. 'That might not have been mentioned on the BBC news. We've had to. We're almost at capacity. It would be inhumane to keep people in cramped conditions.'

Do they still have fingers? I wanted to ask.

I thought, not for the first time, how Cal would respond to them being here if he were still alive. Would he have behaved like I have? Would he have simply let them in, done as he was expected to? Did he watch me now, embarrassed at my docility?

I wanted to cry.

The tall one finished his tea. 'You never paint your fingernails,' he said. The short one still had an almost full mug.

'Sorry?' I was completely thrown. I looked at my hands, dry from manual work, and then panicked and put them at my side.

'Most women I know do,' he said. 'So many pretty colours and designs. I saw some the other day that were like pieces of silver glass. The woman could have put her lipstick on using her fingertips as a mirror.'

'I … my job,' I stammered. 'I can't. All the cleaning products. No good. For hands. Nails. No point.'

He nodded. 'Understandable. And you really need your hands for your job, don't you?'

I nodded because my throat was tight.

'Are you OK, Fern?'

'I … yes … just, unwell today.'

'Anyway, enough of the pleasantries,' he said, holding my gaze, eyes intense. 'You know what's going to happen now, don't you?'

I couldn't breathe. This was it. They were going to do it. Would it hurt? Be quick? Should I scream? Fight? Plead with them? Bargain? Surrender? How many would they take? Was it because I'd gone to Bedtime Stories or because of the notepad?

'Now we're going to search the house,' he said.

I wanted to slump to my knees in relief. In that moment, I hated him, venomously. The pair of them. The tall, lanky streak of piss – as my dad would have said – and the short, squat monster. A bead of sweat trickled down my back, landing on the pages I'd vomited my life into. The short one got up – wordlessly, there's a surprise – and headed into the hallway. I heard him stomping around the house, things falling, drawers slamming. Now I knew what a joke this was. All this time they had been searching the house in my absence. This was a fake search. A just-for-show search. A fuck-you-Fern search.

'Anything else you'd like to talk about?' asked the tall one.

'Not really.'

'You can talk to us about anything. That's what we're here for.'

I shook my head.

'You're the one,' he said.

'The ... *what*?' I asked softly.

'You're the one they'll wait the longest for,' he said.

I didn't dare respond; I didn't know what he meant.

He grabbed my right hand then, so fast I had no time to move. He gripped my fingers tightly in a vice-like fist. I tried to relax, to not give him the pleasure of my resistance, but instinct is strong, and I tried to pull back. Tighter he squeezed. I feared my bones would break. The short one returned. Hadn't it been the other way around for Lynda? Hadn't the short one held her down while the tall one cut two fingers off? The short one sat back at the table, shook his head at the tall one. Another squeeze of my fingers and I'm sure something cracked. Then he let go.

'Not this time,' he said. 'We have our instructions. I can wait. Yours will be a trophy most prized. I think they might let us take them all. Five little piggies.'

I cradled my bruised right hand in the left, close to my chest. He had shared his cards. His hand you might say, if you were being clever with words, like I used to try to be. What was the point in pretending anymore?

'You're fucking monsters,' I spat at him.

It felt good to vent, to fight again, like the old me.

'Very unpleasant language for you, Fern. We're just doing our job.'

'*Monsters*,' I repeated because I couldn't think of anything else.

'Perhaps this is the real Fern.' He smiled. 'I bet you were quite something once upon a time.'

'Get out of my house,' I hissed.

'*Our* house,' he said.

'Fuck you.'

'Well, this was lovely, as always,' said the tall one, like I'd not spoken. He stood and pushed his chair under the table, and the short one did the same. 'I always wish it could be longer, but there are only two of us and so few hours in the day.'

They went into the hallway. I remained in the kitchen, every part of my body shaking. I heard the front door open. Sunlight spilled in, blinding. 'Until next time, Fern,' called the tall one, an alien's shadow against the light.

The door shut after them.

I sank into a kitchen chair and sobbed. Then I wandered around the house, still unable to stop crying. I remembered when Cal died, and I roamed the flat we shared then, wailing and saying his name. I'd never experienced grief like it. A year or two after, when I could think straight, I used that pain to write *Technological Amazingness*. Now the book that saved me during my darkest hours, changed my life, and brought me glory is the foundation of a vile plan to end the lives of many people.

Eventually, I flopped into the chair, here at my desk. I've been here since. My fingers throb. At least I still have them. But for how long? When are they coming back? They can't take my fingers. How will I write? How will I record what's happening, what will happen, what *has* happened?

I'm holding the blue and white trainer, relieved it hasn't disappeared. Was it the tall one and the short one who brought it and removed it after all? I cradle it in my arm like a much-longed-for infant.

Thursday 29 November 2035 – 1.03 a.m.

When I wrote my novels, one of the things I struggled with was knowing how much to impart to the reader. Having to remember at any given moment how much they know. What have I already revealed, what am I still trying to hide, what can I not yet say? The part that came naturally to me was writing inner turmoil; getting inside the head and heart of my characters. Now I'm writing a diary, that's changed. The aspects I struggled with in my fiction are easy here. I tell it all, as I go, and don't have to think hard about withholding information. But I'm struggling to even get close to describing the chaos in my heart, and the constant dread in my head.

The best I can come up with is to say that everyone in my world could be symbolised by a different horse on a merry-go-round. The tall one is a lean, long-snouted horse. The short one is a chunky old pony. Fine-Fayre is a graceful stallion. Hunter is a rainbow-coloured unicorn. And it's spinning so fast I'm relieved the evil horses can't see me, but I'm sad that I miss the good ones too. If it slows down, the long-snouted horse might come after me. But then I'll be able to run my hands through the unicorn's bright mane.

See? I can't just write my feelings, as they are.

It has to be via some literary device. I can't just say, I'm petrified of the tall one and the short one coming back for my fingers. I can't just say, I think about Fine-Fayre in the dark and imagine him lying there with me. I can't just say, I wish Hunter was my boy.

Oh. Look.

I did.

Thursday 29 November 2035 – 11.11 a.m.

They say you should make a wish at 11.11, which it was when I wrote the time. Apparently, when paired together, two elevens are a message from the universe to 'become conscious and aware'. I wish for … I don't know. The old world. The books. The past. What's the point? It no longer exists. I think I prefer bargaining.

Today is my final Bedtime Stories. I called in sick at work again earlier. Now I regret it because the day stretches ahead, full of nothing. I couldn't face seeing Shrivel. I wish I had another job. I guess I wished after all. I need to look for one. I will.

Now, it's time. Time to go. Wish me luck.

I'm back.

Where to start?

I biked to Tinsley's anxious about whether Hunter would ring, realising that *that* should have been my wish. But I have his number now. I knew if he didn't call later, I can contact him. It occurred to me, as I pedalled hard, that the tall one and the short one have never asked to look at my phone. If they had yesterday, they would have seen my new contact. Then I remembered – the whole thing is a facade. They're just *pretending* to look. The real search happens when I'm elsewhere.

I was first to arrive in the basement, given entry by a subdued, no-nail-polish Tinsley. I barely had time to take off my coat before the phone in the time-out room rang. I hurried to it, closed the door, sank into the beanbag, and said, 'Hello, Hunter.'

'Hello, Crazy Lady,' he said.

'How are you this evening?' All my anxieties melted.

He giggled. 'You sounded dead posh then. Like you have pointy glasses on.'

I laughed too. 'I did, didn't I? How do you greet your friends then?'

He paused. I heard the squeak of his chair. 'Dunno. We just say hi. Or nothing. Never thought about it. I'm really low today.'

My heart sank too. 'Really? Why?' I almost called him sweetheart but held it back. Was it my place to do that?

'The chair's broken.'

'Sorry?'

'My mum's chair. When you sit on it, it slowly sinks down, and then you're dead low, near the floor. I can hardly see over the desk right now.'

I laughed. Hard. At both the image of him on a ridiculously small chair and at my misunderstanding of his words. He giggled again too. 'I'm low as well,' I said. 'Probably lower than you. I'm sitting on a beanbag.'

He didn't say anything. I wondered if he was smiling.

'It's my last time here,' I said sadly.

'I know,' he said. 'I might not have been able to ring anymore anyway.'

'Why not?'

'We might be going away,' he said.

'On holiday?'

'I'm not sure. My mum was vague.'

Anxiety rose in my chest. Something I couldn't explain or understand. An urgency that I must stop it. He could not go. He must not travel anywhere. 'When?'

'Next week I think.'

'Which day?'

'Dunno,' he said.

'And you don't know where?'

'Not really.'

'What exactly did your mum say?' I tried to keep the panic out of my voice.

'Um ... she said ... *we might be going away next week*. I never thought to ask about it really. I'm not that bothered.'

You can't go, I wanted to say, but I mustn't scare him. 'I have your number now,' I managed to say, sounding calm, not inexplicably scared. 'I can send you a message. Shall I do that at the weekend?

You might know where you're going by then and we can see ... well, what happens then ...'

'OK.'

'Shall we continue the story then?' My voice broke on the last word. I glanced at the door. Could I finish it tonight? Would someone disturb me? I hoped that if so, it would be Lynda.

'Yes,' he cried. 'I remember. I've been wondering how Hunter's gonna make them see him. Trying to figure it out. Will it be pouring paint on himself? Will it be kicking over all the furniture?' He paused. 'This is why you're the best storyteller *ever*.'

'Am I?' I can't deny that this meant more to me than any long-ago award win or rave review or message from an enamoured fan. I realised that a small part of me has been trying to prove I'm worthy of being *his* storyteller. I didn't need to write for *all* the children; it was enough to create for him.

'Yeah,' said Hunter. 'You know when I rang before I got you, sometimes I could hear how like totally bored the person was. You've never sounded bored of the story. That's why I like it so much.'

'Thank you.' I didn't know what else to say. I wanted to remember every word he'd said. I have, it's here, imprinted now on these pages forever. 'If we don't finish it tonight,' I added, 'if suddenly one of us is gone, I'll message you, and I promise we'll finish the story. OK? We *will*.' I felt I had to repeat it, reassure him. Reassure myself.

'So, Hunter's mum was about to take the parcel off him,' he said.

'She was,' I agreed.

Once again, I'd forgotten to grab a book. Then I remembered. I had my notepad. I went in my rucksack and took it out. I turned a page. It made a far crinklier sound than the ones in a regular book do because my handwriting had added texture to the thin paper. A sentence caught my eye. *Except when I told Hunter that story, I saw flashes of sunflower; I saw those three shades of yellow in the painting and nothing else ...* How profound to see it right now, in this moment.

'Are you comfortable in your very low chair?' I asked cheerfully.

'The world is different down here. I can see the wires behind the desk.'

'OK. So, Hunter's mum had reached for the parcel even though she still couldn't see him. She got hold of it and he let her take it. "I'm here," he said again, but she didn't even look his way.'

'Or his dad?' asked Hunter, hopeful.

'No. Very carefully – even though it said Hunter's name on the front and really it was very rude without his permission – she opened the parcel. She pulled out the contents, very slowly, like she was a magician trying to keep everyone in suspense for the big reveal. It was a large red book.' I turned one of the crinkly pages.

'That was loud,' said Hunter.

'Sorry.'

'I think I know,' he said, thoughtfully.

'What?'

'It's you, isn't it?'

'What is?' I asked.

'*You* did the story.'

'Well, of course,' I said.

'No, I mean you're making it up? Right now. As we go. Is it true?'

Did he sound disappointed about it, or hopeful? I didn't know what to say. Lie? Be honest?

'I don't mind,' he said, as though hearing my thoughts. 'It would be cool. That I'd had a story no one else ever has.'

'I made it up,' I whispered.

'I could help you with the end,' he said.

I heard movement in the other room. No. Not now. 'I have to go,' I whispered. 'But I'll call you, I promise, soon.' And for the first time I hung up on Hunter. I heard his soft 'OK' before I pressed END CALL, desperately frustrated. Then I jumped up and switched on the kettle. When Jasmine came in, I was making tea for everyone, avoiding the unopened carton of milk because the use-by date was tomorrow.

'No Lynda?' She frowned.

'No. Why?' I handed her a mug.

She wrinkled her nose. 'It's black,' she said, and went to the fridge. 'Not like her to be late. It's ten to six. She's always here. And if she can't get here, she always calls me.'

'Should we ring her?' Concern fluttered in my chest.

Jasmine took her now creamy tea into the other room, and I followed. Alfie was putting a packet of cheap cakes on the coffee table. *They won't be Fine-Fayre quality*, I thought. Jasmine took her phone out of her bag and called someone, I presumed Lynda, and then talked in the other room.

'Last night, eh?' said Alfie.

'I know. My time's only been brief, but this must be sad for you.'

'We did some good for a while, I think,' he said softly.

Jasmine came back. Her face was as white as first snowdrops. 'She's gone,' she said.

'Who?' I asked, dumb.

'Lynda.'

'What do you mean gone? Where?'

'He doesn't know. Her husband, Tom. He's going spare.'

'He doesn't know where? What do you mean?'

'He came home from work yesterday.' Jasmine dropped into a sofa, blinking over and over. 'She wasn't there. There was a half-empty mug of tea on the worktop. All that was missing was her phone. He rang it – nothing. Dead. Then he called everyone he knew. But no one had seen or spoken to Lynda all day. He waited up all night. Poor, poor Tom. She never came home. And she's still missing.'

'*Shit.*' My mind raced. It had to be the tall one and the short one. They had come for her. But why? What had she done? Where had they taken her? 'Has Tom rung the police?'

'Yes, just now. He wanted to wait. Make sure. They're on their way there.'

I sat opposite her; Alfie joined me. It was six o'clock but none of us said anything. We had to find out the outcome of our real-life story before we could concentrate on reading happy-ever-afters.

'I doubt they can do anything,' said Jasmine.

'Why?' I asked.

She looked at me, pointedly. 'The police probably know what's *really* happened, but they'll have to pretend they don't and go through the motions of looking for her.'

'Really happened?' I repeated.

'*They*'ll have visited her.'

'The two of them,' I said.

She nodded. Alfie must have known about the visits we writers have because he nodded too.

'They came to see me yesterday,' I said. 'I thought they were going to—'

'What?' asked Alfie.

I looked at my hands. Did he and Jasmine know the truth about Lynda's fingers?

'You must have been scared,' said Jasmine, softly. She knew. But Alfie still looked perplexed.

'What can we do?' I cried, ignoring his confusion. 'We must do *something*. Where've they taken her do you think? Who can we speak to?' I started to get up. No one had even looked at Alfie's cheap cakes. 'I should go to Lynda's house. Comfort Tom. Help somehow.'

'You can't.' Jasmine looked horrified. 'It'd be far too dangerous.'

'I don't care. She's my friend.'

'It's too late.'

'It's because of the plan for ALLBooks, isn't it?' I said. 'You need to tell whoever's taking part to call it off. And then we can tell the tall one and the short one that we're not going to start any fires, and they might let her go.'

'It isn't about ALLBooks,' said Jasmine. 'If it were, they'd have come for all of us, wouldn't they? I'm sure Lynda told you, they *want* the fires to happen; then they have better reason to never retract the fiction ban. Don't you see? They'll be able to say that those of us who want to bring novels back are dangerous vigilantes. And they'll be right.'

'Even more reason to stop it then.' I was hot with rage.

'I've tried.' Jasmine sounded exhausted. Resigned.

'Do you think they've taken Lynda ...' Alfie's words trailed off.

'What?' I asked.

'To one of those re-education centres?'

Jasmine looked like he'd spoken for her.

'Where are they?' I asked. 'What do they do there?'

'Haven't you read about them online?' asked Alfie. 'No one seems to know exactly, but I read that they do some sort of extreme, barbaric ECT treatment so that people forget everything.'

'But ... isn't that illegal now?'

He shrugged. 'You think that would stop them? There's a woman up my street who worked in publishing. She's been missing for three months. Her husband and children are distraught but no one else gets involved. It's like they're ... afraid.'

'That's awful,' I said. 'Someone shou—'

'Look,' interrupted Jasmine, 'speculating like this isn't helping.'

'I can't sit here and do nothing,' I cried.

'What do you think you *can* do?' Jasmine didn't speak unkindly. It was like she felt she had been in my shoes and wanted to prepare me for it.

'I don't know.' I didn't. I had no way of contacting the tall one and the short one. If I could, what would I say? Tom had rung Lynda's phone to no avail so I doubted she would answer if I tried. And I had absolutely no idea where she had gone so how could I even begin searching for her?

'Did you watch that new documentary on CineTime?' asked Alfie. 'It's called *A Thin Line*. It's about how the desire to write fiction is a personality disorder, like schizophrenia or BPD.'

'What?' I cried. 'That's ridiculous!'

'I agree. But they interviewed all kinds of renowned professors and scientists who support the theory. They've done major studies and—'

'They never asked me,' I said. 'And those so-called experts were paid or persuaded to agree.'

'Look,' interrupted Jasmine again, 'we have to decide what to do tonight.'

It was now six-fifteen.

'I don't think I can read tonight,' I admitted. I felt guilty, but having spoken to Hunter already, I'd done my duty, for want of a better word. I could leave.

'I'll try,' said Alfie. 'But it's up to you, Jasmine.'

'I feel we should. This is what we do. It's about the children.' She looked at me. 'But I understand if you want to leave. Lynda was a dear friend of yours.'

'*Is* a dear friend,' I corrected.

'Yes. Sorry. But listen. Don't do anything silly. Don't put yourself at risk. Go home. Sit tight. Maybe Lynda will come home, and all will be well.' I think we both knew that that wasn't going to happen. Jasmine stood up and I joined her. 'Thank you for volunteering with us,' she said.

'It was an honour,' I said. 'Can I give you my number, and if you get news about Lynda, will you let me know?'

We exchanged numbers. Alfie and I too. Then Jasmine turned the phones on, and they both became Cinderella and Peter Rabbit. I got my rucksack and climbed the basement stairs for the last time. No more Bedtime Stories. I glanced back at the time-out room. No more talking to Hunter from the beanbag. No more Tinsley with minty nail polish. No more Lynda. That thought made me miss a step and almost fall.

I biked home.

Now it's 11.11 at the opposite end of the day. What do I wish, here in the dark, the steam from my Fine-Fayre tea dampening my face? I wish I could see where Lynda is, that she's OK. I wish I knew what they're doing to her, and why? Will I be next? No. I don't want to know that.

I said I'd message Hunter at the weekend. That's two days away. How can I wait? I must. I'm thinking again of the reaction I had to the thought of him going away. What was it about the idea that

caused such fear? It's the thought of him getting into a car. That's it.
And I don't know why.

    We must finish our story first; then I feel sure it will be OK.

    He's going to help me with the end.

    I'm glad I won't do it alone.

Friday 30 November 2035 – 7.03 a.m.

I dreamt that Hunter was in a car.

He slept in the back, reddish hair that's really 'more blond' stuck to his forehead, a toy robot bouncing gently with the motion of the vehicle, moving dangerously closer to the edge of the seat. He remained oblivious when his mum – who was driving, I noticed, so it must have been an older car – turned the air conditioning up to max, switched radio stations, and started singing along to Dolly Parton. He wore blue and white trainers. The left shoelace had come undone and dangled precariously, the shoe at risk of falling off. I could smell off milk and wasn't sure why. Then I saw a half-full bottle of chocolate milkshake on the floor, some of the liquid seeping out.

Even in the dream, I gagged.

Then his mum's phone started ringing. *Don't answer it*, I thought in panic. I tried to say it. To warn her. Hunter slept on. She chatted animatedly to whoever had called. *Look at the road*, I wanted to scream. *Look at the road*.

A smash. A flash of searing light. And then it all went blood red.

I woke, strangled, choking, the sheet about my neck. I had been sick in my sleep. It stank of fetid milk even though I'd not consumed any for weeks now. I sat up and tried to get my breath. Then it came to me. Absolute. I could not let Hunter go on the journey with his mum.

It's ridiculous. Now I see it written down. But I *can't*. How can I stop it though? I could take him. Find out where he lives and go and get him. These ideas came to me like a naughty child's plan to steal from the sweetie jar. Take him. Save him. Stop it happening.

What the hell is wrong with me?

I'm actually considering stealing an eight-year-old boy because of a dream. The blue and white trainer is still on my desk. I imagine it for a moment, falling from Hunter's foot, an explosion, smashing metal, fire, screams, death.

I'm losing my mind.

Saturday 1 December 2035 – 2.04 p.m.

It's Saturday but I had still forgotten. I guess that's the thing about a non sequitur; it doesn't follow logically from the previous. Even with his knock – not gentle, not intrusive – coming bang on noon, I had forgotten. It must be the week I've had. Lynda, gone. Hunter, possibly going. Bedtime Stories, over. The tall one and the short one, gloves off now. (Not a funny image any more.) I opened the door, exhaustion making me barely bothered if it was the two of them today, prepared to face my fate, and there he was. My wheel-chair-bound, tea-selling, Saturday non sequitur.

He looked tired too, his scar once again an angry slash against wan skin. But he still had his fingers. My eyes went there after his face: to his hands, resting on the bulging, treat-laden basket.

'These Christmas Crinkles are brand new.' His jolliness sounded forced. A gaudy green and red pack of something sat on top of his many products. It felt surreal to be discussing the festive season when it was so hot that even wearing only a thin vest and some linen trousers made my back damp. 'These cakes are full of all that's best about this season – there's a dash of sherry, juicy raisins, orange, dark chocolate and fig. They're a real favourite with strong tea drinkers.'

'With all those ingredients, you'd *need* strong tea to wash away the aftertaste.'

'Take a sample.' He handed me a small pack.

'I hope it doesn't ruin my appetite.'

'It won't. They're a light between-meal snack and yet nutritious enough to help you last until dinner.' He spoke like he believed every word, no hint of jest.

'*Light*?' I laughed. 'They'd sink to the bottom of a river in seconds. Do you make it up as you go along?'

'It's all true.' Now he raised one eyebrow as though to assure me he knew how funny some of the descriptions were.

'I suppose I could stick a candle in it to celebrate,' I said.

'What are you celebrating?'

LOUISE SWANSON

'My birthday.' I could not have felt less excited. Every birthday
since the fiction ban has been spent alone. I thought suddenly of the
last birthday before it all changed; at the end of 2029, turning for-
ty-seven, having won the British Fiction Prize, sharing champagne
with Shelly, Cass, and Lynda.

'Many happy returns of the day,' said Fine-Fayre.

'I've always thought that's a weird thing to say. What does it
mean anyway?'

He looked up at the scorched blue sky. 'It's referring to the sun
returning to exactly where it was in the heavens on the day you
were born.'

'Oh.' I prodded my Christmas Crinkle. 'Are these in date? The
edges look dry.'

'All our products are at least six months in date. It's policy. Have
another pack on me.'

I shook my head.

'For your birthday, Fern.' He said my name so softly. I remembered then. He knows who I am. He admires me. I wondered about
his home life. His daughter. Is there a girlfriend or boyfriend if there
isn't a wife or husband? Was I jealous at the thought?

'Who wants to celebrate being fifty-three?' I asked.

'You don't look it.' He blushed. It was the loveliest thing. My
heart melted. 'What are you doing to commemorate the day?'

'Nothing,' I admitted.

He didn't speak. Did he pity me despite past denial? I hated the
thought of it. Anger surged at the idea, but I quashed it. I was being
unfair. I shouldn't care how he felt towards me. But I did. I do. It
crossed my mind to invite him to dine with me, but I was embarrassed. What could I offer? I had no fridge. Nothing but tins and
packets.

'It's fine,' I said briskly. 'I'll open some wine, read …'

'What are you reading?'

'*Technological Truth For Tots and Teens*,' I said, though I still hadn't
opened it. In that second, I saw myself buying it, and my heart leapt.

'Don't go to ALLBooks on the next Book Amnesty Day, will you?' I whispered, leaning closer to him.

'Sorry?' He frowned.

'It's on Friday, isn't it?'

'I don't know.'

'It is. Promise me, you won't go. *Please*. I heard about something ... something bad ...'

I know they're going to start the fire before the shop opens, but people queue early on Book Amnesty Day. I need to warn everyone I know. It isn't many people. I should tell Laura next door and my work colleagues ... and Hunter.

'I don't generally go there anyway. What did you hear?'

I shook my head. Maybe I should tell the tall one and the short one if they come again that it isn't going to happen at Christmas like they think, but on Friday. Isn't that betraying 'my own people' though? I tried not to think of it then, with Fine-Fayre there. I needed to enjoy his company while I had him.

'I read the original,' he said.

'What?' I asked.

'*Technological Truth*. Ade Woods clearly had issues with your novel.' He paused. 'I saw a news report about a One Death Policy the other night. Is it true, do you know? If so, they're literally stealing an idea that was supposed to show how extreme things were getting. That would be madness.'

I thought of Shrivel then. Of surgery. Of what it might have done for Fine-Fayre's scar. Then I remembered he had made peace with the childhood injury that reminded me of badly tied shoelaces. I recalled how long it took me to learn to tie them correctly. My dad would patiently show me, crossing and un-crossing, again and again, but my fingers failed. In the end he gave up.

'Do you know what your scar makes me think of?' As soon as I'd said it, I realised it was insensitive, and shoelaces were a cruel comparison.

'Tell me,' he said, unfazed.

I tried to think of a better analogy. 'A war hero. Like you fought in some big battle and that's what you came home with.'

'I guess scars are proof we survived.'

'Better than a war medal, I suppose.'

'I suppose.'

'My friend lost her fingers,' I said before I could think.

'What do you mean?'

I wished he would come in. That I could unburden myself of everything. Tell him my life. Hear his. Share my pain. Feel his. Have his thoughts. His affection.

'I get questioned, you know. These two government men come. To make sure I'm not writing. They visit all writers. They …' I shook my head, felt nauseous again at the thought of Lynda's poor hands. 'My friend, another writer. They cut off her fingers.'

'*What*?' Fine-Fayre's face was aghast.

I nodded. Couldn't speak. 'Now she's missing,' I said eventually.

'I saw someone like that,' he said.

'What do you mean?'

'Without fingers. I was in the supermarket.' It was hard to imagine him there; to see him anywhere but here on my doorstep. 'She was reaching for a tin of peas. Held it between her thumb and fourth finger. The gaps in between were stumps.'

I didn't know what to say. Was this a new thing they were doing? Or had I simply never noticed because I had no reason to?

'How is something like that *allowed*?' he said.

'I don't know. How did any of this happen? How did we get here?'

'I hate this world,' he said quietly.

'Me too.' Sensing a moment of us sharing, being vulnerable, I asked, 'How did you end up in the wheelchair?' I was intensely curious; I felt that the story behind it might show me more of the real man.

'Let me give you the teabags free of charge today; for your birthday.' He handed me my customary gold pack. He obviously didn't want to answer the question. I felt that it didn't matter if I repeated my query nine times or rephrased it – he would calmly change the subject every time.

'You don't have to,' I said. 'You'll have to pay for them, won't you?'

'Isn't that how people give a gift?'

'Flowers tend to be a more traditional gift than teabags. But thank you.' I thought of something. 'Do they have any jobs at your place?'

'Selling tea?' he asked.

'Yes. It must be quite pleasant?'

'It is, yes. My job might be available soon.'

'You're leaving?' The idea of him no longer calling by filled me with a desperation to press pause on the world.

'I had an interview,' Fine-Fayre said. 'I find out if I got it on Monday.'

I could have asked what the new role was, but I only cared that I would lose him. He patted his basket. I realised that he always did just before leaving, as though signalling for me to prepare for his departure. I wasn't ready.

'You're not going to try and get me to sign up for any competitions today?' I asked, buying time. 'No buy-one-get-one-free offers or free teacups or seductive hampers?'

He shook his head. 'Not today.'

'Are you ill?'

He smiled. 'No.'

'Today might have been your lucky day. I might have signed up.'

'I doubt it,' he said. 'You don't strike me as so fickle.'

'A good salesman wouldn't let that put him off.'

He backed his wheelchair up and drove it down my path to the securely shut gate, which he opened and went through, and then fastened again.

'If these Christmas Crinkles give me indigestion, I'll put a serious complaint in,' I called after him.

'Happy birthday,' he said.

I left my step. 'We know the day we were born, and we celebrate it every year. But imagine if we knew our death day too. I mean, we all have one. It's there, in the future.' I was rambling, talking nonsense, trying to keep him a bit longer, before my small house swallowed me up again.

'But who'd want to know that?' he said.

I walked down my path, reached the gate for the first time when he was departing. 'I don't think I would,' I admitted. 'But we'd know how much time we have left. We could do all the things we wanted to. And if we knew *how* we were going to die, we could avoid doing the thing that killed us.'

'Like what?' he asked.

We were each on opposite sides of the gate.

'Not getting in a car we know will crash,' I said.

'That's specific,' he said. 'But I suppose.'

I thought about asking him his name. I've never wanted to know it. When I first met Cal, I didn't know his for ages. We kept seeing one another around the university campus, him popular, confident, thick hair and big smile, me quieter, less outgoing. We crossed paths at a party or two and I was thrilled when he smiled once and made the effort to come and talk to me, only to be dragged away by bawdy friends. I remember trying to imagine what his name was. Hoping it wouldn't disappoint me. That it would fit who he was. It did. Unusual. Bold. Him. What would suit Fine-Fayre?

I decided I'd rather leave him anonymous.

He looked thoughtful. 'Can I ask you something?' he said.

'OK.'

'What was it like?'

'What was what like?'

'That kind of success. Your book. The accolade. The glory. Winning.'

'Brief,' was the word that came to me first. 'I didn't have time to appreciate it before it was over. But also … in truth … it really was magnificent.'

He smiled. 'I bet.'

I bent down, picked the only tulip whose petals weren't dry, and handed it to him. 'For your daughter.'

'Thank you.' He put it on top of his basket and drove his chair towards the van.

'If you get the new job, how long is your notice with Fine-Fayre?' I called after him. Some places only demand a week nowadays. He should get one more visit in. But I had to be sure.

'Two weeks,' he said.

'Good luck.' I wasn't sure I meant it, because I'd never see him again.

And then he was gone. I was sure the temperature dropped, just for a moment. I came inside and put the free teabags and Christmas Crinkles sample on the kitchen worktop. I wasn't hungry but I made some black tea in my festive cup. And brought it to my desk. This is where I live these days. It's the weekend. It's my birthday. But there's nothing to celebrate.

I can message Hunter though.

I said I would on the weekend.

And I do.

I sent a message to Hunter at one o'clock this afternoon. I had to think carefully about what I wrote. I had no idea who might see it, who might question what a middle-aged woman was doing sending messages to a child who isn't hers. I thought briefly, *they*'ll read it anyway on this page. They come into the house. Then I remembered that I take my notepad now every time I leave.

I hate having my phone on for a long period.

But this was an exception.

This was my message: *Hi Hunter. Hope you're OK. If there is a moment when you're free to talk, send me a quick text, and I'll call you.*

Then I sat at my desk with the phone, repeatedly checking the volume was on max, like a teenage girl waiting for a crush to call.

There was a knock on the door at half past one. My heart stopped. The two of them. Who else could it be? Not now. Please. No. I said these words aloud. I bargained with the universe; let it not be them when I must talk to Hunter, and I'll give any of my fingers up. I thought about pretending I wasn't there but then they would have just come in anyway. I hid my notepad in the back of my trousers and put the phone in my pocket and went to the door. It was just the grocery delivery, no milk.

I had to wait two hours for a response from Hunter.

He wrote: *hi crazy lady I am got ma friend here talk soon.*

I smiled. I had to wait another hour. I made more tea, nibbled on my birthday Christmas Crinkle and spat it out. Too bitter.

Then he wrote: *talk now.*

With trembling fingers, I dialled his number.

'Hello, Crazy Lady,' he said.

'Hello, Hunter,' I said. It was just like at Bedtime Stories except I'd called him. And no beanbag. No worry that Jasmine would come in and disturb us. No other children needing me. Just him. 'Are you in your usual spot?'

'I'm in my bedroom.'

I imagined blue and white curtains fluttering in the breeze. Saw a favourite chair, one that rocked, where his mum used to read him stories when he was a baby and couldn't sleep. Isn't that how I described Story Hunter's bedroom weeks ago?

'How are you?' I asked.

'OK. I've been thinking about the end.'

'The end?' My heart went cold.

'Of the story. We never got there. You said I could help with it.'

'Yes. Of course. Now? Should we maybe think some more?'

If we finished it today, would he want to talk again? To meet? I saw my car crash dream again. The smash. The flash of searing light. And then blood red.

'I've been thinking about it,' Hunter said. 'I'm ready.'

I needed to meet him. But can I trust myself not to take him away? Yes. Of course I can. I just want to make sure he's OK. I need to find out where he's going, and when. I need to keep him safe.

'Hunter, I have to ask you something,' I said.

'OK.'

'Have you ever been to ALLBooks?'

'Yeah. Once. Why?'

'Can you promise me you won't go anywhere near an ALL-Books on Friday?'

'I won't be here,' he said.

'What do you mean?' I knew what he meant.

'We're going on Tuesday,' he said.

'Where?'

'I know now. My mum said she got this better job and so we're going to stay with my Aunty Loulou who lives in … I can't remember the place. Not London. Then if she is happy in this new job, we will get our own house.'

Tuesday. Three days away. Too soon.

'Is it far away?' I asked, hoping to work out where.

'Mum said it'll take all day to get there.'

That could be anywhere. I could hire a car, follow them. I don't think my driving licence is in date now. I could hire a driver. Ridiculous. I don't have that kind of money. I have to find a way to go with them then. No. That's ridiculous too. The smash and flash of the dream wouldn't let me go though. I saw it, over and over, felt the heat from the flames.

'Is it a driverless car, Hunter?'

'No. She doesn't trust them. I told her she should get with the programme, everybody has them now. Marley's mum has one that even recharges itself from your breath. That's what he told me anyway.'

I paced the room.

'What are you doing tomorrow?' I asked. He was only eight. Was he even allowed to leave the house alone? My heart pounded. Guilt flooded my veins. I had no right to do this, to ask him to meet me, but I simply couldn't *not*.

'Dunno. Why?'

'Shall we finish the story properly?'

'OK. How?'

'Let's meet,' I said.

He didn't speak. Had I made him nervous? This was so wrong of me. So unfair. Then he said, 'Where?'

'Does your mum let you go out alone?'

'I play on the street with Harper from number nine. And I'm allowed to walk to Marley's because he only lives three streets away.'

Was it fair to ask him to lie to his mother? What choice did I have? I *had* to protect him.

'Tell your mum you're going to Marley's, and I'll meet you there.'

He didn't respond.

'I'm sorry to ask you to lie,' I said softly. 'It's always wrong to do that. But I think this time, we have little choice if we want to finish our story before you go away.' I paused. 'If you really feel uncomfortable, I can just call you again.' *A last time*, I couldn't help but think.

'I was going to Marley's anyway.' He sounded unsure. 'I could leave a bit earlier.'

'What time?' I asked.

'I was going after lunch.'

'Do you know his address to give me?'

'Oh.' He thought. 'I know the street.'

'That's enough.'

He told me.

'I'll wait at the end of the street from twelve,' I said. 'Don't worry if you're late. Just come when you can. If you're definitely OK with that?'

'But I don't know what you look like,' he said, voice small.

'No. But I know you.'

'Do you?'

'The description, remember,' I said. 'In the story. It was you.'

'I have to go,' he said, and more guilt engulfed me. He was just a boy. Not my boy. Someone else's boy.

'Tomorrow,' I said softly.

'Tomorrow, Crazy Lady,' he said, and I smiled.

'Happy birthday,' I said to the room when he had gone.

Sunday 2 December 2035 – 6.31 a.m.

I dreamed of flames again. A car, engulfed. I was somehow above it; next to it; near; far; not quite there. But the heat. It singed my face, then followed me into consciousness. Awake in the dark, I touched my cheeks, expecting welts or pain. Nothing.

I remember flames.

A few weeks after I came to this house. I woke in the night to the cloggy, thick smell of smoke. It curled in through my bedroom window. I went to the back door. It was coming from Laura next door's garden. Fire frantically flickered and frolicked in the darkness.

'I'm burning my books,' she cried, her face manic in the glow.

The next day I thought I'd dreamt it. Until I saw scorched earth like the entry to hell in the middle of her lawn.

I was a flame once. A fan with red ribbons woven through her plaits called me her fire. I was signing *Technological Amazingness* for her, in a festival tent, rain pattering on the awning above us. 'I can't wait to see what you write next,' she gushed. 'Please never stop.' I haven't, Red-Ribbon Girl. I haven't. I won't.

Flames are coming. Unless something happens. Unless something changes. This is a feeling in my gut. Is the ALLBooks plan causing this hunch that simmers like dying embers? Is it only five days until Book Amnesty Day? It must be that. Could I stop it?

Should I?

Sunday 2 December 2035 – 6.09 p.m.

I woke so early that I had to wait five hours before I could bike to meet Hunter after twelve. Time is cruel when you want it to pass; it drags its heels like a child dawdling on a routine trip to the dentist. There was so much I didn't want to think about. Lynda. Where *was* she? Didn't the answer nag at me? Didn't the words *re-education centres* whisper in my head? I turned my smartphone on but there were no messages, not from Lynda or from Jasmine with news. What was I going to do? Wait to hear? What *could* I do? If there was something, *would* I do it?

Time continued to drag; I tried to fill it.

I drank Fine-Fayre tea. I stood on my back doorstep and watched the sun come up. I made a deal with the sky, asking that if it always let me see it I would … I didn't know my side of that deal. I finally flicked through *Technological Truth For Tots and Teens*, curiously landing on a page that included twenty-five 'facts' about time. The reader had to decide which were true and which were 'ridiculous fiction'. Number nine was *time can't drag*. I slammed the book shut and put it in a drawer.

Finally, it was eleven-thirty, and I could leave.

When I tried to open the front door – notepad in rucksack, bike at my side – the key wouldn't turn. What the hell? I tried again, forcing it roughly. Nothing. Stuck.

Fern, you don't have everything; you know this.

The words came to me. I realised I *didn't* have everything. I went to my desk. The blue and white trainer. Still there. I picked it up. Hadn't I known all along? Didn't it feel like an idea formed loosely at the start of a novel and then remembered later, at the relevant moment? In the past, I often unknowingly laid the foundations for a big reveal and thanked my previous self for her foresight.

Take the trainer for Hunter.

It's his.

Of course it is.

Now the front door opened easily. I biked with the shoe in my rucksack, digging awkwardly into my shoulder blades. The sun beat down on me as though to try to send me home, but I pedalled harder, sweat clouding my view. I found the street Hunter had said his friend lived on. There was a bench at the top. I chained my bike to it and sat there. Waited. Heart in mouth. Would I know him if he came?

I did.

Hunter rounded the corner just after twelve-thirty. His reddish-blond hair, that I knew he told everyone was 'more blond', was ruffled on top and short at the sides, clearly freshly cut there. He was chunky, in a good way, like he'll be a strapping lad when he grows up. Not tall yet, but who knows? Only the future. He was dragging a red rucksack with a comical cartoon face on it. The straps trailed the floor. His mum must nag him when she sees the dirt on them. I saw all this like I'd seen it before. Like I knew him. For a few seconds, he didn't see me on the bench, and I had a chance to drink him in. My heart ached. I wanted to leap up and squeeze him tightly. But I didn't. I waited.

He saw me. I smiled and waved so he'd know who I was. His smile in response was shy. He crossed the road, looking carefully both ways, and came to the bench, red rucksack swinging by his legs.

'Hi,' I said.

'Hi,' he said.

'Hunter,' I said.

'Crazy Lady,' he said.

It should have felt strange, but it didn't. It felt like the most natural thing in the world. He sat on the bench too and put his rucksack on his lap. One sock had fallen down; his knee was bruised.

'Here we are,' I said. Now I felt shy. I was the adult. I was supposed to make sure he was OK. 'Are you still going away on Tuesday?' The question choked me.

'Yup. Mum's packing now. She was glad I was getting out from under her feet.' He said it carefully, like he was quoting her exact words. He paused, then said in a soft voice, 'I hope I make friends where we're going.'

'You easily will. You're very likeable. Trust me.' I paused. 'You still don't know the name of where you're going then?'

'Mum did say but I've forgotten. Begins with N.' Hunter took a bottle of chocolate milk out of his rucksack. I winced as he unscrewed the lid; gagged as he chugged a mouthful. 'Are you OK?' he asked.

'Yes. Sorry. I just hate dairy stuff.'

'I can put it away.' He did. But I could picture it inside his bag, growing warm, going off, thickening, putrid. 'I won't ever get you again, will I?'

'What do you mean?'

'You said you don't know how long Bedtime Stories will go on for – and they don't have room for you anywhere else.'

'No, but I'm here now,' I said.

'Do you already know the end of the story?' he asked. I must have looked blank. '*What Happened to All the Bloody Books*?' he said.

I smiled. 'No,' I admitted. 'Do you?'

He shrugged. 'Not sure. Good job I know you made it up or I'd want to see the book now, wouldn't I?'

'You would.' I could have stared at him forever; at the slight flush in his cheeks; the nails that needed cutting; the crease in his cut-off jeans.

'How are we going to do it then?' he asked.

'Where were we up to?'

'Story Hunter's mum still couldn't see him, and she had taken a big red book out of the parcel the postman gave them.'

'You're good,' I said. 'Here's what I think happens. I think his mum opens the red book and starts to read the story aloud.'

'Yes,' cried Hunter. 'That's what I think too! I can see it. I know.'

'What do you see?'

'I don't know the exact words of the story in the red book,' he garbled, excited, 'but I know what happens when she says them. Don't you?'

Suddenly I did. 'It doesn't matter what the exact words are, it only matters that they are from a book Hunter's been excited for weeks to receive – a book that he would've taken straight upstairs and read from cover to cover under the duvet.'

'But that isn't what he really wants,' said Hunter quietly, fiddling with his rucksack straps.

'Isn't it?' I asked.

'No. He really wants his mum to read it to him. Because no one can do it like her.'

I nodded.

'And now she's doing it.' Hunter shivered with joy. 'And when she does, Story Hunter slowly begins to appear, bit by bit, first his nose and then his ears and then his shoes ...'

'And finally, he is there,' I said 'Fully visible. She can see him. In some ways, more than ever before.'

'What about the books?' cried Hunter. 'Have they come back too?'

'What do you think?'

'They have, yes. And I think his mum knows—'

'Knows what?'

'That she should never have stopped reading him stories.' Hunter looked sad.

'But she's not allowed to,' I said kindly.

'What?'

'*Your* mum. Your real-world mum. She's not allowed to.'

'I know. I miss it.' His voice wavered. He must have been barely three the last time his mum read him a story, yet he hadn't forgotten. That was its power. I longed to move closer, comfort him, but I knew I shouldn't. 'But in our story, Hunter's mum can read to him any time. And that way he'll never be invisible again. And that's what they did. Together, out loud. Every day after.' He looked at me, his eyes baby blue. 'And I think that's the end of the story, isn't it?'

'I think it might be,' I said.

'It was a good ending.' He nodded as though to agree with himself.

'It was.' It was better than anything I could have hoped to have written for my long-ago commission. It had been natural, raw, improvised, *perfect*.

'Your mum loves you,' I said.

'How do *you* know?' He was huffy now. 'You never seen her.'

'I just know. Even when she's busy, or she snaps, or she …' I couldn't finish. I felt I would cry, and I had no idea why.

'Have you got your own boy?' asked Hunter.

'No,' I said quietly.

'I hope you get one. You deserve one.' He stood up. 'I better go to Marley's now.'

'Of course.' I couldn't stand up. I thought my knees would give. *Let me get one last good look at you,* I thought. 'Oh, wait,' I said, remembering. 'I have something for you.'

'Really? What is it?'

I went into my rucksack and took out the blue and white trainer, the tiny speck of dark red still there, slightly scuffed. I put it on the bench. Hunter stared at it; his mouth hung open like an old hammock. Then, without a word, he went into his own bag and took out the other one. He put it on the bench. The right to my left; the *right* one. We both looked at them, and then each other.

'Where did you find it?' he asked, eyes wide.

'It … appeared. In my house.'

'But that's crazy. I lost it, like, I dunno. Two months ago. They're my favourites.' He picked them both up, his face alight with happiness. 'I've had this one in my bag ever since I lost that one. Mum went totally mad. She said she wouldn't get me any more, but she had to 'cos I can't walk about in my socks. I. Am. So. Happy.' Then Hunter kissed my cheek with a wet smack and ran up the street, holding both trainers to his chest. I touched where the kiss had landed. He stopped and turned briefly before he went into a house, calling, 'Thank you, Crazy Lady.'

And then he was gone.

I sat there for ten minutes. Did I think he would come back? Maybe. I had never felt more alone. I didn't want to come home. What was waiting for me here? Nothing. No one. But I felt sure Hunter was safe. I feel sure now. I can't explain it. He has both of his trainers. We finished the story. We made Story Hunter visible again. He is safe. Hunter can travel with his mum, and he'll be OK.

Even if I'm not.

I'm too tired now to write anymore. I'm beginning to wonder who I'm doing it for. What I'm doing it for. Why? Who cares about my story? Who cares about the books? Who cares if any of it is true or not?

Monday 3 December 2035 – 2.33 p.m.

It was quiet this morning when I woke. I had forgotten to turn the fan on. I realised that it was the first night where the temperature had dipped a little, where I didn't wake to the relentless whirring blades and damp sheets. I went to the window. The sky had no colour. The trees did not move. It was like the world was waiting for something.

I too had no colour or movement. I felt flat. Still. Drained. Like if I exerted myself too much, I'd collapse. The events of the last few weeks have taken their toll on me. I've quietly got on with my life in this new world ... until recently. Now it's impossible to do that. I know too much. I've seen too much. But I have no energy. I had two cups of Fine-Fayre, hoping to revive myself. I knew I had to go to work – I hadn't been since last Tuesday – and I dreaded it.

I biked there, notepad in rucksack, grateful for the cool turn in the weather. Festive lights led the way; silver flashes punctuated the colourless world, woke me, said *everything is coming close*. It's hard to believe that Christmas is just three weeks away when your face is still tanned, and you haven't worn a coat in months.

My boss wasn't happy with me. She reminded me I wouldn't get sick pay without a doctor's note. I didn't care. I hadn't the strength. At the end of the shift, I pushed my cleaning trolley to Conference Room 3a; the wheels *squeak-squeak-squeaked*, reminding me suddenly of Hunter's chair. I had to stop to get my breath.

He's leaving tomorrow. Should I let him be now or stay in touch? We never talked about that. Do I let him go? Is that it? Once composed, I continued. I'd left the conference room until last, hoping someone else would do it, but no. As I approached, music drifted along the corridor, an orchestral piece, all drums and brass band.

I should have just turned and left.

I reached the door. Inside, was all the colour that had been absent so far today. Red and gold and black balloons – ghastly bloated things, the kind from horror stories – had been tied to every chair and cupboard handle. A sequinned cloth covered the long table, and trays of food filled it: mini quiches, and pineapple and cheese on sticks, and crisps spoiled there; a grotesque 1980s spectacle. Doctors, nurses and other medics milled around in Union Jack party hats, some drinking champagne, some more sedate, all red-faced with celebration. The music soared. I realised something was written on the balloons.

#OneDeathPolicy.

And on others …

#ODP. #WeDidIt. #GoShrivel.

Something banged into the other side of the door. I leapt back with a shriek. Shrivel. Wearing a bow tie, unfastened, around his neck like a black snake, as though he was a singer from the last century on a break between Vegas shows. He put both palms on the glass and grinned at me. I shook my head, backed further away. He opened the door. The music was deafening.

'Come inside and join us, Fern,' he cried, manic.

'I have work to do,' I yelled over the din.

'I know.' He lurched for me. 'This room. Come in! Regale us with your tales while you scrub the floor. Weave a tapestry of lies for us while you pick up the rubbish. It is your success as much as ours.'

'No.' I shoved him roughly off me.

He feigned hurt. 'You reject me. My darling muse. My inspiration.' His eyes widened dramatically as though he'd realised something. 'I know why you're upset, Fern. You think we only care about the One Death Policy.' A black balloon that had come free bobbed by his head and he grabbed it. #WeDidIt. The words sickened me. 'Please don't think for a moment that we're neglecting the Pre-Surgery Care Mortality Policy. That one is just taking a little more time to get off the ground. It lacks the beautiful simplicity of the One Death Policy, you see. Too many words. Not as concise.' He fingers dug into my arm. 'I do wish you'd join us. The film crew from CineTime are here.'

'I don't care.' I pulled free. 'You're insane. This whole thing is insane.'

And I ran, leaving my trolley. His laughter followed me. I looked back, just once, and he was tap dancing in the corridor, balloon in one hand, the other positioned as though it held a delicate teacup.

I was done. I knew I would never go back to the hospital.

I went through the main waiting area on my way out, heart still pounding too fast. It was busy; small children played on the game consoles near the finger scanners; elderly men coughed into the air, to the disgust of those nearby; bandaged limbs were everywhere. One woman cradled her hand in her lap – at least, what was left of it. It was barely a palm. A torn tea towel stemmed the blood flow from the remaining stumps of all four fingers. I caught her eye. I knew her. I recognised her. Could not recall her name. A writer, once upon a time. Of horror, maybe? The irony. Did she recognise me? She did. I saw the light in her eyes.

This should not be happening, she said without words.

No, it shouldn't, I said back without words.

I pedalled home, anxious about how long I had, not even sure where the thought came from. I wasn't late for anything. I had no appointments. I sped past the square, saw the blur of a queue at the ALLBooks doors, not caring what it was for.

It'll be gone on Friday.

This thought stopped me, had me skidding to a halt, causing a car to blast its horn at me. Gone. Burned to the ground. Will I do anything? I don't know. But I should. I *should*. But what? Go there, warn them?

I continued along the high street – now home to more cafes and charity shops than department stores – and that's where I saw him: Fine-Fayre. It was too late to slow down. To stop and talk to him. He was alone, in his chair, wearing a smart grey suit. How different he looked. Handsome almost.

What's your name? I wanted to shout. *Where are you going? What was your novel about? Do you have a wife or husband?*

But I had passed him as soon as I saw him, another aspect of my life flashing past.

When I got home, they were there.

The tall one and the short one.

On the doorstep.

I've written this entry so far without giving away what happened when they came into my house. I wrote it the way I used to write my fiction when I knew full well what I was leading to but needed to keep the reader in the dark. I had to concentrate on writing the events before the two of them arrived in order to get the words down in some sort of coherent way. I didn't minimise my foreshadowing as a shock tactic or for surprise; it wasn't an intentional literary device. In life, we get no warning for tragedy. We might look back, long afterwards, and see the signs. If we're sensitive, we might even see them beforehand. But for most, when tragedy comes, it rips a hole in our world without anaesthetic or warning.

I'm sitting at my desk. They left an hour ago.

I'm shaking.

I dread when they come back and yet now, I want them to.

Monday 3 December 2035 – 4.45 p.m.

I pushed my bike up the garden path and unlocked the front door, ignoring the two of them. Last time, the gloves came off. I called them monsters: the truth. I told them to get out of my house; the tall one said it was theirs. I've been terrified about their return, but now I felt calm. Ready. Defiant. Laura next door was in her garden, cutting some yellow roses from her bush, but she didn't look up.

'Good day at work, Fern?' asked the tall one, following me into the hallway.

Did he know I'd left for good? No. How could he? Even my boss didn't know yet.

I nodded and walked ahead of them into the kitchen. Usually, they led but I felt bold. My notepad was in my rucksack, but if I left it in the hallway with my bike, that would draw attention to it.

Hide something in plain sight, is what they say.

Let them find it, I thought.

I don't know where this new fire came from. It was as though their arrival had flicked a switch in my head and now I was on full power. If they felt this subtle change, they didn't let it show. The tall one took a seat at the kitchen table and the short one followed. I put the kettle on. We began our dance; this time I was the lead.

'I haven't been writing,' I said, answering the questions before he asked them. 'I haven't been reading, aside from a quick flick through *Technological Truth For Tots and Teens*, which I found ridiculous. I haven't been to the government news site. I've been sleeping quite well. Work is fine. Would you both like tea?'

'We would.' The tall one seemed unruffled by my cockiness. 'And thank you for your candour. You've saved me perhaps three minutes there. Time is precious. Tell me, what other questions do I have today?'

The kettle clicked off and I made three teas, no milk, theirs in mugs with sugar, mine in my festive teacup without. I brought them to the table and sat down.

'At some point you're going to say, *you know what happens now,*' I said.

'Ah, not yet.' He sipped his tea. 'You know we like to chat a bit first. See how you are. Catch up.'

'Of course – if by chat you mean that you ask questions and I lie.'

He studied me. 'What if this time I have a question I've never asked you before?'

'That'll be fun,' I said. 'I might even answer it honestly.'

'The blue and white trainer,' he said. 'Where is it?'

'You've asked me about that before.'

'That's not my new question. Where is it, Fern?'

'I don't know,' I lied.

'Not quite as candid now, Fern.'

I didn't respond. I suddenly wondered how much they *really* knew. I tried to work out when I started taking my notepad with me each time I left the house, and therefore how much they hadn't read. I should have worked it out before now. Did they know the ALLBooks fires were going to happen on Friday and not at Christmas? Had I written that only after I'd known they were searching the house in my absence? Should I tell them in case anyone ended up hurt? Or did I actually want those fiction-hating shops destroyed?

'Do you have plans for Friday?' asked the tall one, and I shivered. Could he read my mind? What else was happening on Friday?

And I realised I *did* have plans.

I was going to go to ALLBooks at dawn. I did *not* want the fire to happen. How could I? Books were books. Humans were humans. I should at least *try* to stop the flames. How could I live with myself, knowing it was going to happen and doing nothing?

'Fern?' The tall one was studying me.

'I … I don't have plans for Friday.'

He held my gaze.

'I have a question,' I said.

'OK.'

'What did you mean last time when you said I was the one? When you said I was the one they'd wait the longest for.'

'That's for you to figure out,' he said. 'It's your story.'

'My story?' I frowned.

'Figure of speech,' he said.

'Well, it must mean *something*,' I insisted.

'If it does, you'll find out when the time is right.' Then, after a beat: 'You know what's going to happen now, Fern?'

I nodded. The short one got up and disappeared. I heard him opening drawers and wardrobes. The tall one sipped his tea; neither of us spoke. The short one returned and resumed his seat, without the usual shake of his head. He ignored my rucksack on the table. Something occurred to me then.

They didn't want to 'find' my diary.

It was too curious that they have never once mentioned it when they *must* know it exists; there's no question they would have found it in the early searches without me here. Yet they have never questioned me about it. They want me to keep writing it. That must be it. They're waiting for my full story, whatever that might be.

'Aren't you concerned about your fingers?' asked the tall one.

Now my façade faltered. Now I must have paled. 'No,' I managed to say. 'There's no point. If you've come for them, you'll take them. I can't change it or stop it.'

'We haven't,' he said. 'Not today.'

I was relieved but tried to hide it; tried to breathe slowly. I realised. It was because they wanted me to continue writing. But still, they could have taken the fingers on my left hand.

'Time *is* running out though,' the tall one said.

'That's the case for all of us,' I said. 'Time doesn't run out though. It goes on without us. *We* run out.'

'Do you want to know where Lynda is?' he asked.

'*What*?' I spilt my tea. Was this it? The new question. But it wasn't fun. It wasn't fun at all.

'Do you want to know where Lynda is?' he repeated.

'I do.' I mopped up the tea with my sleeve.

'She's in our newest re-education centre.'

The floor gave way beneath me. I *knew* it. Fuck. 'Is she OK?' I stammered.

'Yes. She is. She's fitting in very well.'

'*Fitting in.*' I thought I might be sick. 'What the hell does that mean?'

'She's … progressing.'

'Where is it?' I demanded.

'This particular one is on a small island off the coast of northern Scotland. It's remote. Beautiful. Perfect. I don't think she'll ever want to come home.'

'Of course she will. She won't want to be with you bastards. She'll want her husband, Tom. He's distraught.' I paused. 'Does he know?'

'He does now, yes. They may let him visit her soon.'

'I want to see her,' I said.

'Very well.' He made a great show of going into the inside pocket of his black jacket, not finding what he was looking for, and going into another, and then another. My heart hammered. Finally, he pulled out a photograph and placed it face down on the table, avoiding the damp patch left by my tea spillage. I snatched it up. Looked at it. I barely recognised the woman whose dead eyes stared out at me. I didn't know the grey-haired female whose face was emaciated, whose mouth was pulled down as though weighted, whose colour was pallid. Her deportment reminded me of those black and white pictures of Auschwitz survivors emerging from the camps in history books.

'What have you *done* to her?' I cried, pressing the image to my chest.

'Just a partial lobotomy,' he said.

'Just a …?' I couldn't finish.

'It's a very simple procedure.'

'*Simple?*'

212

'I'm no surgeon, but I believe it involves surgery on the front-most portion of the cingulate cortex, which is an area associated with creativity. Lynda still has all her main functions, but her emotions, empathy and creativity are now … well, shall we say suppressed. After some recovery time, she'll be able to go home to Tom.'

'Her main functions?' I cried. 'So, she's a … a *robot*?'

'Not at all. She can still enjoy food.'

'You're fucking animals, all of you!' I jumped up, away from the table, away from the picture of a woman who wasn't Lynda. 'This isn't even legal!'

'It is,' he said calmly.

I thought of something else; someone else; two people. 'That's where Shelly is, isn't she?' In that heated moment I couldn't remember if Cass was missing too. Hadn't she surrendered her four fingers? I paced the kitchen floor. 'What about Cass? Where is she?'

He ignored me; he sipped tea.

'If you're going to take me away to one of your re-education centres, just take me now.' I came back to the table, offered myself, palms out. 'I'm ready. I want to see my Lynda.'

'It's not your time,' said the tall one, matter of fact.

'It is. I have nothing left here. Take me.'

Hunter was safe. Fine-Fayre might never be coming back. Bed-time Stories was over. I knew I was never going back to the hospital and had little chance of getting another job with the reference they would likely give me after walking out.

There. Is. Nothing.

'You may think that,' said the tall one. 'But you're wrong – you still have something.' He paused. 'Soon you won't. And then we'll come back.'

'I want to see Lynda,' I cried again.

'Patience,' he said. 'You know about the five stages of grief don't you, Fern?'

'*What?*'

'Patience is required to get to the final stage – acceptance.'

'I'm not grieving.' I swiped my festive teacup off the table, and it smashed against the wall, splattering good tea everywhere. Another part of me broke too. 'I'm fucking raging.'

'The anger should have passed by now,' he said. 'But I guess you still have flashes of it. That's understandable. It's never a precise thing. Some miss out on the anger altogether. I think you might miss out on the depression part, or at least suffer that the least. You'll fight that aspect the hardest. That's next.'

'Let me see Lynda and I'll … I'll …'

'See, you're in the bargaining phase now, with remnants of the anger still flickering.'

'Fuck you.' I kicked the table leg.

He stood, and the short one followed. 'We have to go now, Fern.'

'I'm writing,' I yelled, grabbing his arm. He looked at my hand with mild disgust, before removing it from his sleeve. 'Yes. I'm writing two novels. Thinking about a third. And I've been reading fiction. I've been reading it aloud, singing it, shouting it. I love it. And I've joined a book group.' I almost screamed that I had plans on Friday, that I knew things they didn't, but I bit my tongue.

'We both know that none of this is true.' The tall one spoke like I was a six-year-old whom he was trying to keep calm during a tantrum. 'You're wasting your time and my time. We have our instructions. For now, we leave you.'

'And there are more than five stages of fucking grief.' I followed them into the hallway. 'Those textbook stages are helpful, but they don't tell the whole complex agony of actually living with it.'

'Take care, Fern.' The tall one looked back before they stepped out into the sunlight. 'Next time, maybe we'll take you.'

And he shut the door.

I threw myself at it, sobbing hot tears. I wept until there was nothing left in me. Then, finally, I went back to the kitchen. I couldn't look at the picture of Lynda. It wasn't her. I tore it up and dropped the tiny pieces of what was once my friend in the bin. How could they do that to her? To anyone? To humans? To their glorious brains? To *Lynda's* glorious, unique, creative brain? Why was I even shocked? Was it any worse than the One Death Policy? Than whatever else Shrivel had planned?

What if they did it to me?

Would I even know they had, afterwards, when it was done?

If so, did it even matter?

Yes. How would I write? For now, I am. I can. I must.

I will.

Tuesday 4 December 2035 – 6.06 a.m.

I haven't slept since they left. It's been thirteen hours. I raged for the first half of the night. I tried to switch off but all I could see was Lynda's dead eyes staring out of that photograph. I got up and paced the house, burning up, pushing over chairs as I swept like a tornado through the rooms. The heatwave may have finally abated, but now it's inside me.

In the second half of the night, I wept. The tornado died and the rainfall came. I was cold then. I shivered under my summer duvet but hadn't the energy to find my thick winter one. I remembered my first night in this bed, when I was awake until dawn, shocked, afraid and wondering what the future held for a writer stripped of her career. Then, I clung to hope. Today, I can't get a purchase on it.

Now I'm watching the morning news while writing this. They interviewed Daniel Mills about the One Death Policy earlier but though I saw his mouth moving, I couldn't understand the words, as though he was speaking another language. I've been tornado and rainfall; now I'm fog. After him, there was a report on a new (and apparently safe) drug to help children sleep and then an 'uplifting' story about how the trees we planted ten years ago, during Tree Love Week, are now having a positive effect on the city. There has been no mention of any re-education centres. No mention of lobotomies being performed on decent human beings.

I need more tea.

I'm heartbroken about my festive teacup.

Am I going to see Fine-Fayre one more time before … *before* …?

Oh, a news flash. Not often they break into a programme these days. Must be a local story because it's the regional news now. There's a pile-up on the new motorway just outside the city. My fog dissolves. I can see the crash. The cars. The carnage. Not just on the screen that's showing scenes from far above, shaky, perhaps handheld by someone rather than recorded by a drone; ten cars, maybe more, haphazard, smashed up, flames beginning in some of the ones at the front.

I can *see* it, like a future memory.

I know that one of the cars is old, being driven by a woman whose face I can't see. I don't need to. I know. It's Hunter's mum. And I know he was sleeping in the back, reddish hair that's really 'more blond' stuck to his forehead, a toy robot bouncing gently with the motion of the vehicle, moving dangerously closer to the edge of the seat. I know he's wearing the blue and white trainers, that the shoelaces of the left one have come undone. I know a half-full bottle of chocolate milkshake has spilled some of its contents on the car floor, and I gag. I know his mum's phone started ringing. I knew she answered it, because it was an important call, and lost her concentration for a moment. I know that was when she hit the car in front.

I just screamed.

Like I'm burning too.

Like I'm with him, trapped in a crushed-up, no-hope, hot car.

I should call him. His phone. Check on him. Hunter. *Yes*.

But that's the door. My door. Knocking.

I should go.

Today. It is still today. Now.

I'm in a van. The outside was chrome, wheels like a truck's, big enough to transport frozen meat. Inside, it's cold. Just me. No windows. Not much light. Barely enough to see the page. This will be an unreadable scrawl. But it's all I have. My notepad. My pen. They didn't let me bring anything. Not my shoes or a coat. I need to pee. They didn't even let me go. This seat belt's too tight and won't unclip. I don't know where they're taking me.

Yes, you do.

OK. I do. I just don't know which one.

Yes, you do.

Of course. Yes. I do. Obviously. The one where Lynda is. But it's hundreds of miles away. I could be in here hours. Should I scream? Will they stop?

It was the two of them.

They didn't even come in. They just said they knew about Hunter.

I begged them to check if he was OK. I begged them to go to the scene of the accident. Ring the hospitals. Find out if he made it. But they marched me out of the house. The tall one on one side. The short one on the other. Said I should calm down. Said I was making a scene. I clawed at them, begged to go back in my house and find out about the crash.

They opened the van door and asked where I'd hidden *Technological Amazingness*. I never wrote that down in here. I know this. I remember. I know exactly where my last copy is. I didn't tell them though. Fuck them. We all know they haven't come for me because I still have a copy of my novel. That's what they *want* to say is the reason. I won't give it to them; not the book or the chance to use it as excuse for my detainment. I didn't. Fuck them. That's what I said.

They shoved me in the van. The short one fastened my seat belt.

Now we're moving. It's smooth. Must be on the motorway. My teeth chatter. I need to pee so bad. I wish I had my phone. I wish

I could ring Hunter. My hand is shaking. I can hardly write. But if I don't, what am I left with? If I don't record my thoughts, what is there? I'll have to look at myself then. Inside, at my heart. And I'm scared to.

I have no shoes on.

And Hunter only has one now.

We finished the story. Together. It should have saved him.

I'm cold.

What if he is too now?

Part Four

Depression

Wednesday 5 December 2035 – 6.35 p.m.

I think I've written the correct date. I'm sure I've had one full day here. I know that's the right time because there's a clock on my wall. It's old-fashioned, mustard and black, out of place in this sterile room, and it ticks too loudly and kept me awake most of the night. I'm in a small, square room. It's plain. White walls, glossy, the kind they always have in sci-fi films, so you know things won't end well. There's a narrow bed shoved up against the wall, single pillow and sheet on top. A chrome toilet and sink in another corner. No windows. One door.

I haven't been out of here since we arrived.

It was dark when I was dragged from the van. It wasn't the tall one or the short one, so they can't have joined us for the journey. A well-built lunk of a man handled me like I might fight; I didn't. I'd hidden the notepad in the back of my jeans, which were damp with urine because we hadn't stopped once. I was glad of the lack of light so he couldn't see this. He led me roughly up a path towards a building that looked grey and flat and nondescript. I could hear the sea crashing nearby, but the area was so shadowy I couldn't see it. I longed to. I don't know when I last saw that blue. Salt filled the chill air as we got closer to some double doors. I drank it desperately in; I didn't know when I'd next be outside.

Inside the building was a bland foyer so brightly lit it hurt my eyes. The lunk pressed a buzzer and after a moment a young man with oil-slicked hair and wearing a doctor's jacket emerged through glass doors. He looked at the wet patch on my crotch, and then avoided my eyes. Without a word, the lunk left.

'Come this way,' said the doctor.

'What is this place?' I was exhausted now, weak with hunger. 'Why am I here? Where are you taking me?'

'Please just follow me.' He said it so calmly that I had to wonder if he'd had some sort of lobotomy. 'If you create a fuss, I'll have to call the guards and you'll be taken to the ward. If you behave, you'll go straight to your room.'

I followed him along a white corridor lined with doors, each numbered. I didn't want to find out what the ward was; the word alone sounded sinister. It's about context. Mention a ward in a hospital and it raises no concern; mention one in in a horror film and visceral fear builds.

'Can't you just answer my questions?' I tried to sound composed. I realised what I must look like – dirty feet, no shoes, no coat, wet crotch, unbrushed hair. 'I'm not trying to be unreasonable, I'm just ... I just ... I'm scared.'

He ignored me. Eventually we stopped at a door. Number forty-eight. We hadn't seen another human. The place was deathly quiet; it unnerved me. Was anyone else here? If they were, what kept them silent?

'This is your room,' he said. 'Food will be delivered shortly. Someone will visit you tomorrow and explain the plan.'

'*Plan*?' The word came out as a croak.

He opened the door, and a light came on.

And here I am.

He locked the door after me. I perched on the corner of the bed so I wouldn't dampen where I had to sleep. After a while, a flap opened in the bottom half of the door and a small tray was pushed through.

'Can you tell me who you are?' I called out. 'Where am I? Can I talk to someone?'

But the flap closed as fast as it had opened.

I carried the tray to the bed. On it there were fresh clothes – white linen slacks and a loose white blouse. There was a carton of milk (did they know? They must.) and a pack of sandwiches. There was a toothbrush, toothpaste and some soap. I washed and changed into the clothes – glad to get out of my wet jeans – and then ate the sandwiches and washed them down with handfuls of tap water, ignoring the milk. I put my notepad and pen beneath the pillow. Pointless since there are cameras in opposite corners of the room, but it felt like the right place for it. Then I sat on the bed and waited.

No one came. Nothing else happened. The light went out at midnight. I tried to sleep. The clock ticked. It only emphasised the silence.

Today no one has come. At seven a tray with cold toast and a carton of milk on it came through the door. I couldn't eat it. At noon a tray with more sandwiches and another carton of milk arrived. I didn't eat them. Then, half an hour ago, another with milk and a banana. I haven't eaten that either. I can't. I feel light-headed; I'm not sure if they gave me something while I slept or put drugs in the sandwich last night.

Or is this depression?

Has this confinement opened the door on it; freed it?

It feels like it. Like I left all my emotions in the corridor when I came into this room. I should be angry, screaming my rage, pacing the floor, pounding the door. Have they sedated me? Wouldn't that make me sleep though? Aren't a lack of appetite and insomnia signs of depression? Perhaps it's simply the monotony of being in the same room for almost twenty hours with zero stimulus.

They must be watching me.

Are they waiting to see what I do? They must want me to write or they would have taken this notepad weeks ago. I am. It's hard. My hand feels like it isn't even mine. If words can be slurred on a page, these ones are. I guess they might want to study me. Use me as the reason for why fiction is bad. And yet I don't think that's it. I don't think that's it at all.

Hunter.

I see him. Suddenly. Remember. No: I haven't forgotten. I buried it. I pushed it down to the bottom of my gut. It's too much. The crash on the news. Yesterday. I need to know. Is he OK? It's easier to not think of him. But I can't unsee him now I've looked. He's here. Somehow. In the air. A ghost. And I'm comforted. I remember the end of our story, on the bench, his red rucksack with the dirty straps. I hear him say those final lines.

Hunter's mum can read to him any time.
And that way he'll never be invisible again.
And that's what they did. Together, out loud.
Every day after. And I think that's the end of the story, isn't it?

I'm tired. I think I'll sleep now. It must be the story. When I whisper it aloud, I'm as drowsy as a child after a busy school day. What was our conversation that time, when Hunter realised I was making the story up?

'It's you, isn't it?' he said.

'What is?' I asked.

'*You* did the story.'

'Well, of course,' I said.

'No, I mean you're making it up? Right now. As we go.'

Was I making it up? I don't know anymore. The words are fading now. I must sleep. I hope I don't wake. What is there to wake for? What is there?

Thursday 6 December 2035 – 11.16 a.m.

I slept heavily. I woke when a tray came through the door, screamed at the arm to tell me if Hunter is OK. If it was only one night I slept through, and not longer, then the date above is correct. This is my second day. Is it Thursday? Yes. Friday. Tomorrow. Shouldn't I be doing something tomorrow? Stopping something happening? Still no one. I nibbled the toast on my tray and gagged. Then I washed, cleaned my teeth, and walked back and forth to stretch my legs. How long before a person goes crazy in isolation? I asked myself this aloud. Not a politically correct question with the use of the word crazy. *Crazy Lady.* I heard the words as though whispered behind me and turned with a gasp. Hunter? No one there. Of course not. Don't prisoners forced into isolation start hallucinating after a while? If I focus hard on writing this and take my time scribing each letter carefully, it fills the time. If I pause to think between the lines, it fills the time. But thinking is dangerous. Is that what they want me to do? I won't. I get up and walk about between sentences. I look at the clock. The uneaten food on the trays in the corner is beginning to smell. How long before milk goes off? That would be torture. I'd go crazy trapped in here with sour milk. I've opened the cartons and poured it away. Then I swilled the sink until it was clean. Do I sound crazy? Already? Am I ranting? If I do start screaming, will they come then? I want to scream Hunter's name, but what's the point?

Thursday 6 December 2035 – 1.32 p.m.

They came. I didn't have to scream. I'm back now and I don't know if I feel better or worse. They let me out; *he* let me out. The young doctor with oily hair. He came just before noon and said I could eat with the other residents. I thought it was an interesting word. Not patients or prisoners but residents. Like this is a place people happily choose to live. I followed him along the door-lined corridor; it felt like weeks since I'd last walked down it.

'Can't you at least tell me your name?' I asked.

'Dr Cartwright,' he said, briskly.

'You said someone would come and see me, but they haven't.'

He didn't respond. We rounded corner after corner, onto the same stark corridor. Is this building just an endless maze of doors and rooms? I couldn't figure out its shape from our walk. Perhaps it was designed to confuse. Perhaps it's so that if we ever leave, we can't describe it beyond saying white and repetitive.

Eventually we stopped at some double doors. Dr Cartwright put his palm against a scanner, and they swung open onto a large canteen where dozens of people wearing the same white slacks and blouse as mine were getting settled at rows of long tables. The noise was sudden and shocking, even though it was just chairs scraping bare floor. The room must have been soundproofed because there had been no warning as we approached. I wondered if all the rooms were, and that's why the place is so quiet?

What don't they want us to hear?

'Your seat is here.' Dr Cartwright led me to the end of one of the tables. They were set with plastic cutlery and plastic beakers of water. I sat in the empty chair he pulled out. The woman next to me didn't look my way. Her hair was pulled back in a tight bun, she was perhaps mid-twenties, and she stared at the table. The woman opposite was older and did the same; she seemed fascinated by the space between her knife and fork.

I turned to Dr Cartwright, but he had gone.

I looked around. There were no windows. The walls were, once again, white. The fluorescent lighting only made the scene harsher. Stony-faced men – perhaps ten or twelve – were dressed in black shirts and trousers and stood guard; their wide-legged stance and the batons at their side made it clear that guarding was their role. I wouldn't have argued with them.

A rapid clacking sound made me jump; a hatch in one of the walls went up to reveal what looked like old-fashioned school dinner ladies with trays of steaming food.

'Table one,' barked a guard, and the people at the table nearest the hatch got up.

I'm struggling to find words that describe their movements. Sloth-like. Slow. Without heart. A row of soulless apparitions queuing for a meal they didn't care about or want, only doing so because the alternative probably had consequences. I didn't know what they might be. Not then. No one spoke. Were they drugged? Was it the lethargy of this utilitarian place? Or worse? The procedure they had performed on Lynda? I watched the scene the way you do a horror film. I covered my eyes and peeked out between my fingers.

Then I realised.

Fingers.

I looked at their hands. Many had missing digits. They had to pick up a platter for the food and one woman – tall, willowy, probably graceful once upon a time, in another life – had only a thumb on each hand. She secured the receptacle between her palms. I realised these platters had a device attached that clamped onto the wrist. Those with fewer than two fingers let another, fuller-fingered resident attach the platter for them. They were then able to collect their food and take it back to the table. I wondered what the point of knives and forks was. The people at table one with fewer than two fingers put their faces into their food to eat it. Like dogs. I could not take my eyes off them.

'Table two,' barked a guard, and the next lot went up.

What was mine? Table seven if we were going by position. No resident had spoken to anyone else. I wondered what would happen if I did. One of the guards eyed me as though he could see my thoughts. I kept quiet. When I looked around, I tried hard to be inconspicuous. I noticed that there were far fewer men than women. Is it because women break the rules more often? Because they get caught? Or is the current government angrier at the women who once expressed their opinions via fiction?

'Table three,' barked a guard, and the next lot went up.

And then I saw her.

Lynda. *My* Lynda. Leaving table three; one of the soulless apparitions heading for the hatch. I stood. It was a reflex. My plastic knife clattered to the floor.

'Take your seat.' The guard nearest my table approached, his voice low but firm.

'But I know her,' I said. 'She's my friend. Can I ju—'

I didn't even finish my sentence. He hit me in the back with his baton, a movement so swift I wondered if he'd taken amphetamine. Pain fired hot up my spine. I bit my lip to stop myself screaming. No one has ever hit me like that. I wanted to cry, the way you do when you're five and you fall over. I felt humiliated and indignant. How dare he? Despite my fury, I resumed my seat. No one even looked.

Lynda had reached the hatch. She looked so thin. I couldn't see her face. I wanted to. I wanted to try to catch her eye, but I was afraid. She still had fingers on one hand so picked up her platter without a problem. When she returned to her table, I willed her to look over at me, but she sat with her back to me once more.

At least I know she's here. Still alive. There is hope. As soon as someone comes to see me – they have to at some point – then I'll ask if I can speak to her. Surely I have the right to a lawyer if I'm being held here against my will? I'll ask that too.

Suddenly it was my table's turn to go up. I tried to blend in, to be nondescript. Like the one living human in a zombie movie, I had to pretend to be dead so I didn't stand out. I helped a resident without fingers attach a tray to her hand. One of the dinner ladies ladled food that looked like stew into my tray. She wouldn't look at me. Did she know I was one of the still human ones? That I might be difficult?

I tried to eat. The stew was bland. The room was so quiet I wanted to scream. The guard nearby, baton at hand, kept me silent. Halfway through the meal, a high-pitched shriek had me choking on my mouthful. No one else reacted. A man with fire-red hair stumbled out of his chair and staggered towards one of the guards. Two of them were upon him, with the speed of predatory tigers pouncing on their long-watched prey. The man was removed from the room before he could make another sound. I don't know what happened to him on the other side of the doors, but I knew I wouldn't stand up or speak in here again.

When the meal was over, our table numbers were called one by one, and we had to file out of the canteen as a group. We were met by another doctor and instructed to follow him. The people at my table were clearly housed on my corridor. We were each deposited in our rooms along the way, no conversation, no fuss. The pain in my back meant I couldn't walk fully upright.

'Just tell them,' whispered a voice.

Was I imagining things again? I glanced behind me. It was the young woman who'd been sitting next to me at the table, her hair pulled back in a tight bun.

'Talk about it,' she said softly.

'About what?' I asked. The fire? Tomorrow? At ALLBooks? Or did she mean about my writing? *Hunter*? But how could she know about all that? There was so much I could express but I didn't dare.

'No communicating,' called the doctor, without turning around.

'If you tell them,' she whispered, 'you won't stay here long.'

Was she pretending to be like the others? Was she trying to blend in like I was? I wanted to ask her again what I was supposed to talk about, but we arrived at my door. The doctor opened it without a word, and I went inside.

And here I am. I feel better for having left these confines, even just for an hour, but worse for having seen what's out there. What have they *done* to these people? It surely can't all be partial lobotomies? Why? What are they trying to achieve? I need to speak to Lynda. To see if *she* is still there, inside that strange, soulless shell. The her I know and love.

I want to cry, just to feel something, but I'm dry. I want to scream, just to cause a commotion, but I'm listless. I want to continue writing, just to exist, but I'm sleepy.

Just tell them.

Talk about it.

You won't stay long here.

What did the woman mean? How does she know anything about me? Was she at Bedtime Stories? Does she know about the arson plan?

Does she know about Hunter?

Thursday 6 December 2035 – 6.47 p.m.

I just woke up and opened my notepad. There are four pages of words, all violently scribbled out. I can't read a single sentence. I don't remember writing them. I *didn't* write them. How could I? I was asleep. Did someone else come in and do it? Or did I sleepwalk? Did I sit up while unconscious, record some strange dreamland story, and then decide my waking self shouldn't see it?

I wish someone would come and see me. Forty-eight hours here now and it feels like a month. If they're monitoring me, what is it they want from me? Is there something I'm not doing that I should?

Wait. *They'll* know what I scribbled on these pages, if I did it. They would have seen. The cameras. They could have zoomed in. Read every word.

It's you, isn't it?

Who said that? Hunter?

You did the story.

They're his words. Am I hallucinating?

No, I mean you're making it up? Right now. As we go.

What the hell? This room is driving me crazy.

Crazy Lady.

Shush.

They need to come and tell me what I wrote on those pages. I just waved at one of the cameras. Pointed to my notepad. Showed them the crossed-out pages. I mimed, come and see me. Tell me. Otherwise, I think I might start screaming and never stop.

Thursday 6 December 2035 – 11.08 p.m.

They came for me. Ten minutes after I waved at the camera. The two of them. The tall one and the short one. It feels odd to say that I was happy to see them. That's how awful this place is. I was glad to see someone from my old life; a life that wasn't even a life but an existence. Yet even that was more than what this place is. I didn't know why they were here, so far from their 'patch'. Then I realised that I don't even know how big their patch is – how far they travel. But they were here. For now.

For me.

'I hope you're going to answer my questions,' I said, following them along endless, door-lined corridors, my back still aching from the blow to my spine yesterday.

It was seven-thirty. I hadn't eaten the sandwich that was waiting for me when I woke from my nap, and I felt light-headed. We went the opposite way to when I was taken to the canteen.

'You have all the answers, Fern,' said the tall one.

'How?' I cried, frustrated. 'I don't know anything.'

He ignored me

'This can't be allowed … bringing me here, against my will. I'd like to speak to someone outside this facility. It's my right.'

He ignored me.

We reached a large, single door. The short one put his palm to a scanner and it opened on to an office, white like all the other rooms, containing a thick Formica desk, four matching chairs, nothing on the walls. There was a window; large, seductive. I went straight to it, desperate to see outside. The sea. Oh, the sea. Choppy, endless, blue where the sun touched the waves, grey where it didn't. I could almost smell it. I put my hands on the thick glass, my forehead to the cool surface.

'Take a seat, Fern.'

I turned. The tall one and the short one had taken theirs. I sat opposite. The desk had nothing on it and was polished to a shine.

I thought of the one I'd cleaned so many times at the hospital. A lifetime ago. I wondered: Has Shrivel noticed my absence? Does he miss me? It's only three days since I was there, witnessing their crass party.

'Why do you think you're here, Fern?' asked the tall one, interrupting my thoughts.

'I don't know.' It was an easy answer; a sort of lie. 'Bedtime Stories,' I ventured.

'You know full well that we've known about that for a while. We let you continue going. Why would we suddenly bring you here now?'

'My diary?' I tried.

'We've known about that since you started it,' he said.

'Because I've hidden *Technological Amazingness* and won't tell you where it is?'

He shook his head. With the sea behind him, he looked quite magnificent. I still could not have aged him, with his smooth face, calm manner. Had I grown fond of him? Was it Stockholm Syndrome? Perhaps.

'Is it because of ...?' I started.

'Yes?'

Should I tell them about the ALLBooks fire? No. *No.* It was all I had. If I get out of here, I could still go tomorrow, still stop it. But did they already know? Was this really such precious information? Could I be sure they hadn't read my diary in the last week? Hadn't I had it with me at all times since then? I couldn't think straight.

Silence.

'You said you had questions, Fern,' said the tall one eventually.

'Before you came for me,' I stammered, my heart racing now that I had to think about it again. 'There was a car pile-up on the news ... I think I know someone ... a boy ...'

'Hunter?' said the tall one. 'You mentioned him.' Of course. They said they knew about him when they brought me here. I'd begged them to find out about the crash, hadn't I?

'Did you find out if he was OK?' I felt sick.

'You know more than us.'

'I don't,' I cried. 'How can I? I'm stuck here. I have no phone, or I'd ring him. I have no access to the news.'

'I think you know.'

'I don't. *Tell me*. It's cruel. You're playing some sort of game. You're torturing me.'

'You're torturing yourself,' he said.

'What the fuck? It's you. Not me.' I realised there were tears on my cheeks.

'You had another question.'

'Did I?' I was too upset to think straight.

'Why did we come to your room just now?'

I remembered. The diary. The scribbled-out pages.

'What do you think is on those pages, Fern?' He must have seen in my face that I'd realised this was my other question.

'I don't know. I think I wrote it in my sleep. But you must have it on video. The cameras must have recorded it.'

'They did.' He paused. 'Do you want to see?'

'No.' The word came before I even knew it was there. Suddenly the idea of seeing the prose beneath that black filled me with abject dread.

'No?'

I shook my head vigorously.

'Your stay in this place could be very brief,' said the tall one, gently. 'You just need to *tell* us. Talk to us. And you can leave. You'll go ... well, you'll go home.'

'Home like my own, beloved home, or home the crappy place you gave me?'

'Perhaps the home where you'd like to go.'

'I don't understand.' I put my head in my hands. 'None of this makes sense. If I talk to you, you can just turn back the clock, undo all that's happened, and I can have my house on the river back? I can write. I can be Fern Dostoy again. Is that what you're saying?'

'You're in charge of your own release. You're here because of you.' He paused, said more carefully, 'You're depressed.'

'Am I?"

'Yes. That's expected. After everything this last year. That's why you need to talk.'

'You keep saying that. A woman from the canteen said that.' I banged my fist on the table. 'But I don't know what I have to talk about.' Could it really be as simple as telling them about the ALLBooks fire? But that was all I had, if I had it at all. It just didn't feel … *right*. Like that was it.

'I think we're done then.' The tall one stood.

'No,' I cried. 'I don't want to go back to that room.'

The short one stood too. They both approached me.

'Don't make a scene,' said the tall one. 'It won't end well for you.'

'I still have questions,' I cried. 'What the hell did they do to the people in here? What did the doctor mean when he said someone would come and explain my plan to me? What *is* my plan? No one has told me anything.'

'Come with us, Fern.' The tall one led me by the arm out of the office. 'If you fight, I'll have to call the guards. You don't want that. You know what they can do.' He paused. 'And they might take you to the ward.'

'The ward?' I went cold. I let myself be taken down the corridor, too afraid to cause a summoning of those cruel guards. 'What do they do on the ward?' I whispered. 'Is that where they operated on Lynda? Can I see her? *Please*?'

The tall one ignored me now.

When we got to my door, he opened it.

I looked into the white, windowless room.

Then I went in, and they closed the door.

Friday 7 December 2035 – 7.01 a.m.

I had three dreams. In one, I kissed Fine-Fayre. I knelt before him and put my mouth to his. In another, I stood in front of the framed picture of Van Gogh's sunflowers in my mother's hallway. *If you saw the real thing, the colours would jump off the canvas at you.* Then the light died. The colours washed away. In another, Hunter was lying on a bed drawing with a variety of yellow pens, each shade slightly different, so the sunflowers he created were the most vibrant I'd ever seen. He looked over his shoulder at me.

'I'm not a dream,' he said.

I woke with those words still in the air around me.

Friday 7 December 2035 – 2.46 p.m.

Just after one, my door opened. It was Dr Cartwright.

'Come with me,' he said.

I did. I knew not to create a fuss. He could call the guards. I knew what they were capable of. I was conforming already. How long before I became one of the soulless creatures in the canteen? Is this depression or is it my reaction to being isolated here?

We reached some double doors.

'You're allowed some fresh air,' said the doctor.

I wanted to clap my hands for joy.

He put a palm to the scanner and the doors opened on to a dull grey square of concrete surrounded by a high wall in the same shade. But there was sky; brilliant blue and cloud free. And there were people. They wore the usual white uniform; it reflected the wall-grey more than the sky hues. Dead humans, wandering in repeated circles, not looking up or connecting with anyone else. Then I saw the guards – perhaps twelve – their stance saying *we won't take your crap*.

'Half an hour,' said Dr Cartwright. 'And then …' He seemed to change his mind.

'And then what?' I asked.

He shook his head.

'*What?*'

'I think they're going to take you to the ward.' He closed the doors.

I banged on them. 'Come back!' I cried. 'I'll tell you.' My knowledge of the arson plan was no bargaining tool now though. It would have already happened, hours ago, this morning. I wondered if they had succeeded, if the building I'd passed so many times was now embers and ash. 'I'll talk, but it's too late, they'll have do—'

Pain then. In my back. Just above my previous injury. I folded in on myself. One of the guards. 'Are you going to be quiet now?' he asked.

I nodded, afraid even to say an affirmative.

239

He moved away. I got up, gingerly, wincing at the new fire in my spine. For a moment, I couldn't even move. I leaned against the grey wall by the doors.

'Start walking.' The guard came back towards me.

I assumed the lethargic pace of the other residents, meandering back and forth across the square. I passed face after face, all devoid of expression, none catching my eye, Lowry's matchstick men and women, off the canvas, in this facility. And then I saw Lynda. I gasped. Swallowed the reaction down. She passed me. I longed to reach out and touch her. To rouse some response. But she was gone.

I looked up at the sky.

Was anyone else looking up at it too, out in the real world, at that exact moment?

Was Hunter?

Or was that where he was now?

No. *No.* I collapsed to my knees. The ground was gritty through my slacks. The pain in my back when the baton hit earlier was nothing like the pain when I imagined Hunter had … *say it.* When I imagined Hunter had… *say it.* I can't. I can't. *I can't.*

'Stand up.' One of the guards.

'I can't,' I sobbed. What was happening to me?

'Stand up,' he repeated.

The living-dead stick-humans continued their walk without looking my way.

'I'm …' I didn't know what I was. I hurt. Not where the guard had attacked me, but in my limbs, in my heart, in my head, in my throat. A heavy blackness descended on me, sliding into every orifice, slick and sickly. My body shut down. I could not stand. I could not move. I could not speak.

Two guards lifted me, roughly, and carried me to the doors.

I was as limp as a shopping bag between them.

I couldn't get my breath.

Dr Cartwright arrived and asked them to take me to Room Forty-eight. The journey is a blur. They must have put me on my bed because I came around, alone, in my room, just half an hour ago. I went straight to my notepad to see if I'd done any more dream writing and was relieved that my last entry was this morning's. Now I can't stop shaking. It's taking an age to record these details. What was my breakdown about? It was terrifying. I had to shut my mind to deal with it.

If I start crying – properly, barriers down – I'll never stop.

This could be the perfect place to do that.

Is that what they want?

No.

They want me to talk.

About the fire? Too late. It's done.

Not the fire. Other words.

But those are stuck in my throat with the tears.

What words?

Fern. You. Know. What. Words.

Look at the words under the scribble.

Hunter? *Hunter.*

Friday 7 December 2035 – 5.32 p.m.

They came for me a few hours later. The tall one and the short one. They must have been watching me on the cameras, seen me stop writing and curl up in a ball on the cold floor of my room. When they opened the door, I stood up, knowing my hair must be wild, my clothes creased, my cheeks flushed.

'Please don't take me to the ward,' I begged.

They ignored me.

I knew that this was it. Not just the ward but the last time. Our final chat. How did I know? Is this awareness a gift from this future me, writing this entry, after the moment? No. Something in the air had altered, like the atoms and particles had shifted position, and made room for what I must look at.

'Bring your notepad, Fern,' said the tall one.

'*What*?' I looked back at the pillow where it was hidden. What a ridiculous word; hidden. It never had been. Not really. Despite knowing that they had likely read most of it, I felt … protective. Like all my secrets were in there, hidden (proper use of the word) between the lines. It was all I had.

'No,' I said.

'If you don't bring it, we will.'

'I don't want to look at the scribble under those words. Not yet. Pease don't make me.'

'Fern, I'm only going to ask one more time.'

I got it and they took me to their office, ignoring me the whole way. The sea beyond the window was calm. Gulls settled on the water like there was nothing to fear. I couldn't look at the sky. I couldn't think about the sky and who was or wasn't looking at it. I turned; the two of them had taken their seats. I took mine.

'They're going to take you for surgery,' said the tall one, matter of fact.

'Is that the … the *ward*?'

The tall one nodded.

I thought I might be sick. 'What kind of …?'

'You *know* what kind of surgery, Fern.' He sighed like he was losing patience already. 'Is that really what you want?'

'Of course not,' I cried. 'Are you *insane*?'

'It doesn't have to happen,' he said. 'There's something you can tell us before it's necessary.'

'Was it necessary for those other souls?' I asked. 'For Lynda, and those poor people they clearly did it to. Why did they do it? It can't just be to remove their creativity. It's about control, isn't it? Punishment.'

'You've been in that room so you had time to look at yourself.' He was ignoring my questions again. The short one hadn't moved. He seemed to stare at me without blinking. 'We hoped you would come to your senses. This can all end if you just talk to us.'

'*Talk* to you? What am I doing now? Exactly that. What else do you want to know? You've read my notepad.'

'You didn't write everything in the diary,' said the tall one.

'I did. It's all in there. My whole life. I poured my heart out. How can you say that?' Even as I said the words, I began to feel like I was reading a script that had been given to me. I started to doubt myself. I *have*. I've written every important thing, as it happened.

Haven't I?

'I know you're afraid, Fern,' he said, so gently that I welled up. I'd never heard him speak that way. I couldn't cope with the response it evoked in me, the overwhelming sadness. 'But you've dealt with the other stages so well.'

'Other stages?'

'The denial. Then the anger. That was the longest stage for you, I know. Your anger was fire. Really, there was a fine line between that and the bargaining; they overlapped. And now, the depression. I know this is the hardest part. But you're so close.'

'To what?'

'Acceptance.'

'Of what?'

'Talk about it, Fern. Look at it. And all of this can end.'

'I thought it was about the fire … ALLBooks. I thought that was what you wanted from me, but I wasn't going to give you that. And now it's too late. I can't stop it happening.' I paused. '*Did* it happen? Did they burn them down?'

'None of it happened,' said the tall one.

'Oh, thank God,' I cried.

'*None* of it happened,' he repeated, holding my gaze.

What did he mean?

'Now talk to me, Fern, and this will all end.'

I frowned. 'What will end?'

'This place for a start.' He looked around the room.

'But how is that my responsibility? Why is it all on me? I didn't ask for any of this. I'm not the only one who wrote fiction.'

'No, but you are the only one writing *this* fiction.'

'*What* fiction?' I cried.

'Speak to us, Fern.' It was the short one. His voice was like melted chocolate. I was speechless. He had never said a word in years. His smooth tenor made me feel like I was sinking into a feather mattress. I felt I could tell him things I didn't even know yet. 'We're here to listen. Unburden yourself. Finally. It will all go away. This place. The fiction ban. The books being over. The sleepless children. I know that what you've lost is worse than all of those things, and you're afraid, but carrying it around all this time without facing it will destroy you in the end.'

I think the walls moved then. I heard a scraping sound. I'm sure the one to the right moved closer, maybe the one on the left too. Would they crumble? What would I see? The boundary between fiction and truth disintegrate?

Truth. Fiction.

Did I know the difference?

I glanced at the two men; they were looking at me.

'Let's go through your diary,' said the tall one. I didn't like him anymore. I wanted the short one to talk now.

'Why do you keep saying it like that?'

'Like what, Fern?'

'Like … I don't know. Like you don't believe it's a diary.'

'But it isn't, is it?'

'I don't want to look at the scribbled-out words,' I cried. The sandwich I'd nibbled at lunch threatened to rise and be released across the perfect white Formica.

'Please pass me the notepad.' The tall one held out his hand.

It had never left me. It had been my companion for over a month. I didn't want to part with it. I was terrified to look at my hidden words, but even more than that, I realised it was the visible sentences that I refused to analyse. I've rarely looked back while writing it. Now they wanted me to.

'Fern?'

I gave it to him. He flicked through it. The crinkled pages made a sound like pattering rain. I remembered using the notepad, so Hunter believed I was reading from an actual book.

It's you, isn't it? You did the story.

Hunter? I looked behind me.

'Who do you think is here, Fern?' asked the tall one.

I didn't answer. I could smell Hunter. It was agony.

'Look at this part,' said the tall one, stopping about a quarter into the notepad. 'You dreamt about Hunter before you even met him. Does that sound real to you?'

'It *is* real,' I said. 'It happened.'

He flicked through more pages.

'Bedtime Stories is interesting – that you banned fiction so that you could find a way to be the one who told the story to Hunter.'

'I didn't ban fiction.' I was tired now. Exhausted. '*You* did.'

He ignored me.

'Look at how you well you knew Hunter. Look at how you felt about him.'

'We had a connection,' I said.

'The blue trainer bothered you so much, didn't it?'

'I want to go back to my room,' I said, voice tiny.

Did the walls just close in a little more? If they crumbled, would I step over the rubble into … what? The truth?

'You empathised with Hunter's mum, didn't you? When she didn't have time. When work kept her busy. When she couldn't tell him bedtime stories. You knew she loved him with all her heart, didn't you?'

'Let. Me. Go.'

'That's down to you,' said the tall one.

'Fern.' It was the short one again. I felt better. Safer. I might have even smiled. 'The grief you're feeling is so huge, so unbearable, that you wrote an entire novel to deal with it. You're a writer, Fern. You hid inside your own words. You hid inside this notepad. It's time now to look at the real story though. You haven't written the end yet. You need to. And then you can write the truth.'

'But this *is* true.' Even I didn't believe it now. A brick fell from the left wall and smashed. Then another. And another.

'What was the very first sentence you wrote, Fern?' The tall one again.

'You know what it was.'

'Tell me though.'

I braced myself. 'If you tell a story well enough, it's true.'

'Well?' he asked. 'What does that mean, do you think?'

I was crying now. Quietly. Another brick fell.

'Who are you really?' asked the tall one.

'Fern Dostoy.'

'No.'

'*Yes.*'

'End this story, and then you can look at the truth.'

I couldn't speak. My tears got in the way. I had to look now. Hadn't I written all these words so I *could*?

'Do you want to see beneath your scribble?' asked the short one.

Finally, I nodded. He took a tiny smart device from his inside pocket and opened a video file. It was dark at first. Then the lights flicked on. I saw myself, in my room, sleeping. After a moment, I sat up and reached for the notepad. Staring ahead, I began writing. Faster and faster, I scribed, filling four pages, my face dark with pain. Once done, I looked at it. I threw the notepad across the room. Then I got it and began scribbling out every sentence.

'I can't see what I wrote,' I said softly.

Did I want to?

It was time.

The short one opened a picture. It was a close-up of one of the pages as I was writing. The same sentence, over and over and over, each time ripping the paper more, each time darker as though the ink began to flow more freely.

'It's the same on all four pages,' said the short one.

'What does it say, Fern?' asked the tall one.

I thought if I spoke, my words would come out like bullets: uncontrolled, irregular, deadly, flying wildly around the room, never to be undone. I would have to face the carnage. The aftermath.

'What does it say?'

'It says …'

'Yes?'

'I didn't have time to read him bedtime stories, and I'm sorry.'

The words came out carefully; the hastily swallowed meal that wouldn't stay put, that had blocked me all this time, that I'd dreaded vomiting, came up more easily than I expected. But now, the clean-up.

'Who were you talking about?' asked the tall one.

I shook my head.

'Who, Fern?'

Still, I couldn't.

'We'll keep this notepad now. You can have a new one. Write the real story.'

'I won't be able to.'

'You will. You have to now. Acceptance. You're getting there.'

'It will kill me,' I whimpered.

'It won't,' said the short one.

'I'm a terrible … *terrible* person.'

'You're not.'

'He must hate me.' My sobs were ugly, rasping things. 'He'll never forgive me. He doesn't love me now.'

'Who?'

I inhaled. 'Hunter.'

The tall one nodded. 'And who is Hunter, Fern?'

I said just two words. Each one tore another strip out of me. Each one was a severed finger. A forced lobotomy. A banned story. A forced isolation. A made-up future to deny the past. Sour milk. A lost shoe. A found shoe.

'My son,' I said.

He was here. I turned round. It was him. In the rubble, bricks scattered around his feet like discarded Lego. Real. Here. Alive again. Chocolate milk around his mouth. Chunky, but you know, in a good way, like he'll be a strapping lad when he grows up. Reddish-blond hair, though I know he tells everyone it's more blond. Blue eyes. Not tall yet, but who knows, one day?

'Crazy Lady,' he said. '*Mum*.'

And I collapsed.

Part Five

Acceptance

Psychiatric Evaluation Report – Fern Dalrymple (DOB – 01/12/66)

DATE OF CONSULTATION: 09/09/2020
REFERRING PHYSICIAN: Dr Patrukal, GP
REASON FOR CONSULTATION: Psychiatric evaluation for follow-up.

BACKGROUND DATA: The patient is a fifty-three-year-old female who was admitted to this facility by Dr Patrukal after weeks of insomnia, severe anxiety, extreme depression, an inability to eat, physical pain, and repeated suicide attempts, the final of which she was rescued from by a neighbour. At this time, the patient is being considered for a Section 2 – she is resistant to being detained in the hospital, but the crisis team hope to persuade her and not enforce it. The patient is a bestselling author. She has lived alone since the sudden death of her only son Hunter (aged eight) five weeks ago. The boy's father died before he was born. Prior to this tragedy, the patient was in good health and had never visited her surgery for anything other than her routine smear tests. The patient is taking Sertraline (50mg daily), Zopiclone (3.75mg), and Propranolol (10mg, three times daily). This will be assessed. For further information, please refer to the record and psychiatric assessment from the outside facility.

PSYCHIATRIC INTERVIEW: The patient was generally co-operative in the interview. She spoke with some degree of slurred speech. She stated that she does not need help. When asked about the most recent suicide attempt (by taking large quantities of her Propranolol) she said she 'just wants to be dead'. She admitted that she will try again 'to die'. She talked a lot about guilt. But when I brought her son up, she refused to speak or look at me. The patient stated that, at this point, she does not want to leave her home and stay on a 'crazy ward'. She admitted to a lack of appetite and major sleep disturbance. She denied any substance abuse, of which there is no evidence, and denied any depression, which it is clear she is suffering from. She denied having hallucinations or any homicidal ideation. The patient was advised that a Section 2 will be raised if she does not agree to stay here. She eventually agreed.

PAST PSYCHIATRIC HISTORY: None.
ALLERGIES: None.
PHYSICAL EXAMINATION: Blood pressure 100/60, heart rate 80BPM, and temperature 37C.
PERSONAL AND SOCIAL HISTORY: The patient was born in East Yorkshire and lives in South Cave. She grew up in the Hull area. There is one brother who lives in Canada. He could not, however, come to the UK and support the patient due to the ongoing travel restrictions. There is no known family psychiatric history. Some history of addiction (paternal family).

DIAGNOSES:
Complicated Grief Disorder.
Anxiety.
Acute Insomnia.
Depression.
Suicidal Tendencies.

RECOMMENDATIONS: At this point, the patient is cooperative in being referred to River View, length of stay to be assessed. Social workers will work closely with us. The patient will benefit from ongoing psychotherapy, Cognitive Behavioural Therapy (CBT) and grief counselling, and at this time, she should remain on her current medication.

SIGNED BY – *Dr Shrivel*

From Dr Shrivel's Private Notes

Fern Dalrymple's method of dealing with extreme grief has been like nothing I've experienced in many years of helping patients through trauma.

She was provided with a large notepad on the second day of her stay here by Susan Price (Crisis Team) who supports the idea of writing through pain. Writing therapy is a form of expressive therapy that uses the act of processing the written word for re-habilitation, analysis and healing. This practice also aids self-awareness and self-development. It was hoped that Fern might share on the pages what she could not face or talk about with myself or the other counsellors. Usually, the process is monitored.

Susan Price suggested she set Fern writing assignments (such as an unsent letter to her dead son, free writing for five minutes, a dialogue with God) and that Fern would then share each day what she had written, and together they would discuss it further. Fern refused. Her unspoken wishes were respected. It was then noted that, privately, she wrote fervently, alone in her room, for many hours into the night and took the book with her everywhere she went, seemingly afraid it might be read.

For the first three weeks of her stay at River View, Fern did not speak during our sessions. Though she did all that was expected/requested of her with regards to treatment (she attended all of her CBT, grief counselling, group therapy and art workshops) she remained mute there too. She did not interact with any of the patients. Her main visitors have been her three friends (Lynda, Shelly and Cass) but even with them it was observed that Fern simply sat with them, from a safe social distance, though she did listen when they talked. These women are also authors and we have asked them to encourage Fern in her writing therapy, which they have been doing.

It now seems that what Fern could not say to me during our many silent sessions, she channelled (via her many nights of intense work) into creating what I can only describe as an epic work of fiction. On the twenty-second day of her stay we had a major breakthrough in the session. She began responding to some of my questions. Then, at the end of our hour, she finally handed the notepad to me.

Transcript of Session – Fern Dalrymple – 01/10/2020 –
22 days into her stay

Dr Shrivel: How are you feeling today, Fern?

Fern: (silence)

Dr Shrivel: Susan tells me you're sleeping a little better this last week. I imagine that's a relief.

Fern: (silence)

Dr Shrivel: Is there anything you need today? Is there anything you would like to talk about?

Fern: I guess … uh … I'm a … story.

Dr Shrivel: Oh (pause). You're a story. Can you tell me a little more about what you mean by that?

Fern: You said on our first day in here that you're … recording these sessions. Someone will … you know … listen perhaps. One day. I'll be a story. To them.

Dr Shrivel: I suppose that's true. Stories, um, yes. I understand you're a writer. What kind of books do you write?

Fern: I never… (emotional) …should have.

Dr Shrivel: Can you tell me what you mean by that, Fern?

Fern: (silence)

Dr Shrivel: Why do you think you never should have?

Fern: (silence)

Dr Shrivel: You've been writing while you've been here. Would you like to tell me about that?

Fern: (silence)

Dr Shrivel: How are you feeling about being at River View in general? What have you got out of your stay here?

Fern: I'd like to … go home.

Dr Shrivel: You will, Fern. But do you think you're ready yet?

Fern: (silence)

Dr Shrivel: You've been suffering from extreme anxiety. Susan tells me you get particularly anxious at mealtimes. Is there a trigger then?

Fern: (silence)

Dr Shrivel: Would it be fair to say that you have an issue with milk? Do you want to talk about that?

Fern: (silence)

Dr Shrivel: Anxiety is an interesting experience. It has a huge physiologic component, in that anyone can experience it at any time. Yours, I believe, is due to acute grief. Can you take a moment, right now, to be aware of the anxiety you feel … to think about it … and describe to me where it starts in your body?

Fern: In my … um … my heart.

Dr Shrivel: And how does it manifest?

Fern: (silence)

Dr Shrivel: Shall we talk about your general life – and maybe your books? They were very successful. What were they about?

Fern: Why don't you just … go … and … maybe read … them yourself?

Dr Shrivel: I've ordered them both. I'm very interested. You had two bestsellers – *The Dark Room* and *A Sort of Homecoming*. Writing must have been a huge part of your life.

Fern: (silence)

Dr Shrivel: And you've been writing now, here. It must have been some comfort, doing a thing that you enjoy. Has it been helpful?

Fern: (silence)

Dr Shrivel: Would you like to talk about what you wrote in your notepad?

Fern: (silence)

Dr Shrivel: Do you want to talk about Hunter?

Fern: (silence)

Dr Shrivel: I understand you haven't spoken about him to anyone.

Fern: (silence)

Dr Shrivel: (gently) Would it be fair of me to say that you find it impossible?

Fern: (silence)

Dr Shrivel: Denial of a traumatic event is a natural response. A self-protective mechanism. Being in denial gives your mind the opportunity to absorb distressing information at a pace that won't send you into shock. It can take weeks or months to come to grips with the … with the … *tragedy*.

Fern: (angry) I know about denial.

Dr Shrivel: Yes. Of course. We've discussed it a fe— … that is, *I've* mentioned it a few times here. Psychiatrist Elisabeth Kubler-Ross developed the theory of the five stages of grief, and it's a very helpful list, though many do feel—

Fern: I was listening.

Dr Shrivel: Yes, of course.

Fern: I mean … the whole time. Here. I took it all in. At least … parts. When it … got through. I know you talked about denial. Anger. Bargaining. Depression. The other one. I just …

Dr Shrivel: Go on, Fern.

Fern: I just couldn't … if I had spoken … I would have …

Dr Shrivel: Yes?

Fern: I was afraid he would …

Dr Shrivel: He would?

Fern: (very emotional) Leave. And yet I want him to …

Dr Shrivel: (softly) Who?

Fern: (silence)

Dr Shrivel: Do you mean Hunter, Fern?

Fern: (silence)

Dr Shrivel: Could you see him?

Fern: Can I leave now?

Dr Shrivel: You can leave at any time. But this really is for your benefit. We can talk abo—

Fern: I want to go to my room.

Dr Shrivel: OK (pause). Can you see Hunter right now? Can you tell me more about what you mean by *see* him?

Fern: (silence)

Dr Shrivel: Before you go, can you—

Fern: I'm finished.

Dr Shrivel: You have at least another week here.

Fern: No ... my story. I'm ... done ... with that.

Dr Shrivel: Your story?

Fern: The one ... I've been ... writing. It's done. And maybe ... maybe ... I think I'm closer to ... to, um, some sort of ... acceptance. Not of ... of ... you know. That. But of ... my guilt (pause). So, I can start a new notepad. Maybe I'll ... I don't know. Maybe ... (pause). Do you have one?

Dr Shrivel: Oh. No. Not here. Susan can give you another (pause). You've been writing a story? Do you want to stay and talk about that?

Fern: I don't need to. I'm going to give it to you. To read. If you would like to?

Dr Shrivel: I would like to very much. Thank you.

Fern: I haven't ... read it ... not fully.

Dr Shrivel: Why do you think that is?

Fern: I can't. I'm not ready for that.

Dr Shrivel: If I read it, can I discuss it with you? I think that would be very helpful for both of us.

Fern: I don't know ... *no* ... um, I don't know.

Dr Shrivel: There's no need to decide now, Fern. We can meet as usual and just take things from there (pause). Would you like it back? Is this something you will publish, like your others?

Fern: Oh ... no ... I don't know. I think ... it's too ... *no*.

(Fern leaves)

From Dr Shrivel's Private Notes

I don't know what I expected when I started reading Fern Dalrymple's notepad. I think perhaps I thought it might be some kind of diary, even though she used the word story in our session. But that still did not prepare me.

I stayed up the whole night reading it. I made notes as I went along, questions I had, thoughts that came to me, reactions to certain scenes. I felt a mixture of intense emotions, from sadness to awe to surprise to excitement. I felt that I saw more of the patient in those pages – in the story of a lonely woman coping with the banning of all books and her own childlessness – than I might have done with even the most intense counselling. I saw what she has hidden during our sessions. It seemed to me that using the safety of fiction, Fern was able to address her trauma.

As I turned the pages, I found myself forgetting that these words had been written by one of my patients. Instead, I read it as a strange, dark, sad and complex novel. I felt closer to Fern. Her fiction did that. Halfway through, I realised I was beginning to care for her, and I had to remind myself that I'm her doctor, and that I had crossed a boundary in letting her in in this way. After that, I had to assess the work objectively, more clinically.

It had me thinking about Narrative Exposure Therapy (NET), a psychological technique used to help survivors of trauma make sense of their experiences, while acting as a form of exposure to painful memories. After writing about the facts of a trauma, the patient can slowly add more detail. They can read through their narrative, taking as long as is needed, adding information about the thoughts and feelings they experienced during their distress. As they become more comfortable telling their story, they can focus on the uncomfortable memories.

The 'story' is then reviewed. The patient revises any sections as they see fit. Finally, the patient writes one last paragraph about how they feel now, as opposed to when their trauma was occurring.

What have they learned? Have they grown stronger? What would they say to someone else going through the same experience?

I realise that Fern has written her own trauma narrative, without prompt. There is very little crossed out (aside from the four pages near the end), which suggests that she took her time and was careful. The key now would be to get her to review it. Discuss it. To rewrite the parts that need rewriting as fact. I hope we might together use it as a tool to help her open up. If so, I think this case could be the most unique and eye-opening that I've ever experienced, one that I hope can help others in the future.

I don't think I will ever forget the story I've just read. It is as real to me right now as the office I'm sitting in, and the sun that's warming my back.

Transcript of Session – Fern Dalrymple – 03/10/2020 – 24 days into her stay

Dr Shrivel: How are you feeling today, Fern?

Fern: (silence)

Dr Shrivel: Susan tells me you've had two very restless nights again. I imagine you miss the story you were writing in your notepad. It must have been strange to have let it go; to have handed it over to me. Susan said she gave you another one. Have you written anything there?

Fern: (silence)

Dr Shrivel: I read the whole thing, Fern. I can see why you found success as an author. You really have quite a way with words. I found it extraordinary. Tell me, how much of the story was true?

Fern: (silence)

Dr Shrivel: Knowing your background, and what happened to you two months ago, I think that a great deal was. I was hoping you could answer some of my questions. How about if I open it now and we read together?

Fern: (silence)

Dr Shrivel: The banning of books put me in mind of *Fahrenheit 451*. I think I understand it as you wanting to punish yourself somehow, for being a writer in some way, but I'd like you to tell me, Fern. Only you know.

Fern: (silence)

Dr Shrivel: And the endless heatwave. I have my theories on that, but I need to hear from you.

Fern: (silence)

Dr Shrivel: Naming a deranged surgeon after me, and his accomplice after your doctor ... (laughing). That tap-dancing scene ... most amusing. I wonder if perhaps you dislike being here, if you feel these sessions are invasive somehow, and you expressed that via those characters. Am I wrong?

Fern: (silence)

Dr Shrivel: OK (pause). I'd now like to talk about each aspect of your … *story*. The characters and who they are or what they represent. For example, the tall one and the short one. Who are they to you? What do they symbolise?

Fern: (silence)

Dr Shrivel: Is … what was his name … the tea man … Fine-Fayre, is he real?

Fern: (silence)

Dr Shrivel: Some parts were clearly inspired by real life. The fact that you were a writer in the story, and that two of the books were your real-life novels, is important, though I found the third – and clearly invented – novel interesting, especially its themes. A story within your story. Your three friends, Lynda, Cass and Shelly, are present too, and I know they visit you here. That they are very dear to you.

Fern: (silence)

Dr Shrivel: Another character that I know to be real is, of course, Hunter. He's at the core of the story. Its beating heart, you might say, which I understand (pause). You did, however, separate yourself from your son by writing him a different mother. You made yourself childless. Not only childless, but unable to have children at all. Do you feel you were … um, punishing yourself somehow, Fern?

Fern: (silence)

Dr Shrivel: (gently) Was this the only way you could address your relationship with Hunter, do you think?

Fern: (silence)

Dr Shrivel: And yet you were the one who read him the story he needed. You were the one who tried to save him.

Fern: (silence)

Dr Shrivel: Fern … should we talk about the accident?

(Fern leaves, clearly upset)

**Transcript of Session – Fern Dalrymple – 05/10/2020 –
26 days into her stay**

Dr Shrivel: How are you feeling today, Fern?

Fern: (shrugs)

Dr Shrivel: Susan tells me you slept a little better last night. The days must be easier when you've slept?

Fern: (nods)

Dr Shrivel: Susan said you had your new notepad with you at breakfast. Have you written anything in it yet?

Fern: (opens mouth but then doesn't speak)

Dr Shrivel: (waits)

Fern: (eventually) Not yet.

Dr Shrivel: Are you thinking about it?

Fern: Maybe.

Dr Shrivel: Do you think it would be a good idea to try and talk a little again about the previous notepad today? I had the idea that we could chat about certain parts and then you could go away and write the true version – for want of a better word – in the new notepad. Is that something you feel receptive to today?

Fern: I'm not sure.

Dr Shrivel: What you can't yet talk about, you could write. How it really happened. Not fiction this time. Write it. Look at it. Feel it, Fern (pause). This could be a way to begin moving forward.

Fern: I … I …

Dr Shrivel: Are you feeling anxious? We can do some of our relaxation techniques.

Fern: They don't make any difference. I'm not anxious … I'm … *afraid*. It's real. It isn't some mental health disorder that can be soothed with a pretentious technique. I. Am. Scared.

Dr Shrivel: You sound angry too.

Fern: I guess I'm not allowed to be because I'm supposed to be past that phase, eh?

Dr Shrivel: (kindly) All emotions are allowed here.

Fern: And wouldn't you be emotional?

Dr Shrivel: I would, yes. Life has dealt you a shockingly cruel blow.

Fern: It hasn't.

Dr Shrivel: Hasn't it?

Fern: No. It was all on me. Not life or fate ... *me*.

Dr Shrivel: How about we begin by talking about one of the more joyful aspects of your story?

Fern: (shrugs)

Dr Shrivel: Fine-Fayre. He felt like a real person. I felt that in the end you – or at least the narrator you created – began to almost ... *love* him. And yet there was an aspect of him that irritated you immensely too. These very raw emotions, and the detail of the biscuits and the conversations you had ... well, he felt so real.

Fern: He is real.

Dr Shrivel: He is?

Fern: Yes.

Dr Shrivel: Extraordinary. Can you write me a few pages in your new notepad, telling me about him? Why did he end up in your work of fiction?

Fern: You asked me the other day how much of the story was true.

Dr Shrivel: I did.

Fern: To me ... in the moment ... all of it.

Dr Shrivel: Even the made-up parts?

Fern: Even the made-up parts.

Dr Shrivel: Yet you are aware that you were making it up.

Fern: (nods)

Dr Shrivel: If you tell a story well enough, it's true.

(long pause)

Fern: Fine-Fayre came to my house a week after ...

Dr Shrivel: After?

Fern: I was ... I was ... (emotional)

Dr Shrivel: Deep breaths, Fern. Take your time.

Fern: I was ... it was ... I was in pain. He came.

Fern Dalrymple's Diary – the Tea Man

He arrived in a mock-vintage van, *Fine-Fayre* engraved on the side in gold lettering, above a picture of a family drinking tea while eating custard creams. They were a new company, one older or lonely people enjoyed because of that personal touch. I vaguely recognised him; I'd seen him wheel up to my neighbour Laura's door before. I was alone. I'd been sitting with my bottle of Propranolol, about to take them all with a cup of tea. It was one week after. I was in denial. I was angry. I was in agony.

'Would you enjoy having tea delivered directly to your door?' he asked from beneath me.

He was in a wheelchair and had a scar on his right cheek; even in my pain I thought that the joined expanse between his eyebrow and jaw resembled laces when you first try to tie them as a child. The details of his attire, you know already; the wicker basket of produce you are familiar with.

'It's early,' I managed to say. I must have looked a fright; I hadn't eaten in thirty-six hours; I was shaking.

'Our tea is very competitively priced.'

'Laura sent you, didn't she?' I flung my arm towards her house, a large, beautiful Victorian property like mine, one I'd bought with my royalties. Usually – *before* – I didn't mind Laura, even though she was a bit of a busybody. But in my grief, I was angry that her house was often full of family while I wandered mine alone. 'I can't stand *pity*.' After a beat: 'Are you deaf as well as unable to walk?' It was uncalled for. The cruel words came from a black place.

'We offer a full-money-back-guarantee if our products aren't perfectly to your liking,' he said as though I hadn't just insulted him.

I ranted then – you may recall it in my previous fiction – about Laura and him being in cahoots, trying to cheer up this poor grieving woman with teabags. I wasn't in my right mind. I even sometimes got angry at friends – my beloved Lynda, Cass

LOUISE SWANSON

and Shelly – when I thought they didn't understand my pain. They came, often, with poetry and words and love, but I pushed them away.

I admired the tea man for not flinching at my repeated use of *fuck*.

'Have you considered buying teabags from somewhere other than a supermarket?' he asked, unthwarted.

You know this already. He asked how I drank my tea. *With as many pills as possible*, I wanted to say. He said he had the perfect bag. *For suicide*? I wanted to ask. He took a small gold packet from his basket.

'I'll leave a sample and give you time to think,' he said.

I slammed the door and waited until the van left. After a minute or two I went onto the step. I saw a flash of gold on the wall. A piece of sunshine. He had left me a sample after all.

I thought: *who the fuck are you, imagining teabags will ease my grief?*

He came back a few days later. I hadn't slept for three nights. His arrival cut through the fog. I see him now like a bright cartoon, more real in my head as I write it than when it happened. Yet I thought, *the nerve of him*. Torturing me in my agony.

'Did you enjoy the tea?' he asked.

He hadn't closed my gate properly; it swung back and forth with a rude squeak.

'How do you know I drank it?' I noticed the earth-brown hair neatly cut around his ears and brushed to the side. One strand escaped the others. Like … like … I couldn't even face his name.

We argued back and forth about the price of his teabags, and the special offer on his Nutty Speckles, but you know this, you've already read it.

'This is harassment of a grieving woman,' I said.

He simply nodded and reversed his chair with a whirr. I thought my heart would snap – that it was pulled tight with pain and this would break it altogether. The emotion surprised me. He made me angry, but I wanted him to stay.

'What kind of salesman *are* you?' I called.

He paused at the gate.

'How have you sold anything if you crawl off like a puppy in a sad movie when I tell you to?' He returned to my step. 'I'll take a pack of teabags.'

He handed me some Nutty Speckles too.

'I didn't spend a tenner,' I said.

'It's fine.'

'I don't want *pity* Nutty Speckles.'

I started crying. It was the idea of his pity. It was the exhaustion. It was because … it was because … no, I can't write that yet. I can't. I can only tell you about Fine-Fayre. That's when I first called him this name, after he patiently waited until I'd stopped sobbing, after he handed me a napkin when I was done.

'You can come back in four days,' I said. 'If these biscuits upset my stomach, I'll sue you.'

He came back late, after *five* days; I reprimanded him; I was frenzied from lack of sleep. He left the gate open. I asked if he was born in a field. Someone had cut his hair badly as though attempting to detract from his scar; this was in my fiction and it's also true. My pain was physical, but I'd managed a piece of toast with a cup of his tea that morning. He offered me a Lemon Crackle sample and said I looked better than I had done before. I knew it was a lie; I'd caught a summer cold and was red-nosed.

'There's something going round,' he said. 'Lemon teabags soothe the throat.'

'Tea's no remedy for tonsillitis,' I snapped.

'The best cure is to release what's stuck there.' He said it so tenderly.

'So you're a doctor *and* a tea salesman?'

'Just a tea salesman.'

He smiled. I can't deny how it touched me. Light in my dark. He turned to leave.

'Fine-Fayre!' I cried.

I suddenly didn't want him to go. I could not face my empty house. I felt the world might not end up how it should be if he left. That he might never return. He irritated me but his smile; *his smile*. In its brief flicker, the weight on my heart lessened just a tiny, merciful bit, for a fleeting moment.

'Bring me some Nutty Speckles next time,' I told him.

Next time he knocked so loudly I gasped. I was walking the length of my garden, as I often did – on repeat, over and over, trying to loosen my pain, trying not to consume my pills and sleep forever – so maybe he'd knocked more quietly beforehand.

'I should report you for giving me a heart attack,' I said.

He had shut the gate properly after him though. In between visits, I thought of him in random flashes. It meant I didn't have to think about …

'You seem angry,' Fine-Fayre said.

'Don't tell me … you've got teabags for anger?'

He smiled. It was as bright as sunflowers. 'Camomile tea calms anxieties.'

'Did you bring my Nutty Speckles?'

He took out my now usual gold pack and some Nutty Speckles. I'd observed during our interactions that his facial scar hardly moved when he spoke, as though he'd learned to fit talking around its inconvenience. I couldn't take my eyes off the long, thin, imperfect stripe.

'I know you're looking at my scar,' he said, thoughtfully.

'I'm not,' I lied.

'It bothers other people more than it bothers me.'

'You think I don't have bigger stuff to worry about than your ruined face?' I cried, regretting it immediately. But he hardly reacted.

'Why are you kind to me?' I demanded.

He didn't answer.

As he turned to leave, he dropped a packet of Lemon Crackles. I got them for him. I looked up at him and realised that few people probably saw him from this angle. That mostly he had to look up.

Be lower. Be beneath. I wanted to stay there for longer. See him that way. Let him be the bigger one. The scar ran under his chin, like a stream continuing down a hill's curve.

I found that I was crying again. Embarrassed. Snotty. Sobbing. On my knees. I found it hard to cry alone. I was dry then. Now I put my head in his lap; he patted it until my tears finally subsided. Eventually, I moved away, suddenly, wordless now, shy.

He left, stopping at the flowers bordering my fence. 'Red tulips are an expression of perfect love,' he said.

I'd had that. I'd *had* it. And I hadn't appreciated it. Mothers describe what they feel for their child as perfect love; say it is unconditional; say they would die for them. It is; it is; and I would have. Now, all I had was … a … single … blue and white trainer. That I could not look at.

Next time Fine-Fayre's hair was neatly bowl-like atop his head, his basket full, scar less angry. I was determined not to look at it this time. I did wonder, though, why he had to use a wheelchair. Had he been born without the ability to walk or had something happened during his life?

He offered me a sample of some Ravishing Raisin loaf – you remember the fiction; you know I didn't like it – and he admitted he was bored of selling tea.

'I hope your replacement has a better haircut than you. You look like Blackadder.' I paused. 'Your pity was ill-placed,' I added gently. 'That's why you first came here, isn't it? You knew about … my … what happened …'

He shook his head. 'It's you who pity *me*. But I don't mind.'

'I don't.' Random anger was still fire inside me. 'I'm sorry I said that awful thing last time – it was a reaction to the thought of *you* pitying me.'

He told me then about being in care, how a boy in one of the homes cut his face. Had something happened there that destroyed his legs too? I shook the thought away. I could only picture … *him* … *my* boy … going through something like that. My heart.

The pain. It was acute enough to stop my breath. I smelled my son then. Near me. I didn't want it.

I didn't deserve him.

'I do know ... about ... what happened.' Fine-Fayre's words soothed me. 'Your neighbour, Mrs North, she *did* tell me, yes, but only ... well, only out of compassion for you. Pity wasn't why I came. It was ... how could I not?'

For a moment, during my agonising grief, I imagined what it might be like to kiss him. To lean down and put my mouth to his. To touch his face, run my fingers over his scar's pleats and ridges, then feel his flat, smooth skin in contrast. We do not kiss or hug others in this Covid world. We grieve and suffer now without physical support.

He left then.

'I love your tea,' I called when he reached the gate.

Next time, he looked tired, his scar once again an angry slash against wan skin. He didn't speak much. He handed me my teabags and I paid. Did he pity me despite his denial? Anger still surged at the idea. I was being unfair. I shouldn't have cared how he felt towards me. But I did. I had waited all day for him. He was all that existed outside of black grief and abject loneliness. A man, an angel, with teabags and biscuits.

'Do you know what your scar makes me think of?' I said gently.

'Tell me.'

'A war hero. Like you fought in some big battle and that's what you came home with.'

'I guess scars are proof we survived.'

Most are inside, I thought.

'And how about ...' I spoke softly. 'Why the wheelchair? What happened?'

He didn't respond. I wished he would come in. That I could unburden myself of this agony. Share my pain. Feel his. Have his thoughts. His affection.

'I might be leaving,' he said instead.

'Leaving?'

'Fine-Fayre.'

The idea of him no longer calling by filled me with a desperation to press pause on the world.

'I had an interview for a better paid job.' He patted his basket. I
realised that he always did just before leaving, as though signalling
for me to prepare for his departure. I wasn't ready. I was terrified of
being swallowed up by my empty house.

'You're not going to try and sell me weird new biscuits?' I was
buying time.

He shook his head. 'Not today.'

'Are you ill?'

He smiled. 'No.'

He wheeled his chair down my path. I walked after him, reached
the gate for the first time when he was departing, each of us on
opposite sides. I've never wanted to know his name. I'd rather leave
him mysterious.

'If you get the new job, how long is your notice?'

'Three months,' he said.

'Good luck,' I called after him, but I didn't mean it, because that
would mean I'd never see him again.

And then he was gone. I was sure the temperature dropped, just
for a moment. It was the last time I saw him. I came inside. I took as
many pills as I could swallow with a cup of his strong tea. I hoped
never to wake up. But I did. In Laura next door's arms. She had seen
me through the window when she came around with a casserole.
Dr Patrukal admitted me to River View.

And here I am. New notepad. The real story.

As much of it as I can face.

Fine-Fayre was all that kept me from completely losing my mind.

**Transcript of Session – Fern Dalrymple – 06/10/2020 –
27 days into her stay**

Dr Shrivel: How are you feeling today, Fern?
Fern: (shrugs)
Dr Shrivel: Susan tells me you were awake all night.
Fern: I was writing.
Dr Shrivel: That's good. That's what I was going to ask you about today. What did you write about?
Fern: Fine-Fayre.
Dr Shrivel: The tea man.
Fern: Yes. What really happened. Who he really was.
Dr Shrivel: How did it feel to write the truth?
Fern: (pause) I felt like … I was with him again.
Dr Shrivel: And how did that feel?
Fern: (upset)
Dr Shrivel: Take your time.
Fern: Sometimes I depended on his visits … just to … not go … to the train tracks.
Dr Shrivel: (nods) Can I read what you've written?
Fern: Yes. You can have the notepad. I don't want to talk anymore today.
(Fern leaves.)

Dr Shrivel: How are you feeling today, Fern?

Fern: (shrugs)

Dr Shrivel: Susan tells me you slept a little better last night. I imagine all that writing the night before exhausted you. This is an intense process you're going through – writing your truth.

Fern: (silence)

Dr Shrivel: I found the true tale of the tea man ... very moving. Thank you for being honest with me.

Fern: I was being honest with myself.

Dr Shrivel: Yes. Of course. We often form strange and sudden relationships with new people when we're in the depths of grief. Do you hope to see him when you leave here?

Fern: (silence)

Dr Shrivel: Do you think you might ... take the relationship further?

Fern: (silence)

Dr Shrivel: I found it, um, interesting that you didn't end what you wrote about Fine-Fayre in the middle of a sentence. You know, the way you did in the first half of your fiction. To ... I recall ... to ensure you came back to the page.

Fern: (silence)

Dr Shrivel: So, are you ready to write some more ... truth?

Fern: (silence)

Dr Shrivel: Can we go back then to discussing your huge work of fiction? I'd like to know a little more about that third novel – *Technological Amazingness*. Such a curious title. Where did that come from?

Fern: (silence)

Dr Shrivel: The themes in it were interesting. Those of strange surgeries and extreme policies. I know from your history that Hunter died on the operating table. (more gently) I'm so very sorry about

273

that, Fern (pause). Do you feel that your anger manifested in a story where the NHS decide all patients should be dead on the surgical table?

Fern: (silence)

Dr Shrivel: You must have been angry at those surgeons? That's entirely natural.

Fern: Of course I fucking was (pause). And yet I know … I know they tried; I *do*. It's more …

Dr Shrivel: (gently) Yes?

Fern: The pandemic. I couldn't help but think …

Dr Shrivel: (gently) Yes?

Fern: They were tired … all so *tired*. The surgeons, the doctors, the nurses … and maybe if … I don't know … maybe if the government had handled the crisis better… I was just angry, so angry, at all of it… I know now, that that wasn't why … why Hunter … you know. But at the time … it, well, it consumed me …

Dr Shrivel: Yes. Did writing *Technological Amazingness* – or at least the idea of it – help you deal with that? Process it?

Fern: I … maybe … no. It just … it was … it came out of me.

Dr Shrivel: Like free writing?

Fern: (silence)

Dr Shrivel: How about the tall one and the short one. Who are they really, Fern?

Fern: (silence)

Dr Shrivel: You dreaded them arriving in the fiction. Though they visited you often, we never really got to know anything about *them*. There was a begrudging like towards the end, even sudden affection for the short one, but throughout the story you clearly thought they were going to take you somewhere terrible, somewhere you didn't want to go.

Fern: They were …

Dr Shrivel: Yes?

Fern: My family liaison officers. They … were there … for me. After. Sent to me because of the … accident. They supported me.

But I … I dreaded their visits. Because it just … I just … They were kind, they *were*. But I felt … I didn't deserve it. That it was all my fault (sobbing). I hated them being there. What it meant.

Dr Shrivel: Of course.

Fern: I thought they might take me to … a place like this.

Dr Shrivel: A place like this. Hmmmm. Was this what you envisioned when you wrote the … what did you call them? The re-education centres (pause). The body horror of the partial lobotomies and finger removal was so extreme. You made your pain physical, just to be able to look at it.

Fern: (silence)

Dr Shrivel: It was interesting how Fern – the fictional Fern, but we know you also – very clearly went through the first four stages of grief. It's worth discussing maybe how you could identify this as you went. Such acute self-awareness.

Fern: Because you never shut up about them during our sessions.

Dr Shrivel: Quite (pause). OK. Why do you think you set the whole thing in the future?

Fern: (shrugs)

Dr Shrivel: Do you think maybe a 'not happened yet' is easier to deal with? (pause) Do you think that you liked being able to control what might one day happen? That you might change what had gone by looking back in this way? You can't look at what *has* happened, at least not yet, so you … invent a new world.

Fern: You seem to know, so I'm not sure why you're asking me.

Dr Shrivel: Apologies. I'm musing, really. The whole thing was so thought-provoking. But, yes, this is your work. You tell me then, Fern?

Fern: Sometimes … just sometimes … you don't know why you write a certain thing. It just feels … right. Not all of it is directly inspired by my experiences. Some just came from my imagination.

Dr Shrivel: The heatwave. I really felt that. It was a hot day, wasn't it? The day of the accident …

Fern: (silence)

Dr Shrivel: I think the core of the story is the fiction ban though. I think this is what we really need to discuss. I was struck by the plot to burn down ALLBooks. This place symbolised anti-fiction, truth ... you wanted to destroy that, on some level ... but then not. You were going to stop it. In doing so, were you perhaps freeing the truth?

Fern: (silence)

Dr Shrivel: And of course the sleepless children not getting their bedtime stories ...

Fern: (shakes head)

Dr Shrivel: But *you* made sure they got those stories. You were supposed to be a fiction laureate and write something for them, inspired by their own stories ...

Fern: (sobs)

Dr Shrivel: I understand how hard this is, but we have to talk about Hunter here. He is the one you must talk about now. His story is the one you need to write. There is nowhere else to go, Fern.

Fern: I can't ...

Dr Shrivel: I think you can. You wrote this fiction to be with him again, didn't you?

Fern: (sobs)

Dr Shrivel: You miss him desperately.

Fern: (sobs so much she is retching)

Dr Shrivel: Would Hunter want you to remember him only via a made-up story?

Fern: No! Fuck you! That isn't what I was doing.

Dr Shrivel: (more gently) Do you think he would want to be written as he really was? Do you think maybe that's why you still see him, around you?

Fern: (sobs)

Dr Shrivel: You love him so much, Fern, that you wrote an entire book in order to cope with his death. There is no greater love than that (pause). What would he want you to do right now?

Fern: (silence)

Dr Shrivel: Why don't you let *me* meet him now? I'd really like to. Why don't you write him for me?

Fern: (softly) I did. When I wrote my … story … I could be with him again. I could … make right what I did wrong. But I didn't deserve to be his mother. I didn't deserve any child.

Dr Shrivel: And yet you tenderly cared for him.

Fern: (sobs)

Dr Shrivel: The love you had for him emanated off the page, Fern. I was incredibly moved by it (emotional). That aspect was the most real. Please, share your real boy with me?

(Fern stands, shaking uncontrollably)

Dr Shrivel: Please stay until you feel a little better.

Fern: *Technological Amazingness.*

Dr Shrivel: Yes?

Fern: It was … my …

Dr Shrivel: Yes?

Fern: That's the title of the book Hunter said he was writing. When I was … too busy to … read bedtime stories to him.

(Fern leaves)

Fern Dalrymple's Diary – Bedtime Stories

What can I tell you about my boy, Hunter? How should I write him for you, to give him to you the way I had him? Which parts best represent him?

You got a physical description of him in my fiction: chunky, in a good way, like he'll be a strapping lad when he grows up, with reddish-blond hair that he tells everyone is more blond; blue eyes; not tall yet, but who knows in the future?

You saw his room; the one I gave you in *What Happened to All the Bloody Books?* I described his blue and white curtains fluttering in the breeze, and his favourite chair that rocked, where I used to read him stories when he was a baby and he couldn't sleep, and where he often curled up with our cat Geoffrey and his favourite books.

I gave you my desk, where he often sat to draw or play on his mini console; a large oak thing, with a chair that squeaked and was on its way out and slowly sank the longer you sat in it, with a plant on it that I forgot to water, that fried in the direct sunlight from the sash window, and with photos of Hunter aged two, four, seven, in a row, like a picture story of his growth.

I gave you his love of drawing in one of the dreams I had; Hunter lying on his bed drawing a picture with a variety of yellow pens, each shade slightly different, so that the sunflowers he created were the most vibrant I'd ever seen, brighter than Van Gogh's. Him looking over his shoulder at me. Telling me he wasn't a dream.

He isn't a dream

He was my son; he always will be.

I had him late in life. I never thought it would happen. I was forty-four when I got pregnant. Cal and I had only been married a short while. Cal, my love, my heart, who I also gave you in my fiction. As there, he sadly died, suddenly, of a heart attack despite being so young, an undiagnosed heart defect the cause. I was only six months pregnant. Our child kept me going: the boy Cal had excitedly suggested we call Hunter after his favourite writer, Hunter S. Thompson.

Hunter and I struggled for some years, but it made us close. I was his mother *and* his father. I tried to bring Cal into our lives in as many ways as possible, watching videos, sharing photographs, talking to him as though he was still with us. I went hungry some days to make sure Hunter got enough to eat; a domestic job doesn't pay much, though the woman whose house I cleaned let me take Hunter with me.

When he was four, I started writing short stories and sending them out to magazines. I found comfort in creating a better world for myself to live in, late at night, exhausted, alone. I won some competitions, and it gave me the confidence to write a full-length work. My first novel was *The Dark Room*. It's about a photographer who airbrushes pictures for clients. She realises that in making these images perfect it changes the actual memory; that she is *not in fact a magician, but a conjuror of lies*. Though I'd read that most writers take years to find success, I secured an agent on my first attempt, and she got me a six-figure two-book deal in weeks. It was the stuff of dreams.

Hunter danced around the room with me when I told him. God, he looked like Cal. He understood the magic of books. I'd been reading to him since I found out I was pregnant. I whispered fairy tales to him before he could speak, when he lay in my arms – warm, fuzzy, all mine – and the smell of him in the half-light, dozing off, was intoxicating. And he slept … well … like a baby.

'Will your book be in the actual shops, Mummy?' he asked.

'Yes, the actual shops,' I cried.

'And can I read it?'

'Maybe not until you're a big boy.'

'Why? Has it got rude bits in it?'

I laughed so much then. 'No. Just … I think it might not interest you because it's about boring grown-ups.'

With the money from the book deal, our life changed almost overnight.

I gave up my cleaning job. When the novel was released and went straight on to the bestseller list, we moved out of the tiny flat Cal and I had once made our simple home and into a grand, four-bedroom Victorian house with views of the park. Hunter was six by then. I was able to give him a much better life. We didn't have beans on toast for most of our meals. I didn't have to worry when his shoes wore out or his coat got too small. We had our first holiday in Florida.

I wished Cal was with us to experience it.

But I was busy. Busier than I'd ever been. Good busy. Book tours. Library events. Literary talks. Rewrites, edits, the pressure to write a follow-up second novel. TV and radio appearances. I was given my own evening slot on a local radio station three nights a week, reviewing new books. I often travelled, sometimes for days. This took me away from Hunter, and that was hard. My mum was almost eighty and it wasn't fair to expect her to help all the time, so I paid Josie – a young woman I knew – cash in hand to look after him. She was struggling and I wanted her to keep all the money. The woman I'd cleaned for often did that to help me. Josie came when I needed her. She bonded with Hunter; I felt he was safe with her.

She often had to read his bedtime story.

I can't deny that this was the most difficult part of sharing him with someone else. Of my new, successful, in-demand life. If I was away, I called home at the end of the day, but I often missed him.

'He's asleep now,' Josie would say. 'He drifted off to *Thomas the Tank Engine*.'

And I'd hang up, my throat tight with emotion, heart flat with guilt.

I wrote a second novel – *A Sort of Homecoming* – and it sold even better than the first. It won the National Book Award for Fiction. If I'd thought life was busy before, now it went crazy. This was a word I often used, when I was frazzled, packing to go away, responding to the two hundred emails, arranging time off. Crazy, crazy, *crazy*. Hunter would kiss my cheek with a big smack and call me Crazy

Lady, and then I had to say I was a bad mummy, and that crazy wasn't a very nice word.

I can hear him saying it. *Crazy Lady.* Whispering. Now. Here. In this soulless, white-walled, no sharp edges, no mirrors, safe plugs, no phone chargers in case you hang yourself room. Writing those two words just now I somehow … called him. Conjured him up with a mother's desperate spell. And yet, I can't turn and face him. I'm afraid. I'm afraid his little face won't look at me how he used to. He hasn't forgiven me. He doesn't love me.

I'm afraid.

Back then, I tried to create time where there was none. I tried to say no to any work that wasn't essential. But so much of it was if I wanted to maintain our new high standard of living. I feared going back to a flat I couldn't afford to heat and worrying that I couldn't pay for Christmas. Hunter turned eight. For his birthday I bought him the latest designer trainers that all the kids were hankering after. He kissed my cheek with his usual big smack. But he never wore them. They were still in the box a month later.

'Don't you like them?' I asked. 'We can swap them, Hunter?'

'Oh, I do, Mum.' He clearly felt bad. 'I'm saving them for … a special day.'

He always wore his favourites, which had been super cheap from a discount store. Blue and white. Not branded. Not expensive. But so scuffed that I kept saying we should get rid of them.

'No,' he cried. 'I love them. They're comfy and they just feel … right.'

It was not lost on me that despite the lovely things I bought him – often, admittedly, as an apology for being absent – he preferred the simple things. A red rucksack that my mum got him at a market. A yellow T-shirt that was free from one of my book events. The blue and white discount shop trainers.

I gave him everything I thought he wanted but what he really wanted was simple.

Me. That's all most kids want. Their parent.

I overheard him once, talking to my mum on the phone. He was at my desk. I heard the chair: squeak, squeak, *squeak*. 'She's hardly ever here,' he said. 'I mean, sometimes she is, but even then, it's like … like she's not really. She's like always on the phone or saying *just a minute* or waving her hand at me to go and play one of my games.' He paused. 'I feel mean saying this, Nana. Because I know she loves me. But I'm just … sad.'

I sobbed quietly into my fist.

He had her on speaker, so I heard my mum's response. 'Maybe she doesn't realise this, Hunter. If she has lots of work, and it's just her, it can be hard, I imagine. Tell her how you feel. I bet she'll feel terrible and make more effort.'

'I don't want to hurt her feelings, Nana.'

'Shall I have a chat with her?'

'Nah, it's fine.' He paused. 'I'm dead lucky, really. Our house is nice. She always gets me the best trainers and she lets me eat what I want for tea and we have nice holidays, even if I'm always bored 'cos it's just me.'

That night I cancelled a book group and read to Hunter, both of us squeezed into his rocking chair, Geoffrey the cat at our feet. He was a more than able reader by now, but he still preferred to have me tell the story. He could relax then. He could doze off knowing the story wouldn't end because he had fallen asleep. Sometimes I'd look up and feel sure Cal was standing in the doorway watching us. At times, I felt guilty that he might think I wasn't a good enough mother. But there were other times too, times when I was angry he had left me to do it alone.

I tried so hard to make more time. But the demands on me after the huge success of two books only increased. The pressure was on for me to write a third novel when all I really wanted to do was read to my son. Josie continued to read to Hunter in my absence, but after a while he stopped asking. When I was home, he said he was too old now for 'silly children's stories'.

'You're never too old,' I said, sad.

'Marley doesn't have them.'

'What does Marley do then?'

'Play Fortnite.'

'Before bed?'

'Yes,' said Hunter.

'That can't be good for him,' I said.

I never let Hunter play games late at night, but still he insisted he could read himself now at bedtime. I remembered his phone call with my mum and wondered if he was turning down story time to save me feeling bad when I couldn't do it.

'I'm writing my own book, anyway,' he said one day.

'Really? Can I read it?'

'No, it's a secret.' He looked smug.

Was I hurt? A little. Would I try to find his 'book' so I could read it? No. Never. I respected his privacy. But my heart ached to read whatever words he had written.

Hunter began to suffer from sleeplessness for the first time in his life. It baffled me. I wondered if it was something he was eating and tried to eliminate certain foods from our diet. He drank lots of chocolate milk – often leaving half-full bottles in his room that had gone off – and I worried that it was full of caffeine. I researched what else might have caused the acute insomnia, in case he had an underlying condition, and I didn't know. Nothing seemed to fit or answer why. I encouraged him to relax in the evening and insisted Josie and my mum did the same when I was away.

He came into my room one night just after midnight, tearful, saying he couldn't 'drop off', no matter what he did. 'I switched my thoughts off,' he sniffed. 'I really did.'

'Come here, sweetie.' I held him tight. 'Shall I read to you for a bit?'

'No.' He sat up again. 'I'm too old.'

'You're not,' I insisted. 'Who told you that?'

'No one. But I am. I'm eight and a quarter. I can read myself.'

'But don't you miss it?'

He didn't respond. After a moment he said he would be fine now and went back to bed. But I lay awake for hours, worried, checking on him repeatedly, relieved when he finally fell asleep at two. I knew I needed to take two weeks off and spend quality time with him, but I had a book tour down south, followed by a big launch in Newcastle, and then I was guest hosting an awards ceremony back in London. I decided that in the morning I would tell my agent that once I had done these events, I needed some time off. Book three would have to wait. My son came first.

Then the Covid-19 pandemic happened. All my events were cancelled. I can't lie and say I wasn't relieved. Now I could be with Hunter, even though it meant we were separated from my mum and Josie.

But I was still busy. Everything just happened online instead. The pressure continued for a third book. The phone and emails and online meetings filled my days. My mum often home-schooled Hunter over FaceTime when I couldn't. Though we were just the two of us, under the same roof, I might as well have been in London.

'I'm working on my book,' said Hunter one evening, when I asked if he wanted to watch a movie.

'What's it about?' I asked again.

He was quiet. 'It's got a great title,' he said.

'Which is?'

'*Technological Amazingness*,' he said.

I laughed and squeezed him. I'd once said that I fancied the idea of writing a futuristic, dystopian type sci-fi novel but that I had no idea how to. He asked what I'd call it if I did. I picked a random, ridiculous phrase out of the air to make him laugh: *Technological Amazingness*.

'With a title like that, it'll be a huge success,' I said to Hunter now.

'Totally.'

I paused. 'As soon as lockdown is over, let's go out for the day. Anywhere you want.'

'Can we go to that nature reserve with the llamas?' His face lit up.

'Of course we can, sweetie.'

And we did. On a sweltering hot August day.

But only I made it back.

I can't think about that day. Not yet. Don't make me. I can't. Soon.

Not yet.

I think I wrote Hunter better in my fiction; that distance brought him closer. I feel like he's less real here when I try to give him to you. Like he lives in my heart and I can't put him on this page. Maybe I don't want to let him go. He was many things, as every child is. He was a boy who drank chocolate milk so messily he got it all over his nose. He was a boy who called me Crazy Lady, even more when I told him it wasn't a nice word. He was a boy who loved *Thomas the Tank Engine*. He was a boy who loved his blue and white trainers. He was a boy who died wearing only one of them.

He's here now, right behind me, I know it, I feel it. He haunts me.

But I can't look at him.

I'm sorry, I whisper to the wall. *I'm so sorry*.

Dr Shrivel: How are you feeling today, Fern?

Fern: (shrugs)

Dr Shrivel: Thank you for giving me the next entry in your note-pad yesterday. I read it last night. It was … I think … a very brave thing to write. I imagine it was much more difficult than your fiction. How did you feel?

Fern: I cried … a lot. It took a long time. It took twice as long … as any of the chapters … in the, you know, the other notepad (pause). I … I feel … like I should feel better than I do. It's been more than two months since … When my … when Cal died … I hurt so much but … I could, well, I somehow found the strength to go on, because … because I was carrying our child … (pause). When will this agony fade?

Dr Shrivel: There are no answers for that, Fern. A patient I once had said that the pain never died, it just became something she lived with.

Fern: (voice strangled) Why am I alive and he is not?

Dr Shrivel: There are no answers for that either, Fern. We could torture ourselves forever looking for those kinds of answers.

Fern: It's because of me. That's the answer.

Dr Shrivel: It isn't. It's because of you that your son had such a good, loving and safe life while he was on this earth.

Fern: (quietly) I should never have answered my phone.

Dr Shrivel: Tell me more about that.

Fern: That day … you know … I should have ignored it …

Dr Shrivel: I've read the police report on the accident. It wasn't your fault, Fern. The truck driver fell asleep at the wheel and caused the pile-up. There's nothing you could have done to change that.

Fern: I wish we'd never gone out that day.

Dr Shrivel: Hunter wanted to go. You just wanted to make him happy.

Fern: If I'd been there for him more, I wouldn't have had to make it up to him with a stupid day out.

Dr Shrivel: Shall we talk more about this? About your feelings of guilt. You struggle most with not being there for Hunter's bedtime story. It seems important to you, in your fiction, to bring back bedtime stories for sleepless children. It explains why you—

(Fern leaves)

Transcript of Session – Fern Dalrymple– 10/10/2020 – 31 days into her stay

Dr Shrivel: I'm glad you came back today. Susan tells me you were going to leave River View yesterday.

Fern: I decided to stay until today and see you one last time.

Dr Shrivel: Oh (pause). Do you think you're ready to leave, Fern?

Fern: I do. I've been here more than twenty-eight days. You can't keep me here now.

Dr Shrivel: If we thought you're a danger to yourself o—

Fern: I've made no suicide attempts while here. I've done everything that has been asked of me. I've taken my medication. I made a collage out of leaves in Art Therapy. I ate my meals (pause). I wrote an entire novel.

Dr Shrivel: You did, yes. Sorry, yes, I don't see you as a danger in any way, we just have to be sure (pause). Can I … since you mention it, um, the novel. I've been wondering … what would you have written as the end, had you finished it properly? The last pages had you having to tell the truth. Having to face that Hunter was in fact your son and not your … well, your ward, for want of a better word. Would you have been freed from the re-education centre, do you think?

Fern: (shrugs)

Dr Shrivel: I feel sure that once you talked about Hunter, they would have opened the doors and let you go, back to the world you had before the book ban, back to the world they promised you. Or you could have stepped through the rubble of those falling bricks …

Fern: Maybe. I'll never know. What a shame real life isn't so simple, eh?

Dr Shrivel: Quite.

Fern: Here, I *can* open the door myself. I can go home. And I want to now.

288

Dr Shrivel: (nodding) You can. Yes. But what about … the last chapter … in your *new* notepad?

Fern: (silence)

Dr Shrivel: Have you written, um, about … the day of the accident?

Fern: (shakes head)

Dr Shrivel: Do you feel that you should, perhaps before you leave?

Fern: (shakes head)

Dr Shrivel: Do you think maybe this is the most important part of your healing? To look at that day. For you to write it and then we can discuss it here in this safe space.

Fern: I am going to write it.

Dr Shrivel: Good. Good, Fern.

Fern: At home.

Dr Shrivel: Oh. Do you think that's wise? In light of … um, of the recent …

Fern: Overdose? It wasn't recent. I'm not going to do that again. I'm in pain but I'm not in that place now.

Dr Shrivel: OK. But do you maybe think it would be safer to write the last part about Hunter here, so that you can address any issues that might arise? You have no idea how it might affect you.

Fern: I wanted to die when I came here. Then I wrote that … story. And I realised … I had something to live for. It isn't … (softly) Hunter. He's gone. But it's … *something*. I said in my new notepad that I felt I'd made him more real when I wrote my fiction. It's true. I felt him more there. And that's why … I feel hopeful that I might write again. Not just … you know, *that* day. But … something. Because … it means … in a way … he goes on too.

Dr Shrivel: This is real progress, Fern.

Fern: You're going to tell me I've reached the fifth stage of grief now, aren't you? Go on. You can say it. Acceptance.

Dr Shrivel: I don't know if you have. I think today you're having a more, um, positive day. Tomorrow … you could be …

Fern: That's the case for all of us though, isn't it? None of us knows what we'll wake up to. It would be ridiculous if I didn't have black days (pause). No. I'm going home to write my final piece.

Dr Shrivel: OK (long pause). Well, if you're really going to leave … can I ask you first some things that, um, I've had in my head … and that I thought about after reading the last bit you wrote. This is more … well, for me, if you could indulge me?

Fern: Yes.

Dr Shrivel: I wondered … did you ever find Hunter's book? *Technological Amazingness*?

Fern: (upset) Yes.

Dr Shrivel: Do you need a moment?

Fern: (shakes head vigorously) No … I need to . . . (pause). I couldn't open it for days. He had written the title on the cover, in multi-coloured capitals. But not his name. And then I looked inside. And I knew why.

Dr Shrivel: Go on.

Fern: He had written … (sobs). 'My mum is going to write this book one day. It will be a book we can read together because it won't be about boring grown-ups.' I sat with it … I held it … for hours … on the floor …

Dr Shrivel: He must have been quite a boy.

Fern: Oh, he was (sobs wretchedly). He was.

Dr Shrivel: Let it out, Fern.

(long pause, Fern cries)

Fern: He's closer … when I cry. So, I try not to.

Dr Shrivel: Do you want him to go away?

Fern: No. Never. I just … I can't look directly at his face.

Dr Shrivel: Why Fern?

(Fern shakes her head)

Dr Shrivel: You think … he doesn't love you?

(long pause)

Fern: I'm very grateful for all your help.

Dr Shrivel: That's what I'm here for.

Fern: Sorry I made you such a monster in my book.

Dr Shrivel: (smiling) It was quite the tribute, really (pause). Before you leave, can I ask one more thing that interests me? Why did you give yourself the name Fern Dostoy? You kept your first name, but not the second.

Fern: Yes. I was playing with Scrabble pieces. In the common room. The first day. On my own. I made a phrase out of the letters in my palm. It was … E N D O F S T O R Y. I thought that was quite … profound … you know, in light of my feeling … that I had failed Hunter in my lack of, you know … bedtime story reading.

Dr Shrivel: You did not fail, Fern.

Fern: Well, anyway, I was upset, and I dropped the pieces. I saw my own name in that mess. F E R N. So, I picked up the remaining letters and played around. And I made D O S T O Y. And I thought, Fern Dostoy … she sounds like a writer of great books.

Dr Shrivel: End of Story. Very interesting. Could be a title for your fiction, eh?

Fern: (standing) Maybe.

Dr Shrivel: You didn't end your chapter about Hunter mid-sentence. Like with the one about the real tea man.

Fern: Sorry?

Dr Shrivel: When you've written your real story … you've finished, um, properly. No cut-off word.

Fern: (after a moment) Maybe I don't want to come back to it when I'm done (pause). Goodbye, Dr Shrivel.

Dr Shrivel: Take care of yourself, Fern.

Fern: I will. I promise.

(Fern leaves)

Fern Dalrymple's Diary – Our Day Out

It was hot that day.

The heatwave started at the end of July, with the third-hottest day ever on record in the UK. Pavements cooked, lawns fried, sales of fans went through the roof. We were out of strict lockdown, with visits to cafes and restaurants encouraged to help them out, and travel to outdoor parks permitted. I kept my promise of taking Hunter to the nature reserve with the llamas.

He woke up grumpy. He hadn't slept well. I jollied him along, promising a fun day. I was irritable myself though. The heat had kept me awake too, giving me nightmares about a fire raging through the house. The fridge seemed to be faulty; the milk was tepid. I sniffed it and gagged.

Hunter put a lukewarm bottle of his favourite chocolate milk in his red rucksack.

'No, sweetie, it'll go off,' I said.

'Don't care.' He zipped the bag up.

It wasn't worth arguing when he was stroppy. I put sandwiches and fruit into a cooler bag and loaded the car up. I double-checked Hunter's seat belt was in right once he was in the back, with him – as always – telling me he wasn't a baby.

'Are you sure about your milk?' I asked again.

'Mum, why are you obsessed with my milk?'

'I'm not. It'll just curdle in this heat.' I sighed but let it go.

When we pulled out of the drive, I realised the air conditioning was also broken; it was barely a breath of air. Looking back – writing it here, with my heart tight and my throat dry – I feel like the whole day began badly; that these were all signs that we should have stayed home. We were both tired. It was too hot. Nothing was working. But Hunter wanted to go, and I owed it to him. So, I opened all the car windows and we set off.

When we got to the nature reserve, it was closed.

'Mum,' he cried. 'Didn't you check?'

'Oh, sweetie. I never thought. I'm sorry. I really am.'

Maybe he felt bad for me. Maybe I looked utterly dejected. But he said kindly, 'It's fine, Crazy Lady. At least we're out of the house. Can we have our picnic now?'

We sat on a grass verge and ate our sandwiches, playing I Spy and Spot the Caravan, with cars whizzing by and heat simmering over the tarmac. It wasn't a picturesque scene, but it's perfect now, looking on from this distance. We had sweaty foreheads, sticky hands, damp underarms, but the day was bright, and it was ours. I looked up at the sky; Hunter did too.

'My daddy's up there, isn't he?' he said softly.

I could barely nod.

'How many people do you think are looking up at the sky, right now?' he asked.

'It could be hundreds,' I said softly. Who knew? 'All that matters is that, right now, we're two fans of the sky.'

'Crazy Lady.' He giggled.

When we were done, we packed up and set off for home.

I want to stop now. I don't want to write. I don't know if I can. I can't. I can smell bad milk again. I'm going to be sick. He's here. In my study. Behind this chair that still squeaks. I can't look at him. I won't turn. He's whispering in my ear. *Crazy Lady*. Hands over my ears. No. Eyes shut. No. *Write me, Mum*. No. I can't. *You can*. I can't. *You can*.

I can.

Yes.

Fern Dalrymple's Diary – The Accident

On the way home, Hunter fell asleep in the back. I was glad. I knew how exhausted he was. His hair was stuck to his forehead. The toy robot my mum had just bought him bounced with the motion of the vehicle, moving dangerously close to the edge of the seat. He was oblivious when I fiddled again with the broken air conditioning and then switched radio stations and started singing along to Dolly Parton. I kept glancing at him. Did I know to look and to imprint the image of his flushed, peaceful face in my mind forever? Did I sense it might be the last time I gazed upon it?

I noticed that the shoelace on his left trainer had come undone and dangled precariously; that the shoe was at risk of falling off altogether. It eventually did, with a soft clump, and I reached for it. Held it in my lap. Smiled because I knew the scuffed and cheap things were his favourites.

I have it in my lap now.

I have had it all this time. I keep it here on my desk. Where he liked to sit, laughing as my chair slowly sank lower, squeaking as it went down. I don't like the now. The here. Alone in my beautiful house with a single shoe. But I think that until I go back to then, to that day, I'll never like the present, will I? The wreckage needs cleaning up; writing down. I'll never be able to move into a future until I do that. I don't want one without … *him*. But I have no choice, do I?

I'm crying as I write. Each word is a tear.

I realised, as we pulled onto the last part of the motorway, that I could smell off milk. Even the open windows didn't dispel the odour. It made me feel sick. I thought it couldn't be Hunter's chocolate milk; that was safely inside his rucksack. Then I saw the bottle on the car floor by his feet; some of the liquid had seeped out. I gagged again at the sight of it. I knew it would take some serious scrubbing to get rid of the smell. I tried to reach it but couldn't.

Then my phone started ringing.

I get to this moment in my head and every single time I think that I shouldn't have answered it. But that isn't what would have changed our unfolding destiny. What I should have done is pull over to answer. I even looked for a service station, a turn-off, anything, but there wasn't one. If there had been, and I'd stopped for ten minutes, we wouldn't have been in the path of the pile-up. It's torture to think of this. I used to play it over and over and over in my mind. I remember – in my early grief – writing it repeatedly on a notepad page: I pulled over, I pulled over, I pulled over.

But I didn't.

I had to answer the call. It was my agent. A TV company was interested in optioning one of my books and I knew she might have news. Hunter slept on. I glanced at him one final time, glad he was sleeping. How serene he looked. I whispered one last bedtime story to him: *I'll treat us to a takeaway for tea tonight.*

Then I answered my phone.

I don't now remember what we spoke about. My agent told me afterwards that I said I was in the car so we should keep it brief; then it went dead. These words are probably in my head somewhere, stored, squashed to the back, suppressed by the shock my brain took when the car behind shunted us into the one in front, at high speed. A medic later told me that the airbag caused massive impact to my head, rendering me unconscious. Afterwards I was left with neck trauma and upper spine fractures, but otherwise surprisingly intact.

I came around in an ambulance.

I thought it was a dream. A nightmare. A black blur of shadowy figures and the siren and questions I couldn't get past the oxygen mask. Where was my son? Where was Hunter? I still had his blue and white trainer in my hand. They told me later that I wouldn't let it go. The mask-wearing paramedics must have seen the questions in my eyes; one of them told me my car had been involved in an accident and – because they got me out first – my son was in another ambulance.

'We don't know any more,' he said kindly. 'But your son is in the best hands.'

I was checked over at the hospital, not caring about the pain in my head and neck, begging to see my son, begging for news, and being

assured that they would update me when they had any. They must
have given me something for the pain because everything moved more
slowly, like I was watching from just below a water's surface. Finally,
they told me Hunter had arrived at the hospital and been taken straight
to surgery. Those hours were the longest I've ever known. I floated on
painkillers. Someone on the ward had the TV on and I saw the news
report of the accident, it seemed on repeat but that could have been my
mind turning over. Filmed from above, it looked like something out of
a movie scene. How had I survived it? How had Hunter ...

A surgeon came to my bed.

I can't write this.

You can. I can't. *You can.*

I'll try: I'll start with his eyes.

I knew immediately from his eyes. He wore a mask, so his eyes
were all I had to go on, and they were sad. They were sea green. I
remember that clearly. Then I heard the word sorry, muffled by his
mouth covering. I heard *we did everything we could.* I heard spinal
injuries. I heard multiple organ failure. I heard internal bleeding. I
think I screamed. I know I passed out again. I know I had to come
around and relive the agony afresh.

Pain that no drug or word or distance lessened.

Hunter died wearing only one of his favourite trainers.

I survived with the other in my hand; the single dot of blood on
it is mine, not his.

I'm in shock: I have written about that day, and I'm still here.

The sun is still coming through the window to fry the plant
I keep forgetting to water. The layer of dust on my keyboard still
reminds me I don't write there anymore. The half-full cup of Fine-
Fayre tea that I made earlier has gone cold. But I'm still breathing,
if a little more ragged than usual. My heart is still beating, if a little
too fast. My throat is still dry, tight with his name.

Hunter is here too, and he knows I've written that day.

But still, I'm afraid to look at him.

Fern Dalrymple's Diary – The Aftermath

Aftermath is a good word: the consequences or after-effects of a significant unpleasant event. My aftermath was an empty house, cold despite the ongoing heatwave. It was visits from my dear friends Cass, Lynda and Shelly, with a variety of flans and flowers. It was support from my family liaison officers, who told me over and over that the accident was not my fault, that there was nothing I could have done to change things that afternoon. All these visitors had to wear masks, which meant their eyes were more intense, and difficult to look into.

My aftermath was calls from my agent, encouraging me to write something, saying it might help, that the third novel I'd so resisted could ease the pain. It was depending on drugs to get me through the day; crawling through the hours in a fog of not numbed out, still there, not–quite–enough–to–kill–me–pain. It was falling asleep after lying awake all night, forgetting for one brief, blissful moment that Hunter had died; then waking and remembering with an agonised sob.

My aftermath was wishing, desperately, that Cal was there to share my grief, and then thinking, no, *no*, I'm glad he isn't here for this absolute agony.

It was finding some of Hunter's clothes in the linen basket and sobbing into a Thomas the Tank Engine sock for a full afternoon. It was wrapping myself in his unwashed duvet so I could smell and get lost in him. It was not eating, not sleeping, not washing, not trying. It was Fine-Fayre turning up for the first time when I was about to take all my Propranolol pills with a cup of tea, asking if I wanted his tea delivered to my door.

It was wanting to die.

Trying to die.

Failing to die.

I realise now that I didn't want to die. I just wanted to be with my boy. To be out of pain. To be numb. And today? What's different now? Did writing an entire fiction help me process that pain? Did bringing my boy to life in carefully scribed paragraphs take me from one stage of grief to another? I put words in his mouth that I wanted to hear from him; I had him love the story I'd made up for him. I sketched him with my prose. I brought him to life in a place where it was safe to let myself be vulnerable – on the page. I finally wrote the third book my agent had thought might help me. But even though it was fiction, and I had a choice, I didn't rewrite the car crash. It was inevitable. It happened.

Now, I need to be vulnerable here, in my real world.

I need to look at Hunter; and let him go.

You do, Mum. You do, Crazy Lady.

Wait. There's someone at the door.

Fern Dalrymple's Diary – The Tea Man

It was him. Fine-Fayre. I still don't know his name. I don't think I want to. At least for now. Maybe one day. I opened the door, and he was sitting on my path, basket of offerings in his lap, hair grown out, more natural, nice, and his silver van the fairy-tale carriage on the street behind him. For a moment, I was dragged back to that boiling day in August when he first called by, just one week after the accident. It was a punch in the heart. I had to hold onto the door.

'Are you OK?' he asked.

I nodded. 'I just … need … a moment.'

He gave it to me. I took it. The air was cool. The heatwave was over. The leaves on the tree behind him were crisping, golden, dying. Time is passing. It does not drag. Does it ever? I thought of my fictional work – of the imagined book, *Technological Truth For Tots and Teens*, within it – and how it had included twenty-five 'facts' about time. The reader was supposed to decide which were true and which were 'ridiculous fiction'. Number nine was *time can't drag*. I think it can when you're hurting. Then, slowly, as you grow into your pain, it picks up speed again.

'You're here,' I said eventually.

'You're home,' he said.

'I am.'

'I often came by. I've come past the house a few times. I asked Laura about you. It wasn't … *pity*. It was just …'

'You couldn't not,' I said.

'Yes.'

'I don't know who cut your hair this time, but it's an improvement.'

He smiled and summer was back, but gentle, warm, not oppressive or hot. 'Did your stay in the … did it help you?'

'I think so,' I admitted. 'But not the therapy. Not even the medication. I …'

'Yes?'

'I wrote a story.'

He nodded. 'I imagine, as a writer, that helped?'

'Do you have children?' I asked him.

'Yes,' he said. 'A daughter. I have her every other week.'

'Cherish every moment,' I said. My voice broke. 'Read to her, even if life is hectic, and you're exhausted and …' I couldn't finish.

'I will,' he promised, his face serious. 'I *do*.'

I thought about asking if he'd had bedtime stories read to him when he was small and remembered he once said he was in care. A boy there had cut his face. Today, in the fragile autumn light, the scar looked as though it had faded. Maybe back then I just saw it through angry and wounded eyes. Maybe it had always been a soft line that divided his lovely face.

'Did you get the job?' I remembered he'd mentioned an interview the last time he came by.

'Oh, yes. I've got eight weeks' notice to work and then … that's it.'

I could have asked what the new role was. I wanted to. But then I also *didn't* want to think of him doing anything else. I suddenly remembered sobbing in his lap, here on the path; him patting my head. Now – in this slightly better place – I flushed with embarrassment at the recollection. What must he have thought of me?

'You'd better cancel my visits then,' I said.

'From today?' He looked surprised. Or was it disappointment?

'No. When you leave. I don't want your replacement hammering on my door, trying to sell me bloody Nutty Speckles and Christmas Crinkles.'

'Christmas Crinkles?' He frowned.

I realised I had made them up when I wrote about him in my story. I laughed. I began to wonder if anything I'd written about him might come true. How would I have written us if I'd escaped from the re-education centre and gone home? What future would I have carved out for us?

'I just made them up,' I said.

'You're good. You could work for us.'

'Maybe. Could be fun. Creating silly biscuit names.'

'I think stick with your not-silly stories.' He paused. A breeze lifted the fringe of his more natural hair. 'I read your first book.'

'Oh.' I never knew what to say when people admitted this, especially if they didn't surrender their thoughts with the announcement. He might have hated it.

'You're a beautiful writer,' he said.

'Oh. Thank you.'

'Can I ask you something?'

'OK,' I said.

'What was it like?'

'What was what like?'

'That kind of success. Your book. Seeing it published.'

With a slight change in words, he had become the tea man I created. But I answered in a different way to the fictional me. 'It was surreal. It still is. But I'd trade that success in a flash if I could have just one moment with ...' The pain still hit me, every time I tried to say his name.

Fine-Fayre nodded. He looked behind me, into my hallway, as though perhaps he expected to see Hunter there, playing with the robot toy from my mum, feet bare, nagging for chocolate milk. I knew he was there. I could feel him behind me. Still, I couldn't turn and look at him.

'Can I interest you in our new biscuit?' Fine-Fayre went into his basket of wares.

'You can try.'

He took out a glossy purple and green packet with gaudy gold letting on it – I couldn't quite make out the words – and a picture of a dinosaur in the corner. 'This is our enchanting new product,' he said. 'It's proving very popular, especially with ...' I knew he had wanted to say children and remembered my situation. I saw him realise that the product he was offering did not belong in a home like mine and I felt bad for him. He scrambled for different, perhaps child-free words. 'It's, um ... it's a crisp minty biscuit with a layer of cream running through the centre, topped with a light sprinkling of sparkly jelly sweets.'

'They sound awful. I'll just take my *pity* Nutty Speckles.' I gave a brief smile, so he knew I was joking.

He handed them over with my customary gold pack of teabags. I put my card to his machine and waited until it accepted. Our transaction was done. He would leave. I knew it and I dreaded it. The house I would come back into was not the place of two months ago, but it was still a lonely place, even though I knew that Hunter was waiting there for me to look at him. My throat felt tight. I croaked a thank you.

'Remember,' said Fine-Fayre, 'you have to free what's stuck there.'

'Dr Fine-Fayre, eh?'

'No. Just a tea man.'

'For now, at least.'

He patted his basket. That departure signal I knew well. And then he wheeled his chair back down the path. Maybe sometime in a future I hadn't yet imagined I'd find out why he couldn't walk. Maybe he could, but not for long. Not every story ends with all the answers in place. I followed him to the gate and closed it after him.

'My son ...' I started.

'Yes?' So softly the wind could have taken the word.

'Thank you.'

'For what?'

'For persevering. For coming back. For being a great salesman.'

'I couldn't *not*,' he said.

'Yes, you told me that ...'

'No, I mean I had to ... because ...'

'*Because*?' I repeated softly.

'I know,' he said simply.

'You *know*?'

The gate separated us, but I felt closer to him than I ever had.

'I wanted to die once too.' He looked down at his legs. Maybe his story was going to wrap up neatly after all. 'I … when my wife left me and took my daughter … I … I was in a dark place. I went to a bridge …' He let the sentence die; he left that scene for me to write, in my head. 'They said I'll never walk again. But I can live with that. I have my daughter now. My wife agreed to share custody. That's all I need.'

I didn't know what to say.

We both knew pain.

'I should go.' He seemed embarrassed now. I wanted to show that I felt for him, that I thought him brave, but I didn't know how. 'I'll make sure they know you want to stop tea deliveries in December. Until then …'

'Yes,' I said, my voice thick. 'Until then.'

'See you next week.'

Such everyday words after our intimate exchange. Should I have asked what might happen to us after his departure from Fine-Fayre? I wonder now, will we somehow remain friends? Is our connection, his belated baring of his soul, more than just an exchange of cash and teabags? Do some people turn up at exactly the right moment in time? If so, shouldn't we do all we can to keep those people?

But he's coming back next week. And then I'll find a way to work out his place in my future. I need time. I give it to myself. Fine-Fayre drove away, and I walked back up the path. I came upstairs to my desk where I've been writing this entry in my notepad. What is left to write now?

What is left?

Just me, Mum. Just me, Crazy Lady.

I turned around.

Fern Dalrymple's Diary – My Son

I turned to look at my son.

He has been waiting for me to face him. He watched me write my fiction to cope with the grief; I felt him, in that white soulless room. I knew that I should turn and see him but the fear that he wouldn't look at me in the same way he once did when I read to him stopped me. I wondered, how can he still love me when I live, and he doesn't? How can he forgive that I answered my phone that day? How can he forgive me for ending the stories?

I turned to look at my son.

His face was as serene as it had been that final moment in the car. Flushed cheeks. Hair floppy. Eyes open though and full of mischief. Sitting on the sofa in the corner of my study, wearing pyjamas, feet bare, as real as the day I last saw him. I knew it was my mind that had created him. I knew it was my grief. I knew he wasn't there in the sense that my desk was there, that the squeaky chair was there, that the unwatered plant was there. That *I* was there.

I turned to look at my son.

The lack of love that I feared in his face, the sadness I imagined in his eyes, the anger I dreaded in his stance, was absent. He patted the sofa like I always used to when I wanted him to join me. So, I did. We sat. I kissed his forehead. It didn't matter if my grief – my mind – created the sensation because I could smell the unique scent of my boy; slightly unwashed and warm, with a hint of chocolate milk.

'Are you OK, sweetie?' I asked him.

'I am,' he said. 'Because I'm not alone here.'

Of course. *Of course.*

'I'm so sorry *I* didn't have time to read to you.' My voice broke.

'But, Mum,' he said, 'we shared stories every day. You asked about school and Marley and my games. You told me about your book ideas and when you were little and boring stuff I just pretended to listen to. They're all stories too.'

They were. Ours.

Then I told him one last story. That's ours too; and it's private, not even to be recorded here in a notepad entry I'll never show anyone.

And I fell asleep holding him.

Fern Dalrymple's Diary – If You Tell a Story Well Enough, it's True.

I went for a walk today. When I got back, I sat in the park opposite the house for a while, on a bench beneath a tree that shed its autumn leaves around me like gold glitter on a gameshow winner. It's a spot I've enjoyed before, watching Hunter on the swings. I can see the house from here, just the upstairs windows, my room, his. I glanced across, almost expecting to see him there. But he has gone. He doesn't visit me in that physical way now; instead, he haunts my thoughts, my heart, and he always will.

I still cry most days. I still wake and remember with a heavy sadness that I'm alone now. But I don't want to die. I know he wouldn't want that. I'm weaning off my medication. But it would be the stuff of happy-ever-afters – and a lie – to say that I'm OK.

I caught some of the crisp leaves as they floated past my face and thought about my books. My agent asked yesterday if I'm ready to face that third novel. A literary magazine wants me to write a piece reflecting on the grave tragedy I experienced (their words) and how it impacted (their word) my work. I didn't tell my agent that technically I've written my third novel; that I wrote it while I was in the mental hospital. I can imagine how the media would love *that* story; deranged author loses mind on the page.

For now, I'm keeping my story. It doesn't even have a title yet. Shrivel thought 'End of Story' would make a good one. Maybe. Maybe not.

'I fancy the idea of writing a futuristic, dystopian type sci-fi novel,' I said to Hunter months before he died, 'but I've no idea how to.'

He was sitting on the sofa in the study behind me. 'What would you call it if you did?' His brow was furrowed adorably.

I picked a random, ridiculous phrase out of the air to make him laugh: *Technological Amazingness*. And it did. He giggled and said they were two excellent words and that only I could do it.

'But who the heck would read a book called that?' I asked him.

'*Me*,' he said. 'I would.'

After a while, I was chilly and decided to go home. Just before I got up a little girl sat on the bench, brushing it free of leaves first. Her mum – who waved from the slide where she was helping another child up the steps – must have taught her about social distancing because she sat at least a metre away from me. Or maybe she was just shy. Wary. I smiled at her from from our safe opposite ends. She smiled back. She was maybe six. She had a fluffy rucksack on her back.

'Mum's busy,' she said.

I nodded. 'With your sister?'

'Yes. Millie. She cries a real lot. She's annoying.'

I smiled. 'She'll grow out of it, I imagine.'

She didn't look convinced. 'I never cried like that.'

'I bet not.'

'Do you like books?' she asked.

'Very much.'

'I've got a new one,' she said.

'What's it called?'

She went into her rucksack and took out *The Tiger Who Came to Tea*.

'Oh.' I was emotional for a moment. 'It's a favourite of mine.'

'Mum hasn't read it to me yet.' She was clearly annoyed. 'And I've had it two weeks.'

'Can I have a look?'

She nodded and handed it to me. I looked at the familiar story with a smile. It was one I'd read to Hunter when he was very tiny. I was sure it was still in a cupboard somewhere, the pages lovingly folded and creased.

'Will *you* read it to me?' she asked.

'Me?' I was touched. 'Now?'

'Yes. Millie will be ages on the swings.'

'I don't know.' Why was I nervous? I glanced up at Hunter's room.

'Go on,' she pushed.

I knew Hunter would want me to. 'I … I suppose …'

'*Please*.'

'OK.'

I turned to the first page and began reading, slowly, carefully, adding drama to the parts that needed it, speaking gently when the moment required. The little girl watched and listened, her mouth hanging open just slightly, like a wooden flap in a floor covered with coats and leading to a secret storytelling basement. When I was done, I paused; savoured. It had been so long. I missed it.

'You're good,' she said. 'You must have really practised lots.'

I laughed. 'Yes, I suppose I have.'

'I could proper imagine every bit as you said it,' she gushed.

'Thank you.'

'I believed every word.'

'Well, they do say – ' I whispered and leaned a tiny bit closer like I was imparting the greatest secret in the world. ' – that if you tell a story well enough, it's tru—

Acknowledgements

Thank you from the bottom of my heart to Emily Glenister for taking a chance on me and on the book that saved me during lockdown. And it truly wasn't just because of Marilyn Monroe in your Twitter banner that I approached you ... well, maybe a little bit. Thank you also Lily Cooper at Hodder for your passion for the book right from the start, for *getting* it, and for also taking such a chance on it. Lily and Priyal Agrawal, thank you both for the incredible suggestions during the editing process. Like magic, you exposed me to things I didn't even know about my own book! And thank you to Kay Gale for your sharp eye in the copy edits – even after hundreds of reads, there's always something missed, and you saw it all. Kim Nyamhondera, my publicity gal at Hodder, thank you for championing my book.

Thank you to my loyal early beta readers, my sisters Claire and Grace, Madeleine Black, Lynda Harrison and John Marrs. You had, as always, great suggestions, and you were each insistent that it was 'one of my best' and that I should 'go all the way' with it. Thank you Carrie Martin for writing a beautiful song to accompany the story – you're always the music to my words. 'End of Story' the song will be on Carrie's new album, Beside the Evergreen, released in April 2023.

Thank you to all the early readers, reviewers and bloggers, too many to name, but you all know who you are. I so appreciate you for trusting me with my new pen name, for coming on this journey with me, and for continuing to read what I write.

Also thank you to my husband Joe for putting up with me while I wrote this book during the last lockdown of 2020. One day, some time before I began, I said to him that I wished I was clever enough to 'put some technological amazingness in a book'. He asked what the hell that was; I said, 'Oh, you know, sci-fi, inventive, futuristic things.' Joe said I probably (probably?)

was clever enough and asked what I'd call it. After a pause, I said, smiling, 'Technological Amazingness.' Then it began trending that Rishi Sunak had suggested that people in the arts (as well as those in other industries, it later emerged) should retrain. This got me trying to imagine a world without the arts. Without stories.

A conversation with my husband, Rishi Sunak's tweet, and the intense, isolating and frightening experience of the pandemic inspired this book.